To Tina,

…wherever you are now.

"Whoso diggeth a pit shall fall therein: and he that rolleth a stone, it will return upon him."

Proverbs 26:27

"What goes around comes around."

An old English saying.

PROLOGUE

**Leiston, Suffolk, England,
Tuesday, May 8th 1945**

*"...We'll meet again,
Don't know where, don't know when.
But I know we'll meet again some sunny day."*

If it hadn't entirely been a sunny day, it had certainly been one of unrestrained joy. All afternoon, at street parties up and down the land, people had been celebrating the Allied victory in Europe. Likewise, with dusk drawing in and its revellers still in fine voice, the citizens of this little town had also been putting six long years of 'blood, sweat and tears' behind them. Rejoicing that their own war was now over too, some of the Americans from the nearby base had even popped by to join in.

Hence, with the party in full swing and the beer and spirits flowing, nobody noticed the airman and his young sweetheart slip quietly away and make off down a main street that was by now bathed in twilight. By the time they'd reached the appropriately-named Lover's Lane the sound of those voices raised in song had faded until it could no longer be heard. They were alone at last – which was how *they* intended to celebrate VE Day.

Indeed, the airman had many times wondered whether he would live to see it. Yet living each day never knowing whether that day would be one's last had taken its toll – not least upon whatever chivalrous self-restraint this devout young man had once possessed. Tonight, as they continued to walk together arm-in-arm, he was assailed by lingering guilt and vague remembrance of a line that had been crossed many months ago.

The beach was quieter than usual. Many of its coastal defences had been removed and the once-extensive military presence wound down as the threat of invasion had receded. Therefore, these impatient lovers had no trouble locating an abandoned pillbox back from the shingle in which to steal away out of sight.

Never far from their thoughts as they now exchanged kisses was the knowledge that, with war over, soon he would be departing England for his home back in the United States. Thereafter, who could say 'when' or 'where' – or even if – they would 'meet again'. So perhaps tonight really was now or never. And if so, they tacitly acceded, let the Devil take tomorrow.

Looking to him to take the lead, she gazed up at the moonlight now reflected in his eyes. Without saying a word, those eyes signalled her lips to receive his own, the torrid searching of his tongue supplemented by hands that raced about loosening clothing and touching forbidden places.

Liberated from their garments and their inhibitions, the time had come for them to experience real intimacy with each other. He took the lead again, vigorous and strong. Suddenly, it was good – inexpressibly good. Sucking the very breath from her lungs as she panted involuntarily, she begged as best she could for him to do it faster and firmer.

Upon consummation, their manic exertions slowed until there remained nothing else to do except cling to each other and reflect upon what had been done. Meanwhile, unseen, the Devil slipped away to plan how – at some as yet undetermined time and place in the future – he might redeem his side of their bargain.

* * * * *

**Over the skies of Hanoi, North Vietnam,
Friday, December 22nd 1972**

"Turquoise 5's been hit!"
"Nav, Pilot. Get a fix on her."
"Roger that."

Those crew members who had access to a view of its demise could only watch in sober and impotent horror as the giant camouflage-dappled bomber broke apart like a child's plastic toy, whereupon its fuselage and huge wings began a fiery, spiralling descent towards the city's southern suburbs far below them. The only consolation was that at least some of its crew members had managed to eject. Otherwise, time was counting down for the formation's remaining B52 Stratofortresses to commence their final run towards the target. Inside the cockpit of *Turquoise 2* the sickly wail of the surface-to-air missile alarm was whooping incessantly, as if to remind its own six-man crew that it might be their turn next to experience the wrath of the most heavily-defended hostile airspace on the planet.

"*Radar, Pilot. Confirm we need to be at thirty-three five hundred.*"

The pilot's terse request was meant to convey business-like reassurance after the drama they had just witnessed. Ike, the plane's radar navigation officer, woke from the clawing concern that had been on his mind these last few days and blinked exaggeratedly. He spied the consoles on his control panel.

"*Roger that. Thirty-three even,*" he hurriedly replied.

"*Repeat, Eichelberger. Did you say thirty-three?*"

The young navigator blinked again. They all had a job to do. Nobody wanted to be the one who flipped under pressure.

"*Correction, Captain. Thirty-three five hundred. Repeat we need to be at thirty-three five hundred.*"

"*Copy that.*"

As the SAM alarm continued to warble, Ike cursed his loss of concentration. He simply had to put aside his preoccupation with the girl back at the base and with the ominous news she'd broken to him. Meanwhile, the pilot tried to hide his impatience as he quizzed him again.

"*So what's our heading?*"

"*Two-eight-zero,*" Ike replied, endeavouring to mimic his chief's unflappable resolve. Even so, it was taking an act of will.

Just then the voice of the rear gunner burst into the discourse with a piece of news that nobody wanted to hear.

"*Crew. Guns. I got visual on a SAM at six o'clock!*"

Definitely not good news! By now there was an air of agitation aboard the huge plane that could not be repressed. Perhaps the SAM alarm really was tolling for *Turquoise 2*.

"*We need to turn in thirty seconds,*" Ike meanwhile advised.

"*Roger that.*"

"*I can't see that SAM any more,*" the rear gunner confessed. There was an uncertainty in his voice that was not reassuring.

"Maybe it detonated."

"Or ran outta' gas!" someone piped up in a burst of gallows humour.

"Pilot, Radar. I'm centring the PDI. Prepare to make that turn," Ike meanwhile reminded his skipper.

"Crew, EWO. SAM, seven o'clock low... Turquoise cell," the call went out from the B52's electronic warfare officer buried away in the bowels of the mighty bomber.

"I got visual..." the rear gunner confirmed, *"Uh-ho! Looks like there's two of 'em!"* his voice lifted an octave.

"Roger that."

"Uplink... One of them has got lock on us," the EWO weighed in again.

"Target ten miles out. Make that turn, Captain," Ike tried to interject. However, he had the sense that nobody was listening.

"One of those SAMs has detonated," the co-pilot observed, craning around and spotting a flash below them.

"Then it must be the second one that has lock on us!" the EWO tempered their relief, his wide eyes fixed on the warning alert still flashing on his control panel.

"Crew, Pilot. Anybody got visual on it?"

No reply.

Then the rear gunner suddenly hollered *"Crew, Guns. I can see it, I can see it...! PLEASE, JESUS... NO!"*

* * * * *

**St Cloud, Minnesota, USA,
Sunday, September 7th 1975**

"NO...! NO...! PLEASE, JESUS...! NO!"

For one shocking moment Natalie Eichelberger feared a crude profanity might just have tumbled from the lips of her godly husband – a man of otherwise rock-like rectitude. Shaking him vigorously, she finally managed to rouse him from his nightmare and calm his flailing delirium. Then she turned and reached over to flick on the bedside light, the better to behold a man suddenly conscious that the terrible torment that had occasioned his outburst was all in his head.

"Charles…! Charles…!" she shook her spouse some more before he eventually permitted that head to be cradled against her comforting bosom. Whereupon he threw his arms around her and began to weep.

To be sure, her husband had experienced nocturnal flashbacks before during their thirty years of marriage. However, prayer and the passage of time had helped slay whatever demons had once plagued this decorated World War Two veteran (who had seen more than his fair share of horror and carnage). However, of late these nightmares had returned, this time with an intensity that spoke of new demons crowding in to mock Charles Eichelberger.

Not that he would ever speak about them. Born of a generation that eschewed the wearing of ones heart upon ones sleeve, there were some things this man had seen and done that he was determined even now to shield from his family.

Therefore, knowing that his family had always meant so much to him, she held him tight and ventured to second-guess what might be on his mind at that moment, offering him the balm of more specific reassurance.

"Charles, Aimee is gonna' be okay… in England. The Lord will keep watch over her… You gotta' trust Him. She's gonna' be just fine."

The Isle of Wight, England…

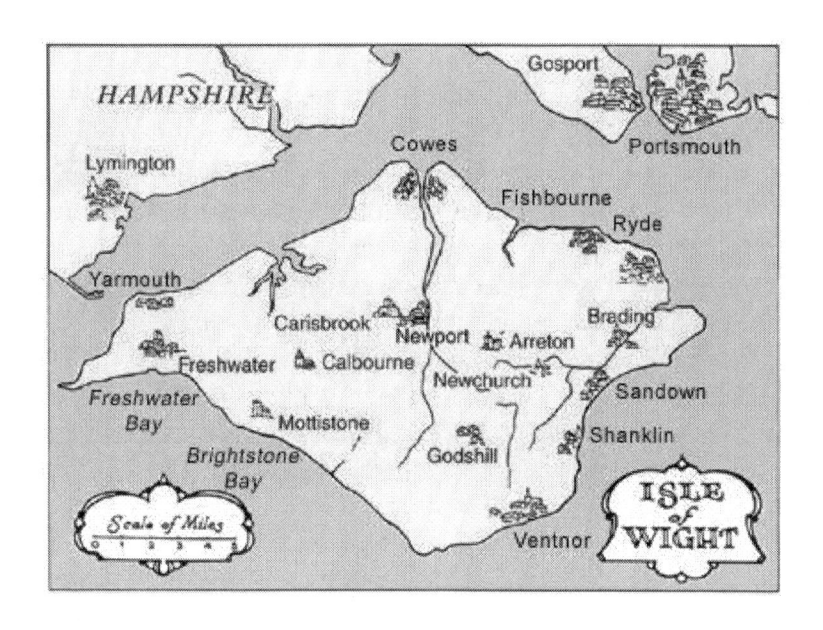

…during the summer of 1976.

1

Saturday, June 19th 1976

"The train now standing at Platform Five is the 0945 service to Portsmouth Harbour, calling at Solihull, Leamington Spa, Banbury, Oxford, Basingstoke, Winchester, Eastleigh, Fareham, Portsmouth & Southsea and Portsmouth Harbour... British Rail apologises that this train is running fifteen minutes late..."

A veritable tornado now swept through the passengers milling about Birmingham's busy New Street Station, lugging its bulky suitcase behind it. Having bounded down the stairwell onto the platform the tornado halted briefly to yank open a carriage door before hurling that bulky suitcase (and itself) inside.

Vaughan Lewis didn't think he'd make it. In fact, with the bus into town also running late he would not have had the train not been delayed somewhere on its journey from Manchester. Thus it was with relief that he located a seat in one of its compartments, heaved that case up onto the overhead luggage rack, and then sat down. Seated opposite, some guy who he guessed was in his early twenties glanced up at him from behind a red-top newspaper. Outside, the platform began to slide past.

The train disappeared into a tunnel to re-emerge criss-crossing a jumble of diverging tracks before gathering speed for its long, four hour journey down to Britain's south coast. Outside the sun was shining again and it promised to be yet another gorgeous warm day. Perfect seaside weather!

"Looks like that rain we had earlier isn't going to do the gardens much good," the guy opposite observed wearily, glancing up to observe the skies.

It was a moot point. What little precipitation the country had experienced during the winter and spring months had failed to top up either the nation's reservoirs or spruce up its foliage.

"They say we could have another fine summer to rival last year's," Vaughan reciprocated, likewise staring up.

"You off anywhere nice?" his travel companion enquired.
"Isle of Wight. And you?"
"Portsmouth," he grunted.
"Navy?" Vaughan made an educated guess.

"Yeah," he explained cagily in his broad Brummie accent, adding "New posting. The promotion will come in handy, like – what with the girlfriend expecting our first child."

The chap smiled regretfully before his gaze disappeared back inside the newspaper, leaving Vaughan to ponder that, in his haste, he had himself forgotten to purchase something to read. He remembered he'd packed his bible in his case somewhere, but couldn't be minded to open it up and rummage for it.

Instead, his gazed returned to the suburbs of Birmingham that were hurtling past – though not before it was arrested by the story on the front page: *'SOWETO ERUPTS – HUNDREDS FEARED DEAD'*. Otherwise, the back page was taken with the shock news that Czechoslovakia had beaten European Championship favourites Holland 3-1 in Zagreb. Meanwhile, with the Second Test underway at Lords, England had yet to make good Tony Greig's boast that his players would make the visiting West Indies cricketers "grovel" (the white, South African-born skipper still smarting over criticism of the racial connotation implicit in his throw-away remark).

Newspaper digested, the sailor eventually folded it neatly, laid it on the seat beside him, and stared out of the window pensively. Finally, he settled back into his seat and closed his eyes. Unsure whether he'd closed them in contemplation or slumber, Vaughan had the sense that he would maybe have liked to have talked further. Something was clearly on his mind. However, one consequence of the IRA's murderous terror campaign on the mainland was that British servicemen had not only been ordered to don civilian clothes when travelling back and forth on leave – as this guy had – but to be wary about divulging too much information about themselves to civilians. That said, the short-back-and-sides haircut and the nautical-themed tattoo on his forearm rather gave his occupation away.

That newspaper looked mighty tempting though. Vaughan was minded to seek the permission of its owner to peruse it. However, that strange reticence that had often gripped him begged him desist. Alone instead with his thoughts, he slid back into his own seat and carried on gazing out of the window. It was going to be a long, boring journey indeed!

To be sure, no one who knew Vaughan Lewis would ever have described him as reticent. In fact, at school he'd had a reputation for extroversion – albeit that this had often manifested itself in a jocularity that bordered on clownishness. But then, like many schoolyard 'clowns', his effervescence was in reality a mask for an innate shyness The kind of shyness that made tomfoolery a substitute for opening his heart; the kind of shyness that made him averse to making a simple request to borrow a newspaper that someone had finished with. In fact, the kind of shyness that meant he would have been perfectly content to laze away the summer months at home had someone not urged him to purchase a ticket and board this train that was now whisking him somewhere else.

* * * * *

At some point after leaving Banbury, Vaughan's vacant gazing out of the window must have given way to brief somnolence. Brief enough so that he was awake again by the time the train rolled into Oxford. Meanwhile, he noticed that the geezer opposite had picked up his paper again, this time to try his hand at the crossword puzzle.

However, before the train had recommenced its southward voyage the morgue-like tranquillity of the compartment was interrupted by the sound of scraping suitcases being dragged along the corridor. Detecting the entrancing lilt of American accents, Vaughan glanced over to spy an attractive young lady poke her head inside the compartment. She possessed long, auburn hair – styled like Farrah Fawcett had worn hers in that new film *'Logan's Run'* – and which swished enchantingly as her eyes now darted to and fro between each of its occupants.

"Excuse me, are these seats taken?"

Mesmerised, before Vaughan could respond the compartment's other occupant had looked up from filling out 'No. 22 across' to gesticulate that they weren't.

With the girls hauling their suitcases inside, at last Vaughan was galvanised into action. He leapt out of his seat to help place their luggage in the overhead stowage racks.

"Why, thank you," said the girl with the Farrah Fawcett hairdo, a bright smile upon on her faintly-freckled face.

Touched by his bumbling act of chivalry, she sat down alongside him while her five-foot-nothing best friend positing her own delicate little posterior on the seat opposite – next to the sailor, who glanced up to offer her a wary smile before immersing himself in his crossword once more. Then Vaughan remembered what the guy had said about his girlfriend expecting their first child – clearly out of wedlock. Perhaps this explained the tar's melancholy. All the nice girls may indeed like a sailor, as the old song goes. However, this particular one was neither 'bright and breezy', nor – it would appear – 'free and easy'!"

If ever Vaughan missed the diversion of being able to bury his head in a good novel, it was now. Sandwiched between a self-absorbed matelot and two American teenagers chattering excitedly, he could only gaze back out of the window again while catching snippets of their conversation.

"… So, like I said. I am determined this summer will be the highlight of my time in England. And I don't care what Mom and Dad think!" the girl next to him was adamant.

"Girl, you've sure turned out to be rebel," her friend opined before conceding that "It's been a tough year though, what with all that studying. We deserve a break."

"Tough indeed! However, I've loved every minute of my time in England. It's been a real adventure. And it's enabled me to get loads of research done for my senior thesis."

At some point, as the train slowed to by-pass Reading, Vaughan glanced over to observe them sharing a moment of amusement – at which point the girl opposite broke to offer him a warm smile. He smiled back before gazing out of the window again, embarrassed that he couldn't think of anything to say.

Once the train had left Basingstoke the sailor wandered into the corridor to light a cigarette and ponder the Hampshire countryside breezing past. Thereafter, he took a walk (presumably see what refreshments were on offer in the buffet car). It left

Vaughan alone with the two girls. However, before he could pluck up the courage to make small talk he was beaten to it.

"It looks like it's gonna' be another nice day," beamed the girl sat opposite, her observation accompanied by a coy grin.

"Er... Yes, looks like you're right," he mumbled.

This time though, he was determined to maintain eye contact. Thoughts re-gathered, he plunged in and asked the question he'd been rehearsing in his head.

"I hope you don't me saying, but you don't sound as if you're from around here."

There was a simultaneous frisson of hilarity on the part of the two girls. However, the one sat opposite responded first, leaning over to rest her arms upon her knees.

"That's because we're not. We're from the United States – but I'm figuring you've probably guessed that. My friend Aimee here is from Minnesota. And I'm Shelby – from Georgia. We're students from Wellesley College... in Massachusetts."

"Hi. I'm Vaughan," he sighed, reaching out to accept the dainty little hand that Shelby offered. He did likewise with the hand Aimee offered too.

Otherwise, they might just have well have alluded to craters on the moon for all the knowledge of the geography of the United States that their new acquaintance possessed. Perhaps reading his mind, Aimee re-crossed her long, shapely legs and explained their presence on his side of 'The Pond'.

"We've been studying abroad for a year – at Oxford University. But now the semester's over, we've both decided to stay for a few more weeks. We've been offered employment on the Isle of Wight over the summer."

"Hey, that's where I'm heading. You've certainly picked the weather," Vaughan chuckled, easing up at last.

"I sure hope so," Aimee sighed. "You see, my mom made me pack loads of coats. Kept telling me how cold and damp the weather is here in England. Like when Dad was over here during the war it never stopped raining. I'm kinda' guessing it did. But, well, you know how parents can exaggerate things sometimes."

Vaughan nodded. His own mother too had fretted over her only son's imminent departure for pastures new: even though, in his case, it was only to stay with a relative for a few weeks.

"Oxford University, you say?" he probed further. "You must be really clever to get in there. What are you girls studying?"

"Me, I'm doing modern history," Aimee shrugged matter-of-factly – as if bagging a place at Britain's most prestigious seat of learning was no big deal.

"And I'm doing English," Shelby enthused, aware instead of the immense privilege she was party to. "And you?" she asked.

"I've just left college. I'm hoping to start a business studies course in September – at Wolverhampton Polytechnic."

"College, you say?"

"Sixth form college," he elaborated.

"Oh, you mean high school!" Aimee twigged.

"See what I mean: two nations divided by a common language!" Shelby joined in the mirth, offering Vaughan another one of her adorable, inquisitive smiles.

"I guess that kinda' makes you, what? Eighteen?" Aimee wondered aloud, eyeing him up and down.

Vaughan grinned awkwardly, wondering whether he was out of his depth even to imagine he might be in with a chance with either of these two girls (who he'd deduced must be a year or two his senior at least).

"So where are you from, Vaughan?" Shelby picked up on this and restarted the conversation.

"From Gornal. It's a little town near Dudley in the West Midlands – well more like a village really. You've probably never heard of it though," he reasoned. He was right.

"Can't say I have," Shelby conceded, observing that it "Sounds a bit like where I come from: Monticello, in Jasper County, Georgia. A few thousand folks in a small town built on red clay soil that no one has ever heard of – and nobody ever sings about. But hey, it's the place that made me. So don't ever be ashamed of who you are, Vaughan; nor where you come from."

Heartened by her kind words, his natural radiance returned. With one of its daughters studying English at Oxford University it was possible yet that somebody might one day pen a song about the red clay soil of Jasper County, Georgia.

"And how about you, Aimee?" he turned to address her. "Where did you say you come from?"

She paused to offer him a teasing stare.

"Me? I guess I come from all over. My folks are from a place called St Cloud – about sixty miles north of Minneapolis-St Paul. However, I was born in Hawaii while my dad was stationed there. You see, he's was in the air force. So I kinda' grew up all over the world – wherever he was based at the time. Korea, Japan, the Philippines, Germany. But for some crazy reason he was never stationed in England – except for during the war, that is."

He could sense from the glint in her hazel eyes that it was a kaleidoscope of life experiences that might just be as bitter as it was sweet. It was Aimee's turn to grin feebly. He responded with a teasing stare of his own – as if to suggest that, with a promising student of modern history at Oxford University, it was possible to believe that one day too someone might pen a song about St Cloud, Minnesota.

Eventually, the sailor returned to claim his seat, his disposition neither improved by British Rail's catering, nor the reflection afforded by dragging on another cigarette in the corridor. Not long afterwards, the shimmering mass of water that was Portsmouth Harbour put in an appearance. Thereafter, the train crossed the causeway to Portsea Island and snaked its way through a jumble of backstreet tenements. The troubled matelot had meanwhile hauled down his case ready for when it drew to halt at the city's main railway station.

"See you 'round, like," he muttered a half-hearted farewell, offering Vaughan and the girls that familiar doleful countenance as he dragged the case out into the corridor.

"Is this our stop?" Aimee enquired, rising to take hold of her own luggage. Vaughan instinctively rose to help her.

"No, not this one. This is the town station. The ferry terminal is the next stop. Just a few more minutes," he counselled.

As he grabbed the handle of the case to steady it he felt his own hand brush against her dainty fingers. For a moment their eyes met. Shyness forced him to lower his gaze – only for it to alight instead upon the gap in her cheese-cloth blouse that permitted him a glimpse of her rotund cleavage. He looked away, conscious she'd spotted him. Instead, he endeavoured to mask his embarrassment by hauling the case down for her in readiness before seizing Shelby's case too.

"Your mama told you about the English weather. Mine told me about the politeness and chivalry of its young men," she winked at her friend, Shelby more than happy to allow her new English acquaintance to demonstrate its practical outworking with regard to her own bulky belongings.

* * * * *

The thirty minute ferry crossing was an opportunity for Vaughan to reflect upon this encounter – more so once Aimee had dragged her friend off to find a bite to eat. Therefore, he availed himself of the solitude to wander the upper deck admiring the views of Spithead – the five-mile stretch of sea that divides the island from the mainland at this point.

To the stern of the vessel the skyline of Portsmouth was receding – though it was still possible to catch glimpses of Royal Navy warships riding at their berths. Vaughan thought about the sailor and the heavy heart he seemed to be bringing with him to that new posting. Meanwhile, ahead of the ferry's thrusting bow he could make out Ryde (the island's principal embarkation point), the tall steeple of its church standing lofty atop the hill upon which the town was nestled. On a perfect day with barely a cloud in the sky it conversely made for a vista that was laden with all manner of exciting possibilities. Just like the two girls, Vaughan too was looking forward to spending the summer on this popular holiday island – courtesy of an offer of seasonal work that would for the next few weeks enable him to escape the hum-drum routine of life back home.

However, there the similarity ended. As he paced the ship and looked down from his eerie up top he spotted Aimee and Shelby sitting in the sun on the lower deck, partaking of the refreshments they'd purchased. Here were two beautiful young ladies who – while they'd been glad to pass the journey in the company of this bashful young man from the Black Country – were looking forward to further adventures he imagined their good looks and self-assurance would undoubtedly bring their way. As such, being reduced to beholding them from afar seemed a worthy metaphor for Vaughan's non-existent love life.

To be sure, he'd made plenty of friends amongst the girls he'd known at school and at sixth-form college – all of whom had been drawn to his sense of humour and his japing ways. However, for some reason that attraction had never congealed into a desire to get to know him romantically. Vaughan Lewis had plenty of 'girl friends'; but to date he'd never had a girlfriend.

Meanwhile, belatedly spotting him, Shelby looked up and waved. Aimee turned around and did likewise, any hint of the regard in which she might hold him masked by the mirror sunglasses that were veiling her eyes.

Vaughan reciprocated with a modest wiggle of his own extended palm. These gorgeous Americans were just two more 'girl friends' to add to the list so far. However – as with all the other female acquaintances in his life – there seemed little prospect of anything more.

Alas, soon enough the ferry docked and its passengers boarded an electric train that was waiting to hurry them to the island's main holiday destinations. Vaughan helped Aimee and Shelby with their cases one final time. Too polite and reticent to ask for an address or a phone number, he stared at them across the carriage and conceded that, amongst the thousands of youngsters who would be arriving shortly to seek work on the island, it was unlikely their paths would cross again.

* * * * *

"'Ere, mate. Yer' wanna' 'and with that case of yours?" the cheeky nipper cupped his hand to his squinting eyes and offered.

Having left the two American girls to travel on to Shanklin, Vaughan suddenly found himself accosted by one of several young boys with go-carts who were touting for business amongst the holidaymakers heaving their baggage across the sun-baked forecourt of Sandown railway station.

"How much?" Vaughan enquired.

"Depends where yer' wanna' go, dun' it," the lad explained.

"Victoria Road?"

"For you, mister. Thirty pence."

"Thirty pence! I could buy a pint of beer for that!"

"It's cheaper than a taxi. And anyway, you don't look old enough to be able to drink in pubs," the youngster observed.

"Well, I am. Old enough, that is. And Victoria Road's not that far. Twenty pence."

"Twenty pence! You taking the…?"

"Go on, then. Twenty-five pence. My final offer."

"Deal!"

Upon which, the lad grabbed Vaughan's case and heaved it aboard the old pram that he'd modified to serve as a makeshift trolley (and thereby a useful source of Saturday income). Then teenage newcomer and prepubescent porter set off together along the backstreets towards their destination. A sufficient walk from the station, Vaughan was glad with hindsight that he'd agreed to have his worldly belongings conveyed aboard the lad's set of wheels – even if those wheels squeaked incessantly!

"So why you over 'ere then?" the youngster commenced an interrogation of his customer. "You on 'oliday?"

"Sort of. A working holiday, you might say."

"'Owzat' then? You gonna' work at one of them 'oliday camps – where you get to wear one of them funny-coloured jackets and make people play silly games?"

"No," Vaughan chuckled. "I'm going to be a bus conductor. I've got an interview on Monday."

"A bus conductor? Cor, I don't envy you. All them' kids monkeyin' about on yer' bus. You'll be a nervous wreck by the time the schools break up," the lad sucked through his lips – and in a manner that suggested he spoke from culpable experience.

"Wots' yer' name then," he probed some more.

"Me? I'm Vaughan."

"That's an unusual name."

"I'm an unusual guy," Vaughan teased. "Handsome, gifted, intelligent; adored by beautiful women wherever I go. Didn't you know I've been invited to play the next James Bond!" he added fancifully.

From the manner in which he glanced up at him, the lad was suitably sceptical. Then he donned a museful expression for the visitor by his side.

"You'll find plenty of beautiful women on this island then. They come 'ere every year on 'oliday or to work. You can see 'em 'anging out in all the pubs around 'ere; and sunbathing on the beach in those tiny bikinis they wear – especially when the weather's like this. Some of 'em 'ave got real nice tits on 'em, I tell yer'."

It was Vaughan's turn to stare down in disbelief.

"You shouldn't be looking at things like that at your age!" he tutted – though mindful that he'd shared exactly the same fascination with the blossoming female form when he'd been that age too – and ever since!

"So what's *your* name then?" he asked.

"I'm Tom. I live on Victoria Road too. That's 'ow I know 'ow far it is. So where you staying?"

"With my auntie. I used to visit her every year when I was younger. She's the one who suggested I apply for a job on the buses. And that I come and stay with her for the summer while I'm working on them."

"'Ere. She's not that old gel' wots' got the parrot, is she?"

"Parrot? Who? My Aunt? No. Not that I'm aware of."

"Yeah. It's right funny, it is. Whistles at all the women as they go past. And it swears like 'ow's-yer-father."

Eventually, they rounded the corner to make the long, gentle descent of Victoria Road – past terraced houses that dated from that eponymous era, as well as quaint bungalows with exotic names and lovingly-tended gardens, most of which had found gainful use as guest houses. Meanwhile, ahead of them Vaughan was granted a tempting peek of an azure blue sea at the end of the road. It set his heart racing once more with the awesome promise the coming summer might hold – the prospect of acquainting himself with some 'real nice tits' included!

"'Ere y'are, mister. Now you wouldn't 'ave wanted to carry yer' case all that way, would yer'," his waggish porter observed, having heaved Vaughan's luggage onto the pavement outside the familiar, imposing frontage of the old apartment block his client had directed him to.

"Thank you. Was it twenty-five pence we agreed?"

"A bargain at 'alf the price," the cheeky youngster grinned.

Vaughan dipped into his wallet and located three ten pence pieces which he deposited in the lad's outstretched palm.

"There's thirty pence then. Keep the change – and invest it in a can of oil for those squeaky wheels."

"Gee, fanks', mister. So shall I see yer' round when it's time for you to go 'ome... if that's alright. Remember, just ask for Tom – Tom Mills. Everyone around 'ere knows me."

"That I can well believe," Vaughan ruffled his curly mop.

Alone again – though this time with his solicitude leavened by the conversation he'd just had – Vaughan grasped the handle of his case, glanced up at his home for the next eleven weeks, and commenced a passage up the steps. Breezing past the cheese plants basking in the sun-drenched verandah, he located a ground floor flat and gave the knocker a hearty rap.

"Coming!" he detected a familiar seductive voice call down the hallway. Then, at last, the door opened to reveal the surprise upon the face of a copper-blonde woman in her mid-fifties – one who, even so, had lost none of her enviable good looks.

"Auntie Angie!" Vaughan cried, dropping his case.

"Well, well. It's my little boy!" she exclaimed, launching herself around him with tearful abandon.

"Not so little now, Auntie. As you can see."

"Nonsense! You'll always be as cute to me as the day I first held you as a baby. Anyway, don't stand there. Come on in. You can fill me in on all the family gossip. First though, I'll show you to your room where you can dump that suitcase."

Observing her purposeful feminine gait as she bade him follow her down the long hallway, he was ushered into the large bedroom at the end of it – to be enthralled again by a ceiling that seemed almost as high as the room was long, and from which was a hung an impressive crystal chandelier. There, too, was the sumptuous duvet he'd once slept beneath; as well as that risqué (or kitsche, depending on ones taste!) *'Wings Of Love'* painting by Stephen Pearson his aunt noticed him studying (and which had scandalised his mother when they'd last holidayed here four years ago). Meanwhile, on the dressing table there was sat a lovingly-framed photograph of Vaughan when he was a toddler, posing on the beach with his mother and his aunt.

"Wow! I remember this bedroom like it was only yesterday," he gasped.

"Yes, well. I keep prodding your Uncle Frank to decorate the place, but I'm afraid my pleas fall on deaf ears," she folded her arms and rolled her eyes, adding "Then again, if he'd listened to me and bought a house when we first moved to the island then, with the way inflation has dwindled away mortgages, we'd have been well on our way to paying it off by now."

"Yes, where is Uncle Frank," Vaughan wondered aloud.

"Oh, doing what he always does on a Saturday – and every day bar Sundays: manning up that shop of his on the High Street."

Vaughan spotted another impatient rolling of the eyes. Aware of this, Auntie Angie moved to allay his concern, light-heartedly reminding him that "I still love the old duffer though. Frank and I can look back on some happy memories during our thirty years together – not least when you and your mom used to stay with us, sleeping in these very same beds!" she fondly ran her fingers across the duvet of one of them, before adding, "Maybe you'll come to love living on the island as much as we have."

"I hope so, Auntie," he smiled.

"Anyway, leave your unpacking for now and come with me into the parlour. You can have tea, you can have coffee; you can even have a beer if you like. Frank usually keeps some in the fridge. Maybe tomorrow, if the weather stays fine, we can have a ride out somewhere nice. There's so much to see and do on the Isle of Wight, as you well know."

"Yes, that would be nice."

"You know, I offered to help you and your mother move to the island too – after the split with your father – but she declined. She must be so terribly lonely still. She knows I've only ever wanted what's best for her and my favourite nephew."

"Mom's doing fine. She keeps herself busy with the church. I guess it helps take her mind off things."

"Hmmn," his aunt was unconvinced. "Sometimes when relationships end they can take a lot of getting over. I could write a book about it! So you bear that in mind, young Vaughan, when you're courting girls. Never go for the ones who trample all over your heart. Instead, you find yourself one who has your heart uppermost in her thoughts. And when you do find her, make sure you treasure *her* heart too."

Her nephew smiled in affirmation. Auntie Angie had always been a refreshing repository of wisdom: about life, about love, about most things, in fact. After such a long time apart, he was looking forward to the opportunity of savouring that wisdom again.

2

Tuesday, June 22nd 1976

"Pay attention, ladies and gentlemen. I'm going to demonstrate to you how a Setright ticket machine works. This is the standard ticket machine used throughout the National Bus Company's various operating divisions."

With those opening words barked across the training room, the inspector beckoned the cohort of new recruits to draw in closer so that they might observe the said device.

Having passed the medical test (to see if he was up to climbing stairs and assisting with luggage) and the aptitude test (to see if he was numerate and possessed the requisite communication skills), Vaughan was overjoyed that he had been successful in his bid to become a conductor with the Southern Vectis Omnibus Company ('Vectis' being the name the Romans had given this splendid little island). Hence, this morning he had turned up to join the other successful applicants who'd been ushered to the depot stores to receive their new uniforms. Suitably attired, it was time to get down to the practicalities of the job.

"Right, to change or insert a new roll of tickets you first remove the ticket roll cover here... like so," the inspector held out the chunky metal machine to show off what he had just done. "Then you turn this small wheel anti-clockwise so that the groove in it clears this small catch here. This will release the machine's grip on the tickets, allowing you to gently pull out any of the remaining ticket strip ready for the new roll to be inserted."

Ticket machines, waybills, company rules and regulations, depot procedures, duty rosters, routes, timetables and fares – there was so much to learn! However, this being Vaughan's first venture into the world of work, he hoped the studious demeanour he now donned would further assure his new employer that he was eager to play his part getting the island's commuters to work, its shoppers into town, and its holidaymakers back and forth between its various resorts and attractions.

"...So once you have tickets coming out of the top of the machine, turn the wheel clockwise to engage the slot with the catch. This will prevent the tickets moving without the handle being turned. Then after you've tightened the roll, replace the cover and secure it with the catch. Any questions so far?"

As there were none, the inspector offered the machine to his pupils to take turns trying it out. First off was one of the two pretty girls in the group, who attempted to hoop the harness and its back plate over her head and onto her curvaceous torso, flicking her flowing light brown hair free once it was in place.

"That's right, love, adjust the straps here and here to make sure it fits nice and snug... and that it doesn't ride too low down. You don't want the thing bashing against your knees," he cautioned.

"It fits snug alright!" one of the lads muttered to another under his breath, observing how her ample, well-corralled cleavage certainly kept the straps in place.

"Neither is it the only thing in danger of bashing against her knees!" his mate tossed out a further innuendo.

"My fist will fit snug into your face, Phil, if you don't shut it!" she shot him a censorious stare, wiggling to get comfortable with the machine now in place, that ample bosom wobbling with her.

"Come on, stop messing around," the inspector turned to quell the nascent amusement.

"Now there are four variable selector wheels below the pence dial. These wheels enable the user to set the fare stage number, the month, the date, and the fare type. Once you've done that, turn the handle, take the ticket between your finger and your thumb, and pull it towards the top of the machine in order to cut it – again, like so," he coached the girl along each step of the operation. "Remember: whatever you do, do *not* pull tickets towards the handle without cutting. Doing this is the most common cause of jams in this type of ticket machine."

Playing with the dials and cranking the handle to churn out some more tickets, the girl was confident she had the hang of the device. Therefore, she unhooped it from her shoulder and handed it to someone else to have a go.

Like Vaughan, most of the recruits being trained up today were students who were anxious to earn a bit of spare cash over the summer, at a time when (fortuitously) the increase in holiday patronage meant the island's principal bus company needed additional crews to work its enhanced summer timetables. Brimming with youthful hormones that rendered them unable to resist casting approving glances at the girls' short, uniformed skirts, it was probably not the only thing the lads would be remembering the summer for.

"Right, now we're all *au-fait* with the collection of fares, if you'll follow me outside I'll show you some of the vehicles you'll be collecting them on."

It was the cue for the recruits to file out of the training room and into the cavernous interior of the depot.

Being early afternoon, most of its allocation of buses was out on the road. However, there were still odd vehicles in the maintenance bays, where a radio playing Dr Hook's *'(Love You) A Little Bit More'* was echoing up from the inspection pit in which an oily mechanic was labouring. Otherwise, two bright green double-deckers were parked up at the entrance to the depot, which the inspector now led them over to.

"Now these buses here are Bristol Lodekkas – so-called because they're built to a shorter height so they can clear low bridges. Lodekkas are the main type of bus that you will be working aboard."

"Wow, man! A nice pair of Bristols!" one of the lads piped up.

"Bristol buses, that is," he then clarified his remark, throwing the palms of his hands up as if to feign innocence when the bustier female member of their cohort turned to entreat him to another of her censorious stares.

"...Older ones like the one behind have the platform at the rear, while this one here is a newer FLF version. It's longer and, as you can see, has the platform at the front so that the driver can watch the doors while you're collecting fares. You'll find we use these buses on our busier Ryde-Sandown-Shanklin routes because of their greater seating capacity."

Once their familiarisation with the buses was complete, there was just time to wander outside to the adjacent bus station for a quick ride out on one that was in service. That way they could observe an experienced 'clippie' in action. Then it was back to the depot to be handed their duties for the coming week, whereupon the inspector wished them good luck in their new roles and released them to head home.

Before he departed, Vaughan paused at the full-length mirror mounted outside the crews' restroom in order to admire his new uniform. *'A Southern Vectis bus conductor must be reliable and punctual; be of smart appearance; and be mindful at all times of the safety of his passengers'*, the inspector had enjoined them. He straightened his cap, brushed down the beige jacket trimmed with a green collar, and took out a handkerchief to polish his little green PSV badge that – as the inspector had also enjoined – was to be worn at all times.

"Quite a dandy, aren't we!" he noticed the girl who'd been the brunt of the lewd jokes admiring him in the mirror's reflection.

"Hi, my name's Tina. I'm over here for the summer. I assume you must be too."

Vaughan turned about and nodded nervously. "That's right. I'm Vaughan. From Dudley."

"Dudley, eh? The place with the castle and the zoo."

"That's right. You've heard of it?" he expressed surprise.

"I used to date a boy from the Black Country – well, from Birmingham, actually. Same thing, I suppose."

Vaughan was minded to point out that there was a difference! However, her amiable chirpiness rendered him forgiving. He listened as she recounted that "Paul was a sailor. We met last summer when he was on leave. We were going out together for quite a while. I did think we might even get married. And then over Christmas the two-timing so-and-so broke it to me that he fancied my best mate instead. The last I heard he'd only gone and got her pregnant!"

"Really?" said Vaughan, recalling that downcast seafarer he'd bumped into on the train – the one with the pronounced Brummie accent whose girlfriend was expecting their first child. No, surely not, he was tempted to ask.

"You a student too then?" Tina meanwhile enquired.

"Sort of. I'm hoping to enrol at Wolverhampton Polytechnic in September – on a business studies course."

"Same as me then. I've just completed my first year doing business studies at Brighton Poly. Two of the other lads here are on my course too," she pointed them out, "As is my friend Sally, who's over there with them. That's how we know each other."

"They were the ones who were making jokes about your…"

"About my big knockers? Yes, that's them," she curled her eyebrows, getting straight to the point. "Forever ribbing me over them, they are! Still, Phil and Dave are good mates – and Sally and I can give as good as we get. The four of us have rented a little terraced property for the summer not far from the depot. We all chip in with the bills. So where are you staying then?"

"With my aunt – in Sandown," Vaughan felt a touch self-conscious about confessing, wondering whether swapping the apron strings of his mother for those of Auntie Angie was really exercising independence at all – at least when compared to the adventure of shacking up with one's college mates.

"Well, there you go – you're not too far away either," she chortled. "Maybe you can come over one night. It would be good for us new clippies to get to know each other outside of work."

"Come on, Tina. You haven't even done a full day on the job yet and you're after the blokes!" they heard Dave call down the corridor impatiently.

"Anyway, like I said. Hopefully, we can get to know each other better," she insisted, nudging him coquettishly before heading off to join Phil, Dave and Sally for the walk home.

The wide-eyed Vaughan agonised. Did she mean what he thought she meant? Meanwhile, his own transport home was propped up around the back of the depot, chained to a metal soil pipe. Aware that his shifts might start at the crack of dawn and finish after midnight, Auntie Angie had very kindly escorted him to the shed outside and unveiled Uncle Frank's old bicycle. Although he could have come to work today on the bus, having spent most of yesterday evening oiling it, polishing it and fitting new batteries in the lamps, he thought he might as well give it a spin and familiarise himself with the route to work and back.

However, he hadn't bargained on the Isle of Wight being as monticulous as it was. With the late afternoon sun beating down upon him it was hard work pedalling – at least until he'd passed through Lake and could coast down into Sandown. He pondered whether the first thing he should do once he'd saved up some money from his new job was to learn to drive.

* * * * *

Arriving back in Victoria Road, Vaughan wheeled his new mode of transport into the shed and locked it away. Removing his jacket and casting it across his shoulder, he removed his cap too and mopped his brow. Then he wandered around the front of the building and mounted the steps that led up to the verandah.

"Give us a kiss!" he thought he heard someone squawk. He looked up from his preoccupations and beheld the culprit.

"Oh… Hello. Who are you?" he marvelled at a parrot that was busily looping the loop inside the tall cage it was clambering around. The bird halted on its perch and scurried over to press its head against the bars, as if to invite Vaughan to stroke it. The smiling busman drew his finger up to oblige.

"Careful. He has a tendency to bite people he's not familiar with," he heard a gentle female voice caution him.

"He's cute. Is he yours?" he looked up, drawing his finger away again.

"He is indeed. His name is Chico. He's an African Grey," replied a wizened, well-spoken lady, who paused from watering the cheese plants to draw up alongside him. "They're renowned for their ability to talk and to mimic what they hear."

"Chi-co!" the bird lifted its head and cooed.

"He can certainly talk," Vaughan chuckled.

"Yes, quite a chatterbox. I wheel him out onto the steps whenever it's a nice day. He likes to feel the sun on his wings. However, I'm afraid some of the school children who pass by have been teaching him some rather naughty words. So I apologise if you hear him being saucy," she drew in close to offer him a mischievous smile.

Vaughan chuckled again, loosening his tie and racing the tips of his fingers across his perspiring forehead.

"Yes, it is rather hot," she noted. "It read eighty-six degrees on the thermometer outside when I looked earlier. Apparently, it's going to be even hotter tomorrow."

"Cor! Sex!" Chico meanwhile interjected, attempting to further show off his dubious mastery of the English language.

"I think he means 'sexy', but hasn't quite learned how to say it properly. It's one of those saucy words the children have taught him. I think he's taken a shine to you though," its owner simpered. "You must be Angela's nephew. Vaughan, is it?"

"That's right."

"Well, I'm Betty – her next door neighbour. Together we take turns to keep all these triffids looking tidy," she joked.

"Ah, there you are," gushed Angie, having overheard the sound of voices on the other side of a front door that was ajar. "So how was your first day then?"

"It went well, Auntie," her nephew enthused.

"Vaughan's a bus conductor, you know," she proudly announced – although Vaughan couldn't help thinking the uniform and the cap in his hand were rather a giveaway.

"Anyway, I suppose you're all sweaty after cycling home in this heat. So I've put the water heater on for a bath. There's just time for one before dinner will be ready," she suggested, fanning herself with dainty swishes of her hand.

"In which case, I won't detain you a moment longer," Betty smiled, returning to her propagation duties.

Meanwhile, Chico whistled a few bars of *'Colonel Bogey'* with which to bid his new friend *bon appétit*.

* * * * *

"She's a good friend is Betty. The kind of neighbour everyone should be blessed with. She used to be midwife before she retired, you know. She worked in Africa. That's how she came by Chico. But just watch what you say in front of that parrot because he's smart and he copies everything he hears. So if you complain about my cooking be sure I'll get to hear about it!"

Thanks to Auntie Angie's easy-going hospitality, Vaughan had settled into his new surroundings. And, for what it was worth, she'd lost none of her famed culinary flair (for which he now complemented her). As she explained, those Delia Smith cooking programmes on TV had tempted her to venture into more exotic cuisine, the beef stroganoff with white mushrooms and a hint of paprika in a small, yet telling way indicative of a woman impatient to be squeezing every last ounce of excitement out of life. He just wished he could say the same for his Uncle Frank.

"You courting yet, young man?" his uncle enquired between mouthfuls, one of several laconic questions and asides he'd tossed out as if to go through the motions of demonstrating avuncular concern.

Vaughan shook his head. "No, Uncle," he replied.

"Ah, well. It'll happen... Soon... I'm sure," was his uncle's equally laconic response.

"Maybe you'll meet someone nice on the buses," suggested Auntie Angie, sensing the plaintive embarrassment in her young nephew's admission and sounding a more optimistic note. "I've seen one or two nice young conductresses working on them over the summer."

"And how's that mother of yours?" Uncle Frank ventured, tossing out another one. "It's been a while since Nora's been to stay. You'll have to invite her down before summer is over, dear," he glanced up at his wife sat opposite, jabbing with his fork.

"I already have," she replied. "When I phoned her the other day she promised she would try and get some time off at the end of August to join us. Won't that be nice, Vaughan?" she beamed, "Just like old times again."

Vaughan nodded. With money tight since his parents' separation, it had been a while since either Vaughan or his mother had been able to enjoy a holiday.

In between his aunt's hopeful banter and his uncle's stilted observations, Vaughan pondered how bizarre it was that his own parents' relationship had floundered – even as the mercurial marriage of Frank and Angela Tring had soldiered on. For though he had fond memories of childhood holidays staying with them, even back then the eyes of a child could detect there was a certain mismatch between Uncle Frank and Auntie Angie. Though on the surface everything seemed a picture of domestic bliss, at times Uncle Frank could be too domestic for his own good. Vaughan discreetly looked up from his meal to cast his eye upon a proper pipe-and-slippers man – someone not overly-fussed that the lithe outline of the dashing naval petty officer he'd once been had long since given way to the paunch, the double chin and the receding hairline of a provincial shop proprietor. And though he was polishing off his own serving of Auntie Angie's stroganoff with gusto, Vaughan couldn't help thinking that he would have been just as content to tuck into a bland plate of meat-and-two-veg.

In contrast, Auntie Angie exhibited an almost religious attachment to tending to her looks and figure – even if the former was supplemented by make-up, lipstick and eyeliner, and the latter by a girdle and a push-up bra. And though a critical eye could discern crow's feet and a head of permed hair that required increasing quantities of dye to hide the grey bits, she was still an incredibly attractive lady. Factor in that seductive low voice and she could surely bewitch any man upon whom she chose to lavish her attention. So why did Vaughan get the sense that somehow it had long ago ceased working on Uncle Frank?

To be sure, one outcome of possessing those looks and that voice was that they had enabled her to find gainful employment as a singer at the many hotels and holiday camps around the island. Though not quite the fame and fortune she'd once dreamt of, at least it had enabled her to sublimate her womanly charms into entertaining others. Besides, as well as supplementing the income the couple derived from the toy shop Uncle Frank owned on the High Street, Vaughan suspected it was also a welcome means of escaping her husband's suffocating mediocrity – if only for a few nights a week. Indeed, with the evening meal consumed, it was for just such a nocturnal engagement that Auntie Angie now glanced up at the box clock on the wall and pleaded the need to get ready.

Feeling obliged to earn his keep, Vaughan offered to do the washing up, thereby freeing Angie to go run the bath. Frank, meanwhile, switched on the television set, sank back into his favourite armchair, and sought to catch up with the opening day at

Wimbledon. Thus it was that, as well as the voice of Dan Maskell in the sitting room commentating on Björn Borg's prospects of reaching the men's finals, he could catch the sound of splashing water drifting from the bathroom at the end of the hall – as well as his aunt humming along to Abba's chart-topping *'Fernando'* playing on the transistor radio she'd taken inside with her. Furthermore, once he'd completed the drying-up, crossing the hallway to join Uncle Frank he perchance did so at the precise moment Auntie Angie crossed it too, catching a glimpse of her cleavage as the bath robe she was wearing briefly fell open. Spotting the trajectory of his eyes, she smiled awkwardly and drew it shut again, hastening to the bedroom and closing the door.

"Nâstase – he's the one to watch..." Uncle Frank entreated him to another of his laconisms. "Much better player... And Chris Evert – a dead certainty for the women's finals."

Vaughan couldn't say he was an aficionado of lawn tennis. So it was with relief that Uncle Frank kept further laconisms to a minimum, instead grunting to himself from time to time to cast aspersions upon the studio commentators' match predictions.

"Right, I'm off now. Another late one, I'm afraid," his aunt chortled, finally emerging to divert into the sitting room, where she placed a dutiful kiss upon Frank's polished head (her husband by now too absorbed in *'The Undersea World Of Jacques Cousteau'* to offer all but a cursory acknowledgement). Vaughan at least looked up and smiled as she slipped her fingers through his dark locks and kissed his head too. Then she grabbed the suitcase she'd deposited in the hall and was gone.

Uncle Frank attention didn't falter from his television – the means by which he chose to unwind at the end of another long day flogging Sindy dolls, Hornby trains and Dinky cars to the town's children. Vaughan laughed along to Tom, Barbara, Margot and Jerry rubbing along together in *'The Good Life'* on BBC1. However, when Uncle Frank bounced out of his armchair and switched the set to coverage of the US Open on BBC2 that was the final straw. Golf was most definitely not the teenager from Gornal's aphrodisiac!

"It looks a nice evening out there, Uncle Frank. I think I might have a stroll along the Esplanade."

Uncle Frank didn't demur, so Vaughan vacated his place on the sofa and made his way out onto the street, past the cheese plants casting silhouettes in the verandah.

"Give us a kiss!" Chico croaked as he flitted past his cage.

One advantage of the Trings having rented an apartment on Victoria Road was that it was a mere hop, skip and a jump to the seafront, where he could now partake of a lazy stroll while gazing out across a becalmed Sandown Bay.

The longest day was remorselessly giving way to the shortest night. With it, one crowd of holiday-makers promenading its well-trod pavements was giving way to another. Back to their hotels and guest houses were heading families that had enjoyed a last roll of their pennies in the arcades; in their place were flocking single young men and women volubly posing in their finest gear, off to search out a bar or a nightclub in which to drink and dance away the sultry first evening of summer.

Vaughan savoured the opportunity to be alone with his thoughts. In particular, he pondered afresh the offer Tina had made that afternoon – about the two of them getting to know each other better. It made him conscious of how sheltered his life had been so far. While his schoolmates had been sneaking into the Catacombs nightclub in Wolverhampton to dance the night away to northern soul, Vaughan had joined the youth group at the lively Pentecostal church in Dudley where his mother worshipped, having dutifully deferred to her desire that he turn his eyes to more edifying teenage pastimes.

His mother had turned to God when Vaughan had started secondary school, a prophylactic (he increasingly suspected) to disappointments in her own teenage years, of which she spoke only elliptically on those occasions when she'd elected to discuss her past at all. Yet there was something in either her disposition or her experience of growing up that had rendered Nora Lewis the binary opposite of her scintillating older sister. Either way (and though an attractive woman herself), following the break from his father in 1970 there had not been another man in her life since. Neither did she seem in any great hurry to find one, preferring instead to immerse herself in the activities of her church.

Wandering through the cacophony of chortling slot machines in the amusement arcade, Vaughan sought out the relative tranquillity to be found at the end of the pier, where waves were rhythmically lapping beneath the deck boards and fishermen were casting lines, waiting patiently for a bite.

As the sun finally dipped, he continued ruminating upon all these things. About girls he'd known (and of his lack of success with them so far); about how he would adapt to the challenge of holding down his first real job; about the chalk-and-cheese personalities of his aunt and uncle; about his mother and the all-encompassing religious faith she'd stumbled upon that had enabled her to blot out unspoken heartache of her own; and finally about his own response to a God who sought obedience from his followers, yet who was daily confronted with fallible disciples who were anything but. And now Vaughan had reached a point in his life when he too would have to tiptoe through such emotional and morally-challenging minefields.

It was certainly going to make for an interesting summer, he sensed. And maybe for a revealing one too.

3

Wednesday, June 23rd 1976

"Say, what was that your mom told you about it only ever raining in England?"

Shelby's ironic observation came when she took a moment out from changing sheets to draw back the blinds and fling open the balcony doors of the most expensive suite in the Shanklin Heights Hotel – the one astride the top floor that offered uninterrupted cliff-top views out across Sandown Bay. Those views she now ventured out to admire.

The fiery yellow ball that she shielded her eyes from was already beating down upon the first morning beachgoers who were staking out deckchairs on the sands below. And it had only just gone nine o'clock!

"Well, it sure doesn't look like rain today There's not a cloud in the sky," she called back inside. Then she stretched her arms aloft and exclaimed to Heaven "Why, I do declare I could almost be back home in good ol' Jasper County!"

Aimee desisted from her weary swabbing of the bathroom floor and propped her mop up in the bucket so that she too could wander onto the balcony. There, the two American room maids enjoyed a long, refreshing moment surveying an azure blue sky and a cobalt sea that met upon a shimmering horizon, upon which was balanced the tiny white outline of a cruise liner steaming off into the English Channel.

"Ever get the feeling that we shoulda' spent the summer bumming our way around Europe?" the Minnesotan opined, her fair hair rippling in the warm breeze.

Shelby smiled, drew in close, and cast her arm around her companion, insisting that "As my daddy used to say to me: 'girl, if you ain't earned it, you won't appreciate it!' Anyway, I think you look kinda' cute in that uniform," she insisted, having unlooped the arm so she could step back and admire her friend.

"Yeah, Shorty. Like your outfit isn't anything like as revealing as mine," Aimee twirled, demonstrating how her own flimsy black skirt concealed very little of her gorgeous long legs.

"Then I guess you'll just have to be careful who's about when you're bending over!" her friend laughed.

"Anyhow," Shelby continued. "Quit whining! Friday will soon be here, and with it our first day-off. So how about you and me head off some place exploring? I'm told you can buy a ticket on the buses round here that lets you to travel anywhere on the island. If the weather stays fine, I say let's do it."

"That's the best idea you've had so far. And when the sun goes down then maybe we can find some place where they play great music and serve ice-cold beers. And where there are plenty of good-looking guys too. I'm sure there must be a cool bar somewhere in this town where we can hang out."

Shelby stared across at her fellow student. "Your folks happy that you wanna' hang out in joints like that?" she frowned.

It was the cue for Aimee to pace a step forward and lean upon the balustrade before returning the stare.

"Give me a break, Shell. I swear you're turning into my dad," she huffed.

"It's just that..."

"Come on. You know how it is. Bars in England aren't like the ones on Main Street, USA. Everyone goes in 'pubs' over here. It's an English tradition. Why, even my dad used to hang out in 'em when he was over here."

Shelby appeared suitably sceptical. Furthermore, she felt obliged to express something that had been on her mind for some time – and certainly during the year they'd spent overseas.

"It's just that... you've changed, Aimee – in the time we've been friends. You used to be so..."

"Yeah, so square – like my folks. Well, you're too right I've changed. I'm a big girl now. And there's so much more I wanna' see and do. I didn't travel all the way to England just to study all week and sit in church on Sundays – like a 'good girl' should. I've spent twenty years playing dutiful little daughter. It's time for that daughter to be her own woman."

Shelby's lingering frown relented. She had done her best to steer her lively and attractive friend away from boys of lecherous intent who'd taken a shine to her at Oxford. And so far they'd both managed to eschew the drugs, drunken soirees and other late-night temptations of varsity life overseas.

And yet somehow Aimee remained a girl who was determined to explore and push boundaries – as if she was on a mission to demonstrate she was 'her own woman' in the most spectacular ways imaginable. Sure, she was in rebellion against her folks and maybe (Shelby feared) her faith also, as well as the expectations of who she should be and how she should behave that both had come to symbolise. For how much longer could her loyal friend (and the most effective brake upon her wilder pretensions) head off the inevitable moment when that restless yearning to 'see' and 'do' collided head on with a fallen world populated by some very fallen people indeed.

Just then their scenic introspection was interrupted by the emergence onto the balcony of a suave and handsome man in an expensive-looking patterned silk shirt. Drawing his fist to his mouth, he coughed to alert the two girls to his presence.

"I'm so sorry if I startled you. The door was open, so I wandered in," he addressed them with the genteel, polished accent of an English gentleman.

"Oh, do forgive us. We were in the process of preparing your room," Aimee apologised, having swung about in alarm.

"That's right," Shelby pleaded. "We were just taking a moment to admire the views from up here. It really is a swell room you've booked – the best room in the house."

The newcomer in their midst appeared vaguely amused.

"It's not *my* room. Though I'm pleased to hear that 'admiring' the views will only take 'a moment'," he teased them – a hint of jest in his manner which Aimee picked up on.

"I'm sorry?" she ventured, her brow crumpling to match her bewilderment.

"John Lawton," he replied, extending his hand – into which the American tentatively slipped hers. He extended it to Shelby too, the diminutive student nervously doing likewise.

"You see, I own the Shanklin Heights Hotel," he then introduced himself.

The girls were thrown by the revelation, glancing at each other in trepidation.

"I've come to apologise," he then announced to their surprise. "For not being here to greet you personally the day you started. I make a point of saying 'hello' to all my new staff. I trust it makes them feel a part of my team. However, I believe you did meet my wife – Veronica. I hope she made you welcome in my absence."

"Er... yeah, she did," Aimee once more took the lead. "We hope we assured her of our gratitude for offering us both jobs."

"Yes, she said you seemed like nice girls, both of you. I trust the arrangements we have agreed will prove mutually beneficial. And you must be...?" he enquired, training his piercing blue eyes upon her more sheepish colleague.

"Er, Shelby. Sh-Shelby Carmichael," she stuttered.

"Ah, yes. Shelby. From Georgia, I believe – Chickamauga, Atlanta, and the March to the Sea."

Shelby stuttered again, as if too overawed to think straight.

"They were campaigns during your country's Civil War," her employer enlightened her, once more a disarming smirk breezing across his sun-bronzed face.

"Oh yes, of course," she remembered, nodding with relief.

"So, by a process of elimination, that means you must be Aimee – Aimee-Marie Eichelberger," his searching gaze returned to her friend, this time with renewed interest.

"That's right, sir."

"The daughter of General Charles F. Eichelberger – retired commander of the United States Seventh Air Force."

Aimee was thrown again, this time her unease borne of wary curiosity rather than a guilty conscience at being caught loafing on the job. She glanced at Shelby, who observed her summon the resolve to match her employer's intriguing gaze.

"You know my father?"

"In a manner of speaking, yes. Well," he chuckled self-effacingly, "let's just say I've been corresponding with him of late. You see, reading and writing about American military history is something of a passion of mine – a pastime I like to indulge when I'm not running a busy hotel," he explained before noting for Shelby's benefit that "A few years ago I had the privilege of visiting your country and some of its famous Civil War battle sites – including those in Georgia."

Then he stared back at Aimee and elaborated upon why he was so taken to being meeting her for the first time.

"So if I may be so bold, your father is quite a stellar presence in the pantheon of American military history: a decorated fighter ace with the 357th Fighter Group during World War Two – including fifteen confirmed kills while escorting bombing missions over Germany, for which he was awarded a Medal of Honor. Likewise some pretty impressive combat citations earned in Korea. It was small wonder that by 1970 he'd risen to be the director of the Joint Chiefs of Staff. Then in 1972 he assumed command of the final US aerial assaults of the Vietnam War. And, last but not least, he directed combat missions over Cambodia in support of its beleaguered pro-American government. By the time those controversial missions were halted in August 1973 the United States had dropped almost three million tons of bombs on the country."

Whatever deference the General's daughter had initially manifested towards this John Lawton fellow appeared to have suddenly evaporated.

"If you don't mind me saying, you seem have made it your business to know all about my father," she replied tersely.

Lawton thought for a moment, as if to choose his words with care, before admitting that "When Veronica first told me she'd taken you on I saw the name and confess I was intrigued. So now you and I have finally caught up, I thought I'd tell you in person how much I admire him. Charles Eichelberger is a brave warrior, a tenacious leader of men, and an outstanding military strategist. He has given a lifetime of loyal service to his country. You must be very proud of him."

Aimee was plainly becoming uncomfortable at the gushing compliments being showering upon someone who she preferred to just look upon as 'Dad'. Maybe her new boss detected this, for his gaze eventually relented and settled upon Shelby instead.

"As I said, I hope we'll enjoy working together. I hope too that you've found your living quarters amenable," he clasped his hands together, a searching smile alternating between them both.

"Er... Yeah. Sure. Y'all made us feel really at home," the flustered Georgian wittered.

"Good. Then I won't keep you from your work," Lawton smirked for a final time, a tilt of his head and the trajectory of his mischievous eyes hinting that it was time for the admiring of the views to cease and for the chores that were awaiting them inside to be attended to instead.

* * * * *

Friday June 25th 1976

When the girls' first full rest day finally came around they did indeed take themselves off to explore the island. However, with the mercury rising in the thermometer and ten weeks ahead of them to complete that exploration, they agreed there was no point in doing it in haste. So on their first outing they chose to hop aboard a Number 46 bus, which took them off along the old military road that traversed the island's wild southern coastline. Eventually alighting in the pretty little port of Yarmouth, they swapped onto an open top double-decker that trundled its way up to Alum Bay at the island's far western tip.

Riding the chairlift down to the bay itself, there they passed a morning taking turns to pose in front of Shelby's Polaroid camera, photographing each other juxtaposed against the albino chalk outcrop of The Needles – the Isle of Wight's most famous landmark – as well as digging amongst the rainbow-coloured sands for which Alum Bay is renowned.

Re-ascending to the top of the cliffs, in the souvenir shop the two students each purchased a miniature glass lighthouse, topping it up with a selection of the said coloured sands to take home as a memento of their perfect day out. Aimee – the more melanin-challenged of the two girls – also purchased a wide-brimmed straw hat with which to supplement the suntan lotion she'd been applying to protect her skin from the fierce midday sun.

After lunch overlooking the boats moored up in Yarmouth harbour, as well as ferries dashing back and forth from the mainland, they then re-boarded the Number 46 bus. However, before heading home – and with its evocative vista of flanking white cliffs and a turquoise sea proving irresistible – they broke the journey at the small seaside hamlet of Freshwater Bay.

It was here – on its small, but inviting stretch of chalk pebble beach – that they could be found relaxing. Supine upon her towel in a slinky polka-dot bikini, Shelby was lapping up an afternoon sun that was turning her already bronzed body a darker shade of olive. Meanwhile, her fair-skinned best friend was trying as best she could to keep cool in the sudden heat-wave, that wide-brimmed hat draped across her face.

From beneath this hat she now emerged to prop herself onto her elbows, taking a moment to survey her surroundings. In particular, she cast an envious eye over an expensive-looking yacht that was riding at anchor in the bay. Upon it she spotted a girl not much older than herself, who had discarded her bikini top to sun herself on deck. Meanwhile, her husband (or sugar daddy, or whoever the older man was) was partaking of a cooling dip in the glistening waters off the vessel's stern.

"Wow! What I wouldn't give to be her right now," she sighed.

Shelby, still basking motionless upon her towel, ventured no response. Therefore – after a moment spent pondering what it must be like to be some millionaire's love interest – Aimee changed the subject and tried again.

"You know, I read some place that Freshwater is one of the 'Seven Wonders of the Isle of Wight'."

This time Shelby proffered a vague murmur.

"Yeah," Aimee elaborated. "'Freshwater you can't drink'."

"No kidding? So what are the other six?"

"'Needles you can't thread'; 'Ryde where they make you walk'; 'Cowes you can't milk'. And I forget what the others are."

"Fascinating," her friend sounded underwhelmed.

"Anyway, on a day like today this place reminds me so much of Italy," Aimee ploughed on unfazed while staring up and squinting as if to spot the faintest hint of a passing cloud. "Capri, I think it was. Or was it Amalfi?" she ruminated aloud.

"You see, I was about eight years-old when Dad was posted to Italy," she continued. "I can still remember that holiday: the sea, the mountains, the green trailing vines, little villages up in the mountains. It kinda' made up for spending the rest of the time stuck on a boring air base in the middle of nowhere."

"You've been so lucky," Shelby opined, finally sounding a note of interest. "I mean to have seen so many amazing places as a child. Until I arrived at college the furthest I ever travelled was to Savannah on 4-H Club summer camp."

With Shelby's eyes still firmly shut, she was oblivious to the envy-laden study her friend was making of the couple on the yacht, the handsome, sun-bronzed man having mounted the Jacob's ladder to towel himself down in front of that topless, sun-bronzed love interest. It prompted the onlooker to snap out her daydream and reach into her bag for some more sunscreen.

"You know, sometimes I get to thinking that you're the lucky one, Shell," she asserted. "I mean, at least you've got a sense of belonging; a place you can call home. Me – I never had that. Home was wherever Dad was posted – invariably a succession of military bases across the United States and overseas. Then later a succession of boarding schools while he was off fighting that ridiculous Asian war. It kinda' made me a loner, I guess; because every time I made a friend we ended up being separated again.

"I guess that's why I really value your friendship. You stuck with me all through college – and here in England. And now you're making beds and mopping latrines with me when you could have passed the summer vacation back home with your folks. I can't tell you how grateful I am. I finally feel that someone is there for me; listening to me; and looking out for me."

Shelby popped an eye open, flopping a limp hand across it to shield her gaze as she glanced up. Then the eye closed again and that arm was extended so that the dainty fingers at its extremity might trail tenderly along her friend's bright red forearm.

"Girl, you sure take a lot of looking out for. I reckon I shoulda' been paid handsomely for rescuing you from some of the hair-raising scrapes we've found ourselves in."

As the trailing fingers retreated Aimee drew herself forward to gather up her knees and rest her arms and her chin upon them pensively.

"So maybe 'Little Miss Perfect' really has become my second dad, after all!" she joked, staring back out to sea.

"Hey, quit saying that. I ain't no 'Little Miss Perfect'. Remember: I'm a sinner saved by grace – just like you," Shelby insisted, though choosing to take her friend's sardonic observation as a compliment.

Upon which, she rose from her semi-slumber, gathered up her own knees, and joined Aimee in a reflective study of that opulent craft bobbing in the bay. There they spent a moment of unspoken communion with each other before Shelby nudged her shades up onto her head and trained her eyes upon her companion.

"Say – and talking of dads – our new boss is certainly taken by yours. It looks like your old man might have become a household name on this side of the Pond too."

The moment she uttered her throw-away remark Shelby could sense it had struck a raw nerve. All through college these two best friends had stuck together; bound by their shared Christian faith, but curiously on account of both being outsiders too.

Shelby Carmichael was the daughter of a rural gas station proprietor from a backwater Southern state – the quintessential outsider who, by dint of intellect, hard work, the sacrifices of her proud parents, and a Pell scholarship had landed a place at her country's most prestigious *alma mater* for aspiring women. Aimee-Marie Eichelberger was the daughter of a distinguished four-star general, who should have been in her element hob-knobbing with the scions of America's wealthy elite. So why was the General's daughter shaking her head and recalling the cruel predicament of finding herself an 'outsider' there too?

"You know, Shell, it still rankles that the girls on campus used to look down on me because I was 'Eichelberger's kid'. To them I wasn't the daughter of a 'brave warrior'; or 'a tenacious leader of men'; or even 'an outstanding military strategist'. No, to them I was the spawn of 'a baby killer'; 'a mass murderer'; a 'war criminal'. I heard the things they used to say about Dad behind my back. And because of the things he was called upon to do, I guess they hated me too. Or maybe they just pitied me instead. Either way, they never wanted to be my friend. It's why I am so grateful to you, Shell," she turned to remind her. "You're one of the few people on campus who accepted me for who *I* am, and not who my father is."

"It wasn't so hot knowing that people on campus looked down their noses at me for being a 'hick from the sticks'," Shelby chafed in her tuneful Dixie drawl. "It rankled too the way they figured that, just because I was a proud, bible-believing white kid from a small Southern town, then I must be the 'spawn' of a cross-burning redneck; someone who lynched negroes and pined for 'the land of cotton'. Hey, I wanted to cry out: my daddy's a good man. He didn't raise me to hate anyone. Besides, it turned out my best friend at elementary school would be one of the first black girls they admitted when the place was desegregated!"

Indignant reminder complete, she flopped back down on her towel and tweaked her sunshades back over her eyes.

"So there you go: I guess maybe you and me were destined to be thrown together for a reason," she affirmed, not noticing that Aimee's attention had meanwhile wandered again to that splendid white yacht that was anchored in the bay.

4

Saturday, June 26th 1976

Boy, it was hot! By the time the elderly double-decker swung onto Ryde Bus Station the midday temperature had already soared well into the nineties. Thus it was with relief that its driver pulled up to the stand, permitting its passengers to disembark. He then bade his callow, perspiring conductor join him trudging off to the welcome shade of the restroom.

"I told you it would come off," he muttered, removing one of the hands he had sunk in his trouser pockets so that he might hold the door open for his colleague.

And so it had. Proud as Vaughan was of his new uniform, the first thing to be discarded had been the jacket. Then the tie had been loosened, the top button of his shirt undone, and the sleeves rolled up. Alas, all that now remained to remind the world that Vaughan Lewis was a conductor with the Southern Vectis Omnibus Company was the PSV badge dangling from the strap of his cash bag and the cap that was sat atop his head of lank, sweaty brown hair – which he removed, puffing exaggeratedly and mopping his brow.

"You should think yourself fortunate, my son," his new friend sniped as they queued for teas. "At least there's a breeze blowing through that open platform. You should be sat next to the engine, like I am. It's like a bloody sauna in that cab."

Colin Garrett was a waggish, twenty-five year-old former soldier who the depot had teamed Vaughan up with, and who had taken it upon himself to mother the rookie conductor during his first week on the job. He was also a 'Caulkhead' – as natives of the Isle of Wight are called (as opposed to 'Overners' like Uncle Frank and Auntie Angie – people from the mainland who have made the island their home).

It had been exactly seven days since Vaughan had arrived on the Isle of Wight and this was the final shift of his first week in his new job. So far, so good: Conductor KK34543 Lewis had familiarised himself sufficiently with the Number 8 route and its fare stages to be able to assist passengers with their journeys without incident or upset. It was a delightful route too, taking in the seafront of Sandown all the way to the cliffs at Yaverland before snaking through the enchanted villages of Bembridge and St Helens on its hour-long sojourn between Shanklin and Ryde.

The worldly-wise Colin possessed a rascalish demeanour that Vaughan had warmed to during the three days they'd been working together. More fascinating still for the sexually-uninitiated teenager from Gornal, Colin was undeniably a lady's man – as evidenced by the suggestive grin he offered the young woman in the canteen as she deposited the teas on the servery (and which lingered as half-an-eye trained upon her once the two crew members had located somewhere to sit down).

"She's a cracker is that one," he leant forward and muttered across the table to Vaughan. "Apparently, her old man's in the Royal Marines. Away in the Med at the moment, he is – or so she's been telling me. I reckon I could be well in with her. Look at her – she obviously up for it."

That was one possible interpretation of the coy smile the amiable brunette emitted as Colin glanced over and caught her attention again. Or maybe, like some of the conductresses Vaughan had watched him also lavishing his charm upon, she was merely flattered and amused by Driver Garrett's comical forwardness.

"So, you had much luck then? On the female front, I mean?" he fixed his concentration upon his conductor, donning an aura of matey concern. Vaughan shook his head regretfully.

"Not a problem, my old mate. We all have to start somewhere. You stick with me and we'll see if we can put that right. You've certainly come to the right place. All these teenage girls on holiday; looking to have some fun on their first time away from their parents. They're up for it too – if you know how to play your cards right. Especially in this weather, what with the way the sun and the heat play havoc with their hormones."

There was always the possibility that the boastful intuition of blokes like Colin was but a smokescreen for their own lack of success 'on the female front'. Though he possessed undeniable rugged good looks, were women really so fickle that they would fall for his preposterous flannel? Vaughan listened without comment as Colin supped tea and continued to wax lyrical about the things he'd learned about women, their ways, and their hormones – the lad from the Black Country hoping to discover useful insights that might further his own ambitions on that front.

"... Of course, talking about the Med," he digressed, "in a few years time things will all be very different. Around here, I mean – on the island. Spain, Greece and Portugal – they're the next big thing in holidays. I watched this programme on telly the other day about how the Spanish have been putting up new hotels like they're going out of fashion. The cost of flights is tumbling too. So why would anyone pay a fortune to spend two weeks in some dismal guest house in rain-lashed Ventnor – and with some old battleaxe of a landlady expecting you to be tucked up in bed by ten-thirty – when for the same price you can enjoy guaranteed sun, sex and sangria on the Costa Brava? Would you?"

Vaughan assumed the question was rhetorical, and so thought it futile to make reference to today's ambient heat, as well as to solitary ceiling fan in the restroom that was making little headway expelling it.

"No, mate. In a few years' time this place will be a ghost town. Spain – that's where it will all be happening; and where all the best young birds will be heading. In fact, one day I'm gonna' move there myself. Maybe set up my very own English pub. Or perhaps a fish-and-chip shop – because not everyone likes all that spicy mush those foreigners serve up."

It was a fascinating glimpse into the future, Vaughan agreed as they drank up and made their way back out into the blazing sun. However, Colin's part in it sounded as fanciful as his supposed prowess with women. As far as Vaughan could deduce from the monologues he'd proffered recounting his life so far, the cheeky, blond-mopped busman possessed no particular catering expertise; and his experience of the licensed trade amounted to the supping he undertook in local pubs when not on duty. Still, he was a highly capable bus driver, confidently manoeuvring his steed around the island's narrow, winding lanes – a skill he'd no doubt honed during his time driving tank transporters in the army (or so he'd recounted during yesterday's restroom monologue). Perhaps that was why he felt able to speak with authority about the sexual frustrations of lonely servicemen's wives.

While Colin mounted the cab of his Lodekka and fired up the engine, Vaughan reached up from the bonnet step to change the front destination blind. As he was doing so, a pair of teenage girls in mini-skirts and vest tops staggered up to him on their platform heels, looking on while he cranked the blind handle through the place names on the roll.

"Ooh, good. Your bus goes to Shanklin then. That's where we're staying," one of them exclaimed as he stepped back onto the heat-softened tarmac.

He turned about to behold both the bonny prospective passengers and the suitcases in their hands, reasoning they must have alighted from the hovercraft that had just arrived from Southsea (the roar of which was present in the background). Consulting the mental filing cabinet of the island's buses he was now carrying around in his head, Vaughan donned a boyish smile and helpfully pointed out something they needed to know.

"If it's Shanklin you're heading for you'd be better taking the Number 16 from that stand there. It's quicker and more direct. I'm afraid this bus goes the long way round."

Having overheard the exchange through the open cab window, Colin rolled his eyes and shook his head, despairing at the naivety of his young crew member.

"That bus might be more direct. But, listen here, girls," he called over, craning out onto the bonnet bearing an unctuous grin, "ours is by far the more scenic route. Okay, it takes a little longer. But if you're not in any particular hurry I'm sure my conductor here will be happy to point out the sights along the way. And tell you about all the many places you can visit during your stay on the island."

"Well... I supposed we're not in a desperate hurry, are we Mand," one of the girls noted, looking to her mate and bearing a suggestive grin.

"No, Trace," she concurred coquettishly, "After all, we can't check in at our guest house until after two o'clock."

"Well, there you go, ladies," Colin crowed merrily, "We'll be in Shanklin in plenty of time for you to be shown to your rooms. So why not hop aboard and enjoy the view from the top deck."

His recommendation was followed by the flashing of a cajoling wink at Vaughan... who eventually cottoned on to what was expected of him, racing after Mandy and Tracy as they were about to board and obligingly grabbing their cases to stow in the luggage bay. Then, after guiltily snatching a glimpse of their knickers as they climbed the stairs it was two rings of the bell and the Lodekka was on its way to Shanklin... via the scenic route.

* * * * *

Monday, June 28th 1976

Alas, the 'scenic route' had not proved to be the productive route for getting off with the opposite sex that Vaughan had hoped.

Insufficiently forward to be able to boldly regurgitate what he had imbibed so far about the island's rich cultural highlights, he had been left to look on in frustration as Mandy and Tracy had plonked themselves down at the front of the bus and thereafter passed the entire journey immersed in a lively conversation about fashion, films and music. Somehow Vaughan guessed jaunty entreaties about the model village at Godshill, the waxworks museum at Brading, or the fibre-glass dinosaurs of Blackgang Chine were never going to tantalise them in the same manner as Vivienne Westwood, Travis Bickle or Leo Sayer. Therefore, he had saved his breath and carried on collecting fares.

Today though he was about to encounter a whole lot more pretty teenage girls on the Ryde-Sandown-Shanklin run; and teenage boys for that matter. For it was approaching four o'clock on another simmering afternoon when Colin drew the Lodekka up alongside a bus stop that was positively teeming with them.

It was the first time Vaughan's rosters had involved him having to wave aboard the riotous oiks waiting outside the local secondary school. Staring back at him in commiseration through the glass partition, Colin was content to be hidden away in his cab. As the bus began to fill with excitable pupils he hastily unclipped the driver's night blind behind him and rolled it down.

"About time!"

"Call this a bus service!"

"Yeah, we've been sweatin' buckets standin' around 'ere."

With these and other disdainful felicitations, the hordes of hot and bothered pupils pushed and shoved their way aboard the bus, the rougher elements jostling their way up the stairs onto the upper deck. With everyone safely on board, Vaughan sounded the bell and the lumbering Lodekka pulled away.

The more polite and scholarly youngsters on the lower deck proved a delight to take fares from – eager to be sped home in time to catch up with what John Noakes, Peter Purves and Lesley Judd were making this week on *'Blue Peter'*. However, it was with trepidation that the rookie conductor returned to his platform and stared up into the convex viewing mirror at the top of the stairs, there to observe the pandemonium that had meanwhile engulfed the upper deck. Swallowing hard, he seized the handrails and commenced a passage up the stairs.

"Fares please," he called out upon ascending to the top.

As well as dodging a squadron of paper aeroplanes, he noticed smoke wafting about now that the fifth-formers on the back seat had started passing round the fags. With these now bobbing between their lips, they grudgingly trawled their pockets for passes and change. Coins and tickets were passed back and forth as fast as Vaughan could take and issue them, the handle on his little machine spinning furiously.

"Haven't you got anything smaller?" he challenged one lanky kid with ginger, feather-cut hair who rather fancifully offered him a crumpled pound note. "And where's your term ticket?"

"Don't need one, do I. I ain't fourteen yet," was the terse reply as the lad jabbed the note in his direction again.

Vaughan curled an eye, but chose instead to scoop a selection of coins from out of his cash bag, painstaking counting out the change while the bus was jolting him about.

"'Ere, mate, where you from?" another kid probed, discerning that the accent wasn't local.

"Me? I'm from Dudley – in the West Midlands," he replied with the obliging smile of innocence.

"What? From Dud-lay? Cor! Listen, lads. He's from DUD-LAY!" the lad riposted, cruelly exaggerating Vaughan's mild Black Country ling.

"DUD-LAY!" his mates joined in the mockery.

As he progressed down the bus Vaughan attention was arrested by another spotty youth, who blew smoke in his face when he requested a closer inspection of the moth-eaten term pass he'd flashed at him. Some of the girls looked on and giggled.

"No problem is there, mate," he grinned cockily, having exhaled another ascending billow. "It sez' in the rules yer' can smoke on the top deck."

The girls giggled again.

"It also says in the rules that radios and musical instruments shall not be played to the annoyance of other passengers," Vaughan turned his attention to one of them, who was clutching a transistor radio in her hand that was warbling a tinny refrain.

"I ain't annoying nobody, am I Sharon," she protested, turning for moral support to her best mate sat next to her.

"Nah, we like this tune, don't we, girls," Sharon concurred.

"Yeah, it's Queen, in' it."

"... *Mama, just killed a man... put a gun against his head, pulled my trigger, now he's dead...*" the girls joined in the chorus.

"'Ere, Michelle. Don't yer' fink' Mr 'Dud-lay' 'ere looks a bit like Freddy Mercury...?" said Sharon, pressing a fingertip against her lips and weighing him up forensically.

Michelle eyed the blushing conductor up and down too.

"Nah, Shazz," she scoffed. "'E's more like Brian Deacon, this one – the boring one who plays bass guitar?"

Her dismissive observation prompted titters on the part of the other girls. However, Vaughan's blushing was about to reach new levels when Michelle began wiggling to get comfortable on the double seat she had bagged for her exclusive use, her long bare legs draped across it so that her wedge shoes were dangling into the aisle. As she did so the buttons were tugging on the school blouse her generous chest was heaving inside.

"Tell yer' wot' though. You can ask me out if you like," she winked at him, those artful eyes mellowing into a seductive stare. "I've always wondered what it's like to play with the conductor's little 'andle."

She wiggled again and the short skirt she was wearing rode up a little further to reveal more of her spectacular fleshy thighs, the subtle parting of which revealed something else that she reasoned might get Vaughan's 'little handle' turning.

"Bloody 'ell, Chell. 'E's got a boner!" the cry suddenly went up. Eyes wide and mouths agape, the other girls gasped.

Vaughan looked down in horror, quickly manoeuvring both his ticket machine and his cash bag into fig leaf mode just in case. All the time, Michelle was smirking gleefully.

"Oy, mate. Yer' don't wanna' be goin' with an ol' slapper like 'er. Yer' might catch somefink'!" one of the lads called out, his mates on the back seat exploding in a riot of lecherous guffaws.

"Watch who you're callin' an ol' slapper, Robert Jones," she sat up, leant forward, and screeched down the aisle. "Otherwise you'll be catchin' my knuckles in that ugly, fat gob of yours!"

"Ooooh!!!" the lads chanted in unison.

It was with relief on the part of its flustered young conductor that his bus progressively emptied of its tormenting juveniles – Michelle included, the six-foot sex siren sauntering down the stairs and pinching his buttocks as she brushed past him on the platform.

"DUD-LAY! DUD-LAY!" her male classmates chanted after him as the bus pulled away. Michelle, meanwhile, blew him an exaggerated kiss before it disappeared from view.

* * * * *

"Blimey! Thirty-six degrees centigrade... in the shade!" Colin exclaimed, pausing to study the thermometer inside the depot as they trudged past it on their way to clock off. "That's ninety-seven degrees Fahrenheit! No wonder the roads are melting!"

"Now I know why everyone dreads the school run," was the shell-shocked reply that otherwise bore no connection to his driver's startling observations.

"'Ere, mate. You look like you've gone twelve rounds with Joe Bugner," Colin opined, examining the emotional dishevelment etched into his fellow busman's cherubic face.

"I feel like I have."

"Yeah, well. Someone's gotta' get the little horrors to class and back each day. Anyway, it's not that long since you were their age – getting up to all the same pranks too, I wouldn't mind betting. And was that Michelle Hardman I saw blowing you a kiss back there?" Colin nudged him.

To be precise, it had been just two short years since Vaughan Lewis had left school. It rendered him barely three years older than the precocious Michelle. And yet it seemed like a lifetime ago. Somewhere across that yawning chasm the eighteen year-old clippie had left his adolescence behind.

"Big girl though, ain't she… if you know what I mean," Colin meanwhile juggled his cupped hands against his chest – as if to emphasise *exactly* what he meant. "However, you wanna' steer clear of the likes of her, mate. Remember: she's jailbait – even if she does strut about like she's Mary Millington."

"Mary Millington? Isn't she that woman who complains about sex and bad language on television?"

Colin fired his innocent conductor a disbelieving stare before shaking his head and returning to the matter in hand.

"Look, what I'm trying to say is if you think that Michelle's built like a brick-shithouse, you should see her old man," he sucked through his teeth with foreboding. "Hardman by name; hard man by nature!"

After today's mauling Vaughan couldn't say he was in a hurry to bump into either Michelle or her father any time soon.

"Tell you what though," Colin struck a more positive note, alighting a hand upon Vaughan's shoulder, "if you're looking for a bit of skirt that's not dodgy, how about you and me go out on the town one night – when we ain't on shift? I know one or two places on the island where we can go to pick up some decent birds. Who knows: we might even bump into those two stunners we were chatting to the other day. How's that grab yer', mate?"

* * * * *

Thursday, July 1st 1976

The sun had finally gone down on yet another scorching day. What's more, the weathermen were promising even more exceptionally hot weather to come. However, sundown brought little respite from the stifling heat. Therefore, as Vaughan readied himself for bed he took a moment to stroll across the room in his pyjamas, where he lifted away the net curtains in the hope of catching the faintest hint of a breeze. Poking his head out of the window, at the end of the street he spotted the lights of the Esplanade reflecting upon the blackness of Sandown Bay.

Meanwhile, parked up in Victoria Road was a little green single-decker. Its saloon illuminated, the driver could be observed sorting the content of his fare box, ready to work the last journey of the evening back to Newport – the island's capital. One-man operated 'pay as you enter' buses already comprised a substantial part of the Southern Vectis fleet – including all its newest vehicle deliveries. It meant that one day the role of bus conductor would go the way of chimney sweeps, gas lamp attendants, locomotive firemen and all those other jobs that the relentless march of progress had consigned to history.

For now though (notwithstanding Monday's embarrassing tribulations), Vaughan was well-pleased with his new job. It was not only providing him with the wherewithal to enjoy his time on the Isle of Wight, but might yet be a means by which he could make new friends with whom he could pass the summer – including those of the female variety.

Just then his attention was taken by a commotion at the end of the road. For there was situated below the apartment block a subterranean nightclub that was so well sound-proofed that the only time it had made its presence felt so far was when the doors on the corner of the street were opened and another posse of inebriated revellers was disgorged into the night. To the escaping chorus of Tavares' *'Heaven Must Be Missing An Angel'* just such a disgorgement now took place. Two young guys in flaired terylene trousers and winged-collar shirts tumbled out onto the street, their sozzled female conquests hanging from their necks and tottering on their platform heels.

Having started up the engine, the bus driver waited while the four of them staggered a passage up to the stop, whereupon loud and exaggerated canoodling took place and final tongue-tangled kisses were hurriedly exchanged.

"Shall we meet up here again tomorrow? Only we go home on Saturday," one of the girls slurred as the guys broke free of their grasps and boarded the bus.

"Go on, please say you will. I love you... Er, whatever your name is," her friend pleaded somewhat implausibly.

Whatever delusions had been induced by the consumption of too much alcohol, the two local lads at least were lucid enough to recognise a timely escape when it had presented itself. As the bus pulled away (and more misplaced expressions of undying devotion were hollered in its direction) it was probable that by tomorrow they would both have put the events of their night on the town safely behind them – save for the bragging in the office the next morning.

As the two listless tarts drifted off to locate their guest house, steadying arms draped across each other's shoulders, Vaughan recalled Colin's proposition about tracking down the sorts of places where they might find 'decent birds'. Alas, the nightspot at the end of road was hardly a glowing advert.

Therefore, he ruminated instead upon Auntie Angie's admonition: about never letting anyone trample on his heart; and of never trampling on theirs either. He was determined that should that elusive girl-of-his-dreams ever stroll into his life – be it on a bus, on a beach, or in a nightclub – he would endeavour to remember her advice.

First though, he had to find her.

5

Sunday, July 4th 1976

> *"Love not the world, neither the things that are in the world. If any man love the world, the love of the Father is not in him. For all that is in the world, the lust of the flesh, and the lust of the eyes, and the pride of life, is not of the Father, but is of the world. And the world passeth away, and the lust thereof: but he that doeth the will of God abideth for ever."*

Aimee-Marie Eichelberger had sat in church often enough to know when a bible verse (in this case from John's First Epistle) was intended for her hearing and edification. Shelby's spiritual ears also sensed that the minister's words must surely resonate in the heart of her increasingly wayward best friend. Accordingly, they each turned from fanning themselves with their hymnals a few rows back from the pulpit and glanced at the other.

To be sure, Aimee had been content to fall in with her friend's insistence that they seek out a regular place of worship while they were on the island – and preferably one within walking distance of the hotel where they worked and were domiciled. Hence this small gospel hall that Shelby had discovered nestled up a backstreet in Shanklin had fitted the bill perfectly – even if the modest-sized congregation and the understated English reserve of that worship was not what they had were accustomed to at their lively student fellowships back home.

Shelby trusted that Aimee might still be open to the Word of God, even if the evidence of backsliding was becoming more pronounced with each 'pub' she insisted they hang out in to escape the sweltering heat; and with each handsome boy she stopped by to flirt with. It would only be a matter of time, she feared, before Aimee decided that drinking and flirting was how she preferred to spend her Sundays too.

* * * * *

> *"...Israeli commandoes landed at Entebbe Airport shortly after eleven o'clock last night. During a thirty minute, close-quarter fire-fight all seven hijackers – including two German terrorists – were killed, along with some thirty Ugandan soldiers. In all, over one hundred hostages from the airliner were rescued; three were killed; whilst one – seventy-five year-old British woman Dora Bloch – remains unaccounted for. In a statement it released, the Israeli government also confirmed that one of its commandoes had been killed during the rescue mission..."*

John Lawton nodded with satisfaction at a job well done. However, his moment of glee huddled over the radio was interrupted by the entrance into the kitchen of an attractive, if bleary-eyed female companion.

"Ah, there you are, darling. I didn't hear you get up."

She filled the kettle and flicked the switch to bring it to the boil, brushing a lock of her bushy blonde mane from out of her face as she turned to face him. Otherwise, she made no further attempt to attend to her post-coital dishevelment, other than to draw tight the short silk dressing gown she had hastily draped around nakedness. Instead, leaning back against the work surface, she took a moment to study him stood there in front of her in just his Y-fronts, his impressive hirsute physique needing no other adornment right then to risk turning her on again.

"Yes, well. It's damned near impossible to sleep in this heat," was his excuse as he switched the radio off and sauntered over.

Taking her in his powerful arms he then thrust his tongue between the lips she had pursed expectantly. When their torrid kiss ceased, he contented himself with the placing of a tender peck of his own lips upon an exposed patch of her forehead.

"As I recall, neither of us got much sleep last night," she looked up at him, her appetitive eyes reminding him why.

"Pray tell me, Sophie. How could anyone possibly share your bed *and* sleep?" he smirked, replying in kind.

"Be that as it may, but clearly you couldn't resist the draw of the morning news bulletin," she noted, drifting away to prepare the coffee.

"It was quite a bold and audacious operation by all accounts. With Soviet-backed forces on the march in Africa, and the Americans still reeling from the fall of Saigon, it's heartening to know that the Israelis at least can be relied on to give the enemies of Western civilisation a bloody nose."

"I might have known: war and military matters – the only things that have ever been able to tempt you out of my bed!" she tutted, catching another drooping lock of hair and looping it over her ear. "Why, John, I swear you only sleep with me because my husband is the Permanent Secretary to the Ministry of Defence. Perhaps these dalliances are your cunning plan to enlist me into wheedling secrets out of him!"

"It's a fascinating hypothesis, my dear," he smiled serenely. "However, you forget: I'm a Cambridge man. On past form, it would appear that those who wish to spy for the *other* side prefer to study at Oxford instead!"

Alas, the joke was lost on her. However, this woman supposedly scorned – who he now sat himself down at the table opposite – had a point. Therefore (and notwithstanding that his presence evidently leavened the boredom of a sexually-frustrated civil servant's wife), he thought it opportune to assure Sophie that he always found both her company and her fashionable London apartment thoroughly agreeable. First though, he sipped the coffee she'd prepared and took a moment to observe the affectation with which she lit a cigarette, exhaled the first drag, and then gripped it between the fingertips of the forearm she now propped on the table while staring him out.

"I confess I make the most of our little 'liaisons' to tour specialist bookshops and peruse the library archives here in the capital. However, being able to spend the night with you is always the most delectable aspect of my weekends in London."

"I bet you say that to every woman you charm into bed. I bet you even say such things to your wife when you need her to mind that seafront hotel of yours," she scoffed.

"Nowadays, it feels more like it's the case of me occasionally minding *her* hotel," he quipped. "You see, Veronica has very much made the business her life's work. I just stump up the money and swan about keeping the guests happy. Quite an agreeable arrangement really."

"Whatever, darling. Anyway," Sophie was curious to know, "what is this new 'project' that you've been busy researching?"

"Oh, nothing that would stir your blood," he shrugged.

"Try me... No, seriously. I appreciate that you probably regard me as just a convenient, if rather cracking shag. But I assure you: when it comes to military campaigns I do know the difference between 'strategy' and 'tactics'."

"So now who's trying to wheedle secrets out of who?" he pondered the irony.

"Another book on military aircraft, perchance? To follow on from the last one you wrote?" she pressed him.

He was surprised by her manifest interest in his other 'pastime' when in London. Shrugging again, Lawton glanced into his cup before looking up at her in earnest.

"If you must know, yes: I am working on another book: this time about the American air war over Indochina – or to be more precise, the role those giant B52 Stratofortress bombers played during the conflict."

"Gosh! We are a clever boy, aren't we!" she marvelled, resting her chin in the cup formed by the hand that was still gripping the cigarette. Staring him out a second time, he glanced away, a hint of frustration in his tone.

"Unlike my last book though, the research I doing for this one is groundbreaking; made harder by the fact that the principal sources I need to tap reside on the other side of the Atlantic – including the man who commanded the most spectacular of those B52 missions. I'm afraid corresponding by long distance letter only takes one so far. Sometimes there really is no substitute for sitting your source down in the same room and bidding him pour out his soul."

"Then if you need to interview this elusive Yank in person you'll just have to make your excuses to Veronica and book yourself aboard a flight to America," she counselled, drawing on the cigarette still smouldering between her fingers.

"Perhaps you're right."

"And no doubt you'll be seducing *his* wife too while you're at it," she grunted cynically, having exhaled a plume of grey smoke. "...Or perhaps his daughter, I shouldn't wonder!"

"Hmmn," he elected to muse in response.

Sophie could detect that beneath that rich head of swept-back fair hair her flippant remark had set wheels and cogs in motion inside that head – evidenced by another of those tell-tale smirks he emitted whenever he was up to no good.

"I was joking! John Lawton, I swear you're an absolute cad!" she shook her head and feigned outrage.

"Maybe I am," he jested, locking those entrancing blue eyes of his upon her. "Or maybe I just possess exceedingly good taste in other men's wives... and their daughters!"

* * * * *

"Happy Bi-centennial!"

"Yay! Happy Birthday, America!"

"Oh, say can you see, by the dawn's early light..."

Though their enthusiastic singing briefly disturbed the repose of dusk, both girls couldn't help but regard their modest picnic as something of a next-best-thing. While thousands of miles away their fellow countrymen were indulging in huge parties, pageants and pyrotechnics, this inseparable American duo were celebrating two hundred years of their nation's independence far from home (and in the very country from which their forefathers had wrested their liberty!), toasting that *'Spirit of '76'* with two cans of Vimto while feasting upon a packet of fish-and-chips each.

"...Oh, say does that Star-Spangled Banner yet wave, o'er the land of the free and the home of the brave!"

That said, once more the British weather was defying all expectations so that 'at the twilight's last gleaming' it was warm enough for the girls to be still sitting on the sand in short pants and T-shirts, watching the waves gently roll upon a receding tide.

"Gee, isn't this romantic," Shelby drew breath, contemplating the seafront strip lazily bidding goodbye to that sweltering sun for another day. Maybe tomorrow it might rain. Maybe.

"It would be even more romantic if we had a couple of hunky guys to share these 'chips' with. Say, do the British really eat this stuff!" her friend grimaced as she picked at the greasy scrags. "Give me a burger, fries and a shake any day," she insisted in between attempts at masticating them.

"So, Miss Aimee-Marie Eichelberger – the girl who's travelled all over the world – has finally gotten homesick!"

"I didn't say I was missing home," she riposted.

"Come on, Aimee. Everyone misses home some time. Who was it who told me the other day that she regretted not having 'a place to call home'? Besides, surely you must miss your folks."

Hoisted on the petard of this previous baring of her soul, Aimee was strangely taciturn. Maybe the life-and-soul of so many of their capers at college (and at university in England) did indeed miss her parents. Or maybe being apart from them for so long had instead drawn her gaze to things that Shelby sensed did not bode well for her forthcoming return to the United States. The 'Land of the Free' appeared to churn up mixed feelings for this girl who yearned for a more consummate freedom from those implicit constraints of parental judgement.

"You know, during the time we've known each other I've gotten the sense that you once looked up to your parents," Shelby therefore probed her again, "…especially your father. But lately it's almost as if you're kinda' mad at him for some reason. And I don't think it's solely down to youthful rebellion."

Aimee huffed and shrugged and carried on munching. Eventually, she summoned up the willingness to open up her heart again to her most trusted earthly confessor.

"Maybe you're right. Maybe I am mad. And mad at my father too. You see, it was always my older brother that Dad was closest to. And upon whom his hopes were riding. Boy, it sure made him proud when Ike followed in Dad's footsteps and graduated from the United States Air Force Academy. Sure, he always loved me;

but I always got impression that what I did was of less interest to him; that I was something of an afterthought."

"That kinda' figures. After all, Ike was eight years your senior," Shelby interjected, the use of the past tense indicative that her line of interrogation was running the risk of trawling up exceedingly painful memories. For now though, having briefly joined Aimee in silently staring out to sea, she endeavoured to match her friend's candour.

"Being an only child I guess all my parents' hopes have ridden on me," she noted by way of contrast, "My father worked real hard to put me through college. I know he will be proud of me too when I graduate – the first Carmichael from Jasper County ever to have something to put after her name. I'm so grateful to my parents for the love they've always shown me; and for the prayers they've spoken over me."

The spiritual inference prompted discernible unease on the part of the General's daughter. She was silent again, and once more it fell to Shelby to restart the conversation.

"I'm guessing too that it's not just your earthly father that you're kinda' mad at."

Chin slumped upon her bunched-up knees, Aimee remained silent for a while longer before deciding that her friend's question-posed-as-an-observation demanded a response.

"I guess I just don't know what to believe any more. Once my life was uncomplicated: Mom and Dad; me and my brother; the air force; the church. Then one morning we received the terrible news about Ike. It was as if the bottom had suddenly dropped out of our world – my own included."

To be sure, these two pals had oft times shared vignettes from their respective childhoods. Past memories of contentment, as well as of disappointments; past landmarks in teenage innocence lost, as well as of unrequited teenage crushes.

"I guess I shouldn't have been surprised," Aimee continued to unburden herself. "After all, flying jet bombers into heavily-defended enemy airspace was always going to be dangerous. My father, of all people, knew that. And yet, as the guy-in-charge who had ordered those crews over Hanoi, he felt personally responsible for what happened to Ike. He really did feel like he had murdered his own son.

"Of course, he could have arranged for my brother to be posted elsewhere. After all, were Ike's plane to be shot down then the enemy would surely milk its propaganda value for all it was worth. Parading the captured son of a United States general in front of the world's television cameras – imagine that! And not just any general! No: the very man who was directing the levelling of their country with every aircraft under his command.

"We'd all heard stories too about the way the North Vietnamese were mistreating our captured flyers. But Dad simply wouldn't countenance posting his own son away from combat while other American sons were dying. And neither would my brother have accepted such a blatant bugging out.

"And so it was on Christmas Eve 1972 we were informed that Captain Lawrence 'Ike' Eichelberger had been officially listed as missing in action. All over that terrible Christmas and New Year Mom and I were praying that it had all been an appalling mistake; and that he'd been found alive – even if it meant he'd been taken prisoner. Of course, it was worse for Dad. After all, he had a job to do. Despite the appalling news about his son, he was still the man in command of the largest air armada the United States had put into the skies since World War Two.

"To this day, I know that somewhere within my father's heart there still dwells the hope that his son might turn up out of the blue. And who can say that he won't! Many POWs who it was thought were being held captive never returned when the prisoner exchanges took place. The North Vietnamese simply denied they were holding them. So, to this day Dad is tormented by the possibility that Ike was *not* killed when his plane went down; but that instead he might be rotting away in some jungle prison camp, abandoned and forgotten. Held as a bargaining chip maybe; but one that our government is unwilling to acknowledge and too ashamed to haggle over."

Once more, Shelby felt compelled to extend the gentle hand of consolation to her fellow student. It was accepted with grace, but also with another glimmer of soul-searching that enabled the ever-faithful Southerner to perceive at last the real reason why Aimee-Marie Eichelberger was 'kinda' mad' with her father.

"Ever since that fateful Christmas it's as if the loss of his precious Ike has finally jolted my father to remember he has another child! Yet it sucks that by shifting all those paternal hopes and aspirations onto me instead – and suffocating me under the weight of them – he thinks he can somehow make up for all the times when I was merely an afterthought.

"Don't get me wrong," she pleaded, a stray tear glistening on her cheek. "I know how cut up my father must be about the son he lost – the son he might have 'left behind' some place. Yet, you know the most horrible thing of all: I really do feel that were that son he 'left behind' to miraculously walk back into his life again after all these years then I would be consigned to being second-best once again – the 'afterthought'. But I am not an afterthought, Shell. I am my own person. I am me! I will never be a substitute in my father's eyes for someone else."

6

Friday, July 9th 1976

Uncle Frank had been forced to eat his own words: to his horror Ilya Nâstase had gone down to defeat at the hand of Björn Borg, the flaxen-mopped Swede triumphing in the Men's Singles at Wimbledon 6-4, 6-2, 9-7. At least he had been right about Chris Evert though, the American winning 6-3, 4-6, 8-6 against veteran Aussie tennis ace Evonne Goolagong Cawley.

However, with the tennis season over, Frank Tring had slunk back into his unvaried television viewing habits. When Vaughan passed the sitting room on his way down the hallway there he was in his favourite armchair, feet propped up on a stool while engrossed (judging by the cacophony of American accents) in *'Starsky and Hutch'*, *'The Bionic Woman'*, or one of the other popular US TV imports that padded out the schedules.

Clutching the bottle of wine he'd purchased, Vaughan popped his head in only to tell him he was off out. He spotted Uncle Frank's raised hand of acknowledgement surface above the back of the chair. He imagined Auntie Angie had been entreated to a similar unadorned valediction when she'd passed that same spot a few minutes earlier on her way to fetch the car from the garage.

Still, at least Chico was up for conversation.

"Cor! Sex!" he chortled as Vaughan wandered out onto the verandah.

"Let's hope so, Chico!" he chuckled, stopping to briefly offer the bird some affection – for which it obligingly nestled its head against the bars of the cage. Vaughan had passed by often enough by now to have gained the animal's trust. He ran the fingers of his free hand along the soft, tiny feathers atop the parrot's grey bonce. Then the bird stepped back onto its perch and shook its plume of red tail feathers.

"Show us yer' tits!" he cawed.

"Wow! Those kids really have been expanding your vocabulary!" the scandalised teenager's eyes popped.

Auntie Angie had brought the car round so that when Vaughan trotted down the steps onto the street her white Austin Allegro was waiting for him, the engine revving on the choke as he opened the passenger door and jumped in beside her.

"It's very kind of you to offer me a lift, Auntie," he enthused as he strapped himself in. "I wouldn't have minded going on the bus, honest."

"I thought you might have had enough of riding around on buses by now," she ribbed him, her eyes scanning the mirrors as she pulled away.

Craning forward to look left and right before turning onto the High Street, a sudden crunching of the gears interrupted her humming along to *'Save Your Kisses For Me'* – Brotherhood Of Man's corny Eurovision-winning hit – which had been softly playing on the car's radio.

"Bloody great heap of junk!" she cursed, finally locating third.

Like many aspects of their haphazard marriage, the Tring's choice of car was a compromise between the wife's zest for life (the colour and the black vinyl roof) and her husband's staid practicality (the car itself). Their bemused nephew imagined Auntie Angie would have preferred to be seen motoring around her adopted town in a silver Ford Capri or a flame red Triumph TR7 convertible. Anything with a touch more style and sex appeal than a dumpy-looking Allegro – even if there was 'plenty of leg room'; and it was 'good on petrol' (as Uncle Frank had reminded Vaughan in two more of his laconisms).

"So how's the job going?"

"Very well, Auntie."

"Good for you! It's nice to know you're making friends too. I assume your workmates will be there tonight."

"That's right. Some of the seasonal conductors have rented a place for the summer. They've finally managed to organise a belated house-warming party – and on a night when most of us are not on duty."

"Good. I like to see you enjoying yourself. I'm sorry if it gets a bit tedious sitting around the flat sometimes – especially when

Frank's hogging the television. I suppose it's fortunate that the weather's been so nice. At least you've been able to spend time on the beach. In fact, you've acquired quite a tan," she remarked, casting an approving glance along his exposed forearms.

Vaughan had indeed. In one of Uncle Frank's more solicitous gestures he'd brought home a blow-up air mattress from the range he sold in his toy shop. Underwhelmed by the gift at first, in the days that followed it had come in rather handy. Sandown's gently-sloping sandy beach and shallow, rhythmic surf was perfect for taking to the water to escape the merciless heat-wave. Arriving home from the week's roster of early starts, Vaughan must have spent hours just idling bobbing up and down on the thing with the water lapping around his limbs.

One unintended consequence was that the bobbing sensation lingered long after he'd left the water – and especially when lying in bed at night staring at the shadows on the ceiling. Another (more painful) unintended consequence was that he'd failed to factor in the power of salt water to magnify the sun's UV rays. So much so that the tan Auntie Angie pointed out had earlier in the week bore a closer resemblance to sunburn!

"So where are you singing tonight, Auntie," he enquired, aware that the flat shoes, denim skirt and patterned blouse she was wearing were destined to be swapped within the hour for stiletto heels and a glitzy dress from the wardrobe full of stage attire she'd amassed, some of which she'd loaded into the suitcase that had been flung in the boot.

"I'm headlining the final night's cabaret at that exclusive Shanklin Heights Hotel. That's why it's no trouble to offer you a lift. You're going my way, after all."

"The Shanklin Heights? I met some girls on the train who are working there – two American students. Very nice girls too!"

"Sounds like you fancy them," she ribbed him.

Vaughan fidgeted with the bottle in his hand. However, a pair of mischievous grins lit up both their faces when Angie pulled up at some traffic lights and glanced across expecting an answer. For some inexplicable reason, he'd found himself able to converse more openly about girls and relationships with her than he ever had with his mother. For example, the bottle of wine was Auntie

Angie's recommendation – her assessment of what would be required to impress this chatty conductress called Tina, who he'd also opened his heart to her about.

"Well, one of them is tall and slim; and with beautiful trailing fair hair – styled like Farrah Fawcett's. But…"

His aunt forfeited a moment of concentration on the road ahead to eye him imploringly.

"But what?"

"Nothing… Well… She's probably out of my league," he admitted, fidgeting with the label on the bottle again.

"Nonsense! Don't ever let me hear you talking like that. You're a good-looking chap, Vaughan. And besides, a person's background shouldn't count for anything. If two people are genuinely in love, then love will always find a way. And anyway, what does her father do for a living that renders her so high-and-mighty?"

"He's an air force officer – some bigwig in their military. He was based over here during the war… or so she told me."

"Uh! Is that so?" his aunt grunted.

For a moment Vaughan thought he detected her composure falter. However, the pulling up of a bus in front offered her the means to unfluster herself by glancing over her shoulder, indicating, and steering around it. When her attention returned so had an expression of disdain.

"So he's a general, or whatever. That doesn't make him God Almighty. And it doesn't make her God's daughter either. Which part of America is she from?"

"Minnesota – wherever that is."

"Up on the Canadian border; the 'Land of Ten Thousand Lakes' – of which the largest is Lake Superior. Minneapolis-St Paul is the state capital. It's also the source of the Mississippi – America's mightiest river," Angie fired back, demonstrating a startling erudition about the geography of the place.

"How do you know all that?" Vaughan marvelled.

She pondered her reply for a moment.

"The Andrews Sisters – they came from Minnesota," she answered improbably, breaking into song "…*Don't sit under the apple tree with anyone else but me... Anyone else but me... Anyone else but me... No, no, no..."*

"Of course, you sang in a band during the war. And you once went out with an American," he chuckled, amazed that magnificent mezzo-soprana voice had lost none of its timbre since she used to sing to him as a child; comforting him whenever he'd fallen off his bike or been stung by a wasp. It was another parental skill in which she had frequently bested his mother.

"That was a long time ago," his aunt chuckled dismissively. "So what's her name then – this girl?"

"Aimee."

"Okay. If I bump into this Aimee tonight then I'll put in good word for you."

Vaughan knew he ought to be grateful for this offer to match-make, but couldn't trawl up the words. However, Auntie Angie understood. She flashed him a warm smile and patted his knee.

"Failing that, it sounds like this Tina you told me about might have a soft spot for you."

Vaughan wanted to say that, even were he to unexpectedly wind up in bed with this forward and more experienced young lady, then she would quickly regret it once she discovered how desperately inept and unversed he was in the art of love-making. However, his aunt read his mind for a second time.

"Vaughan, I know your mother is very religious; and has strong views about the things that go on between young men and young women. But sex isn't a sin. Have you, you know... done it yet?" she cut to the chase, glancing his way again.

The awkward and embarrassed silence that greeted her unexpected enquiry told her everything she needed to know.

"I thought not. Well, if it happens, it happens. And the first time it happens it may well be a little clumsy. But there's no shame. We all have to start somewhere. Just make sure you're 'prepared' when it does happen – if you know what I mean. You can buy them from most chemists. There's even a machine in the toilets of the Shanklin Heights Hotel that dispenses them – if you want me to get you some. Take it from me, Vaughan – being 'unprepared' in these matters can seriously alter the course of your life. And cause you years of pain and regret."

She smiled and tapped his knee again. Seconds would pass before he *did* grasp what she meant. He cursed his lack of acuity. Boy, he was more inept and unversed than he realised.

* * * * *

"Vaughan! How you doing, man?"

"Yeah. Good to see you, mate. Grab a drink, find a space outside, and sit yourself down. Sorry the lawn's in a bit of a state, what with the hot weather and the hosepipe ban."

Phil took the bottle of wine from his hand and escorted him into the kitchen, where an array of other bottles and cans graced the work surface. Vaughan was told to grab whatever took his fancy and make his way into the garden, where everyone was gathering. Meanwhile, the stereo in the living room was belting out that magnificent saxophone riff from Bryan Ferry's *'Let's Stick Together'*.

Vaughan mixed himself a lager and lime and stepped outside, glancing up at the gathering clouds. The air had turned oppressive and the sky had progressively darkened on the journey here. Perhaps relief for the longsuffering lawn was nigh.

"Yeah, looks like we might be in for a thunderstorm," noted Dave as he cracked open a can and joined him outside.

"It's all Colin's fault," said Sally, overhearing them. "The gods have plainly taken a dislike to those legs of his!"

The instant that Colin's squat frame rose from the seat around the garden table (where he'd been chatting with some of the other guests) Vaughan could see why. His tight canary-yellow shorts not only showed off a goodly amount of his hairy legs but a goodly amount of his 'tackle' as well (or at least the outline of it!). The last nineteen days of exceptionally high temperatures had clearly gone to some people's heads.

"Glad you could make it, mate," the libidinous bus driver enthused, offering Vaughan a chunky handshake. "It's about time you started letting your hair down."

Colin's jibe hinted that he had yet to make good his promise to take his conductor friend out one night and introduce him to the delights of the Bird Cage, La Babulu, Coconut Grove, or one of the other popular nightspots on the island where it was all supposed to be happening. Therefore, maybe tonight might be the night when Vaughan Lewis at last stepped out of his sheltered world of church youth activities to sample the more heady diversions that summer on the Isle of Wight had to offer.

"Vaughan!" someone with another familiar southern twang assailed him from behind.

He turned to permit Tina to launch her arms around him. Then she stepped back so that he could behold the vivid, multi-coloured, nylon-print bodysuit she was attired in, the bottoms of which permitted her to display as much leg as Colin (though at least her smooth, shapely pins were more pleasing to the Gods!). The outline of what she'd packed into the outfit up top was just as pleasing too. Vaughan tried not to stare. However, she spotted him the instant his eyes lingered, flashing him a disarming smile.

"I think you'll find most of the guys from the depot are either here or on their way – plus a few people you might not know. For instance, there are two American students over there who Phil has invited along. They look a bit out of place. So how about we go over and introduce ourselves."

Instinctively, Vaughan found his heart racing at the mere mention of the students' nationality. Instinctively too, Tina had snatched his arm and was now hauling him over to the corner of the patio from where these stature-mismatched transatlantic guests were observing proceedings.

"Hi, I'm Tina. And this is one of my fellow bus conductors, Vaughan. Welcome to our little gathering."

"Hi, thanks for the invite. I'm Mark. From Iowa," said the taller of the two, offering them his hand.

"And I'm Dexter – from Albany, New York. We're over in Europe for the summer youth-hostelling. We got chatting with your friend the other day on the bus," explained the short one, doing likewise.

Such was his sudden deflation that Vaughan found himself not really listening to these two bearded nerds recounting their adventures in England so far, as well as the freak happenstance that had enabled them to wangle an invitation to the party. Instead, he began surveying the female guests present, hoping

Phil or Dave might have invited along two other young Americans who might have found themselves at a loose end. Meanwhile, someone had flipped that new *'ChangesOneBowie'* album onto the turntable, the strident guitar overlay of *'Rebel, Rebel'* filling a garden over which the darkening skies were closing in. So much so that, by the time the track had progressed to the more melodic *'Golden Years'*, the first rumbles of thunder had announced their presence.

Suddenly it didn't seem a good idea to be stood chatting next to a stainless steel rotary washing line. Therefore, Vaughan pleaded the need to refill his glass and wandered away, leaving Tina to continue her flirtatious banter.

While the more timid souls were also decamping inside, Colin and the leggy bird he was busy amusing were too engrossed in verbal foreplay to be unduly perturbed by the odd flash of lightning. With his best friend's attention elsewhere for the duration – and Tina still imbibing tales of the Yanks' road trip across Europe – Vaughan was reduced to loafing on the periphery of other people's conversations. The chance of getting off with a girl tonight seemed a remote prospect indeed. Meanwhile, the turntable playing host to Thin Lizzy's *'The Boys Are Back In Town'* had occasioned a lively debate amongst some of the lads.

"Nah, man. Emerson, Lake & Palmer, Genesis, Hawkwind – all that crap will be swept away before the year's out. Me and John here were up to Sheffield last week where we saw two new bands that are gonna' change everything."

"Yeah, the Sex Pistols and the Clash. Bloody brilliant, they were – three-minute, high octane numbers that vent the anger of kids on the dole with no future! So bollocks to all those overpaid and out-of-touch old geezers twanging flatulent twelve-minute guitar solos. Punk rock is here and *it's* the future."

Vaughan couldn't say he'd heard of them – or 'punk' rock. But then he'd only heard of Emerson, Lake & Palmer, Genesis, and Hawkwind because some of the guys at college used to sport their badges and sew-on patches on their denim jackets. Otherwise, his knowledge of rock music was confined to the two Status Quo LPs he'd bought from Woolworths in Dudley (much to the annoyance of his mother, who would call up the stairs for him to 'turn that racket down'). It had been supplemented by those odd occasions when he'd stayed up late to hear 'Whispering' Bob Harris rave about the likes of Bob Seger or Linda Ronstadt on the *'Old Grey Whistle Test'* (ditto his mother calling *down* the stairs!). The more the lads were name-dropping promising new bands, the more Vaughan realised he was a musical, as well as a sexual neophyte. To make the point, another rough-and-ready sound that he'd never heard before was now blaring from the stereo.

"Dr Feelgood," Sally enlightened him.

A sudden flash of lightning – followed an almost simultaneous crash of thunder – finally sent even Colin and his new acquaintance scurrying inside. Some spotting of rain could also be detected. However, it was not going to dampen the party spirit – much less drench the lawn. With darkness proper descending, more beer, wine and spirits were being sloshed. A fug of cigarette smoke had also formed. From the strange aroma in another room, Vaughan detected a fug of something else wafting about. Someone offered him a drag of it, though he declined. He doubted Auntie Angie's willingness to indulge youthful experimentation would stretch to him dabbling in illegal substances!

Meanwhile, some of the girls had tired of grinding rock anthems and had picked out some vinyls from Sally's collection of forty-fives instead. With the turntable hosting Hot Chocolate's *'You Sexy Thing'*, they nudged the lads aside to create an impromptu dance floor on the kitchen lino.

Having ventured onto his fourth glass of lager, Vaughan was tempted to join them (even as he remained unconvinced the world was ready for his take on the rhythm). However, having spotted his prevarication, someone present had more faith in him.

"Come on, Vaughan. Show us what you can do," Tina hollered, for the second time this evening snatching his arm and hauling him along – this time into a space that the girls duly opened up for him in their midst.

"That's the way," she coached him as – bashful and blushing – he sought to copy her moves.

Stodgy and robotic at first, with his inhibitions receding (aided by that fourth lager and lime) his limbs also began to loosen.

"Wooh! Vaughan – 'you sexy thing'!" the girls hollered. At first bemused, the boys too were grudgingly impressed.

The track faded and he was about to return to propping up the kitchen work surface when Tina suddenly had a brainwave.

"Stay right where you are!" she ordered him.

Then she turned about, zipped over to the stereo, and began rooting about in the collection of singles.

"Perfect!" her eyes lit up. She took it from its sleeve, placed it on the turntable, and dropped the needle onto it.

Instantly recognisable, the opening bars of the Real Thing's *'You To Me Are Everything'* suddenly filled the room – and just to make doubly sure of that Tina twisted the volume knob right round. The girls were ecstatic. This jaunty tune had become the sound of an amazing summer so far. The lads too were now joining in. Even the two Americans were tempted, swigging from their bottled beers and pondering that not every great soul record was the gift of their side of the ocean.

With Tina back on the floor and facing him expectantly, Vaughan reasoned that it was safe for him to move again. And this time, move he did. He really had become possessed of that magical thing they called 'the groove'. Arms, shoulders and hips shadowing hers, he had an impish grin on his face that matched that of his lively female coach. The strictures of awkwardness were gone. Vaughan Lewis had arrived!

So impressed was Tina that midway through she dispensed with the distance between them and draped her arms upon his shuffling shoulder blades. Her partner guessed this was the cue for him to gently reach his hands out and take hold of her waist. The impish grin was gone, replaced by an eager smile that she also matched. Was this going to be the night when something else magical was going to happen? Perhaps he should have taken up his aunt's kind offer to run an errand to the hotel toilet.

* * * * *

Sunday, July 11th 1976

"Morning."

"Morning, Auntie."

As they passed in the hallway – Vaughan on his way to the bathroom, and Angie having just vacated it – both aunt and nephew glanced at each other with hang-dog eyes. Angie had also made sure that her silk bathrobe was this time securely tied around her.

Breakfast was a similarly muted affair. That Uncle Frank had little to say was a given. While his uncle nibbled at his toast and turned the pages of his newspaper, Vaughan caught the headline about three British mercenaries having being shot by firing squad by the victorious new Marxist government in Angola.

Strangely though, Auntie Angie too seemed reluctant to engage them with her usual lively banter. He began to wonder whether she and Uncle Frank might have had a row.

"It was kind of the manager to offer you a lift home," his uncle eventually grunted from behind his *'Daily Mail'*.

"It was," his aunt ventured. "We waited and waited for someone to turn up. Eventually though, I called back and told the breakdown people to send someone in the morning instead. So John brought me home. I'm glad you didn't mind."

"No, not at all. Very sensible, my dear."

"It was good of him to pick me up again yesterday so I could collect the car once they'd got it starting again," she added, meanwhile glancing across at Vaughan with a sheepish smile.

Ah, well. No hint of marital discord in that conversation, Vaughan noted. Buttering some more toast, he continued to maintain a low profile.

"Bloody cars nowadays," Uncle Frank then piped up. "Probably a 'Friday afternoon job'... No wonder the British motor industry is going to the dogs... All those strikes... Bloody communists...! And that Harold Wilson was a bloody communist, you know. Resigned and left the country in an even bigger mess than Ted Heath did in 1974 – and that's saying something! The 'Sick Man of Europe': that's what they call us nowadays. No wonder more and more people are emigrating and leaving all those Arab sheikhs to buy up the country..! Talking of which, we should have listened to Enoch Powell. He was right about immigration, you know. All these bloody darkies coming over here... Meanwhile, all these long-haired, left-wing teachers in our schools are churning out kids who can't read or write... and who eff-and-blind in the street like troopers. No wonder the bloody country's a laughing stock!"

Vaughan smiled feebly when his uncle laid his paper aside and glanced his way, having rounded off one of his more lengthy and impassioned breakfast table deliberations to date. He was tempted to enquire whether, being a small businessman with an old-fashioned outlook, Uncle Frank might have joined the growing legion of disgruntled 'middle Englanders' who were looking to Margaret Thatcher – the Conservative Party's feisty new woman leader – to fix Britain's social and economic malaise (and which at that moment included IRA bombs, football hooliganism, simmering racial tension, rising Celtic nationalism, bolshie trades unions, industrial decline, lengthening dole queues, punitive taxation, rampant inflation, and a pound in people's pockets that had lost almost half its value in the last five years).

However, first she had to get shot of the country's Labour government – newly-led by the bluff, avuncular 'Sunny Jim' Callaghan, who (like Wilson and Heath before him) had received the ultimate accolade that could be bestowed upon a 1970s prime minister: to be caricatured by popular TV impressionist Mike Yarwood. Meanwhile, gloomier souls – including the androgynous pop idol David Bowie – were wondering whether Britain's litany of woes was so daunting that only the firm hand of a fascist strong man could put them right. As it happened, the country's far-right National Front party had been gaining support by capitalising on fears about the recent influx of Asian immigrants who had been expelled from Africa.

With the last slices of toast polished off, Vaughan volunteered for washing up duties. Then, with nothing else planned for the day, he drifted off to esconce himself in one of the wicker chairs in the verandah. Though the heat-wave had abated, it was still pleasantly warm. More worryingly, what little rain had fallen over the weekend was unlikely to revive the nation's parched gardens, much less refill its depleted reservoirs.

Being the Lord's Day, he guessed he should by now have found himself a little church to worship in – as his mother had urged when she'd waved him off a few weeks back. Instead – and in a half-hearted attempt at piety – this morning he could be found flicking through the pages of that bible he'd eventually unearthed in his suitcase. His sporadic meditation was disturbed only by Chico fussily picking at the seed pods in his feeding tray.

However, this exercise in prevarication only served to compound his inner spiritual turmoil – especially when, still aimlessly flicking the pages, he alighted upon the words of the Apostle Paul in Romans Chapter 12...

> *"Don't copy the behaviour and customs of this world, but be a new and different person with a fresh newness in all you do and think. Then you will learn from your own experience how His ways will really satisfy you."*

Though not as poetic as it probably read in his mother's King James Bible, the message was clear: Vaughan Lewis's Christian faith was flagging and he knew it.

To be sure, nothing had transpired with Tina at Friday night's party, though she'd clearly enjoyed dancing with him. The feeling was mutual. However, she'd also danced with other boys too. If nothing else, this spreading of her favours meant Vaughan was still *virgo intactus* when the time came for him to stagger to the bus station to board the last journey home.

Alas, the same could not be said for that young beauty that Colin had paired up with – who, at last sighting, had been dancing around the kitchen floor with him to Rod Stewart's supremely appropriate *'Tonight's The Night'*, arms draped around each other and with their tongues down the other's throat. *"Spread your wings and let me come inside"*: no doubt Vaughan would hear all about it when he ran into him in the depot tomorrow morning. A part of him couldn't resist the urge to feel envious though.

Yet if Vaughan had rolled up in Victoria Road the worse for those six lagers and lime, it had been well into the small hours before Auntie Angie had rolled up from her cabaret performance at the Shanklin Heights Hotel. The combination of humid heat, a lingering storm, a gathering hangover, and the undulating sensation induced by that accursed lilo had left Vaughan tossing and turning in bed. When he had finally nodded off, he'd been assailed by another of those terrifying nightmares he'd been having lately: of himself swimming out on that lilo, desperately trying to reach out and grab his mother's hand to save her from drowning. However – and though their fingertips had almost touched – as in those other nightmares, he had once again been left looking on helplessly as she had mouthed a final 'I love you' before slipping beneath the waves.

Thus it was that he'd awoken with a start to hear a car pull up outside. Peeping from behind the curtain, he'd observed his aunt alight from the passenger seat of the manager's opulent coupé.

Ever since, she'd been wearing that discomfited expression that she had at the breakfast table just now – despite having a valid alibi in the form of a car that had stubbornly refused to start (an excuse which Uncle Frank had apparently accepted at face value).

The Shanklin Heights Hotel: come to think of it, Vaughan had forgotten to ask his aunt if she had perchance bumped into a room maid there called Aimee.

7

Thursday, July 15*th* 1976

"So how do I look?" she broke from humming along to 10cc's haunting *'I'm Not In Love'* (which was playing on the radio), swirling about proudly in front of the full-length mirror that was affixed to the closet door,

There was no doubt that, with her luxuriant, styled hair and fabulous figure Aimee-Marie Eichelberger would look good in almost any outfit. Tonight was no exception – the bright red vest top and diamond white, fanny-hugging 'hot pants' certainly complementing the weather. Meanwhile, the heeled sandals she was wearing served to make her legs appear even longer than they already were! However, it was not this that was troubling Shelby as she leant against the door post and studied her friend still admiring her reflection in the mirror. She nudged herself away from it and stood erect, digging her fists in her hips.

"You wearing a bra?" she frowned.

At first, Aimee appeared offended before admitting that "No, I'm not. Why? Is that a problem?"

"Not wishing to sound like your dad again, but..."

"And before you say anything, it's all the fashion these days. And it's so much more comfortable."

Shelby seemed unconvinced but proffered no further comment. Instead, her mien of censure moderated into one of anticipation of what the night would hold.

It was the first time since arriving on the island four weeks ago that they'd finally bagged an invitation to a party. One of the bar staff had turned twenty-one, and had arranged a get-together with friends at his parents' house. Hence it was with a sense of excitement that the two girls set off along the back streets of Shanklin. They had not been walking long before their animated banter was interrupted by a long, sleek luxury car drawing up alongside them. As it halted, the electric passenger window was powered down to reveal John Lawton leaning across the passenger seat to cock an eye at them.

"You girls look like you might be going somewhere," he suggested, pointing out the blindingly obvious.

At first chary of this unexpected off-duty encounter with their boss, the two friends looked to each other.

"Only to the bus stop. We're off to a party in Sandown," Shelby then ventured to reply.

"Sandown, you say. Well, that's on my way. Why not save your bus fare and hop in. I'll give you a lift."

Looking to each other again, it fell to Aimee to purse her lips approvingly.

"Sure. Why not," she nodded, duly opening the passenger door and tipping the seat forward so that her more diminutive friend could squeeze herself into the back. Aimee herself then jumped into the front seat, strapping herself in.

"Say, it's a real cool automobile you got here," she opined, her sparking eyes roaming across the plethora of dials, switches and buttons at her boss's fingertips.

"It's an XJS – Jaguar's latest sporting coupé," he informed her, "Thankfully, it has air-conditioning too," he added, reaching across to tweak a knob on the fascia.

All of a sudden, ice cold air came roaring from the dashboard vents, trailing Aimee's hair evocatively around her shoulders and drowning out the Doobie Brothers' *'It Keeps You Runnin''* that had been playing on the stereo.

"See. Literally 'cool'," he smirked.

"Yeah, especially in this weather," she puffed exaggeratedly.

"We don't often get summers like this. So I guess it's been a perfect opportunity for you girls to try out all these latest skimpy fashions."

Eyes closed as she revelled in the refreshing chilled blast, Aimee failed to spot the prolonged sideways glance her boss awarded himself of her gorgeous thighs; or of those pert little breasts quivering inside that bra-less vest top. Shelby did though – even as she was feigning to observe the street scene as it passed. Neither had the sudden and disturbing familiarity she had witnessed between the urbane hotelier and his coquettish front seat passenger gone unnoticed.

"So how are you girls enjoying living on the island?" Lawton enquired, purposely calling up to rope his rear seat passenger into the conversation.

"It's okay," Shelby noted with wary understatement, his bright blue eyes meeting hers as she spotted them in the interior mirror.

"Okay? We're loving every minute of it!" Aimee enthused, glancing over her shoulder to playfully rebuke her friend.

"Good," Lawton smiled. "I like to know my workforce is contented. A contented workforce is a productive workforce," he chortled, subtly reminding them of who was boss.

"We've been looking forward to tonight's party. Plenty to eat and drink, plenty of great music… plenty of boys too – we hope!" Aimee cast her own kittenish sideways glance at him.

"Yes, well. I guess 'all work and no play makes Jack a dull boy'. And Aimee a dull girl too, for that matter."

If the object of his interest had made it abundantly clear that she had no intention of allowing their time on the Isle of Wight to wind up being dull, Shelby remained more circumspect, listening with unease while this ingratiating character continued his sportive, probing discourse with her friend.

"I also own a private plane, you know," he informed her matter-of-factly.

"Wow! You do!" he'd calculated she would enthuse.

"I use it to fly back and forth to the Channel Islands – sometimes for pleasure; but mostly on business. I've set up some bank accounts there. What with the way our present government taxes everything that moves, it pays to put one's money where Mr Healey can't get his hands on it."

Shelby guessed he meant finance minister Denis Healey (or Chancellor-of-the-Exchequer, as the British quaintly titled the politician in charge of their treasury), who had been misquoted as wanting to squeeze the country's wealth creators 'until the pips squeaked'. With corporation tax at fifty-two percent, the top rate of income tax at eighty-three percent, and tax on investments at an eye-watering ninety-eight percent there was certainly a good deal of squeaking going on amongst better-off Brits – be they financiers, rock stars or aggrieved hoteliers! Otherwise, she was not blind to the way her boss was dangling his wealth (taxed or otherwise) in front of Aimee like bait, following up the aside about his private plane with a suggestion that she might care to let him take her up in it some time. Ingratiating indeed!

"Is this close enough for you?" Lawton joked, eventually drawing the car to a halt directly outside the address that the girls had been given.

"And don't get doing anything I would!" he winked at Aimee through the passenger window he'd powered down once the two girls had hopped out.

While Shelby was busy surveying the frontage of the large Victorian town house, Aimee offered Lawton a tender smile and a delicate wave of her hand, watching as that risqué smirk disappeared behind the window being powered back up.

"You know, there's something about that guy that bugs me," Shelby muttered once the car had pulled away, abruptly dragging her friend's attention back to the here-and-now.

"He's okay," Aimee hummed with a blasé shrug of her shoulders. "Besides, hasn't he got the most adorable, oh-so-polite English accent that you've ever heard!"

"Creepy, if you ask me," Shelby huffed, ringing the bell.

Upon which, their host threw open the front door and launched his arms around them both. Having then urged them inside, it was almost as if he had purposed that the party should have an American flavour, mindful that the two girls had been invited. For in addition to the unwatched television set in the living room beaming coverage of the Democratic National Convention gathering in New York, Lynyrd Skynyrd's *'Sweet Home Alabama'* was pounding from the record player as they made their way out into the garden (where a barbeque was already aflame). More pertinently, no sooner had they each filled a plate with food and grabbed a beer from the buckets filled with ice than they found themselves being introduced to two more American students who their host had also rather thoughtfully invited along.

"Hi, great to meet you guys. I'm Mark – from Iowa."

"And I'm Dexter – from Albany, New York. We're over in Europe for the summer youth-hostelling. We got talking with your friend the other day in a line for the bus."

Once the tall, laid-back Mark had recounted the uncanny coincidence that had enabled them to wangle their way into yet another of the island's summer parties, Shelby was pumping her fellow countrymen for the latest gossip from home. However, neither the hippy from Des Moines nor the dweeb from upstate New York held any particular fascination for Aimee – even less so when the conversation drifted onto politics. The Eagles' *'Take It Easy'* was playing in the background as those bright tawny eyes were soon roaming the garden to spy out handsome young men to whom she might introduce herself.

"... So if Jimmy Carter wins the nomination, that'll be peanut-farming outsider to presidential contender – all in the space of six months," Mark observed with as much awe as his downbeat manner could convey, adding for good measure that "everything now hangs on whether the Republicans choose President Ford as their candidate; or plump for that Ronald Reagan guy instead."

"Not that it really matters, I guess. The fall-out from Watergate means that, come November, we really could have a new broom in the White House," Dexter opined gleefully, looking to re-engage Aimee's wandering eyes by asserting that "It's just too bad we didn't get to impeach Nixon though. Man, what he, Kissinger and that Eichelberger guy did to all those innocent Cambodians was a war crime."

The pocket-sized student was oblivious to the sensibilities he had just stamped on. All at once, those feelings of ostracism and shame that had dogged Aimee through her time at high school and college surfaced again in eyes that ceased roaming and began to glisten instead.

"You okay?" enquired Mark, donning a demeanour of concern.

Aimee lifted up and stared at the almost-empty bottle of beer in her hand. She blew hard, fighting to hold back a snuffle.

"I gotta' pee!" she replied, begging her leave.

As soon as she could without appearing rude, Shelby also disengaged from the conversation in order to chase after her friend. She caught up with her upstairs, the bathroom door ajar and Aimee staring into the mirror at her reddened eyes.

"You know, it sucks how that crazy war – and my father's part in it – has to follow me wherever I go," she despaired when Shelby stepped inside to offer her a hug.

"Come on, Aimee. That nerd couldn't possibly have known that he was talking about your old man. Forget it. We came here to party, remember?"

At first grudgingly, Aimee wiped away another tear before sighing and nodding.

"Anyway, what was it you told me? You're not your brother; nor your dad; nor your mom. You're your own woman."

Aimee nodded again. Then suddenly an expletive escaped past her lips. She drew a hand to them when Shelby blinked in dismay.

"My mom! I completely forgot. I promised I'd call her today. What's the time?" she twittered, staring at the watch draped around her delicate wrist.

"Just after nine o'clock. That's three o'clock in the afternoon Central Time," Shelby beat her to it, glancing at the clock on the bathroom wall and doing the math.

"I better try and call her. She'll only worry if I don't," Aimee insisted, wiping away the dampness from her cheeks and racing out onto the landing.

"Say, you guys, is there a phone booth around here I can use?" she waylaid the first people she encountered at the foot of the stairs – a young man who was busy making small talk with some girl he'd paired up with.

"You mean a phone box? Er… Yeah, man, there's one outside the library at the bottom of the road," he replied.

"Thanks," Aimee smiled, hollering up the stairs to Shelby as she opened the front door.

"I'll be back in about fifteen minutes. Then we'll party, right?"

* * * * *

Aimee strode out onto the tree-lined avenue and headed down the hill towards the seafront at a brisk pace, cursing her forgetfulness as she went. Meanwhile, dusk was drawing in apace. Birds were warbling their evensong. The first lamp standards were flickering to commence their nightly vigil.

She arrived at the said phone box only to discover it was already occupied by two teenage girls, leaving the anxious student to stand about impatiently, glancing at her watch.

Eventually the lasses vacated the booth, permitting Aimee to step inside as one of them held the door open for her. Delving into her purse and laying out a selection of coins on the top of the cash vault, she lifted the receiver and dialled.

"Come on!" she muttered under her breath, praying that her mother was home to take the call. She recalled that on Thursday afternoons Natalie Eichelberger normally attended the women's prayer lunches at the church where her family worshipped.

"Hullo," a voice at the other end finally answered.

Aimee promptly fired coins into the slot.

"Mom...? Hi, it's me... Aimee," she exclaimed.

"Aimee? Why, I thought you'd forgotten about us," her mother chided her in her usual dry humour.

"No, Mom. Things have been kinda' hectic lately. What with work and other things."

"Other things? You mean boys and parties, more like?" another ambiguous barb shot back down the line. *"I know you want to have a good time while you're in England; but just remember what your father told you. You know we never cease praying that the Lord will keep you safe."*

"I know that, Mom."

"And is Shelby looking after you too?"

"Yes, Mom. Shelby is still my 'second dad'!" she groaned, rolling her eyes and shuffling from one leg to the other.

"Don't be so cocky, young lady. Shelby is a good Christian girl who loves the Lord. You'll never find a better friend."

"I know that too, Mom."

"Just remember what I told you too: who you hang out with pretty much determines who you will turn out to be..."

Dutifully, Aimee listened while her mother once again itemised the moral perils waiting to assail the unwary Christian: drugs, alcohol, promiscuous sex, unwanted pregnancy. How easy it was for a believer to shipwreck their faith should they be tempted to 'hang out' with the wrong kind of people.

"... *Aimee...? You still there?*"

"I'm here, Mom," she replied, though pumping a few more coins into the phone just in case.

"*...By the way, your father has been approached by one of the Vietnam MIA groups. They want him to become their president. They're looking for someone with a high profile in the media who can press the government to look again at the issue of those guys who might have been left behind...*"

Aimee listened patiently again as her mother recounted how torn her father was between clutching at the straw of Ike being found alive somewhere in deepest Indochina (and of wanting to pull out all the stops to extract him if he was); and of this staunch Republican not wanting to make waves during a year in which his party would struggle to retain the presidency, much less make headway in the fall's congressional and gubernatorial elections.

"*... And, hey, I got some good news before you go. There's a reunion taking place in England for the flyboys of the 357th who served there during the war. The organisers have invited your father to join them; so we've gone ahead and booked the flights. We thought while we're over there we might as well try and meet up with you. Wha' d'ya say?*"

"Sure, Mom. That'll be cool," Aimee enthused (though another rolling of her eyes belied her unease that, having travelled to England to escape the suffocating over-protectiveness of her parents, suddenly she might find it enveloping her again before the summer was through). Meanwhile, she noticed that someone else had wandered up to the phone box, the woman pacing about, wallet in hand, waiting to talk to loved ones.

"*Your dad thought it would be nice to stay at that swanky hotel you and Shelby are working at. What's it called?*"

"The Shanklin Heights."

"*That's the one. Apparently, he knows the manager there. Why, the guy's even managed to book us a top-class room...*"

Suddenly, her mother was interrupted mid-sentence by the bleeping of the phone indicating that the call was running out of time. With no more coins left to pump into it there was barely seconds left to frantically conclude their conversation.

"I love you, Aimee. See you soon."

"Yeah, I love you too, Mom."

And with that the call was terminated. Aimee exited the booth and held the door open for its next customer. Head in a whirl at the sudden prospect of her folks rolling up on the island, she crossed the road and wandered over to spend a few minutes resting upon a whitewashed wall that overlooked the beach.

The broad sweep of Sandown Bay was alive with the sights and sounds of its two seaside towns relaxing on this warm summer evening. Aimee could even make out the tall, illuminated outline of the Shanklin Heights Hotel in the distance. However, with darkness closing in her doleful introspection was cut short by another glance at her watch. Aware that Shelby was waiting upon her return, she lifted herself away from the wall and re-crossed the road, making her way back up the avenue.

Any lingering introspection was rudely interrupted when she suddenly heard someone wolf-whistle her. She turned and looked about, but couldn't see who. Tugging the neck of her top up onto her chest, she carried on walking. Maybe Shelby was right about the unwanted attention going bra-less would occasion.

"Show us yer' tits!" the onlooker this time called after her.

Enough was enough! She swung about again in a fury, eyes scanning the street for this elusive male chauvinist pig. Once again, there was no one there. Well, not quite. Sat inside a raised verandah overlooking the pavement, she spied a teenage boy with his head buried rather unconvincingly in some book. Overcome with indignation, she strode up the steps to confront him.

"Young man, do you have a problem with women?" she screeched, digging her fists into her hips.

Startled, this studious wolf-whistler looked up from what he was reading and offered her a mystified glare. However, this only enraged her even more.

"So you want to see them, do you?" she demanded, seizing the base of her top and hauling it up. "Well, here! Take a good look, you pervert!"

"Cor! Nice arse!"

Save for her exposed boobs wobbling like jellies, Aimee froze. The guy she was accusing had just said that without even moving his mouth – which remained agape in disbelief at being unexpectedly confronted by her proud pink nipples. His own frozen body twitched only to point out something behind her that she had failed to spot. Hurrying her top back over her breasts, she turned about in manifest trepidation.

"Chi-co!"

The chortling bird may or may not have been disappointed not to have also caught an eyeful of Aimee's orbs. However, he wasn't going to pass up the chance to nudge his head against the bars of his cage in the expectation that his new human friend might care to twiddle his feathers.

"Oh – my – god! A parrot! You mean to tell me that he...?" she pointed to the animal and then stared aghast at its companion.

Vaughan Lewis gulped and nodded. Aimee gulped and, in a flash, all that ruddiness in her cheeks had turned from indignation to crushing embarrassment.

"I am *so* sorry," she shook her head, subconsciously drawing in her arms to further cloak her bosom.

"No, it sh-sh-should be me apologising," Vaughan rose from his seat and stuttered. "I'm afr-fr-fraid the local school kids have been teaching him all manner of rude words. You should hear the way he calls after the traffic warden," he then joked limply.

At last, Aimee's eyes softened and her demeanour completed its transition from indignation through embarrassment to a dawning appreciation of the comical absurdity of this encounter.

"Well, I guess that's one way of attracting attention," she tentatively grinned, succumbing to Chico patiently gesturing that she stroke his head. "Does he bite?"

"Only strangers. But he's obviously taken a shine to you," Vaughan joked again, his own dark brown eyes softening too. They both broke into nervous laughter.

"Say, don't I know you?" Aimee then studied his boyish good looks again.

"You're Aimee, aren't you? We met few weeks back – on the train to Portsmouth."

"Yeah, that's right. I remember now. Where was it you said you came from?"

"Dudley – in the Midlands. Or Dud-lay – as people pronounce it when they're taking the mickey out of my accent," he wittered.

"I know the feeling."

"Hardly. You've got a beautiful accent... if you don't mind me saying so. In fact, a beautiful accent for a beautiful lady," he wittered again, mindful he had spewed out the mushiest of chat-up lines (but past caring anyway).

"Why, thank you. You're kinda', well... handsome yourself."

It was moment infused with the most spine-tingling magic. Both wistful young man and flattered young lady gazed into each other's eyes and wondered what they could possibly say next that would move the stalled conversation along. When their eyes finally flitted elsewhere in awkwardness, accompanied by another nervous laugh on both their parts, Amy noticed the bible he had left upturned on the easy chair he'd been relaxing in. She was about to comment upon this when into the verandah in a fit of panic there hurried a mature, well-spoken lady.

"Oh, Chico. I'm so sorry," she warbled, rushing up to the cage. "I was listening to *'Any Questions'* on the radio. I completely forgot it was getting dark and you were still outside. Anyone could have made off with you. It's a good job Vaughan and his young lady friend were here keeping an eye on you."

"Betty. This is Aimee," he thought he'd better enlighten her. "She's from the United States."

"Really?" Betty enthused. "Which part, my dear?"

"I'm from Minnesota, ma'am," she beamed proudly.

"Minnesota. Fascinating! My sister lives in America, you know. She married an American serviceman who was based over here and moved to San Francisco after the war. They've built a wonderful life together and have never looked back since."

"Wow! Now that *is* fascinating. You see, ma'am, for my university senior thesis – or 'dissertation', as you call it in your country – I've been researching the experiences of British women who dated GIs during the war: how they met, how they fell in love; what happened to them when the war was over – that kinda' thing. Studying in England has provided me with a fantastic opportunity to meet all sorts of women who have shared their stories with me. Maybe I can come around and chat to you about your sister some time,"

"Yes, that would be lovely. I do so love Americans."

"My Auntie Angie went out with an American during the war. You can talk to her too if you like. I'm sure she wouldn't mind," Vaughan ventured, recalling what sparing details she'd shared with him to date.

"Wow! Thanks. So many kind offers!"

Then Aimee glanced again at her watch.

"For now though, I guess I'd better go. I've left my friend by herself at a party while I went to make a phone call. She'll be sending out the search parties for me. But it's been nice talking to you, Betty. And it's been good to see you again... Vaughan."

"You too... Aimee. Auntie Angie sometimes sings at the Shanklin Heights Hotel. I'll tell her to look out for you."

"Sure. I'll look forward to meeting her."

The love-struck young man could see from the puckish gleam in those hazel eyes that – as well as wanting to 'chat' to his aunt – she might also be partial to wanting to chat with him too again at some point. Meanwhile, Betty commenced the ritual of wheeling Chico's cage back into her flat for the night. As she did so – and if by some incredible intuition – the amazing bird bade his own farewell to their visitor by whistling the opening bars to *The Star-Spangled Banner*! It prompted a heart-melting chuckle on the part of the American as she shuffled down the steps onto the street, waving to Vaughan as she headed off up the road.

* * * * *

"Say, you been to St Cloud and back?" Shelby quipped sarcastically upon Aimee's return. "You were gone ages."

"If you must know, I've been showing off my boobs to a hot young man," she replied matter-of-factly as she strolled past her.

It was a fanciful boast that induced another weary shake of the head on Shelby's part. Her incorrigible friend sure knew how to wind her up.

"Anyway, I thought you said we were gonna' party. So let's do it, Shell!" the wanderer cheered, grabbing another beer, cracking it open, and sauntering out into the garden, where the Bee Gee's *'Jive Talkin''* was blaring out.

Stubbornly supping her lemonade, Shelby might have had her misgivings. However, when somebody flipped The Commodores' *'Slippery When Wet'* onto the turntable even she couldn't resist her best friend's call to come join her on the patio slabs. Arms aloft and hips wiggling, Aimee and Shelby continued to boogie with abandon when the other partygoers joined them dancing to Wild Cherry's *'Play That Funky Music'*. Only when the track finally faded did both breathless American party animals also desist from their gyrating, taking a moment to whoop and high-five themselves on a job well done.

* * * * *

Having just made the last bus back, it was well past midnight when the two girls finally rolled up at the tradesman's entrance to the Shanklin Heights Hotel.

"My head hurts!" Aimee groaned, trying to keep the noise down, but (like inebriated revellers the world over) failing miserably.

"Shhhh!" Shelby rebuked her, twisting the key in the lock and ushering her tipsy friend through the door that she held open.

"Shell, I need a man!"

"You need a strong coffee and your bed, young lady."

"No, Shell. Take it from me, I need a man; a big, hunky man!" Aimee slurred, her weary eyes swivelling in their sockets.

Just then their attempt at stealing inside was abruptly blown by the switching on of the light and the appearance of the last person they wanted to bump into just then. Both girls froze to the spot like rabbits in the headlights... until Aimee involuntarily broke the suspense when a hiccup surfaced. Guiltily, she slapped her hand to her mouth.

"Oh. It's you two."

Though Veronica Lawton shared the same surname, same refined tastes, same sartorial elegance, and the same well-heeled, upper-class affectations as her husband, there the similarity ended. Where he was courteous and convivial, she was invariably curt and to-the-point. Where he was charming and easy-going, she gave the distinct impression of being highly-strung – a woman just waiting for an excuse to explode in a fit of terrifying histrionics. It was their first taste of just such an outburst that her two American employees now feared their clumsy post-midnight entrance might be about to occasion.

"I heard voices and thought it might be John," she explained peevishly (though mercifully without raising her voice). "I don't suppose you've seen him on your travels, have you?"

"Er, no ma'am. We haven't," Shelby riposted stiffly.

"Well," said Aimee, having promptly sobered up, "we did see him earlier in the evening. In fact, he very kindly gave us a ride to a birthday party we were heading for."

"Yeah, then he drove off some place. Meanwhile, we've been at the party until now. We're sorry we're late. We do hope we didn't startle you," Shelby added.

"I just wish he wouldn't keep disappearing without telling me," her boss cussed. "It would be nice if he remembered that we still have a hotel to run. Or rather I've ended up running it."

"It's a fine hotel, Mrs Lawton," Shelby forced a smile to placate her. "All the guests we've spoken to have really enjoyed their stays here."

"Yes, ma'am. So fine that my parents have booked to stay here too when they visit England next month," Aimee piled on the flattery.

"Oh, is that so?" Veronica seemed surprised to hear.

"Yes ma'am. In fact, the best room in the house. Your husband has very kindly seen to that," Aimee boasted.

Meanwhile, observing her boss's look of surprise furrowing into a frown, Shelby discreetly nudged her best friend lest she boast too much.

"Well, thank you, girls – for your kind words." Veronica forced a smile too, before lecturing them in her silky, no-nonsense voice to "Remember though: you need to be up bright and early tomorrow to help me keep this a 'fine hotel'. So I suggest you keep the noise down and head for your beds."

"Yes, ma'am."

"We will, ma'am."

And with that she wandered off, perchance to await the return of her husband from whatever nocturnal distraction he was attending to. Thereafter, the two American students breathed a sigh of relief and scurried off to their room.

"Boy, she sure is one fearsome dame when she's on the warpath," Shelby noted afterwards once the lights were out and they were both safely tucked up in their beds.

"Yeah. I wouldn't want to be her husband when she catches up with him," Aimee concurred.

"Say," Shelby then broke the ensuing silence to turn and address her friend in the half-light, "did I hear you say your folks are coming to England?"

"That's right – end of August. Apparently, Dad's flying in for some air force reunion. They thought they'd pop by and say 'hi' while they're over here."

"Doesn't that bug you?"

"Not much I can do about it. I guess we'll just have to be on our best behaviour. No more parties, eh?"

"No," Shelby growled, "I mean don't you think it's kinda' spooky that this Lawton guy is so taken with your dad? First he's writing to him and now he's invited him to come and stay at his hotel – and in its most luxurious rooftop suite too!"

Aimee shrugged. She hadn't given the matter much thought since that first awkward encounter with him that day on the balcony of the room in question.

"I dunno'. I guess he just wants to the chance to talk to Dad about this history project he's working on. Anyway, if my folks *are* coming over then, Shell, we are just going to have to pack in as much fun as we can before they roll up," she insisted, hastily changing the subject. "So how about you and I go check out a few of the island's hotspots some time. I'm told there's an old paddle steamer moored up in Newport that's been converted into a nightclub. That sounds exciting. The *Ryde Queen*, they call her."

"Well… I dunno'."

"Oh, come on, Shell. You can't kid me you don't like dancing. I saw you at tonight's party: *"Do a little dance… Make a little love... Get down tonight...Get down tonight...*" she sang, shuffling in her bed and insisting "Why, that cute little butt of yours was just made for 'grooving'!"

Her friend thought about it for a moment before offering vague and reluctant assent. After all, didn't the Bible say that 'to every thing there is a season' – including 'a time to dance'.

8

Monday, July 19th 1976

> *"Faultless! Absolutely faultless! So what are the judges going to say about that...? Yes, that's perfection! Nadia Comâneci has just scored a first in Olympic gymnastics – a perfect ten!"*

Alas, it was the turn of the Summer Olympic Games to break Frank Tring's customary television viewing habits. For the next two weeks this supple fourteen year-old Romanian – along with David Wilkie, Nellie Kim and Olga Korbut – would be the subjects of his laconic predictions about who would achieve gold medal success in Montreal.

Angela Tring wasn't into sport. Music had always been her abiding passion, and tonight she was off out again to indulge it in the modest way that was permitted to her. Dutifully, she reminded her husband of this, popping her head around the living room door as she made her way down the hallway bearing that suitcase that in a few hours' time would once more transform her into a glamorous singing sensation. Meanwhile, a familiar raised hand above the back of that favourite armchair was the all acknowledgement she was going to receive from her husband.

With Vaughan working a late shift on the buses, this evening she passed the short drive to the Shanklin Heights Hotel by herself. One of several summer performing contracts she had secured, at least it involved less travelling than to the farthest-flung of the island's hotels and holiday camps where she also put in regular appearances.

Even so, the journey afforded her time enough to reflect again upon how she had ended up passing thirty years of her life in a stale and unhappy marriage. And why, cruelly, the very words 'marriage' and 'happiness' were so often mutually-exclusive terms. Then again, they do say 'act in haste; repent at leisure'.

What would have happened had she turned a different corner that day in 1945 when, on the rebound, she had hitched her star to a man with whom she would soon realise she had little in common?

To be sure, Frank Tring had held out the promise of security at a moment when her aspirations for professional and emotional fulfilment had turned to dust. In that respect, she acknowledged, he had been good to her. Though no thrusting captain of industry, he had nonetheless made a modest success of Tring's Toys on the High Street, the business he'd established when they'd first moved to the Isle of Wight in the 1960s. Thanks to his hard work, she'd never gone without. In time, she'd been able to restart her singing career too; and to thus realise at least some of those once-promising professional aspirations. Yet otherwise, she remained very much the emotionally-unfulfilled wife of a provincial shopkeeper. How leisurely the repentance had proved. Surely there had to be more to life than this.

It was a fate made all the more stark when, upon arriving at the hotel, she had bumped into the manager's elegant young wife. Sexual and career liberation for women had come not a moment too soon for Veronica Lawton, the attractive socialite revelling in her role as *de facto* manager of one of the island's most exclusive hotels. She'd definitely ended up wearing the trousers in this establishment; and maybe (Angie mischievously surmised) in her marriage too – her courteous and convivial husband content to show his face from time to time, alternately flattering and amusing the guests with his foppish bonhomie.

Once ensconced in her dressing room, in no time at all Angie was out of those everyday clothes and into a backless, silver-sequinned evening dress and matching open-toed stiletto sandals. Putting the finishing touches to her make-up and hooking a set of large, shimmering ear rings in place, there was just time to puff up her hair in the mirror as she did so.

Satisfied there was not a strand out of place, she stood and ran her splayed-out fingers down the outline of the dress to admire how, by dint of exercise and diet, she'd managed to hold onto her impressive figure. Not bad for a fifty-four year-old, she commended herself! However, a closer inspection in that same mirror revealed how the crow's feet and the wrinkles were deepening with each passing summer. Her complexion was slowly, but surely deserting her – or at the very least reminding the world that she was fast approaching pensionable age.

Her wistful introspection was cut short by a tap on the door.

"You're on in two minutes, Angie," the portly compère advised, having gingerly poked his head around it.

She turned and offered him a jittery nod of the head. Consummate professional though she was, it was funny how – even after all these years – she still found herself afflicted by stage fright.

"And by the way, love. You look absolutely fabulous," he must have picked up on her latent insecurity, addressing her over his shoulder as she followed after him. Blushing, she smiled.

Then suddenly, the four-piece band that had been playing middle-of-the-road melodies wrapped up their routine. The time for stage fright had passed.

"Ladies and gentleman, let's hear it for the Mike Manners Showband!" the compère raced on stage, grabbing a microphone from its stand and waiting for the polite applause that greeted his exhortation to subside. Meanwhile, cupping a hand to his eyes, through the lingering fug of cigarette smoke he could make out drinks being replenished, banter being restarted across tables, and the flutter of beer mats and bingo carnets being waved in front of faces in an attempt to supplement the work of the ceiling fans that were spinning monotonously throughout the room.

"Without doubt the highlight of this summer's programme of entertainment so far has been the incredibly talented lady who'll be rounding off tonight's show. So without further ado, let's give a great big Shanklin Heights welcome to the peerless, the breath-taking, the superlative ANGIE ASHBY!"

From the moment she strode onto the stage, the audience sensed that maybe those florid adjectives had basis in fact. Once they heard her break into the opening stanzas of *'Do You Know The Way To San Jose?'* any doubt was removed. An awe descended as they beheld the animated smiles and wagging fingers by which she sought to engage with them, expounding from bitter experience how 'all the stars who never were' soon enough end up 'parking cars or pumping gas'. Or maybe passing their days crooning to chain-smoking, middle-aged holiday-makers at seaside hotels?

As if seeking to recapture past glory, Angela Tring had chosen to resume her singing career under her maiden name – the name she'd been known by when she'd been a pin-up girl to thousands of Allied servicemen. From time to time, people she'd once entertained would recognise her or recall the name, surprised to discover that Angie Ashby was still around. In fact, enthralling tonight's audience with her own touching rendition of Cole Porter's *'Every Time We Say Goodbye'*, it was possible to detect an eye or two glistening at the thought that, yes, this was indeed the same Angie Ashby – the one who had mesmerised them all those years ago while performing that very same rueful lament on military camps the length and breadth of wartime Britain.

Tonight though, the repertoire had moved with the times to include hits by Carly Simon, Roberta Flack, The Carpenters and Helen Reddy (*'Angie Baby'* – what else!). However, it was her dramatic performance of Shirley Bassey's *'Diamonds Are Forever'* that really had the house applauding.

Dusty Springfield was another artiste whose style she could mimic to perfection. It was no surprise therefore that – at her behest and encouragement – couples soon drifted onto the dance floor to shuffle arm-in-arm to her smouldering rendition of *'The Look of Love'*. Heartened by the response, it was while perchance glancing past the blinding stage lights that she picked out the silhouette of someone else up the back of the room who was spellbound by her performance.

John Lawton had heard on the grapevine about Angie Ashby and her talent. Perched on a stool by the bar next to a whisky-and-dry, he emitted just the faintest smirk of self-satisfaction that it was *he* who had then badgered his wife to hire her. Yet it was more than just the promise of stage excellence that had drawn him to the name. Sipping from his glass, he savoured how intimately she now mastered every twist and turn of this quasi-erotic composition. Perhaps the 'look of love' really was capable of saying 'so much more than words could ever say'.

It rounded off the evening perfectly. Well, not quite. With the audience on their feet clapping and cheering there was no way she was ever going to deny them an encore. Sure enough, half-a-minute passed before those stage lights captured her again hurrying back out to the microphone – her very last song of the evening an electrifying interpretation of *'Alfie'*. It was yet another timeless Burt Bacharach & Hal David classic that demanded the very highest standards of vocal dexterity in order to pull it off. Angie Ashby did not disappoint them. Once again, the rapturous and prolonged standing ovation that erupted at its conclusion attested to this. Wiping grateful tears from her eyes, she took her final bow and retreated to the dressing room.

* * * * *

She had not long commenced removing her jewellery and stage make-up when she heard a gentle tap on the door. In the reflection of the mirror she looked up to observe that door inch open. John Lawton was making his anticipated appearance. Glancing over each shoulder, he stepped inside and closed the door behind him, commencing a passage over to where she was sat. She rose from her seat to gaze up into his azure blue eyes.

"How did I do?" she implored him, almost childlike in her yearning for reassurance.

"You heard them stamping and applauding," he replied.

His hands reached up to clutch the soft, bare flesh of her upper arms. She smiled nervously, feeling like putty in those hands as they drew her forward so that he could launch his arms more fully around her. As he rocked her tenderly in his embrace, her head resting safe and secure against the firmness of his chest, she heard him sobbing tears of pent-up emotion. She too was fighting to hold back such tears – party as they both now were to a terrifying secret that neither of them quite knew how to handle.

"Does Veronica know you're here?" she fretted as she reluctantly prised herself from his grasp.

"Maybe," he shrugged, seemingly unperturbed. "She knows that most evenings I take it upon myself to offer a welcoming face to the guests – and to our visiting entertainers. It frees her up to attend to the more practical aspects of running a successful hotel.

Like managing the staff; or pouring over the accounts; or making our finances more 'tax efficient'."

"The kind of jobs that are beneath a millionaire playboy, eh?" she ribbed him in an attempt to lighten the mood. She reached up to straighten his tie – as would a fussing aunt.

"In this life each of us will excel at something: you're a singer; I'm an aviation historian; Veronica – bless her – is able to get her head around VAT returns."

"An aviation historian, you say? Can't say I've met one of those before," she sat back down, continuing to remove her make-up while addressing his reflection in the mirror.

"That's right. I write articles about military aircraft. I've also had a book published: an account of those magnificent P51 Mustangs of the United States Eighth Army Air Force that were based in England during the war – as well as the daring exploits of the brave young men who flew in them."

She observed his eyes aglow with pride upon recounting this abiding passion of his life (beautiful women aside). Conversely, he thought he detected a hue of cynicism in hers as she carried on divesting herself of her stage finery.

"Should I assume you have no interest in classic World War Two American fighters?"

"The aircraft were impressive enough," she conceded. "Living in East Anglia at the time I saw plenty of them coming and going. But let's just say not all the exploits of those 'brave young men' were daring. In fact, some of the things they got up to on the ground were downright contemptible. But I dare say, being an *aviation* historian, you were not overly concerned with that."

She presumed correctly, given that he then proceeded to witter on instead about a new book he was working on – one which would chronicle the story of another iconic American warplane: the Boeing B52 Stratofortress bomber.

"How come you don't write books about *our* planes – Spitfires and Lancasters?" curiosity compelled her to probe. "I thought you might want to, what with your father being in the RAF."

He shrugged. "For some reason, I've always been drawn to all things American," he then explained dreamily. "The United States is such an amazing country. And Americans are such an amazing people too. Maybe I should have been born one!"

Once more, Angie seemed underwhelmed. She stared up at his reflection again, prompting him to remember something she'd shared when they'd first been alone in each other's company – about American servicemen and their often fraught and tangled love lives. Suddenly, her cynicism made sense.

"Anyway, if you don't mind, right now I need to get changed and go home. There are only so many excuses I can make to my husband for rolling back late," she insisted, rising from her seat to usher him towards the door, adding "You best make yourself scarce too. After all, being found with me in a state of undress might also take some explaining should your wife decide she too prefers welcoming entertainers to filing tax returns."

For a moment he was minded to feel hurt at such a rebuff. It was almost as if this much older woman, who had so captivated him, was playing hard to get.

"Yes, well... maybe another time," he nodded, though the disappointment was etched into his doleful features.

The instant he was gone she slid back into that chair and stared at her pallid reflection in the mirror. This was madness. It certainly risked opening up a veritable Pandora's Box of repercussions that might prove impervious to their control. And yet crossing paths with Angela Tring – aka the dazzling Angie Ashby – had transformed this otherwise urbane, laid-back charmer into a pitiful little-boy-lost.

* * * * *

It continued to exercise her thoughts once she'd slipped back into her ordinary clothes and had made her way out onto the car park. In particular, she wondered how she could keep such a momentous thing secret from her husband – for now, at least. For surely Frank had a right to know about her newfound relationship to this dashing hotelier-cum-amateur historian.

Opening the boot of her car and hauling the suitcase inside, her head was in such a whirl that she wasn't giving the task the attention it deserved. Hence when the corner of that suitcase clipped the lip of the boot, the jolting sprang the clips that held it shut. She could only watch in horror as its contents – her make-up bag, her shoes, her backing tapes, and that silver, sequinned dress – spilled out over the car park. She mouthed a voluble expletive.

"You okay, ma'am?" she heard a voice respond in the midst of her panic. She looked up to observe two young girls racing over to help retrieve her possessions.

"Gee, this dress is beautiful. I'm guessing it must have cost a few bucks," one of them marvelled, loving scooping it off the tarmac and dusting it down.

"It's my stage attire."

"Stage attire? So you must be Angie Ashby?" the girl replied, staring at its owner and matching the face to the one that graced the posters she'd seen about the hotel advertising the entertainment on offer. She handed the outfit to her to fold and place back in her case.

"That's right," Angie replied, likewise clocking onto the American accent and wondering if "You must be Aimee then?"

"No, she's Shelby. I'm Aimee," the other girl interjected, still gathering up odd items of accessories that had come to rest dotted about the car park. "Why do you ask?"

"You've met my nephew – Vaughan," Angie rose to her feet, suddenly remembering his description of a 'tall, slim girl with trailing fair hair'. She recalled too the promise she'd made to him that had been overlooked amidst the excitement of her dizzying encounters with John Lawton.

"So you're his aunt?" the student also rose to her feet, handing back to her the items she'd collected up.

Those items all accounted for – and with the suitcase snapped shut and placed safely in the boot – Angie held out a hand of belated gratitude and greeting, firstly to Aimee and then to her baffled best friend.

"Your nephew told me all about you the other day," the Minnesotan cheerily explained. "He said you once dated an American airman. I hope you won't mind me asking, but, you see, the subject of my university dissertation is the social aspects of my country's military presence in England during the war. And, in particular, the effect it had upon the lives of women of your generation. I would really appreciate it if you and I could get together some time for the purpose of furthering my research. Maybe we can chat about your own experiences of Uncle Sam and his GIs... It could be in strict confidence, if you prefer."

Her qualifying assurance hinted that Aimee had witnessed her subject's eyes strangely darken at the suggestion. However, not wanting to appear rude or ungracious towards a Good Samaritan who'd helped her in a moment of need, Angie's frown mellowed and she appeared to warm to the idea.

"I'm afraid what I have to tell you may not always paint your countrymen in a flattering light," she cautioned even so.

"No problem. We Yanks have our skeletons in the proverbial cupboard too – as you Brits might say," Aimee snickered.

"Well, if it helps you with your project, then, yes – of course I'll happily chat with you."

Then she halted the conversation to reach inside the glove compartment of the car, emerging with a small business card.

"Here's my number. Give me a call and we can arrange a date when you can come round for tea. Then when we've finished *our* little chat you can maybe spend the evening chatting to Vaughan too. I know he'll look forward to that very much."

"Sure. I'm guessing your nephew likes what he has seen of me so far!" her smile broadened. "And I'm real flattered that Chico thinks my butt looks good in short pants!"

Angie grinned knowingly. However, with each startling revelation Shelby's big brown eyes had been opening wider. This last snippet caused her mouth to gape too – which at least prevented her from articulating her dismay that both her best friend and this intriguing woman were party to some kind of esoteric joke from which she was excluded.

"Anyway," Aimee concluded, "it's getting kinda' late. So if you'll excuse us we better head inside before that dragon of a manager's wife is on our case again. It's been nice meeting you, Mrs Ashby."

"It's Mrs Tring actually. Angela Tring. 'Ashby' is just my stage name. Oh, and my maiden name too."

Warm parting words exchanged, Angie jumped into her car, started it up, and reversed out of the parking space.

"So, like, is there something I oughta' know?" Shelby snorted as they observed this Angie Ashby (or Angela Tring, or whoever she was!) waving to them as she sped off. "Such as: who's this 'Vaughan' fellow who you've been seeing behind my back? Is he by any chance the same guy we got chatting to on that train not long back? When might you have found the time to have had all these jolly conversations about his aunt's wartime romances? And last, but not least: who the heck is this Chico guy who's been commenting on your ass?"

"It's a long story, 'Dad'. A long story," Aimee assured her clucking pseudo-parent, draping an arm around her shoulder.

With this in place she then hauled her off in the direction of the tradesman's entrance of the hotel, praying that punctilious dragon wouldn't catch up with them sneaking in late again.

9

Saturday, July 24th 1976

"Hoy! Wait a minute!"

The breathless, middle-aged man was only an arms-length from the grab pole of the platform. However, Colin Garrett was in no frame of mind to be generous. The bell had been rung, the indicators were flashing, and a motorist had very kindly gesticulated for the Lodekka to pull out into the traffic. Therefore, out into the traffic it pulled, the intending passenger realising the driver was not going to wait for him.

"Bloody useless bus service!" he halted and fumed.

From the platform of the bus Vaughan offered him a guilty smile. He knew Colin was in a hurry to get back to the depot. For tonight both driver and conductor were eager to be out of uniform and into clobber more appropriate for what they had planned.

Colin did indeed arrive back to the depot smack on time. Fortunately too, Vaughan was able to book in his waybill and his takings without the eagle-eyed supervisor spotting the kind of discrepancies that might have required explanation. Mounting Uncle Frank's trusty old bike, he was therefore able to speedily pedal home, grateful that (though the heat wave had abated) the weather remained warm and sunny. There was no respite in sight yet for the island's fading lawns.

"Give us a kiss!"

"No time to stop and offer you one, Chico," Vaughan replied, breezing through the verandah to leave the expectant bird offering its head against the bars of its cage in vain.

The evening meal was a similarly brisk affair. Uncle Frank was his usual gruff self, laden with foreboding that formal water rationing on account of the prolonged dry spell could only be days away. Why, Betty next door had already taken to sating the triffids in verandah with water she was recycling from the bath! Meanwhile, Auntie Angie was sporting that same anxious look that told him she desperately wanted to tell her husband something, but – conscious that her nephew's ears were wagging – elected to sit on the news instead.

* * * * *

Mindful of his duty to conserve the stuff too, after an equally brisk bath in shallow water Vaughan had changed into his favourite cheesecloth shirt, brown Oxford bags trousers, and platform shoes. While dabbing his chops from the bottle of Uncle Frank's *Old Spice* aftershave that he'd purloined (and the music charts were counting down on Auntie Angie's transistor radio that he'd also purloined) he found himself singing along to *"Don't Go Breaking My Heart"* – that annoying new tune by Elton John and Kiki Dee. It had turfed Demis Roussos and his cloying *'Forever And Ever'* off the Number One spot – something else that had vexed his Auntie Angie, who possessed a soft spot for the warbling Hellenic love god. Indeed, this corpulent Greek was the reason her appetite had been whetted to maybe try a first holiday abroad next year (or so she'd intimated earlier at the meal table). Assuming, of course, that she could prise Frank away from his toy shop first!

At last he was ready, preening himself in the mirror one final time before switching off the radio and loading his pockets with his wallet and comb. As if on cue, he noticed a little blue MGB GT sports car pull up at the bus stop beneath his bedroom window (and which was Colin's set of wheels whenever he was off-duty). However, before departing to join him Vaughan paused to pick up that lovingly-framed family photograph that was posited on the dressing table.

Taken not long after Frank and Angela Tring had moved to the Isle of Wight (and just a few hundred yards from where he now found himself gazing wistfully at it again), it captured the infant Vaughan on the beach in his swimming trunks, posing in front of the giant sandcastle he'd just built. Happy and smiling, he was flanked by the two women he loved the most – his mother and his Auntie Angie (both of them looking svelte in their own 1960s bathing attire). Uncle Frank – who he recalled had helped him construct it – had presumably been behind the camera taking the photograph. Meanwhile, in the background, his father was lounging in a deckchair with his trouser legs rolled up – head buried in a newspaper and disinterested (as always) in his son and his creative achievements.

The more Vaughan had studied that photograph these last few weeks the more he was convinced it alluded to something unexplained at the heart of his family. In particular, though she never let on (and he was too reticent to ask), Vaughan was convinced Auntie Angie had invited him to spend the summer with her for an ulterior reason – one that had nothing to do with gaining work experience on the buses. Furthermore, he was convinced that his mother was somehow in on the scheme too. Indeed, he found it strange that this strait-laced woman seemed uncharacteristically relaxed about her one-and-only son passing these weeks in the company of his breezy and irreverent aunt – someone who had no qualms about him growing his hair long, frequenting pubs, or stopping out late at parties, nightclubs and other havens of carnal temptation (her only stipulation being that he should be 'prepared', that is!).

"Come on, mate. I nearly got ticketed waiting for you," Colin berated him – as he did so spotting the woman who was waving Vaughan off from the verandah of the apartment block.

"Cor! She's a bit of alright. She that next-door neighbour of yours who owns the parrot? Uh! I can see why the dirty little creature's always talking about sex!" he guffawed, slotting the car in gear and sprinting up to the junction – though not without taking a final crafty glance at her in his mirrors.

"That's my Auntie Angie," Vaughan enlightened him, the poker face masking a nephew who was unsure whether to feel flattered or aggrieved by his friend's smutty inference.

"Oh, sorry, mate. You can't deny she's a good-looking woman though. She's certainly got one crackin' figure for her vintage!"

Vaughan was only too aware of that. In fact, he had his suspicions that Colin Garrett wasn't the only younger man who had warmed to his aunt's sensual delights. In truth – and given that Uncle Frank gave the impression of being more in love with his television set than he was with his longsuffering wife – who could blame her were she to treat herself to a spot of extra-marital diversion (for which her frequent late night absences as an entertainer would provide the perfect cover).

"Anyway, enough of beautiful women – at least until we reach our destination. For now, pin back your ears and listen to this," Colin insisted, taking a music cassette from the console box and inserting it into the stereo system he'd installed in the car.

All of a sudden, an urgent, brooding guitar riff filled the car from the customised speakers mounted in all four corners of it.

"Brilliant, eh...! Blue Oyster Cult – their new album," he cried as vocals broke over the music track.

It was Vaughan's turn to be enlightened. Colin hit the accelerator to dart around one of those Number 16 buses that on any other warm, sunny evening he might have been driving. Meanwhile, his passenger was content to tap his hand in time on the sill of the window he'd wound down – and which permitted cool air to trail up strands of his brown locks...

"Come on, baby...
Don't fear the Reaper...
Baby, take my hand...
Don't fear the Reaper..."

Music (unlike girls) was one topic where Colin's proffered insights had proved more dependable. Britain might be perched on the precipice of a music revolution – with spitting, spiky-haired punk rockers challenging the existing order – but Colin Garrett was unapologetically old school: prog-rock outfits like Supertramp, Jethro Tull and Tangerine Dream, certainly; but also heavier stuff by Led Zeppelin, Uriah Heep and Rainbow. However, his musical tastes were even more eclectic than that. At the other end of the spectrum he was also an authority on genres as diverse as reggae, ska, disco and northern soul; a veritable walking encyclopaedia of popular music that Vaughan felt privileged to be imbibing.

All this meant that, once they had rolled up at the nightspot in Ryde (and had cleared the bouncers to gain admittance), the young conductor was at least able to distinguish his Philadelphia soul from his Latin Hustle; his George Clinton from his Barry White. Indeed, as they strode into the club – Colin treating his blonde mop to a quick flick of the comb and then glancing around as if he owned the joint – the old 'Walrus of Love's' *'You See The Trouble With Me'* and *'Let The Music Play'* were pounding back-to-back from the sound system. It was a wall of noise that was complemented by a battery of kaleidoscopic strobe lights picking out young people who were already on the dance floor.

"This is more like it, mate: ace music and fabulous birds. Oh, and the beer's just about drinkable too."

Pints in hands, after a quick reconnoitring of the club's darkened nooks-and-crannies they located a spot along the balcony from which to observe proceedings. There Colin leaned against the balustrade to eye up a posse of chicks dancing around their handbags to Candi Staton's *'Young Hearts Run Free'*.

"So how come you and Tina haven't got it together yet?" he enquired above the din. "I reckon she fancies you."

Vaughan didn't have an answer. He was too ashamed to confess that it was part of a pattern in his life: girl 'friend' breezes in; girl 'friend' pays him a few compliments; gets him all going; then breezes back out of it again – leaving him to despair of ever finding a 'girlfriend'. The same thing looked set to happen with Aimee, the jolly American lass who he'd not heard from since their surreal encounter the other evening on the verandah. Neither had Auntie Angie made mention of having 'put in a good word' since their conversation in the car.

"Looks like we better try and fix you up with one of this lot then," Colin gestured with his glass, having spotted more young things boogieing below them. "How about that one there: the one in the glasses with the red stripey tank top? If you like, I'll move in on her mate first. Then you can join me."

As if on cue, the girl in question smiled up at them. Colin winked suggestively. Nice girl, Vaughan agreed. But... well...

"Uh! Fussy, are we!" Colin rolled his eyes, sensing his friend's procrastination. This risked being a very boring evening.

"Alright, how about those two there? You take the short one and I'll go for the leggy one with the blow-waved hair."

Suddenly any hint of ennui was gone. Vaughan's brown eyes – which had been in danger of glazing over – were suddenly ablaze with possibilities. And with thanksgiving too!

"No, mate," he insisted, shoving Colin aside as they proceeded down the stairs that led onto the dance floor. "*You* take the short one and *I'll* go for the leggy one!"

Van McCoy's *'The Hustle'* added an enchanting touch of frivolity to the niftiness with which Colin and Vaughan circled the two stunners before closing in for the kill. Then the 'leggy one' with the blow-waved hair suddenly recognised one of them and halted to throw her arms around him. The 'short one' too seemed bowled-over to be setting her eyes upon this boy from the Black Country again.

"Blimey! You don't hang around!" Colin cried, disconcerted that Vaughan appeared to have pulled before his skirt-chasing workmate had even had time to unleash one of his chat-up lines.

"Colin, meet two friends of mine. This is Aimee... and Shelby. They're working at the Shanklin Heights Hotel over the summer," Vaughan introduced the two girls.

"What? That place up on the cliffs overlooking the Esplanade – the one you can see from the Number 44 bus?" Colin replied.

"Sure is. That's where we're spending the summer while we're over here in England," Shelby cheered, offering him a great big girlish grin.

"Blimey! She's an American!" he marvelled.

"We're both Americans – from the good ol' U S of A!" Aimee informed him with a similar cheery smile.

Suddenly the night had taken a turn for the better – even if Vaughan was pairing up with the bird that Colin had had his eye on. However, with Shelby certainly not lacking in the looks department, the smooth-operating bus driver conceded his mate his wish and sidled up to the jolly little Georgian instead. The DJ helped things along by serving up Lou Rawls' *'You'll Never Find (Another Love Like Mine)'* on the turntable.

"Do you come here often?" Vaughan meanwhile summoned up a hackneyed chat-up line of his own.

"About as often as you, I guess," was Aimee's vacuous, knee-jerk riposte, the General's daughter wrestling with the same shyness and realising that she was not always as confident in the presence of a boy as she liked to kid herself.

In the end, they both settled for nervous smiles – as well as that certain look in each other's eyes that told the other that the gods were smiling down on tonight's encounter. Or should that be *the* God? Aimee now put a question that had been on her mind ever since this handsome young man had had the dubious fortune to have witnessed her in a less than becoming comportment.

"Was that the Bible I saw you reading the other day?"

Flummoxed, Vaughan could think of no better response than to confess that "Yes. It was."

"So do I take it you're… a Christian?"

"Yes. I am," he felt almost embarrassed to admit.

"Snap!" she then grinned. "Though Shelby's keeps telling me I'm backsliding."

Vaughan would have liked to have confessed the same – but his crestfallen expression said it for him anyway. Recognising this, Aimee treated him to another reassuring smile. They carried on dancing without returning the matter. Instead, when the DJ mixed The Miracles' *'Love Machine'* into The O'Jays' *'I Love Music'* all four new friends both availed themselves of the spritely tempo to demonstrate how adeptly they could groove.

To be sure, Vaughan had further honed his dance skills since that day he'd surprised both himself and his work colleagues at Tina's housewarming party. Since then, turning up Auntie Angie's transistor radio and practising his moves in front of her full length bedroom mirror when no one was around had paid off handsomely. Aimee was certainly impressed.

Both couples were having so much fun that, in no time at all, the evening had flown by and it was time for the DJ to slow things down with a selection of more intimate melodies, opening with Earth, Wind & Fire's clawing *'Reasons'*. The ever-lustful Colin seized the opportunity of slow-dancing with Shelby to repeatedly sneak a hand down to rest upon a cheek of her pert little bottom – only for her own hand to intercept it each time and draw it back up to her waist.

Aimee had no such problem. Vaughan was the perfect gentleman, content to fold his arms around her and sway in time to the music. It was a response predicated as much upon his naivety in such matters as his desire to behave chivalrously towards a member of the opposite sex.

Staring into her eyes as Boz Scagg's dreamy *'Harbor Lights'* wrapped up a perfect evening, he recalled Auntie Angie's words: find yourself a girl who has your heart uppermost in her thoughts; and when you find her, make sure you treasure *her* heart also.

Aimee stared back at him wistfully and blinked. Then she rested her head against his shoulder, the prompt for both of them to close their eyes, draw in tighter, and imagine they really were all alone on the dance floor. All the time, Vaughan was praying that he might just have found that girl at last.

* * * * *

If the slow dances had been divine, the journey home was rather less so. Of course, Aimee and Shelby had the money on them to hail a taxi back to Shanklin. However, Colin was most insistent that they avail themselves of the offer of a lift home in his car. Vaughan too was eager to prolong the time he could spend with his new 'girlfriend' (thereby hoping to summon up the courage to seek one further indulgence: to exchange phone numbers!).

What the two Americans hadn't bargained for was that the rear seat of Colin's MGB was little more than a small bench crammed against the sloping rear windshield. Given that she was the shortest of the four of them inevitably it fell to Shelby to occupy one half of the bench seat (which least spared her the attention of Colin's wandering hands), while Aimee volunteered to squeeze onto the other half.

It was during the twenty minute journey home that Vaughan discovered to his surprise that Aimee already had his phone number – courtesy of Auntie Angie, who had invited her to tea next week (and on an evening when he was off-duty too!). Maybe *the* God really was smiling down on their budding friendship; or at the very least his aunt had been supremely thoughtful.

* * * * *

All too soon the little sports car was back in Sandown – though the girls sandwiched together in the back were hardly sorry (relieved that, with Vaughan stepping out onto a deserted High Street, Aimee could hop in the front, thereby enabling Shelby to stretch out in the back).

"Thank you. For a wonderful evening," Vaughan seized Aimee's fingertips as she was about to jump into his vacated seat.

"Thank you too. It's been most enjoyable," she simpered.

"I'll look forward to you coming round."

"I'll look forward to coming."

"Come on, you two lovebirds. It's well past midnight. And I'm back on duty at eight," Colin called over, revving the engine.

Aimee smiled regretfully, broke loose from his grip, and jumped back in the car, waving to him.

"Take good care of them both," Vaughan called back to his colleague through the open passenger window.

"Blimey! What do you think I'm gonna' do with them? Take them up Culver Beach?"

"What happens on Culver Beach?" Shelby piped up naively.

"On a warm, moonlit night like tonight, love? Don't ask!" their chauffeur turned and offered her a wicked grin.

"In which case, we'll head home, if you don't mind."

"And don't spare the horses!" Aimee tapped the dashboard and cried out in her best impersonation of an English toff.

And with that they were gone, the sound of the MGB's throaty exhaust echoing off the shop fronts.

Vaughan crossed the road, hands in pocket, making his way back to his own summer abode. As he did, he halted to peer inside the frontage of Tring's Toys. Amongst the Lego bricks, Scalextric cars and Holly Hobbie dolls – as well as seaside staples like buckets, spades and fishing nets – he spotted a huge box mounted behind the counter. It was a 1/72 scale model of one of those gigantic American Stratofortress bombers.

In a moment of sheer boyhood regression, he recalled that it had been a while since he had pieced together a model aeroplane – his bedroom back in Gornal still home to the handful he'd crafted that had managed to avoid losing cockpits, rudders or weapons pylons to the attrition of his mother's feather duster.

Perhaps he could butter up his Uncle Frank to offer him a discount – or at the very least throw in a tube of glue, a brush, and a few tins of Humbrol paint. Then again, for all his uncle's faults, lack of generosity towards his nephew had never been one of them. On past form, he'd probably end up giving him the massive plane for free – glue, brushes, paint and all – along with a wink and an admonition not to tell his Auntie Angie.

Hands in pockets, he resumed the short journey home, turning the corner into Victoria Road. As he did, he spotted the glowing sidelights of a long, sleek Jaguar coupé that had parked up in the street. Thinking he recognised at least one of its occupants, he hastily ducked behind the phone box outside the library, watching as they continued their discourse. The guy in the driver's seat seemed agitated – tearful even. It was an upset that appeared to resolve itself when the woman next to him reached over and planted a kiss upon his brow. Then she grabbed her handbag and opened the door to step onto the pavement.

Vaughan pressed himself tighter into the shadows, observing her more clearly now that her face was no longer obscured by the glare of the street light on the windscreen.

His heart skipped a beat. It was indeed Auntie Angie! Sartorial as always, her evocative gait covered the few dozens yards to the verandah steps as stealthily as her clicking heels would permit. Once she was inside the block and out of sight, the Jaguar likewise pulled away as stealthily as the low-pitched growl of its colossal 5.3 litre V12 engine would permit. As it passed him, Vaughan caught sight of the blonde locks of its driver. Then he too was gone, leaving the dumbfounded young bus conductor more convinced than ever that his beloved aunt really was having an affair with a much younger man.

10

Sunday, July 25th 1976

The minute Aimee sliced through it the sounds above the surface became a muffled hum. Opening her eyes and hauling herself through the water, it was as if she had returned to the succour of her mother's womb – a place she sometimes yearned to retreat to; a place where the complications of life outside of it could no longer trouble her.

Eventually, the need to take in air compelled her to break the surface – where, along with the hubbub up top, Cockney Rebel's *'Come Up And See Me (Make Me Smile)'* was piping through the speakers dotted about the terrace. She swam back and forth in the deep end of the pool a few times before spending a moment in idle contemplation while clinging to the side.

Being not yet nine o'clock, most guests were still wolfing down breakfast in the restaurant. Hence only a few eager souls had gathered around the pool so far. At the shallow end a father was coaching his children to swim, the little boy and girl splashing about in their water wings. Now that the schools had broken up for the summer she guessed they would be the first of many more children whose excited squeals were going to echo around the swimming pool of this popular hotel.

Thrusting herself towards the ladder, she clambered up and wandered back to the sun lounger where she'd left her things, trailing water as she went. Squeezing the stuff from her hair, she then towelled herself down and readjusted her bikini top to better corral its contents.

"Nothing like an early morning dip to invigorate the old constitution," smirked someone else who had meanwhile noticed both the corralling and the contents.

She turned with a start to observe John Lawton looking his usual dapper self, sporting a patterned open-neck shirt, fawn bell-bottomed trousers, and with his ogling gaze veiled by a pair of mirror sunglasses upon which the morning sun was glinting.

"Just don't let Veronica catch you," he muttered *sotto voce*, removing them to reveal those familiar, penetrating blue eyes.

She smiled obligingly. While Lawton himself had no issue with the staff making use of the pool during their free time, his persnickety wife had made plain her preference for them doing so at times of the day when the paying guests weren't. Aimee carried on drying her hair in his presence, the thought occurring to her that maybe husband and wife were putting on some kind of cunning 'good cop, bad cop' routine – intended to alternately charm and browbeat their employees to keep them on their toes.

"Still, I'd make the most of it, if I were you. If the drought continues it won't be long before some petty official turns up and orders me to shut the pool. That said, I'm told there's a quiet beach somewhere near Blackgang where a pretty young thing like you can swim as naked as the day you were born," he ventured, looking on while she hastened to wrap the towel around her torso.

"I dare say your friend wouldn't approve though. Talking of whom, being Sunday would I be correct in assuming she's occupying a church pew somewhere?"

"Uh-uh," Aimee acknowledged perfunctorily, deciding she had tired of showing her boss a deference he didn't always deserve.

"And you're not?"

"No. I'm not."

From the leery stare she fired back him he deduced that she had no intention of volunteering an explanation for this sudden faltering of religious observance. Then again, he mused, perhaps a distancing between the pious Shelby and her companion was no bad thing – especially if it meant the more fun-loving half of this previously inseparable duo would be spending more of her spare time parading around the pool in that revealing white bikini.

"Ah, there you are, darling. I've been looking for you. Listen, I've arranged for the repairman to come round first thing tomorrow to take a look at that troublesome boiler in the laundry room. I need someone to be about to show him around."

A mien of annoyance flashed across Lawton's face that his musing had been interrupted by Veronica flapping about some accursed piece of plumbing (as well as by the inference that he spend less time chatting up the hotel's female staff and more time attending to the business of actually running the place).

"Of course, dear. I was just enquiring why young Aimee here isn't at church this morning," he explained, donning a faux smile.

His wife appeared unconvinced that their employees' spiritual well-being was the reason she'd again caught him sniffing around this lissome young American. However, she said nothing – instead firing Aimee a testy stare that told her she was in danger of outstaying her welcome beside the pool now that more guests were arriving to stake out the sun loungers.

The chastened room maid took the hint and gathered up her belongings, offering Veronica a faux smile of her own. Her condescending manageress sure had way of putting her back up!

* * * * *

With Vaughan working today and her husband watching Edwin Moses readying himself to go for gold in the Men's 400-metre Hurdles, Angie knew her window of opportunity would soon pass. Therefore, sloping out into the hall on the pretext of making herself another drink, she waited until the starting gun was fired and the television set came alive to Olympic crowds cheering the athletes on. She picked up the telephone receiver and began to dial. Huddling over the mouthpiece, she kept an eye on the back of Frank's favourite armchair for signs of sudden movement.

"Hullo... Is that you, Nora...? Yes, I'll have to make it quick, I'm afraid... Yes, Vaughan's doing just fine. Loves his job, he does... Found himself a girlfriend too... Of all things, the daughter of an American air force officer!"

Catching a nervous titter from down the other end of the line, she knew that snippet of irony would amuse her sister. Then she dispensed with the gossip and cut to the chase.

"Look, I've found him...! Yes, he's the one alright. His name is John Lawton..." she enthused as much as she dared given the conspiracy she was caught up in. She heard Nora breathe an almost tearful sigh.

"Yes, he's very handsome. And a right charmer with it! Made his fortune dealing on the London Stock Exchange. Nowadays though, he's a historian. He writes about aeroplanes and war. In fact, his 'father' was a fighter pilot in the war – Air Marshall Sir Hugh Lawton VC. He was quite famous, apparently. Well, I supposed he must have been to have won a Victoria Cross!"

All these details about her subject's colourful background had come tumbling out during their late night assignations – and which the woman he'd confided them too was eagerly relaying now to her disbelieving younger sibling.

"...Yes, he manages one of the posh hotels I sing at each week. That's how I ran into him. Since then we've been discussing how we're going to announce this momentous news...! Of course, he can't wait to meet you, Nora... What? Have I told Frank? No, not yet... I know I must... Of course, the old duffer has a right to know."

She glanced across again at the flickering hues of the TV picture reflecting off the walls of the sitting room. Perhaps the old duffer had fallen asleep in his chair.

"Absolutely... Yes, I can foresee that Vaughan is going to be the problem. He has a right to know too; but how on Earth do I break this kind of thing to the poor boy? Unless... unless I try and keep it under wraps until you arrive. Then we can decide which one of us is going to tell him... Yes, it might be difficult. I think he already suspects something... And then, of course, there's that other little matter that we need to talk to him about."

"Make me one too while you're out there, love," she heard her husband holler from the other side of the seat back.

"I will. Two sugars?" she shielded the mouthpiece and hollered back – somewhat superfluously really: Frank Tring had been taking two sugars in his tea throughout the entire thirty years of their topsy-turvy marriage!

However, his suspicions unaroused, she was just able to discuss a few more practicalities in the time they had left – for she thought she detected muffled sobbing emanating from the Black Country end of the telephone line.

"Look, Nora. Everything is going to be fine. This has happened to thousands of women. Families survive. In some instances knowing the truth actually makes them stronger. Ours will be no different. We just need to stay focussed and let Vaughan know that he will always be *our* little boy; and that we will *always* love him; and be there for him. Nothing we are going to have to steel ourselves to tell him in these coming days must ever change that."

* * * * *

He had been back and forth past the Shanklin Heights Hotel each time the Number 44 bus had wound its way down the steep descent to the Esplanade, where it terminated. From there Vaughan could gaze up at it perched high on the cliff tops – aided by the fact that the route was worked by an open-top Lodekka. Always popular with holidaymakers, now that the schools had broken up this afternoon was no exception. The bus quickly filled with children and their parents all eager to experience the breeze in their hair once Vaughan had rung the bell and it began chugging its way up the hill on its return journey to Sandown.

Taking fares and issuing tickets on the top deck, he found his concentration interrupted by another crazy compulsion to gaze up at that imposing edifice as it sailed past – symbolic, as it was, of the first love of his life; the first girl he'd properly kissed; the first girl who'd ever wanted to know him as more than just a 'friend'. And yet the more he stared, the more the luxury hotel seem to mock such hopes and pretensions – as if to remind him that this girl might yet be 'out of his league'.

Sure, she was just a lowly room maid there. However, she was also the bright and personable daughter of a four-star general, an overseas student at Oxford University, and soon to graduate from one of her country's most prestigious colleges. Thereafter, an illustrious career in journalism, politics or academia beckoned. Meanwhile, Vaughan Lewis was the self-effacing son of hairdresser from Dudley, soon (fingers crossed!) to bag a few 'A' levels, and then to hopefully gain a qualification in business studies at Wolverhampton Polytechnic. A mundane career in the back office of some factory in the Midlands beckoned.

It presented a depressing landscape. He could but hope that Auntie Angie was right: that somehow – if Aimee harboured the same feelings towards him as he did towards her – then love would eventually find a way.

* * * * *

One more trip to Sandown and back and Vaughan's roster was finished. At last he was able to tot up his cash bag, tally up his waybill, and hand them in at the depot.

"Hiya, Vaughan. You look a bit downcast," he caught wind of a familiar southern twang as he was unchaining his bike from the soil pipe outside.

It was Tina. He hadn't really seen much of her since the party, although Colin a man ever with his ear to the ground – had observed in passing this morning that she was still 'available'.

"Just tired, that's all," he blew hard and shrugged.

"Too much dancing and clubbing, I bet," she ribbed him.

"'Ere, a little bird tells me you've got a girlfriend," she then nudged his arm. Clearly someone had been relaying to the rest of the depot what his 'ear to the ground' had discovered.

"I hope I have."

"What do mean: 'hope'? Oh, Vaughan. She hasn't dumped you already, has she?"

"Well, no. But… she probably will when she realises that I'm not… well…"

"Don't be silly. We all fret about whether we're 'good enough' for the one we fancy. But remember: faint heart never won fair lady. Who is this fair lady anyway? Do I know her?"

"Probably not. She's an American student who's working at the Shanklin Heights Hotel over the summer."

"An American, eh? Well, there you go: aren't American women supposed to adore English accents? Even Black Country ones!" she teased. "So why don't you swallow your doubts and go cycle round there right now. Surprise her. Show her that she's surrendered her heart to a right romantic geezer. The convenience store around the corner stays open until six. If you hurry you'll be able to pick up a box of chocolates to take with you."

The ripple of a smile upon his tanned cheeks spoke of an acknowledgement that she was right. There and then it was what he resolved to do.

"Thanks," he replied, running a hand along her arm.

"You're welcome. And remember: any time you need lessons in love you come see your 'Auntie Tina'," she winked.

They both chuckled – Tina belatedly so – upon twigging the unintended innuendo in her invitation. She bade him a successful evening as he mounted his bike and pedalled off in the direction of the said store.

* * * * *

In no time at all Vaughan had rolled up onto the forecourt of the Shanklin Heights Hotel, which was cooling in shade now that the sun had moved around. Chaining his bike up to a convenient lamp standard, he removed his cap and wandered up to the main entrance with his duffle bag containing the chocolates looped over his shoulder. 'And all because the lady loves Milk Tray!' as the famous TV advert might have put it.

However, Tina's helpful suggestion had not allayed all his fears. As he stared up at the hotel frontage, a doubt or two surfaced again. It was while he had halted to mull them over that, out of the corner of his eye, something turned his head. For there, parked in the bay across from him that was marked 'Reserved for Manager' was that same sleek white Jaguar he'd spotted in the early hours of the other morning. The customised registration plate was the giveaway.

Furtively he wandered up to it and peered inside. The leather interior was immaculate. A folded copy of the *'Daily Telegraph'* and the cassette box to a Fleetwood Mac album lay discarded on the passenger seat. Otherwise, a liberal coating of dust upon the paintwork announced that its owner was doing his patriotic duty to conserve water by driving around in an unwashed car.

"Excuse me, but what do you think you're doing?" he was jolted by a supercilious female voice calling from behind.

Sporting a face like a frightened hare, he spun about to be confronted by a woman heading his way on a pair of clicking heels, and who halted in front of him to plant her delicate jewelled hands upon hips that were adorned by a pencil skirt.

"Er... I was just admiring it. It's a Jaguar – one of those new XJS sports coupés," he twittered, hastily regurgitating something he'd seen on a billboard advert.

"Yes, and it happens to be my husband's. Anyway, who are you? And what are you doing here?" she pressed him, staring up and down at his bus conductor's uniform.

"I'm V-v-vaughan. Vaughan Lewis. I've c-c-come to see Aimee. She works here. She's my gir... er, she's a f-f-friend of mine," he twittered again.

"Aimee...? Oh, you mean that American girl. Well, yes, she does work here. But she's out at the moment. She and her friend head off to church most Sunday evenings."

'That Amcrican girl' was beginning to get on Veronica Lawton's wick. As if flaunting herself half-naked around the swimming pool wasn't bad enough, now she was attracting waifs and ne'er-do-wells to the premises as well – including this bumbling specimen upon whom her censorious stare was fixed.

"Oh... I see. Er... well, maybe you could tell her I called by," Vaughan emitted a faltering smile.

He was minded to haul the box of chocolates out of his duffle bag and hand it to her to pass on – if only to demonstrate that he was not some skulking car thief. However, he grinned feebly again and drifted backwards towards his bike. Her suspicious eye remained on him all the time he was unchaining it from the lamp post. Whoever this unsmiling woman was he was sure glad he didn't work for her. Why, she made that glowering inspector on the Number 16 route seem positively benign.

* * * * *

One outcome of his aborted flying visit was that at least he had established who it was his Auntie Angie was having an affair with: the wealthy manager of one of the island's most prestigious hotels, no less. No wonder she'd been behaving strangely of late. Otherwise, the cycle ride back to Sandown afforded Vaughan the opportunity to ponder again his own less scintillating love life.

In particular, he suspected it would take more than a box of melted chocolates to win Aimee's lasting devotion. It was a self-flagellation made more burdensome by the fact that he still knew so little about her – mostly what had been gleaned from their snatched conversations so far. However, he had by now deduced that both she and her fellow room maid were the kind of devout Christians who, on such a warm summer evening, preferred sitting in church to skinny dipping on the beach or thronging the beer gardens of rowdy seafront pubs.

He passed a few churches on his way home, tempted to stop by and stick his head around the door. To search out Aimee and Shelby, of course; but also because he felt ashamed that – after over a month away from home – he'd still not found a church of his own in which to worship. The parties, the nightclubs, the drinking and the dancing had proved more fun than labouring after the kind of upright life that he had tried – and so often failed – to live with any consistency. Compounding this inchoate guilt, he recalled too those nights when he'd hurried himself to sleep by fantasising about Tina's bounteous mammaries!

Or maybe the placing of this beautiful, godly American girl across his path was the Lord's way of reaffirming that true fulfilment in life (as his mother always reminded him) could only be found by surrendering to Christ and living in the redemptive power of His Cross. If so, then seeking after that power through more fervent prayer and a more earnest reading of his bible would not only help him achieve a closer walk with God, but might also win him the place in Aimee's heart that he yearned for.

'Flee the evil desires of youth, and pursue righteousness, faith, love and peace, along with those who call on the Lord out of a pure heart', he remembered reading in one of St Paul's Epistles. Yes, that would be his goal too, he decided. He would prove his worth to Aimee by his own obedience to the Saviour she adored, and by treating her with a Christ-like 'pure heart' at all times. It was nothing less than this wonderful Christian woman deserved.

11

Tuesday, July 27th 1976

Aimee-Marie Eichelberger had spent the last two days mulling over the implications of what she was about to do. She had almost summoned up the nerve to do it on Sunday evening while Shelby had been at church. So when her friend had announced she was taking herself off to the Tuesday night bible study too, her absence presented Aimee with a golden opportunity to finally grasp the nettle, as it were. She knocked on the door and waited.

"Come in," a lazy voice replied.

Aimee swallowed hard and gripped the handle. There she paused for a split second to reconsider one final time. However, she took a deep breath and opened the door.

"Oh... It's you. Well, this is a most pleasant surprise."

John Lawton kept a spacious office in the Shanklin Heights Hotel – as became his role as its owner. However, the business of actually managing this busy establishment took place in his wife's more functional office located across the lobby from the main reception. Instead, the true nature of this opulent bolthole that she now stepped inside could be discerned when she gazed around at the collection of aviation art that hung from the walls as paintings or photographs; or at the bookcases brimming with tomes and magazines; or at the sturdy 'Imperial 66' typewriter on the desk that her gaze now alighted upon, having heard him tapping away at it while hesitating outside.

He noticed the trajectory of her bright tawny eyes, wheeling his reclining swivel chair back and rising from the desk.

"Yes, I'm afraid I'm a somewhat one-fingered typist," he acknowledged. "I keep promising I'll find myself an attractive young secretary. Can you type?"

From his suggestive smirk, she considered the question unworthy of an answer. It reminded Aimee too that Veronica would almost certainly take a dim view of her skulking presence in his private den – with all the implications that risked for her continued employment at this establishment.

"I just came to apologise," she got to the point, shrugging her shoulders and alternately staring at the floor, "...for being off-hand with you the other morning; and for maybe getting you into trouble with your wife. I wouldn't want her to think that I was... well, you know..."

"And why would she think that?" he looked her in the eye.

It was another question that, in her embarrassment, she declined to answer. The awkward silence continued until Lawton decided he'd prolonged her discomfort enough. He advanced around the desk and drew up to her.

"But now you are here, let me take you on a journey into my world. Then you will hopefully see that you and I have more in common than we ever realised."

It was a tantalising invitation that at least took the edge off the simmering sexual tension – and which the gentle slipping off his hand into the small of her back would otherwise have surely heightened. Instead, he employed it to draw her over to a huge, framed portrait of some austere-looking figure with a clipped moustache who stared back at them. From the pressed grey-blue uniform Aimee deduced he was an officer in the Royal Air Force – and quite a senior one at that, judging by the stripes on his sleeves and the array of braid and medals on his chest.

"That first day we met you were surprised that I knew so much about your father," he reminded her. "So now let me introduce you to mine: Air Marshal Sir Hugh Lawton KBE VC.

"Just like your father, mine began his air force career as a fighter pilot – in his case, flying Spitfires during the Battle of Britain. He notched up an impressive tally of enemy kills – until one day over Kent he came off worst following an encounter with a Messerschmidt 109. Though a cannon shell had broken his left leg, he managed to remain at the controls long enough to down another 109 that had a colleague in its sights. Then, when he finally bailed out, he suffered the indignity of having some trigger-happy Home Guard unit mistake him for a Jerry – one of them shooting him in the groin!"

"Ouch!" Aimee exclaimed, blinking exaggeratedly.

"Quite! However, for his courage that day that he was awarded the Victoria Cross – my country's highest decoration for bravery," Lawton pointed out the said medal on the portrait, adding "not unlike how your father would earn his Medal of Honor for his deeds over Germany in 1944.

"However, he was soon back in the cockpit – this time at the height of the campaign to expel Rommel from North Africa," he announced, moving along to point out a photograph of the pipe-smoking Flight Lieutenant Lawton with his comrades, taken against a backdrop of desert and pyramids.

"By June 1944 he was leading a squadron of rocket-firing Typhoons on missions to protect the Allied bridgehead at Normandy," he then progressed, pointing out an image of his father posing in his flight suit beside the said warplane. "The price he paid was to be shot down again – this time breaking his other leg during a forced landing behind enemy lines. Fortunately, the French Resistance sheltered him until Allied armies could overrun the German defences.

"However, they say 'every cloud has a silver lining'. It was while recuperating back home that he met my mother, who was a nurse at the time. Appropriately enough for a man who flew Typhoons, it was a 'whirlwind' romance and they married shortly afterwards!" he joked, directing her gaze to a touching portrait of his parents on their wedding day – the groom in uniform, incongruously sporting a set of crutches.

"Again like your father, mine chose to remain in the air force at the war's end, subsequently posted to commands in Germany, the Far East and the Middle East," Lawton then continued, introducing her in turn to a further selection of photographs chronicling his travels in the service of his country.

"So I'm guessing your experience of having a respected aviator for a father was not unlike my own," he smiled. "Namely, of boarding schools back home; of friendships constantly severed; and of passing summer vacations at a succession of military bases in far-flung corners of the world."

She grinned and nodded. In fact, the similarities didn't end there. In conclusion, he guided her to a photograph of a huge, delta-winged bomber thrusting through a silvery blue sky.

"And, ironically, just as your father was a fighter pilot who finished a glittering career in command of a force of bombers – so too my father retired from the RAF in 1970, after having commanded Britain's force of 'V' bomber strike aircraft. Thankfully though, unlike Charles Eichelberger, he never had to order his bombers into action over hostile skies."

It was a *tour d'horizon* that left the young student heartened to know that there was someone who could empathise with what it was like to be the offspring of a famous military family that had never stayed in one place for long.

"So did you fly with the Royal Air Force too?" she was curious to know – having scanned the walls in vain for any pictures of her boss in uniform. "After all, you obviously love military aviation."

Their eyes having met once more, he looked away in shame, though feigning to study that portrait of his father once more. As he did, for the first time she thought she detected a fragility about John Lawton that left her strangely warming to him.

"It was always my intention to follow in his footsteps; to have flown fast jets – and perhaps even to have commanded a squadron of them on an important mission. I longed to serve my country with all the courage and determination that my father did. But, alas, my childhood asthma proved a bigger handicap than I could ever have imagined. I suppose I could always have applied for a ground-based trade. But, well… to fly was always my abiding ambition. It really was flying or nothing."

"Oh... I see."

Suddenly, to this awareness of childlike vulnerability there was added sympathy for his crushing disappointment. To be sure, John Lawton was an Etonian, a Cambridge graduate, and a millionaire who had made his fortune in the cut-and-thrust world of international commodity trading. As he now recounted, he had then invested that fortune in a jaded hotel and transformed it into one of the Isle of Wight's most exclusive holiday destinations. The hands-on business acumen of his beautiful wife – herself the daughter of an aristocrat – had, in due course, freed him to indulge his love of military history (including having had a book published – about Mustangs, just like her father used to fly – a copy of which he proudly showed off to her).

By any measure he had achieved more by the time he was thirty than most men do in a lifetime. Factor in that he was tall, dashing and exceedingly handsome – a magnet for women on account of his looks alone – and it was inconceivable that this man should labour under any kind of inferiority complex. And yet that was exactly what John Lawton *was* doing – and all because he had failed an RAF medical examination and been frustrated in wish to cut through the sky at the speed of sound. She could well imagine the lingering shame he felt that writing about the flying exploits of others was a pale substitute for having been denied the chance to perform those exploits himself.

As she mulled over his torment – and to her continuing surprise – he had one more uncanny resemblance to the story of her own family to reveal. Thus the hand in the small of her back guided her to another framed photograph – this one posited atop his desk. It pictured Sir Hugh attired in a dinner jacket, his wife by his side in an evening gown.

"This was the last photograph ever taken of my parents," he sighed, looking her in the eye again. Those eyes had meantime glazed over. A melancholy had descended upon him.

"It was taken on Friday, December 22nd 1972 – at a Christmas reunion of my father's old squadron," he elaborated, the date immediately pricking the American's ears. "Shortly afterwards, they were driving home. My father probably only had a split second to spot the car coming the other way on the wrong side of the road. They never stood a chance. Suddenly, my world was turned upside down. As you can imagine, the untimely death of my parents left me questioning an awful lot of things – not the least of which was why a supposedly loving God would so cruelly snatch two such special and utterly selfless people from me."

Suddenly there was more than sympathy between them. These two people from different sides of a big wide ocean really had been living parallel lives. Aimee began to wonder what else they unknowingly had in common. Meanwhile, the object of her gathering fascination had drifted over to a mahogany drinks cabinet, which he opened to unveil a selection of tipples.

"Bacardi and coke? BabyCham? Cinzano and lemonade? There's even some Southern Comfort in here somewhere if it makes you feel at home," he enquired – though he could discern from her hesitation that this mixed-up evangelical Christian was a relative novice when it came to things alcoholic.

"Yeah... I mean, Southern Comfort. That'll do just fine."

He acknowledged her choice and gesticulated for her to sit herself down on a dark leather sofa that graced the wall by the window. This she did, glancing out to observe that the sun had dipped behind the headland. Then, taking a glass and pouring, he wandered over to place it in her hand. Returning to the cabinet, he mixed himself a whisky-and-dry and joined her on the sofa, lazily crossing his legs and leaning back into it to study her. She meanwhile remained perched upright on the edge of it, her elbows propped upon her knees. There she nervously huddled over her glass, avoiding his gaze

"Veronica tells me there was a young man asking after you the other day: someone who looked like he worked for the local bus company. Boyfriend?"

She trained an insouciant eye upon him before shrugging.

"Kind of."

It was a curious answer that merely whetted his appetite.

"I know you Yanks like adding that word to your sentences. But that's rather like saying one is 'kind of' pregnant."

"Yeah, so he's my boyfriend."

There ensued a pause that was also 'kind of' pregnant.

"If I may be so bold, that's not exactly a rousing endorsement of this young man," Lawton scoffed haughtily, drawing on his glass. "But then it tells me you're maybe wrestling with the dilemma that young women have always faced when choosing a mate: to go for the one who's reliable, but boring; or instead seek out someone who's exciting – but most probably dangerous."

"Well, he is. My boyfriend, that is," she replied, stung by the inference. "Like me, he's over here for the summer. He's staying with his aunt – who happens to be that Angie Ashby woman who sings at this hotel most weeks."

Lawton paused again – this time to take in her resumé.

"Well, well," he eventually smirked. "So Aimee's new boyfriend is the nephew of 'the dazzling' Angie Ashby."

"You sound like that's some kinda' big deal."

"No, No. I'm just intrigued, that's all," he jovially protested. "It's a small world, as they say."

There was another awkward silence before he swigged from his glass and asked "Is he your first boyfriend then?"

She glanced at him in surprise. It seemed a bizarre question to ask – impertinent even! She was almost twenty-one years-old. Why would he assume she was so callow and unversed?

"I'm not a virgin, if that's what you mean!" she fired back petulantly.

It was the turn of Lawton's face to blanch with surprise. For once, his flair for a swift and witty riposte had deserted him. He looked her up and down for a moment before responding – a process aided by another swig of that stiff drink. In the time it took him, Aimee's indignant scowl abated. She began to regret owning up to something that her boss didn't need to know.

"Then I guess that makes two of us," he smirked again.

He placed his empty glass down on the coffee table in front of them and sat up himself, drawing in closer to her.

"Somehow I suspected you weren't. Unlike that Miss Goody Two-Shoes you hang around with, you give the impression that you can be a bit of a naughty girl… when you choose to be."

"Are you implying I'm some sort of floozy?" she snapped.

This conversation was most improper. Or at least that was what the angel on Aimee's right shoulder was screaming in her ear. This man was her employer; he was a decade her senior; and he was a married man – and she was alone with him in his office drinking alcohol and engaging in sexual banter! She must get up and leave the room forthwith.

"No, far from it," he placated her. "Just that you're a human being… with needs – like the rest of us ordinary mortals. It's nothing to be ashamed of. We can't all be saints."

She was not so naïve she hadn't twigged what kind of 'naughtiness' her boss had in mind. Neither was she unaware of the way he'd been ogling her these last few weeks. It was why she'd wisely turned up this evening in a long skirt and a buttoned-up blouse – underneath which she was wearing a bra!

And yet a different voice on a different shoulder was chiding her to ponder those things she'd discovered they had in common – and which she might never have found out had she heeded the angel that had begged her not to come here tonight in the first place. This other voice pointed out too that John Lawton was an intelligent and thoughtful man who – for all his success in life – was burdened by a residual sense of failure. Was it any wonder that he yearned to escape the hen-pecking of a cold and imperious woman who Aimee too had come to despise? And perhaps escape with someone who was more attuned to where he was coming from? Who could blame him? It was why, the voice reminded her, his relationship with his wife was functional rather than romantic. And besides, the voice whispered in her ear, Aimee couldn't deny that – married man or not – she was drawn to her boss; intrigued by him; had the hots for him even!

"Look, I really oughta' go," she slammed her glass down on the table and rose to her feet.

"So soon?" he rose too and squared up to her. "And just when we were getting to know each other so well?"

'Trust me, I gotta' go', she meant to say. But somehow the words never came out. Frozen to the spot by his piercing blue eyes, that voice on her other shoulder bade her stare into them. This she did, unperturbed that his lips were drawing ever closer to hers. Then those lips touched. A moment of fleshly exploration ensued as he drew his hands around her waist and she clasped his shoulders. Then all too soon the moment had passed.

"Trust me, I gotta' go!" the words finally came out.

Too late. She knew a line had been crossed. She wriggled from his grasp and sprinted for the door in shame and remorse, determined not to look back as she slammed it behind her.

Lawton smirked and wandered over to the cabinet to pour himself another drink. A sixth sense told him she'd return – sooner or later. Women like her always did.

12

Friday, July 30*th* 1976

The little blighters were everywhere. Ladybirds (Latin name: *coccinellidae magnifica*) might be the cute little spotted insects that had lent their name to a series of popular British children's books. However, to Aimee-Marie Eichelberger they were 'ladybugs' and – like something from a Hitchcock movie – the little critters were swarming over the island by the millions. They were in people's hair and down their shirts, as well as smothering walls, pavements and parked cars.

Most annoyingly, this afternoon they had also found their way in through the open window vents of the bus that transported her to Sandown High Street. There she alighted, continuing to swat them away as she rounded the corner and spied out that raised verandah where Chico was standing sentry duty in his tall cage (which, now as then, had been wheeled to its customary spot atop the steps that led up to it). Standing alongside him, Angela Tring had spied Aimee's approach and was waiting.

"They say it's the continuing warm weather," she called out, "And an easterly breeze that's blown them in from the continent."

"Well, let's pray for rain and a westerly gale!" Aimee replied, picking yet another one from a strand of her glorious fair hair.

"Not much chance of either, I'm afraid," her host sighed.

Chico too shook one from his battleship grey plumage. Then he looked on as Angie inserted a hand in the small of Aimee's back to guide the American visitor inside her flat, brushing another ladybird from her shoulder as they went.

"I sure am grateful to you for agreeing to be interviewed, Mrs Tring," Aimee reiterated once she had been refreshed with a welcome cup of English tea.

"That's okay. But do call me Angie," she replied, bidding the student make herself at home on the settee. "I was going to suggest having our little chat in the verandah. But with all those blessed insects flying about maybe we should do it here instead."

Angie relaxed into the embrace her own armchair, looking on while Aimee reached down into the shoulder bag she'd laid at her feet. From it she trawled up a folder of notes she'd accumulated, along with a biro to transcribe another entry. As she looked up, she thought she detected trepidation in her subject's eyes.

"Mrs Tring, I mean, Angie... I know you said your experiences of Americans in England were not always positive," she reminded her. "So if this is going to be painful for you to discuss, then I'm happy for us to just skip the interview. Trust me, I have enough personal recollections in here with which to complete my dissertation," she insisted.

"After you've come all this way? No, I'm fine. Let's start, shall we. What do you want to know?"

Aimee glanced down at her notes, if only to psyche herself up. Her ambition was to enter journalism once she graduated. These kind of interviews had been good practice that would enable her to maybe work her way up one day to be a reporter with the *'New York Times'* or NBC television, where she might get to interview all sorts of influential people. For now though, it was the stories of ordinary people – and, in particular, those ordinary English girls who'd once dated GIs – that she was eager to transcribe.

"So tell me," she opened, "what did you do during the war?"

"Well, I grew up in a small town in Suffolk. I was seventeen when war broke out. For a time I was a Land Girl. Those were young women who were drafted to work on farms, replacing young men who'd been called up."

"Sure, I've interviewed a few of those," Aimee glanced up from scribbling on her notepad.

"However, someone heard that I could sing, so eventually I found myself being volunteered to join an entertainment party. We used to tour the local villages; boost morale; that kind of thing. Then in 1943 I was invited to be the female vocalist with a swing band that toured more widely. We mostly played on military bases – including the US Eighth Army Air Force fighter station near my home town of Leiston. It was where I met an American fighter pilot one night following a concert the band had performed there. We got talking – as you do. The next thing I knew, we were 'dating' – as you Americans call it."

"Hey, my dad was based in Leiston in 1944 – he flew with the 357th Fighter Group!" Aimee looked up again and announced.

"Oh… really," Angie appeared surprised.

"Yeah. His name's Charles – Charles Eichelberger. You heard of him by any chance?"

Angie paused for a moment as if to interrogate her memory. Then she smiled awkwardly and shook her head.

"No, can't say I have."

"He was quite a guy – used to fly long-range P51 Mustangs on escort missions. He was awarded the Medal of Honor following a hair-raising dogfight over Germany."

Either her train of thought had been broken or Angela Tring really was having second thoughts about this interview. Aimee's mien of excitement was swiftly replaced by one of earnest.

"I'm sorry. I interrupted you. Forgive me. Please continue."

Angie drew her thoughts together and pressed on.

"We saw each other when we could – in between his missions and my performing engagements. I have to confess it was quite a passionate affair – right from the beginning. I know you baby-boomers like to think you invented sex; but I assure you it's not so! I suppose when you never know from one day to next whether you'll ever see each other again, then self-restraint tends to go out the window. Lots of wartime romances were like that."

"Yeah, I can appreciate that. Dad kinda' never talks about the war much; but I reckon he must have had at least *one* English girlfriend," Aimee pondered aloud with a wicked glimmer in her eye. She apologised again for interrupting.

"Well, 1944 drifted in 1945, and it was obvious that war would soon be over. It was time to start thinking about what peace would bring. For me it looked like wedding bells. To my surprise, this fellow had bought a ring and asked me to marry him. I'd never been so happy. Everything was set for him to take me back with him to America, where we talked about building a new life together. I even dreamed of maybe making it big on Broadway. In the meantime, I was practising saying 'sidewalk' instead of 'pavement', and 'trash' instead of 'rubbish'!"

Aimee warmed to the romance of it all. However, from her subject's select use of tenses she sensed this story had not ended well. She waited while Angie struggled to dam a stray tear.

"Then one day in June his squadron upped sticks and returned to the United States. And *he* returned with them," she almost spat. "I never heard from him again – no letters, no telegrams, no nothing. It was as if he'd vanished into thin air. Suddenly, it felt like those nine months we'd enjoyed together had all been a cruel illusion. I wrote to the only address I could find; but all my letters were returned unopened. In fact, all I had to remind me that our time together had been real were a few photographs… and this…"

Aimee watched as she leant over to the sideboard and opened a drawer. She took out a small velvet box and opened it in her presence to reveal a diamond engagement ring.

"Wow!" the Minnesotan gasped, the sparkle of the tiny jewel bringing this tragic tale of abandonment to life better than words ever could. "You have kept his ring all this time?"

"Thirty-one years and five months, to be precise. I'd had boyfriends before; but then they say you never forget your first love. And this man was my first real love."

"If you don't mind me asking: what was this guy's name? And where was he from? Can I see those photographs?"

Angie closed the box and buried it away amidst the jumble of her personal effects, from whence it came. All the time Aimee was on tenterhooks waiting for her to reply.

"I'd rather not," she was surprised to then hear.

"It would be in confidence," she assured her.

"No, if it's all the same. As for where he came from, well… it was some insignificant and unpronounceable place out west. You Yanks will give your towns these bizarre and exotic-sounding names," Angie tried to summon up a smile.

"It left me devastated. Added to which, my singing days were brought to an abrupt end by the break-up of the band and the entertaining work drying up. I was hoping to be taken on by a music producer, but it never happened. So it was as if my entire life had crashed down around me. At one point I even contemplated ending it all. If all those historical accounts that have been written about the 'Mighty Eighth' and its 'flyboys' had devoted a thousand chapters to it, they could never have conveyed the heartache and misery men like my ex-fiancé left behind by way of love betrayed, promises unfulfilled and… well, other more tangible reminders."

Aimee knew what she was alluding to. She'd listened to similar stories being recounted during her year in England. With five times the spending power of British servicemen, it was no surprise that the million-and-a-half American military personnel who passed through between 1942 and 1945 proved such a magnet to the ration-bound young women of the host country. Allies John Bull and Uncle Sam might have been; yet 'oversexed, overpaid and over here' was the common refrain amongst envious locals regarding this sudden influx of affluent, testosterone-fuelled GIs from across the Pond.

It was not all heartbreak, of course. Many of these Yanks were perfect gentlemen, whose exquisite chivalry simply bowled English girls off their feet. Seventy thousand of them would go on to marry their American boyfriends and make the crossing to the 'Land of the Free'. However, pity the nine thousand illegitimate children left behind – many of whom would languish unloved in orphanages long after war's end. They were the most painful legacy of the American military presence in Britain during those three critical years – the forgotten human detritus left behind by the mighty expeditionary force that had helped liberate Europe from one of history's darkest and most bloodthirsty tyrannies.

"You mean babies?" Aimee eventually pressed her.

"Yes… And no, I wasn't one of those mothers!" she piped up to deflect the inference.

"In which case, do you know any women who did? End up getting pregnant by their American boyfriends, I mean."

"Oh yes," Angie sprang back. "One in particular: someone very close to me. She too discovered she was pregnant. We never did find out by whom, though we had our suspicions it was a Yank from the local camp. The girl in question was hidden away until it was time for her to give birth. Then her child was taken and put up for adoption. The poor girl felt she had no choice. There was a terrible stigma attached to such things in those days. She certainly never got over having to give away her child."

"I'm sorry. So very sorry," Aimee was genuinely moved. "I can only apologise on behalf of my country."

Angie breathed deeply and shook her head.

"For what? That your young men were only human? Forget it. Besides, you Yanks did give us Glenn Miller!"

"And you Brits gave us The Beatles and The Rolling Stones!" Aimee returned the wisecrack. The amusement they shared helped lift the despondency and unease.

"Anyway, you seem to have made a good life for yourself," she noted, eyes roaming the room to admire the photographs and heirlooms that graced it.

"I met Frank not long after. He helped me through a very bad patch. We married at the end of 1945. It was our intention to raise a family, but it never happened. Then, in 1957, I suffered what today would be termed a nervous breakdown. I couldn't have blamed Frank had he walked out on me. Once again, the fall-out from another bad patch took me perilously close to the edge," she tossed out further allusions, Aimee endeavouring to read between the lines. "However, we pulled through. I guess had we been today's generation we would have battled it out through our divorce lawyers. But, for better or worse, our generation did things differently. 'You make your bed, you lie in it', my old mother used to say. It's just that sometimes you can end up lying in it for a very long time indeed.

"Anyway, in time we made our peace and got on with life. Moving to the Isle of Wight helped. Frank set up his toy shop on the High Street; and I was able to restart my singing career, performing at hotels and holiday camps during the summer. I never achieved international stardom – as I once dreamed of. But at least it keeps me performing in front of audiences. And for that I guess I should be grateful."

"And I'm very grateful to you, Angie. You're a wonderful woman. And Vaughan is very lucky to have you for an aunt."

Angie sniffed and shrugged self-effacingly. Then she glanced up at the box clock mounted over the mantelpiece.

"He'll be home soon. He's so looking forward to meeting you. Have you decided what you're going to do afterwards?"

"Nothing planned. Maybe take a walk along the seafront. As it happens both of us are off work next Tuesday; so maybe we'll go sightseeing somewhere."

"That'll be nice," his aunt smiled. Then she leaned forward in her chair and changed the subject.

"Anyway, permit me to turn the tables in the time we have left – if I may. Tell me about your father."

Aimee placed her file of notes back in her bag, rested her arms on her knees, and poured out what she had gleaned over the years.

"Dad was training to be a minister when he heard that the Japs had hit Pearl Harbor. He was so mad that he quit bible college, enlisted as an officer, and flew Mustangs instead. Continuing his career in the United States Air Force after the war, he was rapidly promoted. He flew F86 Sabres in Korea, and commanded the Seventh Air Force in Vietnam. He retired last year."

Angie chuckled and reached over to pat Aimee's knee.

"No, silly! I mean what became of him in his personal life."

"Oh," the girl from Stearns County was momentarily lost for words. No one had ever asked her that before. Most people wanted to hear about Charles Eichelberger the warrior, rather than Charles Eichelberger the family man. She too chuckled nervously.

"Well, he returned home in the summer of '45 – and married my mom later that same year. They'd been sweethearts before he enlisted – keeping in touch via letters, all of which Mom has kept and treasured. Like I said, Dad doesn't talk about the war much – they say the ones who've seen the real action seldom do. But he never stops talking about Mom – and about how marrying her was the best thing he ever did."

Angie listened politely. However, her *raconteur* was not so wrapped up in what she was recounting that she couldn't pick up on the faint whiff of envy on the part of the snubbed war bride that her father's tale of romantic-bliss-ever-after was so much at variance with her own. Nonetheless, she ploughed on.

"My brother, Lawrence, was born in 1947. He too served in the air force – but was shot down over Vietnam four years ago. Dad was really cut up when he heard he'd been posted missing."

"I'm sorry to hear that," Angie interjected. Maybe Charles Eichelberger had not had life all his own way.

"I came along in 1955. I was a bit of a belated surprise to them, I guess – an afterthought, you could almost say," she tittered. "And that's about it. Mom and Dad are still as much in love today as when they first set eyes on each other thirty-eight years ago – when he was eighteen and she was sixteen."

A miasma of envy had definitely descended upon her listener. But then Aimee guessed the story of her own family must seem idyllic to one who had been so unceremonious dumped at war's end, only to end up trapped in what (she sensed) were far from idyllic domestic circumstances. She longed to explain to her that the Eichelberger household too had been far from idyllic at times – the sibling rivalry, the parental favouritism, the tensions occasioned by her father's many absences fighting an unpopular war. Indeed, there were many times when Aimee herself had felt just as much a prisoner of cruel happenstance as Angela Tring.

"I'm glad everything turned out well for your father," Angie summoned up the generosity of spirit to affirm.

"Thanks. But are you sure you never met him? I can show you some photographs if it helps you remember."

"No," she shook her head gently, but firmly, "that won't be necessary. Eichelberger, you say? I'm sure I would have remembered such an unusual name."

"As unusual and unpronounceable as the place your American fiancé hailed from?" Aimee raised an eyebrow, staring her out.

Just then this sudden terseness in their conversation was interrupted by the sound of the front door being swung open. Then into the hallway marched Vaughan in his uniform. The moment he spotted Aimee his eyes opened wide and the expectant smile that had been on his face broadened.

"Hi, I'm glad you could make it," she rose from her seat and sauntered up to him, grinning. They placed a gentle, decorous kiss upon each other's lips.

"Isn't it supposed to be me saying that to you?" Vaughan joked as he gazed into her eyes. For here she was – his very first girlfriend. And she was beautiful!

His aunt glanced away to spare them their blushes. The joys of young love, she proffered a sardonic, if unseen grin.

Vaughan pleaded the excuse of needing a quick bath. Aimee sat back down to await his scrubbed-up return while Angie begged her leave to attend to the meal in the kitchen.

It afforded the student an opportunity to gather her thoughts; in particular, to ponder again whether her heady decision to date Vaughan risked raising expectations she would struggle to fulfil. After all, in a month's time he would be boarding a train back to the Midlands and she would be jetting back to her family home on the outskirts of the 'Granite City'. How would the relationship they'd struck up survive the four thousand miles between them? Would theirs be destined to go the way of vacation romances the world over? And, more pertinently, was romance what she was really looking for? Or – with her parents' scheduled arrival just over a week away – was time running out for her to cram in some less complicated fun instead?

The time for such portentous musing soon passed when, attired in his best flaired jeans and collared T-shirt, Vaughan reappeared to join her at the dining table, where Angie had brought in a selection of salad dishes for them to help themselves to.

"Hey, you'll never guess who I saw on the final journey back to the depot," Vaughan exclaimed as they tucked in. "It was your friend, Shelby. She'd been shopping in Ryde."

"Is that so?" Aimee noted, nibbling on a stick of celery. "She said she might go looking for presents for her folks."

"With the children off school the bus was quieter than usual. So I managed to have quite a chat with her. She has the most adorable accent. I really could listen to it all day long."

"They call it a Dixie drawl. Most folks from the Deep South speak like that. Some of the girls at college used to give her a real hard time because of it," she recounted.

"A bit like people with Black Country accents!" Angie couldn't resist chipping in.

"She told me you both had a falling out last week; but she's glad it's sorted. She said something about tempting a promise out of you to rejoin her in church again this Sunday! Shelby really thinks a lot of you, you know."

"Sure. We're best buddies," Aimee chirruped, feigning indifference to these insights her loquacious friend had shared about just how tenuous that friendship had been of late.

"Yes, you're a Christian, aren't you?" Angie enquired, picking up on something her nephew had told her.

"That's right. My dad's an elder in our church back home. My mom leads the women's prayer group there."

"Vaughan and his mother are too – Christians, that is. Isn't that right, Vaughan," she looked to him.

He nodded, glancing at Aimee and rejoicing that a point of convergence between them had been established.

"Me? I can't say I'm particularly religious. Each to their own, I say. It's religious hypocrisy I can't abide: when people give the impression of being pillars of righteousness while, out of sight, they're busy committing all manner of sins."

Why did Aimee get the impression that last statement was intended as a barb? However, remembering that religion was one of the three taboo subjects the English supposedly avoid when in polite conversation, she changed the subject.

"By the way, I didn't tell you. My folks are coming over to England in two weeks' time. They've even booked to stay at the Shanklin Heights Hotel – where I'm working. Just think Angie: you might actually get to meet my Dad and chat about the war."

Even before she'd heard her out, Angie's chestnut-tinged eyes had bulged in their sockets and she descended into a fit of violent spluttering. Instinctively, Vaughan rushed in to thump her back.

"You okay, Auntie?" he anguished.

"Phew! Cucumber must have gone down the wrong way... Sorry," she puffed once the coughing had subsided.

Otherwise, she looked up to observe her visitor flash a half-curious, half-sympathetic smile. It masked Aimee's gathering suspicion that it was possible Angela Tring was not being truthful when she had insisted she'd never met her father.

13

Tuesday, August 3rd 1976

The moment had arrived at last: their first full day out together. Owing to the fact that he couldn't drive, Vaughan was mindful that much of it would have to be spent on buses: a 'busman's holiday', as it were (and as he apologised, explaining this British expression to his American companion). It was one further thing to add to the list of reasons why he was fretting again that he might not be 'good enough' for her.

Aimee was unfazed. After meeting up with her at Shanklin Bus Station, they boarded a Number 12 bus to Newport, passing through the enchanted village of Godshill on the way. If nothing else, the meandering thirty minute journey offered them both an opportunity to get to know each other better – supplementing what they'd discovered about the other during their stroll up to Battery Park after tea last week. Overlooking Sandown Bay, it was there that Vaughan had notched up another landmark first: his first proper French kiss – even if she had seemed more knowledgeable about what to put where and how. He had a lot of catching up to do. He feared it showed.

They passed a few moments quietly taking in the countryside that was passing by, Aimee permitting Vaughan to steal another gentle kiss on the lips. However, their canoodling was interrupted by the conductress clumping up the stairs.

"Fares please... Well, well – Vaughan. Fancy seeing you on my bus," chortled Tina. "In the company of a young lady too!"

"Oh... Hello," he looked up with a start, hurriedly making introductions. "Aimee, this is Tina. She's one of my colleagues from the depot. And Tina, this is Aimee – she's my friend from the United States who I told you about."

"She's a bit more than just a 'friend', I seem to remember you telling me. Anyway, pleased to meet you, Aimee," his buxom workmate beamed.

"You too," Aimee acknowledged with a wary smile.

"So 'Auntie Tina' was right then: a box of chocolates *was* the way to Aimee's heart," she winked at Vaughan suggestively.

He smiled too, mumbling from embarrassment. Thankfully though – recognising that she was rudely interrupting their love-in – Tina nudged him playfully before moving along the saloon to take fares from the other passengers.

"What's she mean: chocolates are the way to my heart?" Aimee wondered aloud once the jolly clippie had disappeared back down the stairs. "I don't recall you buying me chocolates."

"Oh, take no notice," her new boyfriend twittered. "It's just a joke going around the depot. They're like that, my workmates – they're always pulling my leg because they think I'm inexperienced when it comes to the ways of women."

"Is that so?" she searched his gentle face.

Why did Aimee get the impression he wouldn't be 'inexperienced' for long if this 'Auntie Tina' had her way? That sparkle in her eye that Aimee had just observed suggested this voluptuous lass was partial to Vaughan being something more than just the butt of her esoteric ribaldry. More that just a 'colleague' too!

He pacified his beloved's suspicions by looping a possessive arm back around her shoulder again. Aimee returned his fawning smile and tilted her head against his shoulder.

"So am I your first boyfriend?" he enquired.

That question again! She looked at him, her eyes flitting about the features of his face once more. Then she trained those eyes out the window again and admitted what he suspected.

"No. I've dated others. Nothing serious though."

"That's understandable," he acknowledged. "You're very beautiful."

"But I am *your* first?" she guessed, glancing back at him.

He nodded apologetically. She squeezed the hand she'd been holding in his lap.

"It's no big deal. There has to be a first for everything. So what do you do with yourself when you're not collecting fares? Do you play soccer? Or that other weird English game – cricket?"

"I'm not really that into sport," he confessed, though fearful it might further demonstrate his unmanliness. "I like swimming though. I've done quite a bit of it since I've been on the island. Uncle Frank gave me a huge lilo when I first arrived. I must have spent hours bobbing up and down on it since."

"Lilo?" she puzzled.

"An air mattress: for floating on the sea," he explained.

"Oh," she noted.

The little nugget of transatlantic incomprehension highlighted yet another yawning chasm that he feared might divide them.

"I like reading too," he ventured.

"You do?"

"Yes, history and things like that. You like history too, don't you. It's what you're studying at university."

"Uh-uh."

At last – something they shared in common. His heart raced as he proceeded to milk it for all it was worth.

"Uncle Frank was in the navy during the war. He's lent me a really interesting book about battleships that I've been reading. Say, wasn't your dad in the war too? He was a famous fighter pilot, wasn't he? Or so Auntie Angie told me."

"Uh-uh."

"The other day I bought a huge model aircraft from Uncle Frank's toy shop. Well, he let me have it for nothing, actually. He's like that. I used to make loads of model aircraft when I was younger. I bought it for something to do on rainy evenings. But as we're still waiting for one of those, I've made a start on it already. I've glued together the wings and painted some of the smaller parts. I just need to put the fuselage together and assemble it."

"Really," his listener tried to sound smitten.

"Yes. It's a B52 Stratofortress. Massive it is – one of those huge bombers that you Americans used in Vietnam."

She turned and fired him a wounded stare that halted his spirited monologue.

"I'm sorry," he mumbled and gazed down at the delicate hand he was still clutching in his lap. "I must be boring you."

She sighed and stared back out of the window.

"Forget it," she sniffed. "It's just me. It's a long story – remind me to tell you about it some time."

Her puzzling *mea culpa* only went so far to allay his fear that he was screwing up badly. He wondered why she didn't want to tell him now – at a point on the journey when they had otherwise run out of things to say. He chose not to press her.

Instead, he joined her gazing out of the window. He'd tried to impress her; to convince her that – though he was two years her junior and his background was humble – he was genuine and had something to bring to their relationship. He'd even been practising saying 'sidewalk' instead of 'pavement'; and 'trash' instead of 'rubbish'! At that moment though, he wished Auntie Angie was sitting on the seat behind him, pointing out where he might be going wrong; and offering her valuable feminine insight as to how he might put it right. Or even 'Auntie Tina' if she'd finished taking fares. Then again, perhaps not, he pondered, studying his girlfriend's inscrutable gaze!

* * * * *

Swapping buses in Newport Bus Station, Vaughan and Aimee boarded the Number 5 to East Cowes. In just over ten minutes it had deposited them at the gates of Osborne House – Queen Victoria's palatial holiday home sat atop a promontory overlooking The Solent. Her consort, Prince Albert, once said the view reminded him of the Bay of Naples; and on a day like today when the sun was shining and ships were busily passing on their way to and from Southampton, it was not hard to see why.

The house too evoked the Italian palazzo style. Meanwhile, the paintings and artefacts on display in the Durbar Room – completed in 1892 – reminded visitors that the widowed queen was by then passing her summers here during the zenith of the worldwide empire over which she had reigned. There was even a miniature fort in the gardens, constructed so that the royal children and grandchildren might be acquainted with the martial virtues upon which that empire had been grounded. Finally, it was in the state bedroom at Osborne that the Queen had passed away on January 22nd 1901 – by which time she had become the longest serving monarch in British history.

"You know, they say that it was all downhill for the British Empire after she died," said Vaughan, striking up a note of erudition in the hope of further impressing Aimee. "Germany was rising to challenge British sea power. It was also the beginning of 'the American Century'. Soon enough, your own country would overtake us to become the most powerful nation on the planet."

Aimee curled an eyebrow and smiled. "I guess you really have been reading a lot lately," the student of history joked.

Vaughan returned the smile and was ready when she reached up to plant a kiss upon his lips. Maybe all was not lost after all.

* * * * *

Completing their leisurely stroll around Osborne House, it was back on the bus to East Cowes, thence to take the floating bridge that crossed the River Medina into Cowes proper.

The first week of August is traditionally 'Cowes Week' – one of the oldest and most famous international regattas in the world. It was the place where aficionados from around the globe arrived to compete for some of the most glittering prizes in the world of yachting – including the prestigious Queen's Cup (further cementing Victoria's association with the Isle of Wight, it had first been awarded in 1897 to commemorate her Diamond Jubilee). This year though, the hot weather and absence of any discernable breeze was making the races especially challenging for the competitors taking part.

Vaughan and Aimee were content to amble along the waterfront and observe the vista of white sails tacking back and forth across the mouth of Southampton Water. Besides, the prices in the marquees servicing those wealthy spectators who'd flocked to watch the races were far beyond the means of either a seasonally-employed bus conductor or a seasonally-employed room maid. Therefore, they both settled for an ice cream instead – to be consumed while sitting on a bench outside the Royal Yacht Squadron, watching the craft sail silently past.

"So how long have you been a Christian?" Vaughan enquired

in between brushing his tongue around the cream in which the chocolate flake of his '99' was embedded.

"Oh, I don't know. I can't remember a time when I wasn't," she replied with a lackadaisical shrug of her bare, sun-reddened shoulders. "And you?"

Vaughan could point to a more specific moment in time and space when he had ceased dutifully mimicking the faith of his mother and had instead discovered one of his own.

"Sunday May 7th 1972. I was fourteen. I'd been going along to the church youth club for some months. I suppose, like you, I thought I'd always been a believer. But then one night the visiting speaker spoke powerfully about how going to church and being good was not enough to earn salvation. In fact, salvation cannot be earned. It's the free gift of God. And 'church' is not a building that Christians go to. It is who we are: a community of sinners who are saved by the grace of God. If I'm honest though, I know I'm not always the best advert for my faith. I'm weak; I'm unreliable; I'm prone to... well... you know: what boys do... when they think about pretty girls... like you... at night."

Tilting her head in the manner of a confused canine, Aimee didn't know whether to laugh or gape in shock. In the end, both emotions got the better of her.

"Vaughan Lewis, are you trying to tell me you've been...?" she spluttered, mercifully declining to spell it out.

With appalled hindsight, Vaughan wondered what had made him confess to such a thing. And to this good Christian girl too! However, even he couldn't resist releasing a crumpled smile. He got his own back by pointing out the splash of ice cream that had been deposited upon Aimee's nose following another attempt by her to slurp her melting cone.

"I really like you, Aimee. I hope we can be good friends."

"Sure, we can be friends."

"I don't just mean friends, as in friends. I mean friends, as in 'friends' – if you know what I mean."

The forensic manner in which she stared back at him and watched him struggle to pinpoint exactly what he had in mind suggested she probably did; but was open to him elaborating nonetheless. He bit a chunk out of his flake for courage and swallowed both chocolate and his reticence.

"It's just that you're very special to me."

"But you barely know me," she pointed out in the same forensic manner.

"I know. But when I first saw you put your head around the door of that compartment – on the train – I felt... well... like I said, you're special. In fact, I love you... What's more, I believe God has had a hand in us coming together."

Oh boy! Her heart sank. He'd been reading that bible again. Once more this conversation was drifting onto dodgy terrain.

"No you don't. You only think you do." she screwed her mouth up dismissively. "What you're actually in love with is the idea of being in love. It's often like that with the first person you date. And anyway, what is love? It's just some crazy feeling we get when we're physically close to someone."

Suddenly, it was the turn of Vaughan's heart to sink.

Look," she then suggested in a bid to prop it up, "why don't we just enjoy our time together and see what happens. And if God really does think that what we have together is 'love', then maybe He'll get round to telling me about it too some time."

Vaughan had made a fool of himself again, though he nodded to signal acceptance of her proposition. However, Aimee was loathed to leave this caring young man with the idea that she was just some shrewish tease who was on a mission to humiliate him.

"Come on," she rose from the bench and suggested, "if neither of us can afford to eat around here, let's head off some other place. And as you very kindly bought me the ice cream, I guess that means it's on me!"

* * * * *

Re-crossing the Medina on the floating bridge, they boarded a Number 4 bus to Ryde and found a little snack bar off Union Street in which to re-victual. It afforded them the opportunity to converse further and to exchange some more tales about their childhoods. Vaughan assured Aimee that his intentions towards her were honourable. Admiring (and yet also daunted by) the sincerity shining out of those cute, adoring eyes he was flashing across the table at her, how could she possibly doubt that.

To his surprise, she then confessed that – far from him needing to feel unworthy of her – she implied she was not good enough for him (or at least not worthy of the pedestal upon which he had thrust her). That said – and for all that she liked him and was humbled by the affection he was showering upon her – she feared Vaughan was simply too naïve and love-struck to be either willing or able to discern a woman who was desperate to lower his expectations ahead of disappointing him.

It was early evening by the time they'd eaten, looked around the shops, and strolled down the hill to the Esplanade, where the sun was bathing the expanse of Ryde Sands in its golden rays. They lingered on the seafront to watch the ferries plying back and forth from the mainland, as well as to pop a few coins in a beachside telescope with which to spy out the abandoned mid-nineteenth-century sea forts that dotted Spithead – relics (or so Vaughan enlightened her) of a fleeting panic on the part of Queen Victoria's ministers that Albion's traditional Gallic enemy might again be poised to invade.

"Look, the night is still young and I'm certainly not in any hurry to get back. So why don't we take the scenic route home," Vaughan mooted, craftily escorting his companion to the stand in the Bus Station from which the Number 8 departed.

Perhaps Colin's attempts to educate his jejune workmate in the art of seducing women had not been entirely wasted. Aimee grinned gamely, willing to fall in with his unsubtle scheme. Perhaps her bumbling boyfriend was partial after all to putting aside all this 'knight-in-shining-armour' malarkey and indulging in some less complicated fun.

By-and-by a familiar leaf green Lodekka turned up and docked at the stand before departing on its circuitous trundle around Nettlestone, St Helens, Bembridge and Whitecliff Bay. There was time enough for the two top-deck lovebirds to admire both scenery and each other – the journey punctuated by a kiss or two (or three or four!) to add to the enchantment.

It was when the bus rounded Bembridge Down and descended into Yaverland that a wicked thought entered Aimee's head. Having spotted a sign by the road, she reached up to push the bell.

"Here, this is not my stop," exclaimed Vaughan, "We're not even in Sandown yet. And anyway, you can't ring that thing. Only the conductor can do that!"

"Well, you're a conductor, aren't you? And, like you said, the night is still young," she pointed out as she hauled herself out of her seat. Tilting her head in the direction of the stairs, she bade him escort her off the bus.

And so it was that they found themselves alone on the 'sidewalk', with the bus they'd been travelling home on chugging off into the distance without them. Meanwhile, a fading westerly sun was casting its long shadows upon the stark white cliffs that overlooked Culver Beach. Inhaling a bracing whiff of sea air, Aimee marched off in their direction, her bewildered boyfriend making haste after her as she kicked off her sandals and jumped down onto the sand.

"Where are you going?" he was anxious to know.

"To a place where magic is supposed to happen," she grinned.

"Eh?"

"Well, that's what your friend Colin told me."

It clicked that she meant the remote expanse of beach that was a favourite summer haunt of skinny-dipping teenagers. Vaughan began to wonder whether this good Christian girl he was so eager to impress was quite so 'good' after all.

Sure enough, on their sojourn they passed isolated clusters of half-naked youngsters, the girls chatting around impromptu bonfires while the guys strummed guitars. When added to the gentle lapping of the waves it made for a lazy ambience that lulled both wily room maid and innocent bus conductor into savouring the romance of it all. Alighting upon a handy piece of driftwood, Vaughan raced ahead of Aimee to bend down and trace the shape of a heart in the moist sand, along with the words *'Vaughan 4 Aimee 4 ever'*. She halted to study it before offering him a bemused smile. John Lawton's inference about her boyfriend being 'reliable, but boring' sprang to mind.

"Wow! Isn't this just awesome," she marvelled, eventually stepping up onto a rock that was some distance removed from the other youngsters. There she turned and stared back at the lights of Sandown and Shanklin that were twinkling in the twilight.

"We'd better be careful. It'll be dark soon. And the tide looks like it might be coming in," her companion carped.

Aimee jumped back down and wandered over to him. With a glint in her eye, she looped her arms up around his shoulders and, with her lips poised, begged from him a kiss. Vaughan responded in kind, their tongues slowly twisting. He squeezed her tighter into his embrace while she sank a hand through his hair.

In fact, her move had not just banished his fussing about time and tides, but seemed to be goading his groin into action too. Aimee sensed his aroused appurtenance pressing firm against her belly. Perhaps Vaughan Lewis really was about to ditch all this silliness about 'love' and just have a little fun. But just to make sure she now reached for the top button of his jeans and sprung it. Helped along by her guiding hand, there began a remorseless riding of the zip over each of its teeth until those trousers hung loose around his waist. Into the gap so fashioned she slipped that delicate, yet determined hand. However – and though it defied his every instinct at that moment – into the gap he reluctantly slipped his own tremulous hand to remove it.

"Aimee," it pained him to beseech her, "I want to treat you right. I want to treat you special."

"I know you do," she panted.

However, it was no use. Hell might have no fury like a woman scorned; but not far behind was a woman whose lustful advances had been thwarted – no matter how tenderly or regretfully.

"What's the matter? Don't you fancy me?" she pleaded, her eyes perplexed and glistening.

"Of course, I fancy you. I love you!" he repeated that doleful refrain for a second time that day. "But look, I want you the right way: God's way."

That three-letter word was like a red rag to a bull. In fact, it was a taunt – a divine taunt, she didn't wonder. For crying out loud, men were not supposed to resist her in this way! Stepping away from him, part-frustrated and part-ashamed, she turned and folded her arms, an angry wrist emerging to dab at her accursed tears. It afforded Vaughan vital seconds with which to readjust his clothing; and Aimee vital seconds to contemplate what she had just done. Now whose turn was it to feel like a fool!

"I'm sorry," he drew up behind her.

"Don't... don't touch me!" she raised another angry hand.

He desisted. For what it was worth, he'd never imagined that a good Christian girl would be this forward. He still had so much more to learn about women, about sex – and, indeed, about where faith and virtue fitted into the equation.

She turned and accepted his apology – adding one of her own. They had both seriously misjudged the other.

With time, tide and dusk advancing, they made a passage back to the main road, hand-in-conciliatory hand – passing again those groups of idly strumming teenage troubadours. Having made their peace – and with time to spare before the next bus was due – Vaughan stooped down to plant a loving kiss upon her forehead. She smiled awkwardly.

However, completing the journey back to Sandown in silence, they were both left to ponder whether their nascent relationship wasn't now somehow, so to speak, a cracked mirror.

14

Thursday, August 5th 1976

> *"It's one o'clock and here is the news.*
> *"The Government has officially declared a State of Emergency in effect from today. With the prolonged hot, dry weather showing no signs of abating, an official spokesman has indicated that from now on, widespread water rationing is to be introduced in response to the worsening drought..."*

It had to happen. In some parts of Britain standpipes had already appeared in the streets – along with broods of housewives in slippers and curlers queuing up with buckets, jugs and pop bottles to take home as much of the precious stuff as they could carry. Meanwhile – in true British *'Carry On'* style – the recommendation that they should consider sharing a bath in order to further save water had set bawdy tongues wagging.

However, the drought was of only secondary interest to John Lawton today. Instead, he switched the radio off, sat back in his expensive leather armchair, and began perusing a book that had been air-mailed to him from New York that very morning.

It was an hour-by-hour account of *'Operation Linebacker II'* – the ferocious, eleven-day aerial assault against North Vietnam in December 1972 that had been a final roll-of-the-dice by President Richard Nixon to exit from a war that the American people had grown weary of. 'Peace is at hand', his chief negotiator, Henry Kissinger, had famously declared a few weeks earlier. However, a stonewalling Hanoi had first had to be bludgeoned into conceding the terms that would adorn it with the fig-leaf of being 'peace with honour'.

To be sure, *'Linebacker II'* had been a race against the clock back home too. For although Nixon had been re-elected by a landslide in November, when Congress convened in the New

Year its Democratic majority looked set to legislate the United States out of the Vietnam War for good – with or without honour.

For the first few months of 1973 it was possible to believe the sacrifices the United States had made had not been in vain. However, Nixon's resignation over the Watergate scandal in August 1974 would embolden the North Vietnamese to launch a final offensive that would ruthlessly sweep aside South Vietnam's beleaguered armed forces. Saigon, the capital, fell in April 1975. Hence this futile war would close with an armada of whooping helicopters ignominiously lifting the last US personnel from their abandoned embassy in the city. The chaotic, American-backed regime in Cambodia had similarly collapsed two weeks earlier.

Looking up from its pages, Lawton reflected that the war had cost the United States dear. Fifty-eight thousand Americans had been killed during the twenty-years of US involvement in Indochina. Three hundred thousand had been wounded. Almost two thousand men remained unaccounted for – including many previously identified on the rolls of POWs held by the communists. Pursuing the struggle had meanwhile cost the United States $352 billion – six billion dollars alone spent on the seven million tons of ordnance that had been dropped by US aircraft during the conflict (twice what had been dropped on Germany during World War Two). The war had also cost two Americans presidents their careers and reputations. Meanwhile, over two million Vietnamese on both sides were estimated to have perished, along with anything up to a million Cambodians.

Indeed, the Vietnam War was above all a human tragedy. Lawton recalled that famous image of a napalm-scarred South Vietnamese girl fleeing an air strike on her village; or the distraught black mother burying her son, his coffin draped in the Stars-and-Stripes (black GIs would pay a disproportionate price fighting what Martin Luther King had dubbed 'a white man's war'); or the bearded amputee who had returned minus his limbs and minus any gratitude or respect from a nation for whom he represented an ugly reminder of an unpopular war; or the vacant stares upon the faces of those half-Caucasian or half-Negroid 'children of the dust' who'd been left behind after the fall of Saigon – orphans long since abandoned by their American fathers. "A child without a father is like a house without a roof," the Vietnamese saying goes. That particular image of the forgotten human detritus of war had a strange poignancy for this hotelier-cum-amateur historian.

Resuming flicking the pages, he encountered another face staring back at him: this time the careworn features of an air force general who had lost his son during the *'Linebacker II'* Christmas bombing campaign – or so the addendum account of Lawrence Eichelberger's fate read. Lawton knew this man still clung to the hope that his boy might be alive somewhere in Indochina. He tried to imagine what it must be like to wake up every day knowing one might have left a son behind at war's end.

Though by now anxiously glancing at his watch, it prompted Lawton to reach across the desk and take hold of another book that he'd earlier brought down from a shelf on his bookcase. Purchased for a previous piece of research he'd undertaken, he'd never really paid much attention to the image on an inside page of Major Charles F. Eichelberger, the famous fighter ace, relaxing with his buddies in a pub in Suffolk at Christmas 1944. There – laughing merrily while nestled up to him – was none other than that once-renowned wartime singer Angie Ashby. What serendipity it was to have discovered this intriguing black-and-white image – for if Angie was a beautiful woman today, then she had been an even more choice beauty back then.

This photograph captured one of many such hopeful gatherings during that final winter of the war. However, studying it he recalled something she'd said: that in his obsession with cataloguing dogfights, combat tactics and aircraft types, Lawton had omitted to account for what the men who'd flown those missions had gotten up to while off-duty on the ground.

Glancing at his watch again, his eyes scanned the photograph one final time, this time to fix themselves upon another choice beauty who was visible in the background – a woman who was staring back at him with an enigmatic Mona Lisa smile; a woman he had yet to meet, but who he hoped would soon help him make sense of the enigma that was his own life.

* * * * *

John Lawton' time-keeping was always impeccable. It was just as well for the ruffled figure sat reading his paper in a Mark III Ford Cortina parked across from the Shanklin Heights Hotel. The minute he spotted that distinctive Jaguar coupé slip out of the car park, he tossed the paper onto the back seat and turned the ignition. Pulling away, he then followed the car up to the traffic lights on the main road. When the lights changed, he too turned right and began to trail after it.

He had not been stalking him long when the Jaguar pulled up sharp at a bus stop. Pulling up sharp too, Lawton's pursuer could only pray he hadn't been spotted. He needn't have feared. Having wound down the passenger window, his quarry was too absorbed conversing with some fair-haired teenage girl in denim hot pants, who was waiting at the stop.

Whoever this attractive young lady might be she was evidently a reluctant conversationalist, folding her arms in a huff as if she wanted nothing to do with his importuning. However, she fitted the description that Lawton's pursuer had been given. Therefore, a self-satisfied smile rippled across his sagging features as he lifted to his eye an expensive-looking camera that he now took from the seat beside him.

John Lawton clearly lived up to his reputation as a smooth operator with an eye for gorgeous women. Whatever cock-and-bull the hotelier had fed the girl finally persuaded her to hop into his car. There was time for one quick shot of this act before Jaguar and pursuing Ford Cortina indicated right and moved off, permitting an arriving bus to dock at the stop they'd left behind.

The guy with the camera now followed Lawton's motor as it cruised through Lake and down into the backstreets of Sandown, where it drew to a halt outside an apartment block near the seafront. Out this young girl jumped, albeit quite clearly in a temper. Standing on the pavement and bawling at her chauffeur, she then slammed the door shut and stormed off, striding up the steps and into the block. Maybe John Lawton's oleaginous charm didn't work on every female who crossed his path!

* * * * *

Friday, August 6th 1976

> *"It's four o'clock and here is the news.*
> *"John Stonehouse, the former Labour minister and MP for Walsall North, has today been sentenced to serve seven years in prison for fraud. Fifty-one year old Mr Stonehouse disappeared after faking his own death by drowning in Miami two years ago. Scotland Yard later tracked him down in Australia, where he had been planning to live with his mistress and secretary, Sheila Buckley – and from where he was subsequently extradited to the United Kingdom..."*

'Another day, another dollar' – as they say. It was a mighty tedious way of earning it though, entailing as it did an awful lot of loitering about in hot, stuffy cars – today (lest his quarry rumble that he was being followed) a silver Hillman Hunter saloon. Still, at least his pursuer had the radio for company. He pondered how quickly he might have tracked down the errant Labour MP by employing his formidable skills as a private investigator.

Today though, our man was once again trailing John Lawton. Hence why his covert pursuit found him parked up across the way from a musty old bookshop in Ryde that specialised in militaria. Indeed, that brief encounter with that American college kid yesterday had so far been the only promising event in a week spent covertly observing the hotelier. Having deposited her on the pavement after that blazing row, Lawton had then driven off to help judge the Miss Shanklin beauty contest (of all things!).

This afternoon's shadowing of the suspect looked set to be an equally damp squib. Emerging from the bookshop bearing a dog-eared book in his hand, the millionaire playboy jumped into his opulent Jaguar and pulled out into the traffic. Unseen behind him, the Hillman Hunter did likewise. Eventually rejoining the main A3055 to Shanklin, so far Lawton had given this sleuth no cause to believe he was up to anything untoward.

Suddenly and unexpectedly however, the Jaguar bore right at Brading and accelerated up a steep hill. Again his pursuer in the

Hunter did likewise, sticking just close enough to tail him, yet far enough back so as to hopefully not arouse suspicion. The road having levelled off as it traversed the escarpment that was Brading Down. This cat-and-mouse game ended when the Jaguar turned off onto a car park where all the sweeping majesty of Sandown Bay could be viewed on this bright, sunny day.

Meanwhile, the Hillman Hunter parked up a suitable distance away. There its driver extinguished the engine and prepared for yet another boring stint of observing nothing much going on. Perhaps this scenic spot was more conducive to his quarry perusing that book he'd just purchased.

Or perhaps this American totty it was rumoured Lawton was knocking off might show up after all. A faint hope really – the car park was too busy to be planning on giving anyone a back seat shag! And it was a long walk from the bus stop if he'd intended for her to make her own way to a rendezvous with him.

It looked set to be a boring afternoon indeed. Several minutes would pass before the sleuth noticed the driver's door of a white Austin Allegro that was parked up nearby open. Out stepped an attractive and mature lady attired in white bell-bottomed trousers and a black halter neck top. She hung on the door for a moment or two as if to savour the breathtaking views.

"Phwoah! I'd certainly give you one, love!" he muttered to himself as he eyed her up and down approvingly. It was good to know that there were old birds out there who could teach today's teenagers a thing or two about style and elegance.

She shut the door and appeared to be about to stroll off along the footpath. It prompted her admirer to huff incredulously. Months with hardly any rain might have banished the mud; but negotiating uneven ground in those heels risking spraining an ankle for sure. It soon became apparent though that an invigorating ramble was not her intention. Instead, she approached the Jaguar. Glancing around furtively, she opened the passenger door and stepped inside.

"Yeeesss!" that admirer now sat up his seat, animated.

All of a sudden, the tedium of his day so far was forgotten. Grabbing the camera from the seat beside him, he twiddled with the zoom lens and took aim. Perhaps now he would have something of merit to hang on the mercurial character he'd been following so diligently.

15

Sunday, August 8th 1976

"Give us a kiss!"

"Oh, my gosh! He talks!"

Shelby's eyes lit up and her mouth dropped open. It compelled her to draw in close to the bars and stare into Chico's beady eye, conversing with him as if to a baby.

"Watch out, Shell. The things this bird has to say are definitely not for the ears of a nice girl like you," Aimee joked, positioning her hands to shield her friend's lugholes in readiness.

"Show us yer' tits!" Chico then squawked, as if on cue.

Mouth gaping wider still, Shelby turned to her fellow room maid in disbelieving mirth and shielded it with her own.

Ever the eager suitor, Vaughan had already spotted the two girls rounding the corner from the High Street and had been waiting in the verandah to greet them. There was the obligatory kiss on the lips for Aimee and a more platonic one on the cheek for her best friend – both of whom had rushed here as soon as the morning service at church had finished

Leaving Chico to spy on passers-by in the street, he escorted them inside, where Auntie Angie too greeted both girls with a kiss. Uncle Frank was content to rise from his favourite chair and offer them his hand, thereafter to sit back down and watch television again. Like many ordinary blokes of his generation, 'Bloody Yanks' was his default opinion of anyone who hailed from the other side of the Atlantic, and this was his way of avoiding having to converse with these two excitable Americans. However, Angie was having none of it. For the first time during Vaughan's stay he watched her march over and switch the set off, ordering her other half to pour their visitors some drinks.

"Are you sure you don't mind having li'l ol' me for Sunday dinner? It sure is good of y'all to make me welcome," Shelby thanked her hosts, taking up a place around the dining table.

Otherwise, she remained self-conscious about playing gooseberry to Vaughan and Aimee on their day out – even though Aimee had insisted on her tagging along. However, Angie couldn't have been more accommodating; and Vaughan had been willing to fall in line with Aimee's wishes. Besides, like his aunt, he found it impossible not to warm to the happy-go-lucky young Southerner, who (unlike his more abstruse girlfriend) was as open as a book. What you saw really was what you got.

"So what time does the boat depart?" Angie enquired once the plates had been brought in and everyone had been urged to help themselves to the vegetables.

"Two thirty, Auntie," Vaughan replied.

Angie glanced up at that ornate box clock on the wall. "Good. Then you still have plenty of time," she observed.

"Cast off," mumbled Frank, in between masticating a mouthful of lamb shank. "'Cast off' is the nautical term… Or you could have said 'set sail'… But not 'depart'. It's not one of the lad's big green buses we're talking about, my dear."

"Uncle Frank was in the navy during the war," his nephew explained for Shelby's benefit. "Aircraft carriers, wasn't it, Uncle?"

"That's right," the bluff sea salt affirmed with a jab at the air with his fork. "*HMS Victorious*… Far East… June 1944 to October 1945."

"Wow! My dad served aboard carriers in the Pacific," the gregarious Georgian informed them, her face lighting up.

"Aimee's father served in the war too. He was a famous fighter pilot," Vaughan then answered on his girlfriend's behalf.

"Yeah. He was based at Leiston, East Anglia – '44 to '45. Flew Mustangs on escort missions," she noted, those russet eyes flitting first to check Angie's reaction and then her husband's.

Like his wife, she thought she spotted the briefest flicker of emotion at the mention of the time, the place and the purpose. Frank hurriedly chewed and swallowed what he was munching, as if impatient to respond. However, when he did, it was about another matter entirely.

"Armoured flight decks," he grunted, with another jab of the fork. "Our ships had 'em… Saved our bacon more than once off

Okinawa... 'Course, you Yanks weren't so smart. Built your carrier decks out of wood to save weight. Jap Kamikazes smashed clean through them... Almost sank the *Bunker Hill*, they did."

"Really? Wow! Dad never told me that," Shelby rhapsodised.

Not as gifted with her friend's good grace, Aimee was visibly unimpressed by this little lecture about the supposedly superior quality of British warship design. When allied to Angie's indecipherable glare, she couldn't make up her mind whether her husband's observation was intended as a dig at her country or at her personally. Why did she get the impression neither of Vaughan's relations held her in much regard.

"Leiston? That's where you and Mom come from, Auntie," her boyfriend innocently rode to her rescue.

Both his aunt and uncle paused from eating and fired a furtive glance at each other. Yet not so furtive that once more one of their guests wasn't left squirming in her seat.

"So, Eighth Air Force, was he?" Frank began dissecting her brusquely, having recommenced the shovelling of fork to mouth.

"That's right."

"What's his name?"

"Eichelberger. Charles Eichelberger."

By now there was a buzz in the room. Even Shelby could detect it, turning to her friend and offering her a supportive smile.

"Eichelberger... Yes, name does ring a bell..." Frank appeared to interrogate himself. "Wasn't he on the news a while back – the guy whose planes were bombing all those Cambodians?"

Aimee looked as if she was about to burst into tears. This time though it was Angie who rode to the rescue, shooting her husband a faux censorious glance.

"Come on, Frank. What those American airmen had to do was no different to what our airmen had to do over Germany during the war: they were tasked with winning it. And anyway, talking of Germany, Aimee's father was a decorated war hero who shot down dozens of German fighters – and a gallant and very handsome one at that," she purposely smiled at his daughter before hurriedly adding "...Or so I'm told."

* * * * *

With both main meal and dessert consumed, Angie waved aside an offer from the two girls to help with the washing-up, insisting that they hurry themselves down to the pier in good time before their boat departed (or 'cast off' or 'set sail', she joked, rolling her eyes in the direction of her husband, who had squat back down in front of the television set).

Diverting into the bedroom once they'd gone, she drew up to the window and nudged the net curtain aside. There she took a moment to observe the three friends strolling off in the direction of the Esplanade – Vaughan and Aimee hand-in-swinging-hand and Shelby the ever-patient chaperone. Though she knew it wasn't the poor kid's fault that she bore the family name, his aunt felt increasingly ill-at-ease with this mismatched relationship between her beloved nephew and the girl he had fallen head-over-heels in love with. It was a chariness heightened by the sense that, when this opaque young lady wasn't sporting a chip on her shoulder, she conversely gave the impression of being party to some guilty secret that she was not about to divulge – least of all to her naïve and fawning boyfriend.

She just hoped it didn't bode ill for Vaughan. For if there was one thing Angie had sworn to herself it was that she would not stand idly by and watch an Eichelberger break his heart and shatter his dreams the way hers had once been.

* * * * *

The minute the small motorboat cast off from the end of the pier Aimee knew it had been a mistake to agree to this nautical excursion – especially after having partaken of a heavy meal. While Vaughan and Shelby were soon pointing out landmarks to each other, the motion of the waves quickly turned their companion's complexion ghostly. Suddenly, the normally becalmed Sandown Bay didn't seem so quiescent when one was sat at the prow of a small launch thrusting its way spiritedly towards Bembridge Foreland.

However, she said nothing when Vaughan squeezed her hand and smiled sweetly, instead greeting it with a languid smile of her own – the large sunshades that she had dropped from her head to her eyes helping to disguise those second thoughts. Supplemented by the commentary offered by their captain (and which was oscillating through the tannoy system), Vaughan carried on regaling Shelby with fascinating insights of his own that he'd picked up during his weeks working on the buses. Suddenly, it was someone else's turn to feel like a gooseberry.

To be sure, it had been Vaughan's idea that they pass their afternoon on one of the boat excursions that sailed from Sandown Pier – this one to take in the sights of Portsmouth Harbour (including its historic naval dockyard). On the voyage out, the captain drew their attention to other things to look out for – those impressive Culver Cliffs; Whitecliff Bay (where fossils could be found in its Eocene beds of soft sand and clay), historic Bembridge; and those abandoned Spithead forts (which the captain quipped were on the market should any of his passengers possess pockets deep enough to be able to purchase and renovate one as a perfect secluded getaway).

During those moments when only the humming of the engines and the lashing of the waves disturbed the tranquillity of this gorgeous sunny day, Shelby glanced across and wondered if it was more than just seasickness that had unsettled her friend. For so long they had shared everything – including insights into each other's thinking. And yet lately it felt as if her best friend was slowly, but surely pushing her away. It hurt to think she was no longer in Aimee's confidence; that she no longer knew for sure what she was thinking – about the faith they shared; about Vaughan and the seeming ambivalence of her feelings towards him (as evidenced by her insistence that Shelby accompany her today); about the imminent arrival in England of her parents; and indeed perhaps about some altogether more troubling matter that Shelby sensed Aimee might be wrestling with.

* * * * *

At last they arrived at the mouth of Portsmouth Harbour – flanked to starboard by Southsea Common, with its bustling funfair and amusement arcades; and off the port beam by the Haslar submarine base at Gosport. Once through the channel entrance and into the calmer waters of the harbour itself, Aimee at last appeared to relax and take in the sights. Meanwhile, her boyfriend had succumbed to that boyish animation that often afflicts grown men who find themselves in the presence of tall grey warships riding at anchor.

"Look! D80 – that's *HMS Sheffield*. She's one of our new Type 42 destroyers. She's armed with those formidable Sea Dart missiles," he pointed out.

Shelby duly swivelled about at his bidding, listening with interest as he reeled off its particulars – and which supplemented the ongoing commentary that was oscillating through the tannoy.

"I wonder if it's the ship that sailor is serving aboard – the one who was sat by us on the train," he then remembered. "From what few words he uttered on the journey it sounded like the poor bloke had got his girlfriend in the family way."

"The family way?" Shelby puzzled.

"Pregnant; expecting a baby – as in out of wedlock."

"Maybe that was why he seemed so miserable," she recalled.

Though underwhelmed by Vaughan's running commentary, Aimee also stared up at the vessel and its bristling weaponry. In particular, those bright red missiles visible in their launcher reminded her again of the fate of her brother. She wondered whether the SAM that had stricken his plane had delivered death swiftly; or whether it might have been a lingering and terrifying one as what was left of the giant B52 had plunged to Earth with Lawrence trapped inside.

"It's an impressive ship, isn't it," Vaughan enthused, abruptly pricking her introspection.

She smiled wanly at him through those mirror shades, resisting the temptation to point out that 'we Yanks have more of 'em – and ours are bigger!'

"I remember Uncle Frank taking me on this same boat trip many times whenever I was on holiday here. Normally he's a man of few words – as you discovered today. But the moment we entered Portsmouth Harbour he would start spouting all these facts and figures at me about the history of the ships, their displacements, their crew compliments, and their weapon capabilities. Once he gave me an Airfix model of *HMS Victorious* from his toy shop. He showed me how to paint it and put it together. He was real proud of me when I finished it. I guess that was what kick-started my interest in model-making.

"He was always good to me like that. In fact, it was at such times that I used to wish Uncle Frank could be my dad!" he opined fancifully. Then Shelby suddenly observed darker recollections clouding the monologue as he confessed that "He was certainly a better father to me than my real dad was. *He* never showed any interest in me. Nor have I seen him in years. It's as if he has erased all memory of me from his life."

Turning about at Whale Island there was time for Shelby to take a few quick photographs of *HMS Victory* with her trusty Polaroid camera. As the commentary explained, she had been Keppel's flagship at the Battle of Ushant, Howe's flagship at Cape Spartel, Jervis's flagship at Cape St Vincent, and finally – and most famously – Nelson's flagship at the Battle of Trafalgar. Nowadays she was preserved as a floating museum. Shelby also trained her camera at Vaughan and Aimee, chivvying them to pose for her and smile. Waving the print-out in her hand until it had dried, she presented it to Vaughan as a keepsake. Then the motors revved up and the launch headed back out to sea.

The voyage home was purgatory for one of its passengers. While Vaughan and Shelby were once more nattering to each other and savouring the views, their bilious shipmate made the first of several lurches over the side of the boat to puke up.

"You okay?" Shelby reached over and grasped her bare knee – the nearest part of her quivering body that was to hand.

"It must be family thing. Now I know why Dad never applied for the navy," she spluttered, embarrassed at having to wipe her mouth with the back of her hand.

"Here, love, try sitting up the middle of the boat; or maybe inside," a fellow passenger suggested, offering her a tissue. "You won't notice the motion quite so much there."

It seemed sage advice. The sheet-white American was by now desperate enough to try anything that would alleviate her torment. She duly cranked herself up from her place at the prow and staggered down the aisle in the direction of the galley.

"Shall I come with you?" Vaughan called out in dismay.

He was confronted with his beloved's hand being waved vigorously behind her back as if to decline his polite offer.

"Hey, d'ya want me to come with you instead," Shelby hollered. She too was confronted with a wave of the hand.

The hapless student then disappeared to the toilet signposted below deck, leaving Vaughan and Shelby alone together enveloped in a guilty silence.

"Oh, well. If she says she wants to be alone, I guess she wants to be alone," Shelby shrugged by way of mitigation.

It didn't prevent Vaughan from gazing culpably into his lap.

"I never thought she might be seasick. Perhaps I should have taken her to see the steam trains at Havenstreet instead," he ventured. To which Shelby guffawed.

"Vaughan, you old charmer! You sure do know how to impress a girl. But, for what it's worth, Aimee ain't into old railroads either!"

Her playful teasing coaxed a smile from him and lifted his gloom sufficiently for him to do some heaving of his own – namely, of the despair from his heart that he increasingly felt.

"I sometimes get the impression she doesn't particularly like me," he confessed to her.

"Sure she likes you. It's just that... well..."

He watched while she formulated her reply. She stared back, desperate to do so as sympathetically as she knew how.

"Vaughan, I guess Aimee's just a little confused at the moment. She's been through some tough times these last few years, what with the death of her brother; getting all kinds of grief at college for being General Eichelberger's kid; and now she's probably worrying about whether she's gonna' be able to live up to all the high hopes you clearly have for this relationship. I guess she just needs a little space to unravel her head."

"Is that why she invited you along today? Because she thinks I'm not giving her enough space?"

However she elected to respond to that stark petition, Shelby's eyes were simply incapable of telling a lie. Vaughan looked away, more disheartened than ever. One minute Aimee was all over him like a rash – even fumbling inside his trousers; the next minute she was cold-shouldering and belittling him. What was he doing wrong? Was love always this complicated? Were women always this complicated?

Shelby looked on in anguish as he sank his face in his hands and wrestled with his own artlessness. Eventually, she felt obliged to slip across onto the bench alongside him and place her own tiny hand upon his shoulder.

"Don't take it personally, Vaughan. You're a real cool guy. You're kind; and you're funny too. If you can make a girl laugh then you're halfway to her heart already. As for you and Aimee, well... I wish I could wave a magic wand and make everything right between you. But I guess all I can do is to pray for you both. I've been doing that a lot lately."

"I've been praying for us both too," he ventured cynically. "Except it doesn't seem to be working."

"Sure, prayer works. But sometimes the Lord prefers to answer us according to what we need, and not what we want. And moreover, according to what *He* thinks we need in order to for us walk more closely with Him. Believe me, that's the only place where true and lasting happiness can be found."

It was while he was gazing into his lap, contemplating what she'd said, that the thought struck him: Shelby seemed so much more comfortable in her own skin than her headstrong best friend. The rattle-brained hayseed façade belied a young woman of formidable intellect and resolute faith who knew her own mind. How else had the daughter of a lowly gas station proprietor from the Deep South wound up studying at Oxford University!

"I am a fool, Shelby – a proper clown. I was the clown all through school too. You say I'm kind and I'm funny. And maybe I am. I certainly made plenty of girls laugh. The trouble was I never managed to convince them I was serious about anything – except perhaps in ways that scared them off wanting to go out with me. The same way I've obviously scared Aimee too. As for discovering a closer walk with God, well... I try – I really do. But I keep failing too. He must be so disillusioned with me. Maybe He regards me as just a hopeless clown too."

"No, He doesn't. God is never disillusioned with us; because He never had any illusions to start with. You're a sinful human being, Vaughan – just like I am; just like Aimee is too. And anyway, you don't need to be perfect to be loved and accepted by your Heavenly Father. That's why He sent His Son to die for you: *'for by one offering He hath perfected for ever them that are sanctified'* – Hebrews Chapter 10, verse 14."

"So are you suggesting I should try a little less hard," he sat up and stared out to sea, nudging away a tear.

Unsure whether he meant romantically or spiritually, but wanting him to comfort and reassure him, she fell back on a piece of advice appropriate to both meanings.

"Be yourself, Vaughan. Not anybody else's opinion of who you should be; not even your own misplaced opinion of who you think other people want you to be. And as for the pain you obviously still feel that your earthly father has rejected you, know instead that you have a Father in Heaven who loves you – despite your faults and failures – and who will *never, ever* reject you."

He looked into Shelby's winsome eyes and felt like crying. In a few short sentences she had done more to encourage him to not give up on his faith than any number of Sunday sermons. She was a true girl 'friend' – in the noblest sense of the word.

For her part, Shelby was heartened to witness the return of his jovial countenance. He was such a fine young man, with a kindly face to match his kindly disposition; and (despite his father cruelly abandoning him) a commendable readiness to look to the good in others – including his erratic girlfriend.

Talking of whom – and with Sandown Pier in sight – Aimee emerged back up on deck and shuffled down the aisle to where they were sitting, looking the better for having settled her stomach. Shelby vacated her spot beside Vaughan so that her friend could sit down and permit him to drape his arm around her.

"I'm sorry if I ruined your afternoon," she whimpered.

"You haven't ruined anything," he insisted, hugging her magnanimously. "Besides, it should be me apologising to you: for Uncle Frank maybe being a bit abrupt with you over dinner. He can be a funny old character at times."

Respecting their right to a moment of privacy, Shelby turned about and shuffled down the bench. Resting her chin upon arms that she had draped upon the side of the boat, there she feigned to study the Esplanade as it drew closer off the starboard bow. Suppressing her own jealousy, instead she silently offered up another prayer for the happiness of her best friend and this boy who plainly adored her.

16

Tuesday, August 10th 1976

"Come in."

The voice behind the door was brusque – as Veronica Lawton's voice invariably was. As he entered her office with the bulging folder under his arm he could tell from the tautness of her frown that she was on edge regarding what it might contain. Poker-faced, his countenance gave nothing away. Perhaps the devil in him wanted to make this demanding taskmaster sweat a while longer. It certainly added to the drama of the occasion.

When he did eventually place the folder on the desk in front of her, she took a moment to stare at it before looking up, her eyes drilling into him impatiently.

"So you've found out what he's been up to then?" she bade him pull up a chair and sit down across the desk from her.

"I have," he replied.

"And does it involve *her*?" she spat the pronoun out.

"Yes... and no."

"What do you mean: yes and no? Tell me straight: is my husband having an affair with that American girl?"

To answer her question, he leant across and flipped the folder open. The very first photograph she set eyes on confirmed her worst fears. For there, in black and white, was her husband's sleek white Jaguar with its distinctive number plate. And next to it, stooping on the pavement to converse with its driver was 'that American girl', dressed in a pair of provocative, bum-hugging hot pants and one of those flimsy vest tops that she was always flaunting herself in. Seething with righteous indignation, Veronica decided there and then that her employment at the hotel would be terminated forthwith – a summary decision merely confirmed when the private investigator she'd hired to keep tabs on her libidinous spouse flicked to the next photograph. This one captured the room maid actually getting into the car. She looked up at him again.

"And now for the 'no' part of my findings," he stared her out, flicking to the next photographs he'd taken.

"Whatever they got up to on that short journey to Sandown, as you can see it ended with her storming out of his car in a right temper. Slammed the door shut and marched off," he explained.

"Lovers' tiff, I suppose!" Veronica huffed, her normally resolute brown eyes oozing hurt and anger.

"Of course, it's always possible he tried to proposition her. And that she rebuffed him. Perhaps that's why she was upset."

She was in no mood to listen to him playing devil's advocate. "More like that vacuous little cock-teaser was making demands that even *he* baulked at! You know, when John is wittering on about his hotel, his private plane, and the fortune he made in the City he doesn't realise that these young girls are swooning over him for one reason – and one reason only. This dumb Yank is no different," she hissed, flicking through the next few images – including the one of Aimee offering her husband 'the finger' as she stepped out of the car.

"If you want my professional opinion, I really don't think she's the one he's seeing," the sleuth insisted. "In all the time I've been stalking your husband that's the only instance I've witnessed of the two of them together. So either they're conducting an extremely well-hidden affair; or she's not the woman you should be worried about. I'd surmise the latter. You see, as you're paying me so generously I took the liberty of tasking one of my colleagues to keep tabs on the Yank too."

To back up his assertion he 'walked' her through a few more photographs – these shots taken by the said colleague. They mostly featured Aimee in the company of some gangling teenage boy. Veronica recognised him as the lad she'd spotted snooping around the hotel car park the other day. For the most part, the two youngsters were captured hopping on and off buses, wandering in and out of tourist haunts, licking ice creams on seafront benches, and kissing and canoodling at various locations around the island. Yes, there were a lot of photographs of the two of them kissing and canoodling.

"I think you'll agree they appear to be very much in love. I'm tempted to say they can't keep their hands off each other!"

She failed to find his aside amusing. "So I've wasted my money hiring you?" she fumed to herself, sinking back into her chair and re-crossing her legs.

"Far from it," he insisted, "Thanks to my colleague, I trust we can safely eliminate the Yank. However, I've continued to maintain a watchful eye on your husband."

She looked on attentively as he drew some more photographs from out of the back of the folder, placing them in front of her and again 'walking' her through each one. First off, one in which she recognised her husband's car again – this time parked up on the beauty spot that was Brading Down. Then another shot in the same location, this time a close-up of its rear windscreen – through which his sophisticated piece of photographic kit had been able to pick out the outline a woman sat in the passenger seat. Veronica leaned in to study the image, her eyebrows curling. He flicked over to another photograph depicting much the same thing; of two people deep in intimate conversation.

Though, maddeningly, there were no shots of her husband and this mysterious woman unambiguously engaging in what might be construed as passion, it reeked of two people up to no good. This was confirmed once her private investigator explained that – prior to swinging his camera into action – he'd observed this woman step from her own car (which had already been there when Mr Lawton had arrived) and hop into her husband's.

It all pointed to what Veronica had suspected for weeks: her husband was indulging in yet another extra-marital affair. For some time relations between the Lawtons in the 'bedroom department' had been fraught – to put it mildly. Veronica knew no sooner she'd married him that John Lawton's wandering eye would never be satisfied gazing upon one woman alone – even an aristocratic beauty who had not that long ago been one of high society's most stunning debutantes. Repelled by his sexual opportunism, she had instead thrown herself into the day-to-day management of their hotel, perhaps compounding the problem. Indeed, for a brief moment she was tempted to blame herself for her husband's wandering eye; and that it was her emotional frostiness that had left him feeling compelled to seek an outlet for his vibrant libido elsewhere.

However, Veronica Lawton was not a woman given to beating herself up. Self-possessed to a fault, when her personal sleuth flipped to the final photograph in the folder – a close-up facial shot of the woman her husband was trysting with – she almost ground her teeth in fury. For far from being the naive, nubile types that he usually chased after, this woman was old enough to be his mother! What's more, it was none other than that ageing nightclub siren – Angie Ashby!

Suddenly, everything fell into place. Now she knew why her husband had been most insistent about hiring this woman – and then upping her performing contract to *two* nights a week! It also explained why, of late, he had taken to spending ever more time working late in his office on the pretext of researching and typing up that ridiculous book about the Vietnam War.

"Will you be wanting to retain me – to keep a further eye on what they're getting up to?" the investigator enquired, reluctant to puncture his client's terrible epiphany.

She shook her head.

"No, I think I have the evidence I need to confront my husband. I trust my remittance has covered all your expenses."

He nodded, rising to his feet.

"If you do need my services again, you only have to pick up the phone," he reminded her.

She nodded again before directing her gaze away to some point in the room that became the repository of her icy glare. As he turned to leave, he took a moment to study those cold, calculating eyes. It prompted him to wonder whether the next phone call Veronica Lawton made regarding her husband's philandering would be to hire the services of a hit man!

* * * * *

Completed at last! The final decals had been applied and Vaughan Lewis could sit back in his favourite wicker chair in the verandah to admire his finished creation. Chico was impressed too, offering his human friend a congratulatory wolf-whistle.

For there, in all its awesome span on the table in front of him, was that 1/72 scale model of a B52G Stratofortress bomber. In the end, Vaughan had decided to finish it off in the dappled camouflage livery that depicted aircraft 58-0183 of the 69th Bombardment Squadron, 42nd Bombardment Wing, and which had flown out of Andersen AFB in Guam during *'Operation Linebacker II'* over North Vietnam in December 1972 – or so the blurb on the box had explained.

Picking the model up and holding it aloft, as if in flight, he tried to imagine what it must have been like piloting this colossal plane into hostile airspace. At least now he knew why Aimee had been so tetchy when he'd mentioned he was building it. He knew her brother had been posted missing over Vietnam; but only lately had she revealed to him the precise circumstances surrounding it. How terrible to have to live with the faintest possibility that one's brother might actually be alive somewhere. And, what's more, that it was your own father who was responsible for him being left behind (albeit that Charles Eichelberger had acted with a heavy heart and from the call of duty).

It still left him wondered if this was the real reason she kept behaving so defensively. Was there something else going on that she was not telling him about? Indeed, was she secretly seeing someone else? What Vaughan had hoped would transpire to be a beautiful romance was fast becoming an emotional minefield.

On that subject, his aunt had lately given up the pretence of conducting her affair with that flash hotelier in secret. Increasingly careless about who might see her, even a dullard like Uncle Frank must know what his wife was up to. Indeed, Vaughan was convinced that Uncle Frank *did* know. More worrying still, he'd overheard snippets of a phone call his aunt had made the other night that suggested his mother might also be in on these sordid goings-on!

In fact, the only person they had omitted to let in on this shady secret was Vaughan himself. Too appalled to shut it out of his head, but too hesitant to demand answers from them, he placed his creation back on the table and slumped back into the chair, his heart burdened with foreboding. He was beginning to wish he had never set foot on the island; and that this torrid, tawdry summer would hurry up and draw to a close.

* * * * *

The medallion-adorned crooner with the chest hair billowing over his shirt had belted out his final Tony Christie hit and taken a bow. To a smattering of applause around the smoke-filled room, this white-suited warm-up act now made haste offstage. In his place, the compère returned, cracking his usual jokes and churning out his superlative hype about tonight's star guest.

There was no doubt that Angie Ashby's twice weekly appearances were the highlight of the entertainment on offer at the Shanklin Heights Hotel. Backstage the lady in question had put the finishing touches to her finery and was now waiting in the wings. Then, having hollered his final superlative, the compère retreated and on stage she strode attired in yet another of her dazzling stage outfits.

It seldom took Angie Ashby long to work an audience. Opening with Burt Bacharach's *'I'll Never Fall In Love Again'* (the bitter-sweet signature tune to her life, she often mused), she was soon parading along the front row of tables, admonishing the wives to beware of guys who'll 'burst your bubble' (yet reluctantly conceding to their husbands sat next to them that – 'at least until tomorrow' – she had no intention of repeating what had transpired to be the biggest regret of her life).

Blinded by the powerful stage lights, this accomplished performer failed to notice one young wife looking on from the back of the room who was equally unimpressed by the web of 'lies, pain and sorrow' that her own guy had been weaving. Less so with the woman he'd been weaving them with him.

Veronica Lawton didn't normally stay behind late at the hotel, preferring to delegate the evening's chores to her 'entertainment manager' (aka the ubiquitous compère). However, tonight she'd made an exception. Making an exception to his routine too was another character who had taken upon himself the role of 'entertainment manager'.

By this point in the evening John Lawton would normally be working the tables and glad-handing the guests (especially the pretty female ones). Veronica indulged him this annoying ritual because so many of the letters of thank-you and promises to return-again-next-year that the hotel received specifically made mention of the warmth and bonhomie of its manager. Hence, with more and more people nowadays jetting off abroad for their summer breaks, she was anxious that the Shanklin Heights retain the kind of free-spending clientele who were now lapping up Angie Ashby crooning *'Bewitched, Bothered And Bewildered'*. It perhaps made up for the fact that the *de facto* manager herself was not exactly renowned for possessing the common touch. Tonight though, her husband seemed more preoccupied than usual with his research work – to the point where completing that book was becoming an obsession. Tonight it had even caused him to forgo his customary gushing welcome for the hotel's glamorous star turn.

All the while that star turn was performing her routine of ballads recounting the up-and-downs of being in love the eyes of the hotelier's jilted wife were trained upon her – pondering whether tonight would be the night that she would confront this chintzy mutton-dressed-up-as-lamb about her dalliances with her husband. She was even minded to march up on stage and snatch the microphone from her, broadcasting to her foot-tapping fans what a shameless slapper this Angie Ashby really was.

Yet what purpose would be served by creating a scene in front of all these paying guests? For whatever Veronica Lawton lacked in human warmth or sexual feeling, this shrewd and premeditating woman more than made up for in her determination to ensure nothing would jeopardise the success of the enterprise into which she had invested her time and industry. A hurried shag with a 'bewitched, bothered and bewildered' young room maid was one thing. However, she would never permit a rival to presume she might be in with a chance of getting her hands on her husband – much less on his money.

No, she *would* eliminate the threat this older woman represented – but not tonight. Instead, leaving Angie to stir those fans with a heart-tugging rendition of *'A House Is Not A Home'*, she made her way out of the hotel.

Jumping into her own red Triumph Stag convertible, she noticed that her husband's car was still in its reserved parking bay next to it. Maybe he really was hard-at-work on his latest book project. Or maybe he was waiting until the coast was clear before once again secreting his menopausal mistress to some private place where they could ravish each other. The very thought made Veronica sick in the pit of her stomach.

"Make the most of her, darling," she smirked as she drove past his Jaguar, "while you still can."

* * * * *

Aimee-Marie Eichelberger had always been a fitful sleeper – unlike her room mate and softly-snoring best friend. She glanced over at Shelby in the darkness and wished she too possessed the ability to sleep soundly – more so of late, when so many preoccupations were crowding into her head. Neither did this oppressive heat exactly aid slumber.

Eventually, she reached over to lift the alarm clock from the bedside table, studying its fluorescent-tipped digits. Then she rolled back into her pillow and stared at the ceiling, minded to pray. However, the tears that trickled from her glinting eyes were those of shame, not supplication.

After a few minutes so spent she rose from her bed. Locating her panties, she climbed into them and slithered them onto her hips. Then she located her denim pants and climbed into those too. Finally, she wrestled a T-shirt over her naked torso. As surreptitiously as she could, she then grabbed her sneakers and tiptoed over to the door, inching it open. Noting that Shelby was still fast asleep, she inched it closed behind her.

No sooner she had, an eye popped open to observe the empty bed. Then Shelby closed it tight again. At least one of the two American room maids would be praying in earnest tonight.

17

Friday, August 13th 1976

Dawn had already broken with an ochre glow by the time Northwest Airlines Flight 3208 made landfall over the United Kingdom on its long overnight flight from Minneapolis-St Paul.

Charles Eichelberger had always been a fitful sleeper – certainly since his days in the air force, when the terrors of combat had often rendered it difficult to unwind after missions. Perhaps that was why he was to be found gazing out of the window while the other passengers were still asleep – including his wife sat next to him.

Of late, other cares had crowded in: most obviously, not knowing for sure whether his son might have survived that missile strike upon his plane. To be sure, the consensus amongst the other B52 crews that had observed *Turquoise 2*'s fate was that he hadn't (indeed, only one chute was spotted emerging from what was left of the fuselage after the initial impact – its rear gunner, who had subsequently been taken prisoner).

Then there was Aimee. It was only after Lawrence's death that he had become burdened by fear for his daughter; that tragedy of some kind might similarly snatch her from him – in the manner of divine punishment. And yet it was such an irrational fear – especially for a man of profound faith, for whom the perfect love of Christ 'casteth out fear'. *"Aimee is gonna' be okay in England. The Lord will keep watch over her. You gotta' trust Him. She's gonna' be just fine,"* he recalled his wife's words.

And finally, there was England itself. Surprisingly for a man who had travelled the world with the United States Air Force, this was the first time in over thirty years that he would set foot again in the country in which he had spent two of the most heady and impressionable years of his life – and two of the most impetuous. An ocean apart from his devout German-American family, back then he had behaved like a kid let loose in a candy store. With combat intensity high and none of them knowing whether each dawn breaking would be the last they would ever see, the flyboys of the 357th had lived and loved like there would be no tomorrow. There were good reasons why Charles Eichelberger had put off making this pilgrimage to the place where he too had done his share of such 'living and loving'.

Meanwhile, the cabin crew trundling the breakfast trolleys down the aisles finally roused Natalie from her slumber. She smiled across at her husband serenely. He grinned rather less so in return before gazing back out at the clouds again.

"Coffee, sir…? Madam?" the stewardess enquired.

Her colleague rolled up a few minutes later to offer them breakfast. Though he was hungry from the exhausting flight, Charles found himself picking at it as fitfully as he had slept.

"Ladies and gentlemen, this is your captain speaking," the intercom eventually broke his contemplation. *"We will shortly be commencing our final approach to London Heathrow, so kindly return to your seats and keep your seat belts fastened until we've landed. As you can see, it's a gorgeous, sunny day out there – indeed, it's been gorgeous in England all summer. So please sit back and enjoy the views of Birmingham and the English Midlands that we're passing over. We hope you've enjoyed flying with Northwest Airlines and look forward to maybe seeing you again on your return flights."*

The retired four-star general continued to stare out of the window – mentally preparing for what the next two weeks might hold, as well as taking a good long look with foreboding at the country he had last set on eyes on as a handsome and headstrong young fighter ace in the summer of 1945.

* * * * *

"Hi, Madge."

"Warro', Nora. Looks like it's gunna' be another bostin' day again, doh' it."

The summer of 1976 would indeed be remembered for the longest spell of hot, dry and sunny weather England had ever experienced. For Nora Lewis these last few glorious weeks had meant not having to wear a coat or carry a brolly as she sauntered down the hill each morning from the council estate where she lived – greeting her neighbours in the street as they passed. It was a fifteen minute walk into Gornal village that she had made most days for the last fifteen years, ever since moving here with her ex-husband from their native Suffolk.

Nestled in a steep valley on the fringe of the industrial Black Country, Gornal possessed an insular feel at times, its people likewise. If even folk from nearby Wall Heath and Pensnett were sometimes looked upon as hailing from a foreign land, how much more so a modest lass from the other side of the country.

However, in time they had taken Nora to their hearts – and certainly the good ladies of the village had, regularly availing themselves of her talents at the hairdressing saloon on Louise Street where she worked. If you wanted your barnet cut, coloured, highlighted, permed, bobbed, shaped or generally re-invigorated, then Nora was the woman who would ensure you really did shine at that party, wedding, job interview or first date.

Alas, after today these ladies would have to make do without her styling skills – at least for the two weeks of her annual holiday. For tomorrow she would take the early bus to Wolverhampton and thence haul her suitcase aboard a train that would retrace the journey her son had made several weeks earlier.

It would be good to see Vaughan again. She missed him so much – his cheeky smile; and even his light-hearted backchat. Yet spending the summer away had been an essential step in his coming of age, she accepted. She was pleased that an important aspect of that voyage of self-discovery had been meeting and falling in love with his first proper girlfriend – and a nice Christian girl at that (or so his phone calls home had intimated).

However, Nora – of all people – knew from bitter experience that first loves don't always end in happy-ever-afters. Often there is heartache; and that sometimes more grievous and lasting repercussions can accrue from the foolish things that young people in love are want to do.

For no particular reason at that moment, she paused from fumbling with the key in the lock to stare up and observe the outline of an airliner silently carving vapour trails through that perfect blue sky above. It brought to mind a day thirty-one years earlier when she had first learned that a foolish thing she had done was going to have similar life-changing repercussions. She remembered lying back on a beach and staring up at a similar perfect blue sky, wishing that – like that gleaming plane – she could fly somewhere far, far away, leaving behind her sin and her shame. Alas, the foolish things that young people in love do.

Meanwhile – high above, and barely noticed by a little Black Country village going about its business – that airliner continued on its southward flight. Nora snapped out of her daydream and unlocked the door, stepping inside to turn about and twist the 'CLOSED' sign hanging from it around to 'OPEN'. Soon enough she would be southbound too – into the welcoming arms of her son and her big sister; but also (the real cause of that excitement mixed with trepidation) into those of someone else too; someone she had not set eyes upon in over thirty years, but whom all this time she had never forgotten.

* * * * *

A woman should always look her best – never more so than when she will be back on stage tonight endeavouring to bring a touch of magic to people's annual holidays.

When she was younger it was to her sister, Nora, who Angie had turned whenever she wanted her hair styled to impress. However, since moving to the Isle of Wight it had been to the busy salon in Lake that she had returned every few weeks so that the girls there could do the honours. It was where she was to be found again on this bright, sunny morning, speed-reading through *'Woman's Own'* while her barnet was encased in a dryer that was humming away and doing its thing.

These last few days she'd found it increasingly difficult to concentrate – and not just because the weather was turning oppressive again. Things that had been weeks in the gestation were about to come to pass. Even now she was not entirely convinced that she hadn't lifted the lid on something that threatened to open up all manner of unforeseen consequences. For the person she had been meeting up with during that time, who –

for all his foppish unflappability – she'd come to realise was a very fragile flower indeed; for her husband; for her sister; and for her beloved nephew (who would shortly have to be confronted with the outworking of his family's rash and foolish decisions).

However, there were ripples on another pond that had spanned out and were about to lap at her feet. And they had to do with the father of that flighty American girl who Vaughan was still dating, and who would today be returning to Britain for the first time in over thirty years. It was a return that she suspected he – like her – had been awaiting with profoundly mixed emotions.

* * * * *

With John away on another one of his 'research' missions to the mainland, his absence presented Veronica Lawton with the perfect opportunity to do a recce of his office – to use the sort of military jargon her husband was fond of employing. Having obtained the spare key to it from the safe, she'd waited until evening before availing herself of the moment to enter unseen into his private lair – for she was by now going out of her mind trying to second guess what he was really getting up to in here. Indeed, had he not been away this weekend she was ready to confront him with the evidence she now possessed of what he'd plainly been getting up to in his car.

Truth to tell, she was no stranger to this place, often breezing in to hand him cheques that needed counter-signing or paperwork that required his attention. Otherwise, with its photographs and paintings of military aircraft, and its shelves piled high with books and magazines about military aviation, it wasn't somewhere that she could say she felt especially welcome.

To say her husband was obsessed by planes was an understatement. Over in a corner of the office there was even one of those newfangled 'Betamax' video cassette recorders that he'd purchased and wired up to a television set (and on which she'd found him watching films and documentaries about the things too!). She switched the television on and bodged the clunky buttons on the front of the recorder. To her surprise though, when the machine sprang to life it did so instead with grainy images from John's childhood that his father had filmed. Yes, she recalled, her father-in-law had been a dab hand with his beloved Brownie sixteen-millimetre cine-camera. She recalled too her husband informing her that he was in the process of transferring these treasured mementoes onto video format – which he'd confidently predicted was the wave of the future when it came to storing moving pictures.

It peeved her that the only thing her husband didn't get up to in his office at the hotel was actually managing the place! There were times when she was convinced he'd only married her for the business acumen she'd brought to the establishment he nominally owned (and which enabled him to pass his days – and increasingly, his nights – indulging his esoteric hobby).

Infuriatingly, she tugged at the drawers to his desk only to discover they were locked; and that the only key to them was presumably the one that was on his person. The absence of the key quickly put paid to that little recce.

Casting about in frustration, she tried her luck instead with the filing cabinet. Its drawers did open – though it wasn't difficult to see why he hadn't bothered to lock them. All they contained were bulging files of notes, press cuttings and magazine articles connected with military aviation – or, more specifically, with America's air war over Indochina. Through these she now waded, puzzling at the titles he'd scribbled on the folders: *'Rolling Thunder'*; *'Barrel Roll'*; *'Arc Light'*; *'Niagara'*; *'Menu'*; *'Patio'*; *'Linebacker I'*; *'Linebacker II'*; *'Freedom Deal'*. Finally, she alighted upon a folder entitled *'Eichelberger'*.

Eichelberger? That was the surname of that American room maid who Veronica was still convinced her husband was carrying on with. So why would John want to keep a file about her hidden away amongst this bumph he'd amassed about the war in Vietnam? Desperate to learn more, she bore the folder over to his desk and laid it out in order to peruse it further.

However, far from unearthing the love letters she feared it might contain, it too was stuffed full of trivia centred upon some guy in an air force uniform. Then it clicked: Eichelberger was also the surname of the guests who were booked to stay at the luxury rooftop suite next week. So this man must be Aimee's father – the man she recalled her husband mentioning in passing that he'd been corresponding with. It was confirmed when, amongst the jumble of papers, she found a photograph of the said General Charles Francis Eichelberger USAF relaxing with his family on vacation in California – replete with his arm around some tomboyish-looking prepubescent girl who Veronica deduced to be Aimee. Even as a child that girl had mischief written all over her freckled face.

She was intrigued. However, though she leafed and leafed, it was the only picture of her that she could find inside the file. However, it did contain letters that John and her father had been exchanging, her husband effusive in his gratitude for the assistance this man had been affording him.

Suddenly, she wished she'd paid more attention to John's tedious ramblings about his latest research project. For it was only now that she recalled him mentioning something about this Eichelberger chap being an important personage in the American military. Browsing through the notes and photographs in the file, she discovered just how important: he was no less a figure than the commander who had been in overall charge of United States air power in Vietnam during the final stages of America's involvement there! Flicking through the articles and newspaper cuttings, her husband had amassed a mighty impressive dossier about the war this man had fought. There was even a heart-rending article about how his son – Aimee's brother – had been shot down over North Vietnam during Christmas 1972.

So perhaps her husband had been telling the truth when he'd pleaded that his interest in the pretty student on their payroll was motivated solely by a fascination with her famous father. Was John Lawton really such a bounder that he would screw the daughter of a man he held in such patently high esteem? And to whom he was indebted for the invaluable insights he'd been able to offer into this war her husband was busy chronicling?

Probably not, she charitably conceded. Gathering up the file she placed it back in the cabinet and shut the drawer. Then she exhaled and drifted over to spend a few moments studying that magnificent portrait of her late father-in-law that was mounted in pride of place upon the far wall of the office: Air Marshall Sir

Hugh Lawton KBE VC. With his clipped moustache and austere demeanour, he looked every inch the kind of resolute, no-nonsense figure upon whom the proud tradition of the Royal Air Force was built. Although she hadn't known him well (John's parents had been killed in a terrible traffic accident shortly after he and Veronica were married), she felt sure that somewhere deep down her husband yearned that he could have followed him into the RAF. Maybe that was why he had made it his life's work to recount the stories of men like his father. It must be kind of propitiation for having never cut it as a warrior himself.

Returning to the desk, she slumped into her husband's expensive swivel chair and spun herself to and fro in a lazy arc. As the private investigator she'd hired had insisted, there was no actual evidence that her husband was messing about with the General's daughter. But that still left Angie Ashby – the ageing songstress who she now knew he'd been meeting in secret during the last few weeks. What game was this pair up to?

It was while spinning back and forth deep in thought that her eyes focussed on the letter rack on the corner of his desk. In amongst the official-looking letterheads that were protruding from it (and which denoted tax returns she'd been badgering him to sign off), she spotted a hand-written piece of correspondence. Leaning forward and picking it out, her first instinct to assume it was another transatlantic missive from Charles Eichelberger.

However, she was mistaken. The stamp bore the Queen's head (though the postmark was too smudged to make out where it might have been posted from). Meanwhile, the handwriting on the envelope was most definitely that of a woman – and the exquisite, copperplate script of a woman raised and educated in a more decorous era at that. Teasing the floral notepaper from out of the envelope, she opened the letter out and began to read. Yet as her eyes raced down the page, so her countenance began to darken. She hurriedly twisted it over to read the second page.

Suddenly, Veronica Lawton was confronted with the terrible truth that her philandering husband most certainly was *not* the man she thought he was. Having read with her own eyes this woman's florid declaration that *'I have never ceased loving you'* and that *'not a day passes that I do not think of you'* she sank back into the chair. There she began to sob like child, clutching the note to her chest. How could John have concealed such a momentous thing from her for so long?

18

Saturday, August 14th 1976

Saturdays were always busy on the Number 16 route – especially during August. There were plenty of holidaymakers piling off the hovercraft from Southsea and milling about for connections at Ryde Bus Station to convey them to their hotels and guest houses in Sandown, Shanklin and Ventnor.

Colin and Vaughan had been obliging as best they could, their Lodekka filling to capacity on each of its visits there so far. It meant that Vaughan had been on his feet taking fares for most of his shift. The young conductor preferred it that way. At least it took his mind off other preoccupations.

This day, of all days, he should have been happy. His mother was due to arrive on the island today – the first time he would get to see her in eight long weeks. So much had happened during that time. He'd held down his first proper job; he'd made good friends; he'd discovered he could dance; and he'd fallen in love with a beautiful girl. However, it was that last little matter that was once more the cause of his melancholy.

"Blimey, mate! You like you've lost a tenner and found a sixpence," Colin picked up on this during one of the afternoon's snatched moments in the crew restroom.

Vaughan shrugged, taciturn as he often was when he was in emotional turmoil.

"Not still getting grief from that American bird, are you?"

Vaughan sighed in the affirmative, grabbing a tea.

"She's leading you a right dance. What's she been up to now?"

Colin joined his boyish workmate at a spare table, looking on in dismay as his forlorn conductor slunk down in his seat to prop his folded elbows wearily upon the table.

"She's decided it's best if we remain just friends. She told me last night. So I guess we're over – as a couple anyway."

For all his unsentimentality when it came to the opposite sex, Colin could sympathise with what the lad was going through. From the sorrow in his rich brown eyes it was obvious the love-struck young man from Dudley was struggling to work out how he could possibly revert to being 'just friends' with someone who meant the world to him – as Aimee clearly did.

"I'm sorry, mate. Look, I don't wish to sound harsh; but life goes on. You need to just forget her – plenty of fish in the sea and all that. Anyway, why don't you try your luck with her best mate instead? What's her name...?"

"You mean Shelby?"

"That's her. I tell you, I'm prepared to put money on her having a soft spot for you. You see, I was watching her that night we first met up in the disco. She was definitely staring at you and wishing. You should've listened to me. Did I not tell you to take the short one? But no, you had to go for the leggy one, didn't you – the mixed-up bird who's been giving you aggro ever since."

Sipping on his tea, Vaughan shot Colin an inscrutable glance, unsure whether he was just prattling on for the purpose of lifting his spirits; or whether Shelby might really be interested in him in the way he was suggesting. It was a tempting thought – though it didn't lessen the hurt he was feeling at that moment.

"She's quite a pretty thing, she is. She's certainly got one cracking arse on her," Colin pined, recalling those snatched moments when he'd got to squeeze it. Then, huffing as if to dismiss wounded pride that Shelby had politely rebuffed his advances, he added "But she's not *my* type... if you know what I mean. In fact, between you and me," he leaned in as if to divulge a secret, "she's sounds a bit of a religious nutter. You know: all that bible-bashin' nonsense. I dare say she'd expect a ring on her finger before she'd let a bloke so much as glimpse her muff!"

Vaughan was indignant. How dare Colin make light of her deeply-held beliefs; or mock that she would want to preserve the ultimate act of intimacy for her wedding night. Then the shameful realisation struck him: why had he allowed the light of his own Christian faith to languish 'under a bushel', as it were – in contrast to Shelby's, which shone so brightly for all to see? To date, he'd offered only oblique evidence to his colleagues that he too claimed Jesus Christ as his Saviour. He yearned for the courage to 'take up his cross' and openly share his faith – as Shelby clearly had no problem doing.

Much too quickly the time rolled around for them to head back to their bus and take their next journey out. While Vaughan collected up the cups to take back to the servery, Colin turned and made for the exit. As he did so, the door burst open and in raced Tina Brown, who only narrowly avoided colliding into him – or rather two prominent parts of her anatomy almost did.

"'Ere, you wanna' watch where you're going with those things. They could do some damage!" Colin suggested, staring down at them as they nestled inside her blouse.

"Cheeky!" she scowled. "Anyway, come out of me' way, will yer'. I'm desperate for a wee; and I've got all of four minutes before I'm due out."

"Running hither and thither like a woman demented? I would have thought it's more like a sign you're due on!"

She scowled again, unceremoniously bundling him aside as she raced over to the ladies' room. However, she was not so desperate that she didn't halt at the door to remark upon the glum countenance of Colin's fellow crewman.

"Yes, it's that bird of his. She's given him the elbow," Colin called over by way of a presumptive explanation.

"Oh, Vaughan! I'm so sorry," her face sank, her hand still hanging on the door handle. "But remember what I said about always being able to confide your problems in your 'Auntie Tina'. Listen, the guys are off out to some party this Friday coming; and Sally has a date with her new boyfriend. So I shall be in all by myself. If you still need to chat to someone – or just want a shoulder to cry on – you feel free to call by."

And with that generous invitation she hurried inside the loo. Meanwhile, Vaughan noticed his driver, hands sunk in pockets, loitering by the exit and giving him that knowing look.

"She's a pretty thing too," Colin winked. "And I'm sure you don't need me to tell you what she's got that's cracking!"

* * * * *

With his shift finished, Vaughan cycled home from the depot. Putting his bike away in the shed, he then mounted the verandah steps to be wolf-whistled by his favourite feathered friend.

"I shall miss you when I go home, Chico," he said, once more taking the time to run his finger through the feathers that the bird had pressed expectantly against the cage.

"I just wish the girl I love was as constant in her affection as you are," the lovelorn conductor then sighed.

All this time, sitting in Vaughan's favourite easy chair, a homely woman with sable blow-waved hair could barely restrain her tears as she beheld teenage boy and parrot in perfect communion. She marvelled a while longer until the boy spotted her at last. She rose from the chair and was ready when he bounded over to launch his arms around her tightly.

"Mom!"

They broke to gaze thankfully into each other's eyes. Perhaps Vaughan was not the only Lewis who had been troubled by recurring nightmares about losing someone special.

"I love you, Mom. I've missed you so much."

"I've missed you too."

"And I never want to lose you," he whimpered, the closest he came to confessing that nightmare.

"Don't be silly. You won't lose me. I'll always be your…" she stalled before offering him a faux dismissive smile. Then she rubbed her soft knuckles up and down his cheek. "I'll always be here for you. You know that."

* * * * *

It was just like old times. Frank, Angie, Nora and Vaughan all gathered around the dining table in the spacious sitting room, exchanging family gossip and catching up on what they'd each been up to in the four years that had passed since they'd last been gathered around it. Yet although on the surface it was a joyful occasion, Vaughan thought he could detect an undercurrent of something that he couldn't quite put his finger on.

Perhaps aware that he was studying them with searching eyes, Angie broached a subject that, out of his own sense of deflation, he had purposely not mentioned so far.

"So tell us, how are you and Aimee getting on?"

"Ah, yes. She's that girl you're going out with," said Nora.

Vaughan's downcast expression answered the question even before he opened his mouth to admit that "We're not any more. Well, we're just friends. It's all she wants us to be."

Angie's first instinct was to damn the girl for stringing him along. However, an almost visible flush of relief instead belied her thankfulness that their erratic relationship was at an end.

"Oh, well. Maybe it's for the best," she said, topping up each of their glasses with what was left of the Beaujolais. "I was loathed to say it before; but there's something about that girl that unsettles me. She's definitely not the one for you, Vaughan."

He said nothing, reluctant to challenge her disappointing observation. For her part, Angie looked up and could detect the troubled look in his glinting brown eyes.

"And before you say anything, it's not because you're not good enough for her. On the contrary, I think *she's* not good enough for *you*. You deserve better, Vaughan – a girl who will treat you right and not toy with your affections the way she has. Why don't you ask her friend out instead? What's her name…?

"Shelby."

"That's her. She seems a much more genuine and down-to-earth character. She's a Christian too," Angie then noted for Nora's benefit (her sister smiling approvingly).

That was twice in one day that someone had told him he had made a wrong choice. What's more, he couldn't deny that he liked Shelby – more so in the time he'd been able to get to know her better. Yet it hurt too much to simply let go of Aimee, who had enthralled him from the moment he'd first set eyes on her. Meanwhile, his mother slid a hand across the table to tenderly fondle his own.

"It can be difficult to forget about someone you have feelings for," she observed, "But you do what I've been telling you to do: pray. Lay it before the Lord, Vaughan. Let Him lead you to who He wants you to be with – and in His own good time."

* * * * *

Sunday, August 15th 1976

> "...The 'peace movement' was hastily put together after an IRA suspect who was being chased by British soldiers ploughed his car into a young family, killing four children – including a six week-old baby in its pram. Their distraught aunt, Mairead Corrigan, later went on television with her friend, Betty Williams, to make an impassioned appeal for peace. Yesterday, answering their call, over ten thousand women from across Northern Ireland – both Catholics and Protestants – marched through Belfast to demand an end to violence in the Province..."

Uncle Frank was absorbed in his usual Sunday evening catch-up of the week's news. However, he was not so absorbed that he hadn't already bounced out of his chair more than once, wandering over to the window to anxiously spy his nephew brooding alone in that sun-drenched verandah.

Sitting back down again, he switched channel in time to watch Viv Richards flick another four-stump ball though midwicket. Beneath a baking hot sun at the Fifth Test, the visitors' master batsman was systemically taking the English bowling apart, cracking the ball off to all four corners of The Oval's parched brown boundary. By the time his innings had topped two hundred runs, the West Indian crowd was exuberant with delight.

However – to the surprise of both Angie (engrossed in her paperback romance) and Nora (engrossed in her knitting) – Frank stood to his feet and switched the television off. Then, without saying a word, he wandered out of the room, leaving his disbelieving wife and sister-in-law to stare at each other and marvel at the sudden silence.

"What's wrong, son," he enquired, seating himself down in the chair opposite his sullen nephew. While waiting for a response, he craned to observe Chico nibbling at a piece of fruit.

"Girl trouble?" his gaze returned, trying again.

This time Vaughan thought it rude to do other than nod his head and frown in frustration. Frank stood to his feet again, this time to stretch while loosening his collar (the taciturn ex-matelot born of a generation that felt underdressed if not wearing a tie – even on a stifling day like today).

"Goodness, it's hot in here. I thought you'd be in the sea again by now – cooling down on that lilo I gave you," he suggested, training his eyes in the direction of the beach. Then he looked down at his nephew and tilted his head in that direction too.

"Come on, son. Let's take a walk."

Vaughan felt compelled to follow after his uncle as he led him across the road. As they strolled along Sandown High Street, both of them hands-in-pocket, he could see Uncle Frank was angling to commence some kind of man-to-man talk with him. He halted the lad outside Tring's Toys to gaze at the goodies on display in the window. Then he stared up proudly at the sign above.

"You know, I've built this business up from nothing. When I arrived on the island fifteen years ago I noticed that – aside from the beachfront bucket-and-spade stalls – there was nowhere in town that sold children's toys. So I thought: that's what I'll do. I'll set up a toy shop and fill a gap in the market – a proper toy shop selling dolls, little girls' prams, train sets... And model ships and planes too – because I knew there were plenty of boys like my favourite nephew who liked making them."

"I hope I've lost none of my skill, Uncle," Vaughan shot him a hopeful smile.

"You haven't. That jet bomber you've put together is fantastic. Rather than risk breaking it by squeezing it in your suitcase when you go home, I was rather hoping you'd let me have it to mount on display in this window – to impress other boys who might be tempted to buy a model plane from Tring's Toys. And when I open up the shop each morning I can see it hanging there and think: 'Vaughan made that'. It will remind me of that special time you spent with us during the long, hot summer of 1976."

Vaughan smiled again. "Of course you can keep it, Uncle. Besides, Mum will almost certainly break it when she's whizzing around my bedroom with the duster!"

His uncle smiled too – one of those awkward, yet touching smiles that he recalled he would don whenever he'd been amused or impressed by something his nephew had said or done. They continued walking, crossing the street to head for the pier.

"You know, it's fashionable nowadays to look down upon men like me – ordinary guys who work hard to create a business; and whose taxes pay for all these big ideas that governments have for doing this, that or the other. I might seem boring to you, son, compared to all these pop stars and footballers who we keep being told are 'successful'. But I hope you'll understand that I too have been successful – even if it's not the kind of success you get to read about in the newspapers."

"You've certainly made a lot of little boys and girls on the island very happy – including a certain 'big boy' too," Vaughan chuckled, recalling how this costive, bottled-up character remained generous to a fault when it came to indulging his nephew with items from his toy shop.

"So what's the story with this American girl then?" his uncle probed as they wandered onto the pier and through the amusement arcade, with its blaring cacophony of sounds.

"I know Auntie Angie is trying to make me look on the bright side. But I really do think I've been a fool to ever believe I could win the heart of a general's daughter who has travelled all over the world and been to Oxford University."

"That doesn't make her a better person than you, son. Deep down she's probably labouring under all manner of insecurities of her own, of which you know nothing. 'Frank,' as my best mate in the navy always used to say to me, 'it makes no difference whether you're an admiral or an able seaman – we're all a little bit mad; and we all crap out of the same hole'!"

Vaughan laughed, the touch of salty humour further bonding a concerned uncle with a nephew in need of his spirits lifting. On they strolled, past the children's carousels, until they reached the relative tranquillity to be found at the end of the pier. There they found a spot along the railings where they could gaze out to sea.

"I say, that's *HMS Sheffield*, is it not – the Royal Navy's newest destroyer," said Frank, straining to identify a sleek grey shape that was making haste along the horizon.

"You're right. She's probably returning from an exercise somewhere," Vaughan suggested. "She's certainly an impressive ship. We saw her the other day on the boat excursion around Portsmouth Harbour."

"It's unusual for a warship to be exercising on a Sunday. Perhaps her captain really is putting his men through their paces. You know, I've come across a few officers like that in my time: ones who are so determined to whip their crews into shape that they drive them to the verge of mutiny. I remember there was this one officer on a cruiser I served aboard who was a right slave driver. He pushed the men in his detail so hard that one of them became flustered and accidentally discharged a torpedo. The poor bugger nearly sank the flagship, he did!" his uncle roared.

"Anyway, we digress," he insisted, returning to the matter in hand, "Your aunt's right though. Maybe this Aimee has done you a favour – even though it doesn't seem that way. But in years to come you'll thank her. She shouldn't have to feel she has to stick around with you out of a sense of guilt; or a fear of hurting you. The mistakes made by remaining in a relationship out of duty or obligation are sometimes the ones people end up regretting the most. That's been my experience," he observed cryptically.

"And whatever you do, don't go dating that other girl on the rebound. That was where your aunt made her big mistake. She'd just broken up with some American guy who'd promised to marry her, but who'd scurried back to the States instead. It's probably the reason why she's never had much time for Yanks," he huffed. "Me?" he then added in a rare baring of his soul, "I guess I felt sorry for her and wanted to help put her world back together again. I so wanted to be her knight-in-shining-armour."

Then Vaughan watched his uncle lean on the railings and stare out to sea with a distant expression, insisting that – in words his jilted nephew could readily empathise with – "I was totally bowled over by her the moment I first set eyes on her. She was such a stunningly beautiful woman back then. She still is now. She was a far better catch, or so I thought, than a modest little man like me deserved – a humble sailor with absolutely no singing talent and no real appreciation of the dreams she still cherished for the fame and success that had eluded her.

"No sooner we were married we realised we'd both made a terrible mistake. We wanted different things. Yet here we were: two mismatched people trapped in boring domesticity. She was still hankering after greater things. I was head-strong and adventurous in other ways – though you must find that hard to believe, looking at me now," he was self-effacingly honest.

"So how come you and Auntie Angie have stuck together this long? Why didn't you just go your separate ways – as my parents did?" Vaughan felt bold enough to wonder aloud.

"We very nearly did," Frank turned and confessed before gazing out to sea again. "We've had our ups-and-downs. In fact, there were times when things were very down indeed. But, well... you could say we eventually found a way of rubbing along. In time, your aunt managed to restart her singing career, entertaining audiences at holiday venues around the island. I threw myself into making a success of Tring's Toys. Perhaps I threw myself into it a little too much at times. Looking back, I accept I may not have paid my wife the attention she deserved. And I haven't always attended to her womanly needs."

It was a painful admission that Vaughan feared might have come too late for his uncle to put right. If indeed he possessed the will to put it right; for the naïve young man found it both baffling and scary to think that this *modus vivendi* that Uncle Frank had alluded to might even now include tacit acceptance that Auntie Angie had 'womanly needs' that could only be attended to by another man – and a much younger man at that!

"Your aunt is a good woman with a good heart. I'm grateful that she stood by me – despite all my faults and failures. And yes, I do love her – in a funny old way. I hope she'd say the same about me too."

"I'm sure she would, Uncle," Vaughan sought to assure him – even as he pondered just how 'funny' that 'old way' had proved. Then he watched his uncle lift himself away from the railings, morbid introspection banished as his tone lifted to match,

"Anyway, coming back to this young lady of yours," he said, "just remember that, when it comes to women, all that glitters isn't gold. I suppose it's only to be expected that the eyes of an impatient young man like you will be drawn to the fancy ones; the ones with the gorgeous legs," (Vaughan instinctively thought of Aimee), "or the shapely behinds," (ditto Shelby), "or the impressive you-know-whats," (ditto Tina – who else!). "But if you're looking for a soul mate with whom you can spend the rest of your life – someone who will prove a loyal and dependable wife, and a loving mother to your children – then you need to go for the girls who possess those noble qualities that aren't immediately obvious when you're eyeing them up across a crowded disco; the kind of qualities that only become apparent once you've taken the time to get to know a girl as a friend – before you even think about sleeping with her. In fact, the kind of inner beauty that your mother possesses... not that Nora isn't beautiful on the outside too, you understand."

The youngster was demonstrably gladdened, for Uncle Frank had unwittingly alighted upon the living embodiment of everything that Vaughan was looking for in that elusive 'soul mate'. His mother did indeed treat people right (few people had a bad word to say about her). She had indeed been a loyal and dependable wife (it was not her fault that the man she loved had deserted her – and deserted their child too!). She'd also proved a loving mother – the best mother a boy could ever ask for, and he wouldn't swap her for the world (not even for his Auntie Angie – the only woman who came close to her in his esteem). And, of course – despite fast approaching her fiftieth birthday – she was indeed an outstandingly beautiful woman in a wonderfully natural and unpretentious way (though it helped that she worked at a hairdressing and beauty salon!).

Vaughan was grateful for his uncle's sage advice. He might be a man of few words most of the time. Yet when he did open his heart and speak with conviction – as he had this afternoon – what he had to say was always worth listening to.

Recalling how cold and dismissive his own father had been towards him, it was at times like these that Vaughan considered it a crying shame that Uncle Frank and Auntie Angie had never been blessed with children of their own.

19

Monday, August 16th 1976

How this place had changed. Where once this stretch of the Suffolk coast had been a heavily-fortified camp fronted by gun emplacements, barbed wire and tank traps, today it was once more a peaceful seaside hamlet – albeit one now dominated by a huge nuclear power station. All that remained to remind sightseers of Sizewell's wartime past were the odd rusting remnants of those defences that had survived the ravages of time, dotted amidst the sandy grasslands aback its expansive beach.

Having strolled here from their hotel in nearby Leiston, Charles Eichelberger had left his wife chatting to a British couple they'd met on a bench overlooking the beach. Ever the quintessential talkative American, surely Natalie retelling her life story would enable him to disappear long enough to confirm something that had been bugging him. Sure enough, he had not walked far along that grassy foreland before he encountered what he was looking for. Standing there gazing at it for a moment, he was strangely unsure whether to feel relieved or chastened – for this particular crumbling concrete pillbox was more than just a forlorn reminder of a world that had once been at war.

First making certain of his footing, he stepped down into the hollow and trudged up to it, casting his eyes over it with a mixture of awe and unease. Then, for the first time since an unforgettable evening in May 1945, he placed a steadying hand upon the portal and stared inside.

A shaft of bright sunlight was streaming in through the aperture where once a sentry had kept watch. By it, he could observe the sand that had blown in and gathered in its recesses, as well as the graffiti that covered its walls. There were discarded cans and bottles aplenty. A whiff of human faeces filled his nostrils. Meanwhile, here and there, the unmistakable evidence of fumbled teenage love-making could be spotted. *Plus ça change*, the General shook his head in wry amusement.

Unable to resist the temptation to close his eyes and reminisce, he recalled how, without saying a word, those eyes had once signalled her lips to receive his own, the torrid searching of their tongues quickly supplemented by hands that had raced about loosening clothing and touching forbidden places.

It was too much to bear. Eyes opened and welling up with tears, he dragged his face away and fixed his gaze instead upon that monolithic power station, biting at his knuckle as he tried in vain to muffle his sorrow.

"I'm sorry…! Jesus…! I am so sorry…!"

His lachrymose utterance was not a crude profanity – far from it. Instead, this illustrious man was again imploring the God he served to forgive a most fateful sin – a secret sin the knowledge of which (his God aside) only one other person in this world was party to. Yet if that moment of weakness had been gnawing at the General's conscience for over thirty years, how much more so had that all-too-brief moment changed forever the life of a young English girl who had likewise been 'weak' that night. Meanwhile, out there somewhere might be a young man or woman who remained oblivious to the part that weakness had played in bringing him or her into the world nine months later.

Charles Eichelberger had been able to walk away from his sin. Returning home a hero, he had gone on to marry and raise a family. In time, his glittering military career had culminated with him commanding the most awesome mission the United States Air Force had ever undertaken. Meanwhile, with America smarting from its post-Vietnam crisis of confidence, there were those in his party who were pressing him to render one final service to his country: to run for the White House in 1980.

Yet, unable to publicly confess his sin or to unravel its consequences, this would-be president considered himself a fraud. This supremely decorated airman, this stalwart of the Republican Party, this iconic embodiment of American Christian values, was concealing a secret that, if revealed, would soil (or at worst negate) every good thing he had ever achieved, and every noble belief he had ever held. As such, Charles Eichelberger was still very much a prisoner of his past.

"Hey, where'd you get to?" his wife could only guess when he eventually returned to the car park, rejoining her on the bench long after that kindly British couple had resumed their hike.

"Gee, honey. You okay?" she probed, the sarcasm of her initial remark giving way to concern that he appeared to have passed his absence in the company of a ghost.

"Yeah, yeah!" he snapped and nodded his head insistently. "It's just that some of the places we've been visiting these last few days have kinda' brought back a lot of memories."

"That figures. And not always pleasant ones, I would imagine. Listen, those folks I got talking to told me that if you wonder along this coast you can come across all manner of abandoned wartime structures."

"Really?"

Having been patiently awaiting his return, it appeared that Natalie was about to inveigle her husband with a regurgitation of everything she'd discussed with her newfound acquaintances while he'd been off tramping the dunes. Therefore, remembrance of those times – or, more precisely, one memory in particular – stirred him to halt her in her tracks.

"Listen, Nat. There's something I gotta' tell you," he interrupted her.

She was all ears, alarmed to observe that this 'something' was clearly agitating him.

"You see, those years in England – while we were apart – well, I wasn't... I mean, I didn't... Oh heck, what do I mean?" he screwed his face up in frustration, twisting this way and that on the bench and clutching at his wiry grey hair as if his head was about to explode. Then he settled on grabbing Natalie's shoulders, determined she should look him in the eye.

"There *were* others. I mean, we were Yankee airmen who weren't short of the odd dime or two. It was inevitable that English girls would want to hang out with us. Look, what I'm trying to say is..."

"You're trying to tell me you dated an English girl... or maybe English girls?" she rounded off his confession for him.

"Yes," he exhaled – and with it his agitation subsiding. "I guess that's exactly what I'm trying to tell you."

She stared at him long and hard for several agonising seconds. Then she huffed, shook her head, and lowered his hands, guiding them into her lap instead.

"Charles Eichelberger – did you think I was born yesterday?" she marvelled. "I worked that one out a long time ago."

"You have? I mean, you did?"

"To tell you the truth, I guess it's high time I made a confession of my own. Do you remember that boy who used to work in the drug store on the corner of West St Germain and Fourteenth?"

Charles nodded. "Earl Wagner's kid, wasn't he?"

"That's him. Well, while you were gone he and I used to walk to church together most Sundays. He never said much. I guess he just enjoyed the company of someone who cared to listen to what few things he did say. Some of the other girls on the block used to think he was a bit goofy; but I guess he was just shy.

"Well, by-and-by he received his draft notice. He stopped by to see me one evening when my folks were out. I remember it was a bitterly cold night. Look, I know I shouldn't have; but I took pity on him and invited him in. He was kinda' at a loose end. He'd received orders to report to camp the following day. Once or twice he'd told me he thought I'd make a wonderful wife. That night he came right out and said it: he wanted me to be *his* wonderful wife! Well, one thing led to another and ... we kissed."

She sneaked the verb out as if grudgingly owning up to the crime-of-the-century. Thereupon, she dipped her eyes in shame. All the time, her husband was sporting a disbelieving, if visibly underwhelmed look.

"You kissed?"

"We kissed. I mean, I told him about you and me; how you were serving over in England. And that you'd promised to come back at war's end and marry me. But..."

"You kissed?" he repeated, just to be sure he'd heard correctly.

"We kissed. And that was all we did, I promise. Next day he shipped out. The next I heard he got killed in the Philippines. His folks never got over the news. He was their only child. A shy, nineteen year-old boy who never got to know the love of a woman; or the wonder of a godly marriage – the closest he ever came that stolen kiss with his pastor's daughter. War can be so exceedingly cruel. It's why I've always hated it.

"Listen, Charles," she tugged their joined hands as if to emphasise what she was about to say, "the Bible tells us *'all have sinned and fallen short of the glory of God'*. You and I are no different. I was human. I'm sure you were too. That's why I really don't want to know what happened while you were over here. We were all young and foolish back then. But *'in Christ we are new creations'*. *'The old has gone; behold all things have become new'*," she asserted, quoting Scripture from memory. "So let's not dwell on what went on while we were apart. The Lord has blessed us with over thirty years of wonderful marriage; and given us two amazing children – even if, for reasons we may never know, one of them He chose to call home to Himself when he too was still young – and most probably foolish too."

He was visibly moved by this resumé of their story together – the kind of thankful testimony she'd probably offered that couple she'd earlier been sat beside on the bench. Maybe Natalie was right: instead of treating their vacation in England as an excuse to wallow in the mistakes of the past, perhaps he should look upon it as an opportunity to offer up those mistakes to Christ's atoning blood, which could indeed make all things new. In two days time they would get to embrace their daughter for the first time in a many months. Till then he offered up a silent prayer for Aimee's safekeeping – as he had done every night since her brother's untimely death. He would rededicate himself anew to his marriage and to his sole remaining child – the daughter he had oft times overlooked, but who he now yearned to tell in person just how deeply she was loved.

* * * * *

Sunset on a becalmed Solent: with its glassy sea, lush crimson sky and fiery amber sun dipping below the western horizon, John Lawton had never before witnessed one as striking as this. Absent the gentle humming of the car ferry thrusting its way towards the island side of the water, there was nothing to disturb the tranquillity with which he and the other passengers on deck were now contemplating this awesome natural canvas.

Truth to tell, he was troubled by what that sky might portend. The pensive Etonian recalled the classics he'd read, and how – according to Ancient Greek mythology – when Typhon was defeated in his quest for mastery of the cosmos Zeus condemned him to become a raging volcano demon, spewing forth fire that had turned the heavens blood red. Lawton pondered whether his own licentious challenge to the gods might be about to similarly unleash a typhoon of deadly consequences, of which this dramatic blood red sky was a herald.

Certainly, he had the sense that things were coming to a head. He'd been in London all weekend, undertaking some final research for his latest book. However, never one to pass up the opportunity for a spot of sensual diversion, he'd spent the night with Sophie, taking advantage of her husband conveniently being in Washington on MoD business. And yet some sixth sense had alerted him to the possibility that someone was trailing his movements. If not, what to make of the car with driver sat inside that he'd spotted parked across the street from her apartment when he'd arrived – both car and bored-looking driver still there when Lawton had peered around the curtains before he and Sophie had retired to bed? Had someone made it their business to find out what the wife of one of the country's most senior and politically-sensitive civil servants was getting up to?

More pressing, in a few days time Charles Eichelberger and his wife would be arriving on the island. He was aware that their daughter viewed her parents' intended stay with mixed feelings. Yet while Lawton himself was looking forward to meeting her famous father in the flesh for the first time, it was unfortunate that his presence would coincide with an even more pressing matter that he'd set aside this week to resolve; one that bizarrely looked set to draw into the reckoning that gormless young bus conductor that Aimee had been haphazardly dating.

Furthermore, ahead of it he'd decided that the time was ripe for apprising his wife of the liaisons he'd been conducting with Angie Ashby. He tried to convince himself that he should feel relieved that his shameful secret would be out in the open at last. There would no longer be any need for ridiculous subterfuge. He felt sure that once the initial shock of what he had to reveal had subsided then Veronica would understand.

It pained him to reflect that theirs had turned out to be such a loveless, if supremely functional union. Of the many spats this had occasioned before their marriage had discovered its sullen equilibrium, he recalled his beautiful, if temperamental wife raging at him for being 'an utter bastard'. He smirked as he watched that blood red sun finally disappear below the horizon. Just a few more days and she would appreciate the irony of her observation.

* * * * *

Tuesday, August 17th 1976

These last few days the temperature had started nudging back up into the low nineties Fahrenheit – close to where it had sat day after day during those record-breaking three weeks at the end of June and early July. Neither was there any sign of rain. Indeed, parts of southern England hadn't experienced a single drop of the stuff for over forty days. As a result, many rivers had dried up. Even 'Old Man Thames' had been reduced to a shadow of its usual flow, with boats along its Middlesex reaches left high and dry on mud banks baked solid by the unrelenting weather.

For Aimee and Shelby the merciless heat rendered mopping floors and making beds a chore made bearable only by the knowledge that if they put their backs into it and finished their rounds early then another long afternoon on the beach beckoned. Indeed, cooling down in the sea was the only respite to be found now that water rationing had closed the hotel's swimming pool.

However, it wasn't just the weather that had made conversation between these two normally garrulous room maids a chore as well. They were increasingly drifting apart. No longer was Shelby willing to play counsellor (much less 'second dad') to a friend and fellow believer who was hell-bent on shipwrecking her faith; who had treated with contempt a wonderful young man who had done her no wrong; and whom she suspected was keeping secrets from her. This morning the dismayed Georgian could be found taking her frustration out upon the bathroom floor, across which she was aggressively wielding her mop.

Shelby's agitation had not gone unnoticed by her friend (who was meanwhile playing out her own frustration wrestling with an uncooperative fitted sheet that didn't want to be fitted). To be sure, Aimee felt guilty that she'd hurt Vaughan. But the die was cast. Maybe it was for the best that both he and Shelby would be distanced from the terrible thing she had become caught up in (and that she feared they might yet discover).

Eventually, Aimee could bear the heat no longer and broke from her exertions to step out onto the balcony. Tugging out the barrette with which she'd swept it back, she shook her hair free and glanced up at the cloudless skies. Upon lowering her gaze – and out of the corner of her eye – she spotted that familiar white Jaguar parked in its reserved bay in the parking lot below.

He was back.

* * * * *

Wednesday, August 18th 1976

> *"That is incredible! Michael Holding – eight wickets for ninety-two runs... Surely England must be asking themselves who's 'grovelling' now..."*

Nora glanced up from clicking her knitting needles, noting the mortified expression on her brother-in-law's face as he witnessed the West Indian they called the 'Whispering Death' bowl out yet another English batsman during the Final Test at The Oval.

Frank Tring had seen enough! As the clock chimed six o'clock, he switched channel to catch the opening jingle of *'BBC Nationwide'*. As he did, Nora thought she'd better lay aside her knitting and see if Angie needed help preparing the evening meal. Her sister seemed to have been gone an inordinate length of time.

However, crossing the hall into the kitchen there was no sign of her – and no sign of the meal being prepared either. Only

Wings' *'Silly Love Songs'* quietly playing on her transistor radio offered a clue that the kitchen had been visited. It was only when Nora wandered down the hall that she caught sight of her sister at last – sitting on her bed, transfixed by a small velvet box that she was holding open in her hand. In an instant, Nora recognised the symbolic token it contained. She slipped herself onto the bed alongside Angie and drew an arm around her shoulder.

"I absolutely adored that man, Nora," Angie snuffled, staring at the ring.

"I know you did."

"I would have gone to the ends of the Earth to be with him – even to St Cloud, Minnesota!"

Her wry admission coaxed a sorrowful smile from Nora, who hauled her big sister in close. It was while Angie's head was rested against hers that tears began to fall. Nora was shocked to discover that the memory of being jilted was as painful as it had been over thirty years ago – when Nora had first witnessed her sister wrestling with the realisation that Charles Eichelberger was not going to be taking her home to St Cloud after all.

"Why did he do it? Why did he make all those promises to me if he never intended to keep them? What could possibly have gotten into his head to make him just abandon me? I could have lived with him being killed over Germany. It would have been hard; but at least there would have been closure – some purpose to my grief; some nobler reason why I had to be denied his love. But for him to survive the war... only to then wash his hands of me completely – as if I had never existed?"

Nora so wanted to cry with her grief-stricken sibling. However, she silenced her own snuffling and tried to fashion an answer that might balm this hurt and anger that her sister had never let go of.

"I suspect he may have had a girl already waiting for him back in America. It happened quite a lot, you know. Remember Joanie Butler? She was engaged to a sergeant from the base who it turned out had been two-timing his fiancée in Baltimore."

True enough – upon which Angie recalled what Aimee had said about her father having all along had a 'sweetheart' who he'd later married – her mother! Yet if so, why had he promised to marry *her* – when she'd never pressed the subject herself during the whole nine months they had been going out together?

"It makes no sense. Yet thinking back now, something changed during those final weeks we were together – around about VE Day if I remember rightly. I'd not been able to make it back to Leiston that day. I was singing with the band at a celebratory concert in London."

"Yes, we all missed you. We had a super time at the street party," Nora explained. Unseen by her sister, she closed her eyes as if to implore that the events of that momentous day not be brought to her remembrance.

"I've never been able to put my finger on it; but something suddenly made him impatient to leave England – and, more tellingly, to never return."

"But he has returned," Nora reminded her, aware that before that box clock in the living room chimed midnight tonight, both Charles Eichelberger and the woman he had gone on to marry would have retired to a hotel bed just a few miles from this very spot. How chilling that a family holiday that Nora and Angie had intended would serve as the opportunity to exorcise one ghost from the past had been complicated, first by the chance discovery in their midst of a second ghost; and now by the completely unexpected return of a third and far more troubling spectre.

"I still hate that man, Nora," Angie gnashed. "I know you Christians are always telling us to forgive; but I hate him. I hate him! I hate him! I HATE HIM!" she screamed, slamming the velvet box shut and hurling it across the room.

Wrestling to bring Angie's flailing arms under control, Nora gripped her sister tight and hushed her voluble wailing.

"You must forgive him, Angie. You can't go on carrying all this bitterness inside. You have suffered long enough. Let go of it. Trust me, only forgiving him will finally liberate you."

"I suppose that's the only consolation," Angie exhaled, calming down sufficiently for her observation to pass for more purposeful reflection. "Perhaps his presence here on the island is your God's way of confronting Charles Eichelberger with just how profoundly he is still destroying our family. And I intend to be the one who is going to confront him."

"*Still* destroying?" Nora's eyes suddenly flashed wide. "And what do you mean: *our* family?"

"Yes – *still*. I hate him because of what that daughter of his has done to *our* family too. My God, she's a chip of the old block, if ever there was. For she has done to my... to your..." she shuddered in frustration before settling upon "... to *our* Vaughan exactly what her father once did to me – shattered the poor boy's heart and then walked away as if it was nothing at all.

"Mark my words, Nora, before this summer is over I intend to find out the truth about why Charles Eichelberger walked away from me and left my own heart in a million tiny pieces. He owes me that much at least."

At that moment, Nora could think of no answer she could give that would beg her to desist from such a vengeful and nihilistic obsession – except to perhaps extol the virtue of forgiveness once more. However, she said nothing. Besides, tomorrow there was a much more pressing matter that they needed to resolve.

20

Thursday, August 19th 1976

The morning had dawned warm and bright again. It was going to be yet another scorching day. Would this blazing summer ever end – and with it the craziness that it had induced in people?

John Lawton jumped into his car and started it up, turning up the air-conditioning as if the chill might dispel his own prolonged season of craziness. Indeed, nothing he had seen or done during his eventful thirty years on this planet had ever prepared him for what he was about to do now. He could only close his eyes and offer up the prayer of the otherwise impious that someone somewhere up there knew how that life would pan out. And to what purpose it would ultimately have been lived.

When he opened those eyes, he glanced up to observe Veronica gazing down at him from an upstairs corridor window. She was offering him a rare tender smile. She accepted too that he had to do this. Who knew: if he could only get it out of his system then he might actually return from this afternoon's encounter a more rounded and contrite individual.

The short drive into Sandown took longer than usual in the traffic. By the time John had parked up in Victoria Road he was already late. He hated being late – whether for business meetings, research assignments, or extra-marital trysts. It was a product of his 'military' upbringing, he liked to joke. However, before stepping out of the car he reached into his pocket to lift a small photograph of his parents from his wallet. They had been good to him, he reflected: strict, but fair; and loving and generous with their encouragement. He still missed them terribly. Neither would he ever forget how they had offered him a chance in life that had bucked the circumstances of his coming into this world. He gave thanks and inserted the photograph back into the wallet.

Angie was already waiting on the verandah when he wandered up. She was stooping and – through the bars of its cage – was gently trailing her painted fingers along the battleship grey plumage of some parrot.

"Sorry I'm late."

"It's okay. No rush. You're here now – and that's all that matters," she stood erect and replied, unfazed.

"Is your husband likely to disturb us?"

"No. He won't be back until six. He tends not to shut the shop for lunch during the holiday season."

"Good. I mean, well..."

"He knows," was all Angie needed to say.

"Good. And Vaughan?"

"Not until this afternoon."

"And he knows?"

"No. But he will... before the day is over."

"Good. I'm glad about that too."

"Shall we go inside?"

John swallowed the lump in his throat and nodded.

"Cor! Sex!" Chico meanwhile interjected, the talkative avian perhaps aware something eventful was about to take place.

Amused, John sidled up to the cage and marvelled at the bird. Angie thought the remark funny too.

"Astute bird, eh," he smirked.

Thereupon, Angie reached out a hand to take him by his fingertips and lead him over the portal of her flat. Once inside, she led him into the sitting room, where she bade him make himself at home upon the sofa.

"Nervous?" she continued their laconic discourse.

"A little," he stared up at her with bright blue eyes that even so conveyed more than a hint of boyish excitement.

"That's to be expected... in the circumstances."

"I suppose."

"Are you ready then?"

"As ready as I'll ever be... I guess."

"Good. You wait here then," she requested tenderly, but firmly, offering him one final knowing grin before making her way down the hall to the bedroom. For when she returned, that was when the real excitement would commence.

In the time she was gone he gazed around at the furniture and the decor, the photographs and the ornaments, trying to piece together what he'd gleaned about her bizarre family so far. Then he spotted something on the dining table in the window bay.

Compelled to wander over, he squatted to marvel at the painstaking handiwork that had gone into assembling it. For there, for his delectation, was a magnificent 1/72 scale model of a B52G Stratofortress bomber, finished off in the dappled camouflage livery that depicted aircraft 58-0183 of the 69th Bombardment Squadron, 42nd Bombardment Wing. Consulting his prodigious memory for such things, he recalled it being one of the planes that had flown out of Andersen AFB in Guam during *'Operation Linebacker II'* in December 1972; one of the planes that would also feature in his forthcoming study of the role these colossal bombers had played in the doomed struggle that the United States had waged in Indochina.

Its presence in her apartment was uncanny. How had she come by it? Could this be some sort of sign affirming assent for the life-changing encounter that was mere seconds away from coming to pass? Was someone up above really trying to tell him that everything was going to be okay?

"Vaughan made that," Angie enlightened him upon her return. "He's very proud of it. He's left it there to allow the glue to set. You see, he's had to stick a few bits back on. I'm afraid his mother is still as lethal with a feather duster as she ever was!"

John turned to behold her standing at the threshold of the room. And stood next to her? Why, the most beautiful woman he had ever set eyes upon – in fact, every bit as prepossessing as Angie had promised she would be. However, right then this comely lady was as frozen in heart-stopping disbelief as he was. She offered him a nervous smile – for clearly what they were about to do would change *her* life just as surely as it would his own. He returned the smile, tears meandering down his handsome face. It was the most handsome face she had ever set eyes upon.

"John," Angie drew him forward until he could slip his hands into those of her sister's, "meet Nora – your mother! And Nora – after all these years – meet John… your long-lost son!"

* * * * *

Evening was drawing in. Most of the beachgoers had long since rolled up their towels and drifted back to their hotels and boarding houses. Only a handful of loyal sun worshippers remained to savour its fading glow; tossing frisbees, kicking balls, or – in a few brave instances – venturing into the sea. Otherwise, the scene could almost have been a throwback to a more innocent time. Vaughan and the two most important women in his life – his mother and his beloved aunt – huddled together on this stretch of Sandown's familiar golden beach.

There were no words to describe what Vaughan was feeling at that moment (though shell-shocked came closest). He had been staring vacantly out to sea for what seemed like an age, only now turning to observe them watching for his reaction to that which they had purposely walked him here to be told.

"So who's his father?" was all he could think to ask, dangling a hand beside him to lazily scoop up grains of fine sand.

Nora glanced across at Angie flanking him on one side, who in turn stared back at her sister flanking him on the other. Then his mother drew a deep breath.

"His name was Paul. He was a soldier who was stationed at the nearby coastal defences at Sizewell. I never knew his second name. By the time I found out I was pregnant the defences had been dismantled and he'd been posted to the Far East."

Vaughan didn't know whether to laugh or cry. He would never be able to look upon his mother the same way again – that was for sure. Shattered forever was the image he'd fixed in his mind of the demure, saintly figure that had nursed him as a child and taught him right from wrong. In its place, he tried to banish the appalling image that now flitted into his head of his mother – skirt hitched up – merrily servicing some sex-starved squaddie.

"Vaughan, your mother was young; just eighteen years-of-age – the same age as you are now," Angie tried her hand at assuaging his hurt. "There was a war on. None of us knew what tomorrow would bring. Because of this, romances were often struck up in haste; the following day a telegram might arrive that would draw those romances to a sudden and tragic end. In that kind of heady existence people snatched love wherever they could find it. It might be the last chance they would ever have."

That he could understand. Indeed, hadn't Aimee spoken of how that 'heady existence' of fearing 'sudden telegrams' had seared a whole generation of young English women (the subject of her dissertation, tales from which she'd shared with him). Yet somehow it didn't lessen the shock of knowing your own mother had indulged in such 'snatched' and unseemly love.

"So how did you find out that he was your son?" Vaughan felt compelled to ask – though reluctant to employ the name of his newly-discovered half-brother.

"For some time Nora had been trying to find out what had become of him," his aunt again elected to do the explaining. "We knew that after he'd been born, John had been passed to an orphanage to be cared for. Apparently, he languished there for almost two years before a couple finally adopted him. However, all your mother's enquiries had drawn a blank.

"Then a few months back, John was doing his usual rounds, visiting the dressing rooms to thank the acts for performing at the hotel. I just happened to mention that, the following day, I would be singing at a reunion of airmen who had been based at the RAF radar station at Ventnor. One thing led to another and the next thing I knew he'd whisked me up to his office, poured me a drink, and was showing me all these pictures on the walls of different planes. You see, he writes books about aircraft. He's had one published already; and he's presently working on another – ironically, about B52 bombers, like the one you've made.

"Well, at first I thought it was all just a ploy to chat me up. I'm told he has a bit of a reputation for being a lady's man. I confess I was rather flattered to think that such a dashing young chap would fancy a bit of old crumpet like me!"

His aunt underestimated her own allure. However, her self-effacing quip at least prompted his mother to appreciate the funny side of this bizarre lucky break. Vaughan, however, was in no mood for humour. He glanced up at Angie as she continued her account of that fateful night.

"Anyway, suddenly he scoops his arm around my waist and draws me up to this huge portrait of his father – Air Marshal Sir

Hugh Lawton, who he told me was a famous fighter pilot. Except Sir Hugh wasn't his real father. Perhaps John looked upon me as some kind of mother figure to whom he could admit such a thing; but he proceeded to tell me how he had been adopted by Sir Hugh and his wife as a toddler. He never knew his real parents – although he'd started to make his own enquiries about them.

"Then I discovered the real reason why he'd invited the 'stunning' Angie Ashby into his office at such a late hour: namely that the mother's name written on his birth certificate was 'Nora Ashby', and the birth had been registered in Suffolk on January 16th 1946 – 'father unknown'. Having told him on a previous occasion that I was originally from that part of the world, he wondered if I might be related to her. To say I almost fainted in his arms was an understatement!"

Vaughan's frown rippled just enough to hint that his anger and dismay might be dissipating. Even he was not so dazed by these revelations that he couldn't appreciate this touching answer to his mother's earnest prayer. But just in case, Nora felt obliged to take up the narrative and explain why the quest to find her abandoned first child had meant so much to her.

"So in case you wondered whether she was having some kind of illicit affair, that's what Auntie Angie has been up to these last few weeks: making arrangements for me to finally meet the little boy I only ever got to glimpse for a few minutes when he was born; the little boy I've never stopped pining for during thirty long years of being apart; the little boy I'd almost despaired of ever seeing again. I had to do it, Vaughan. Just because I have a son that you were unaware of doesn't mean I love *you* any less."

Now he knew what all those awful dreams had portended – the ones in which he was powerless to prevent his mother from drowning. It felt like he had indeed already lost a part of her – even though her plea, along with a more dispassionate assessment of matters, told him such a fear was ungrounded. Nora leaned in and took his hand, squeezing it the way she always had whenever she sensed he was troubled.

"Why didn't you tell me sooner?" he implored her, abruptly tugging it free in order to brush away his tears.

"Those were desperate times in other ways too," she sighed. "Back then there was terrible shame attached to having a child out of wedlock. Nanny Ashby was so appalled that I'd got myself pregnant that as soon as I began to show she had me packed off to stay with a relative in Ipswich. She told the neighbours I'd been offered a job there. And when I returned in the New Year – minus child – she told them I'd left the job because I was 'homesick'. Those were the kind of deceptions people had to engage in back then in order to avoid having fingers pointed at them in the street. Sometimes you had to spin so many little white lies that concealing the truth became second nature."

"Vaughan, I know your mother – after all, she is *my* little sister. She has never been a very convincing liar," Angie insisted, prompting Nora to evince an ambiguous smile, "less so since she's started going to church! She would have told you sooner or later. I know she would."

Vaughan was not so sure. Even though he'd just been flattened by one almighty (and unforeseen) bombshell, he was convinced that both his mother and his aunt were concealing other things from him too. There were just too many weird goings-on; too many whispered conversations that it was plain he was not meant to be party too; too many instances in which his Auntie Angie was slowly, but surely positioning herself more centrally in his life (most obviously, her insistence that he stay with her the entire summer) – even as his mother appeared to be content to take a back seat, as it were.

Perhaps aware that cogs were whirring away inside his head, Angie and Nora glanced at each other in that certain way again. One secret from the past resolved; time to call closure upon another.

21

Friday, August 20th 1976

The very fact that Uncle Frank was already home ahead of him should have been the giveaway. His uncle never shut up shop before five-thirty on weekdays. Yet he here was, in his favourite armchair, pretending to watch news coverage of President Gerald Ford's narrow victory over Governor Ronald Reagan at the Republican National Convention in Kansas City.

However, he would not get to listen to the speeches for long. No sooner had Vaughan returned from the bedroom, having divested of his uniform and wriggled into his shorts and T-shirt than his mother and his aunt entered the room behind him like a phalanx – as if to bar any thought of escape. It acted like some kind of signal for Frank to get up and switch the television set off.

"Take a seat, son," he instructed him ominously.

Though wary, his nephew did as he was told.

"Vaughan, there is something else we have decided it's time you need to know," Auntie Angie opened with sober deliberation.

However, it fell to his mother to actually make the dreaded announcement. She swallowed hard and donned a pained smile.

"Vaughan, there is no easy way to tell you this – but I am not your real mother."

Surely this must be some kind of wind-up, his eyes opened wide to beg them. After yesterday's revelations though, he was in no mood for joking around.

"What do you mean: you're not my real mother? You're my mom. Who else could possibly be my mother?"

The words uttered, a stray tear was the vanguard of pent-up emotions that now prevented Nora from pressing ahead to elaborate. Therefore, the task fell to his aunt. Meanwhile, he noticed that Uncle Frank was wearing an expression that spoke of wanting to be a million miles away at this precise moment. He too now donned a pained smile.

"Firstly," Angie sought to reassure him, "it doesn't mean you're not part of this family. It just means that Nora is not your birth mother. She is instead your auntie."

The lad was still struggling to get his head around what they were trying to tell him. Therefore, she paused to let the statement sink him, watching while he mouthed what he'd grasped so far.

"So… if she is not my mother… but is my aunt… then who *is* my mother?"

Then it hit him. His maternal grandparents had only given birth to two children – both daughters. His eyes locked onto Angie's and his mouth opened wide in disbelief.

"Yes, Vaughan. *I* am your mother," she confirmed.

For several long, tense seconds the boy said nothing – his dumbstruck stare alighting in turn upon those present in the room before his watery eyes lowered to fix themselves upon a point on the carpet where they might dwell. As he began to comprehend the implications of this terrible secret, Angie commenced the invidious task of offering an explanation.

"I guess it all has to do with the decision of that American airman to renege on his promise to marry me – whose name, in case you haven't already put two and two together, is Charles Eichelberger: the man who is at present staying at a hotel just a few miles from here; the man who is Aimee's father."

His eyes flashed wide. "You mean Aimee's father is *my* father too?" he gasped.

It was an appalling thought. For several seconds the tension in the room could have been sliced with a knife before Angie finally offered him a risible frown. She could see how, from her obtuse statement, he might have reached such a hasty conclusion.

"No, Vaughan. Charles Eichelberger is *not* your father. Uncle Frank is your father," she stared him out and put him straight.

Intercepting the trajectory of his eyes as they switched focus to the one person present who had yet to say anything, she observed her husband's awkward gaze briefly alight upon Vaughan, accompanied by an equally awkward smile – as if he was waiting for the floor to kindly swallow him up

"But it's important that you know how I absolutely adored Charles Eichelberger," she continued, this time Uncle Frank (nay, his father!) staring away with a mixture of anger and distaste. "In fact, I never truly got over what he did to me. I carried the hurt from that relationship into my marriage. Unfairly, I know. I know too that Frank eventually became very frustrated with me. It was what probably led him to have affairs with several different women over the next few years."

The after-shocks kept coming strong and fast. The thought of this docile man conducting himself like Don Juan took some grasping. However, that was back then – in the early 1950s – when he had still been virile and handsome (as Angie now elaborated as delicately as she could – to spare the blushes of her once-rakish husband). Vaughan also understood why his aunt (nay, his mother!) had taken such a profound dislike to Aimee – the conduit, perhaps, for her resentment at being so callously betrayed by her father. Suddenly it felt as if every key player in this sordid, unfolding drama had been gathered together on this small island during this sultry summer so that – like an Agatha Christie murder-mystery – they might be present to witness the ultimate villain-of-the-piece being unmasked.

"Things came to a head when I found out about those affairs. The discovery further sent my head all over the place. So all over the place that shortly afterwards I suffered a mental breakdown. I really was at my lowest ebb. Seeing no way out, I attempted to end my life. I took an overdose of the sleeping tablets I'd been prescribed. For better or worse, Frank found me and the hospital managed to revive me. Perhaps it might have been better for everyone concerned if they hadn't," she wept.

It was at this juncture that Nora took up the story while Angie dabbed her tears and Frank sidled up to offer her a hug (the first hint of affection that Vaughan had witnessed during the whole time he had been staying with them).

"It was shortly afterwards that Angie discovered she was pregnant... with you. However, she was in a very bad way. We feared she might even have to go to a place where she could be 'looked after'," she recalled, alluding to the dark fate of people back then whose sanity had been deemed to have deserted them. "She certainly couldn't have coped with looking after a baby. Therefore, having lost my own child to adoption by strangers, I was determined *her* child would *never* suffer such a fate. With Frank and Angie's consent, Jim and I stepped in to adopt you and raise you ourselves. We've never been able to have children of our own – a problem on your father's side... apparently."

Vaughan looked her in the eye – jabbing his wrists to his face to force away further tears, yet letting slip a wicked grin. It meant that there was no genetic basis for having to refer to that despicable man as his 'father'. Nora picked up on this.

"I can't say I blame Jim for walking out," she sighed. "He was never happy with the deal. He just fell in line to please me. Afterwards, he accused me of railroading Frank and Angie into agreeing to the adoption in haste and when neither of them was thinking straight; of not allowing them time to sort their lives out. Maybe too he resented the way I sublimated the affection I should have shown towards him into affection towards my 'new child'," she admitted, staring unrepentantly at the boy who had instead become the repository for the maternal love Nora had been unable to offer her real son. "However, I was desperate to prevent Angie losing contact with her child altogether – as had happened to me.

"Shortly after the adoption went through, all four of us left Suffolk to escape gossip in the street. We knew that gossip would eventually find its way back to you when you started school. Frank and Angie moved to the Isle of Wight. Meanwhile, Jim found a job at a factory in Dudley. We moved there with him. But they were not happy years – as I'm sure you will remember."

He did indeed. The rows, the fights, all those accusations that at the time made no sense to a small boy caught up in the middle of such a hare-brained, if well-intentioned domestic arrangement. Jim Lewis had never taken to a child that was not his – and who he furthermore blamed for robbing him of his wife's conjugal affection. Meanwhile, the man that small boy had matured into now turned to observe Frank still staring shame-faced at the carpet. Sensing this, his real father looked up at his son, attempting another smile. Vaughan could think of nothing else to do but smile back.

Frank now opened his mouth for the first time during these fraught proceedings. He shuffled from his chair, knelt at

Vaughan's feet, looked him in the eye, and then reached across to rest a hand upon his shoulder.

"Son, I can't begin to tell you how sorry I am for the way things turned out. Please forgive me... if you can."

'Son': for the first time the customary term of endearment by which this mercurial chap was forever addressing him had a special and intensely personal feel to it.

"Of course, I forgive you," Vaughan snuffled, rubbing that hand still gripping his shoulder. Meanwhile, Nora looked on with tears streaming down her face as this tentative reconciliation blossomed into a full-blown hug.

"So why was *I* never told any of this? And why tell me now?" he addressed the two women as weeping father and son broke free of each other's embrace.

"In time Angie did recover. And she and Frank patched up their marriage," his mother (nay, his aunt!) replied. "But by then the deed was done. It was just simpler to carry on the fiction. But she never stopped loving you – and neither did Frank. It's why we like to think that raising you has been a joint enterprise – even though the distance between us often meant we've had to endure long periods apart. But it's why I made sure we holidayed on the island every summer when we were able. It's why you have always been a very special 'nephew' to them. And it's why I know these last few precious weeks that you've spent together have meant so much to them both."

He looked across at Angie and smiled at her. Yes, she had always been very special 'aunt' to him too. Now at last, he knew just how 'special'; and why there had always existed such a close – almost telepathic – bond between them.

"As for telling you now," Nora continued, "when you told me last year that you wanted to travel abroad – to maybe go on one of those trips to the Holy Land with the young people in the church – I knew there would be a problem. In order to obtain a passport we would have to let you have your birth certificate. Then you would discover who your *real* parents were. Therefore, I agreed with Frank and Angie that the time was ripe for telling you the truth. It's why I've been happy to let you stay with them this summer: so that the ground could be prepared for us to make this long overdue announcement."

From staring at his hands sunk in his lap, Vaughan now beheld the woman who had selflessly committed eighteen years of her life to raising him as her own child; the woman who even now his first instinct was to address as 'Mom'; the woman who had been his protector, his champion and his role-model; the woman who had – without trace of irony – taught him that great biblical truth that *'ye have not received the spirit of bondage again to fear; but have received the Spirit of adoption, whereby we cry, Abba, Father'*. This woman had made it her calling to be his parent – notwithstanding that he'd discovered that she was also shockingly fallible. Yet if she could love him so unconditionally then how much more so was he loved by a perfect *Abba* Father in Heaven – who had likewise 'adopted' the sinful Vaughan and now called him an 'heir of God; and a 'joint heir with Christ'.

All at once he burst into tears. One last time he pictured himself racing out to sea on that lilo, desperate to rescue his 'Mom' from drowning. Instinctively, now – as in those terrible dreams – he reached out to grasp her outstretched hand, fearing that (knowing what he now knew) she was set to finally vanish from his life forever. However, before he could expel the nightmarish vision from his head he looked down to observe her fingers lock firmly inside his own.

"Vaughan, it's okay. I'm here," she asserted, fighting back her own tears as he gripped her hand tightly. "I will always be here. And I will always love you. You need never, ever doubt that."

* * * * *

Vaughan Lewis had read somewhere of a troubling affliction that had dogged many American servicemen who had returned from Vietnam: feelings of rage, impotence and despair in response to traumatic events. He had no wish to compare what he had experienced this last week with something as horrendous as witnessing death or destruction in battle. However, taking off on a long sojourn alone along the cliff top path that provided a quieter, more leisurely route into Shanklin – and after the initial euphoria of knowing the truth – at last his mood began to similarly alternate between rage, impotence and despair.

Though he had no particular place he wanted to go on this beautiful sunny evening, he was certain he needed to pass it alone. Hence he had declined an offer by his mother (or his 'aunt', or whatever he was now supposed to call her!) to join him. Angie too had stayed her sister's hand, wisely bidding Nora give the lad the time and space he needed. Pausing in Battery Park, Vaughan therefore sat down on a bench overlooking the bay to try and make sense of it all. However, the place reeked of yet more painful memories – of that first proper kiss with Aimee before their fleeting romance had also become for him a source of rage, impotence and despair.

On and on he walked until the path eventually emerged onto Shanklin Esplanade. Soon enough he was passing the Shanklin Heights Hotel. As he did, from the road he spotted John Lawton's sleek Jaguar XJS parked in its usual reserved bay. As he stood there, hands fumbling in his pockets, he found himself rolling a fifty pence piece between his fingers. To be sure, he was smarting to think that not only did he have a half-brother that his 'mother' had never told him about; but that half-brother (well, half-cousin actually – grief, this was so complicated!) had turned out to be his 'mother's' *one-and-only* biological offspring. Vaughan was not so stupid he couldn't reason that, in time, this would inevitably magnify this man in the pecking order of Nora Lewis's affections.

Fumbling with the coin ever faster in agitation, he was unable to resist the temptation to wander up to the car, draw the coin from his pocket, and press it tight between his thumb and his forefinger. One long scratch with it down the length of the panels would certainly make a mess of its paintwork. He might even carve the word 'BASTARD' onto it for good measure! Yet he hesitated to wield the coin and do the deed. Suppressing his rage, he then slipped the coin back in his pocket. It was hardly a very Christian thing to do; and neither would a police record for criminal damage look good on his CV. And what purpose would it serve anyway? To a man of John Lawton's not inconsiderable means the hundred pounds or so it would cost to have the panels repainted would be small change.

Conceding that the wealthy hotelier was as much a victim of his family's foibles and frailties as Vaughan himself, instead he wondered into the hotel lobby. Gazing around and observing the tasteful décor, he lingered at the 'entertainment' board that was propped on an easel situated by the door to the restaurant. He took a moment to peruse the acts lined up for tonight's cabaret.

"Can I help you, sir?" he heard someone with a jolly Irish lilt call over to him.

He turned to observe that the young girl on the reception desk had spotted his presence, perhaps curious how out of place he must look attired in shorts and a T-shirt when everyone else who was drifting into the restaurant was dressed for dinner.

"Er… no, it's okay. I know this woman. I've heard her sing," he explained, pointing to the glamorous portrait of 'The Fabulous Angie Ashby' that took pride of place on the notice board.

"Yes, she's very good. She'll be on at ten o'clock tonight if you'd like to hear her sing again," the girl reminded him.

"Er, yes. I might get changed and pop down," he glanced himself up and down as if to apologise for being underdressed.

The girl on the desk returned to her paperwork. Presumably she was satisfied he was just another guest who'd returned from a stroll on this lovely evening.

With her attention elsewhere, Vaughan subtly shifted his own attention from the notice board to the internal partition window that ran the length of the restaurant – and through which he could make out diners at their tables, as well as the waiters who were busy attending to them. Over in a corner, a jazz pianist was meanwhile aiding digestion with a selection of allegretto ivory-tinkling, strains of which escaped – along with the general hubbub of prandial conversations – whenever the door was flung open by other guests arriving to join them. Then, on a table by the far wall, he spotted two familiar faces.

Aimee and Shelby were seated around a table with an older man of impressive bearing (who resembled the photograph Aimee had shown him of her father), as well as a woman of the same age who was seated by his side (who he assumed to be his wife – Aimee's mother). So this was Charles Eichelberger, he sniffed:

the man whose betrayal of his *real* mother had sent her into an emotional tailspin that had almost broken her.

From the way that Shelby, Aimee's mother and Aimee herself were dolled up the young man now surreptitiously peering in at them deduced it must be some kind of special occasion. Maybe he was just used to seeing the two American girls dressed casually – usually in shorts and T-shirts, as befitted this extraordinary summer. Yet tonight here they were – both resplendent in elegant, expensive outfits, the acquisitions from some serious fashion shopping in Ryde or Newport.

Once again, it was Aimee who drew his attention. She was wearing a white flowing dress with enough exposure around the shoulders to showcase the modest suntan she'd eventually acquired while on the island. As she sat there conversing with Shelby and her parents, Vaughan could tell by the way her golden hair danced on those shoulders that it too had recently been styled and highlighted. Meanwhile, around her slender neck she wore an expensive-looking gold chain, from which was hung a tiny, glinting cross that nestled above her cleavage – and which she broke from conversation to show off for everyone's benefit. Her father looked on well pleased.

Just then the reason for the special occasion became apparent. In from the wings there wafted John Lawton, leading the way for his *chef de partie*, who now placed before them a beautifully-decorated cake that was topped with a cluster of brightly-flickering candles. It prompted the guests on neighbouring tables to turn around in awe. Aimee beamed with incredulous delight. Meanwhile, her mother clasped her hands together to thank both the ever-obliging hotel manager and his talented chef.

Then Vaughan remembered: August 20th – it was Aimee-Marie Eichelbergers's twenty-first birthday. Maybe that expensive chain-and-cross was a gift from her parents. He continued to observe at a distance while she drew breath and blew every single candle out. She then sank back into her seat to savour the applause of her parents, of Shelby, and of the other diners.

Vaughan's heart sank. The symbolism of not having been invited to this milestone birthday party was more than he could bear. Now he knew he really was just a nobody who had somehow managed to gate-crash into the trifling affections of the General's daughter, only to be slung out on his ear when – like her father before her – she'd grown tired of hanging out with some low-born foreigner. As indeed, he feared, he was about to be slung-out on his ear any minute now if the girl on Reception cottoned on to his non-resident status at this upmarket hotel.

However, like a moth to a flame, he simply couldn't pull himself away. When the congratulations ceased, there remained three people around the table staring in marvel at the cake while the fourth was gazing up at the man who'd commissioned it. There was a serene glow in Aimee's eyes that spoke of more than just gratitude to the oleaginous hotelier. Vaughan watched Lawton return that grateful pout with a smirk and a wink of his own. Then, when her father glanced up at Lawton to commend his thoughtfulness, Aimee swiftly lowered her gaze – upon which it made unwitting contact with an incredulous face still staring at her through the glass partition. Suddenly her startled gaze was no longer serene. It was guilt-stricken.

"Vicky, if you want to take your break now I'll watch Reception for you until you come back… Er, I say, young man… young man…"

Only the fear that he'd been rumbled caused Vaughan to wrench himself away from the compelling spectacle. He spun around to witness some officious-looking woman in a pleated fawn skirt come striding towards him, her heels clicking on the polished marble floor – the very same woman who had castigated him for loitering about the hotel on a previous uninvited visit.

"Can I help you…? Oh… it's you!" she exclaimed, halting upon recognising him.

Before Vaughan could engage the brain and formulate a credible excuse for spying on her guests, adrenalin instead fired him up to flee. He scurried out of the lobby without waiting to catch her plaintive cry.

"Wait… Wait… I've been looking forward to meeting you. John has told me…"

But he was gone. Meanwhile, Veronica Lawton turned to observe that the birthday party in the restaurant had been suddenly interrupted by this commotion going on in the lobby.

However, with Vaughan gone and nothing much to see, merriment quickly resumed. Only the birthday girl's perturbed expression lingered – at least until she too snapped out of whatever it was that had briefly caught her eye. She laughed and waved her hand dismissively, re-engaging with the joyous celebration.

* * * * *

"Oh! Hello. This *is* a pleasant surprise!"

It was indeed. When Tina Brown had made her throwaway comment in the restroom of Ryde Bus Station a week earlier she hadn't for one minute imagined that Vaughan would take her up on it. However, it was Friday night; Sally and the lads were out elsewhere; and there was no place she was going. Neither was there anything on the three channels on TV worth watching. Therefore, she invited him in.

"So what brings you this way then?" she enquired, having ushered him into the garden, where she returned with two ice cold beers she'd snaffled from the fridge.

"No particular reason… well…" she watched him hesitate.

"It's that American girl again, isn't it?" she correctly surmised.

Vaughan nodded.

"It was Aimee's twenty-first birthday party tonight. But I wasn't invited."

"Oh, Vaughan. You don't deserve to be treated this way. You're such a nice chap too," it tugged at Tina's heart when he proceeded to recount chapter-and-verse of the evening so far.

"Maybe 'nice' is not what girls are after. Maybe they want the kind of men that I'm quite clearly not," he countered dolefully.

Tina frowned – albeit to empathise with a young man who, admittedly, was not the most rugged, athletic or thrusting specimen of malekind she'd ever befriended. Maybe more of a poet than a rugby player, she smiled to herself.

"That's not always so," she endeavoured to correct him. "I'm sure there must be loads of women out there who warm to the fact that you're kind, you're considerate, and you're loyal. One day you will make a superb husband. And a great dad, I'm sure."

He looked up from his beer to observe the kind of gentle smile that told him she was not just fobbing him off with kind words. Swishing her long brown hair back over her shoulders, she reached over to squeeze his free hand as it rested upon the patio table – which at least put a reluctant smile on his face too.

"Listen," she released it and sat back in her chair, "we women sometimes have the same problem too. Why is it you men always seem to value us primarily for our physical attributes?" she scoffed. "And when you've got a pair of attributes like these proceeding two steps ahead of you, usually that's the *only* reason most boys are interested in you," she added, pressing her upper arms together in order to bunch up those quivering 'attributes' and show what she meant.

They'd certainly never failed to capture Vaughan's attention during the time he'd been working with her – that was for sure. He offered them the obligatory scrutiny that her demonstrative act demanded and then resolved not to scrutinise them again – well, at least not for another sixty seconds!

"At least boys are interested in you for something," he sighed instead, articulating the common male neurosis that when it comes to the ability to physically attract the opposite sex women hold all the best cards in their hands. And they know it!

"Maybe so, but why are boys nowadays so superficial. All they ever seem to think about is sex!" Tina continued (Vaughan tempted to ask: 'twas it ever thus'). "For instance, why do they assume I must be 'easy' just because I've got big boobs and enjoy male company? I guess that's why I feel comfortable around you, Vaughan. I know you respect me and wouldn't try anything funny. When it comes to girls you're able to distinguish between a come-on and a playful expression of trust. Unlike your friend, Colin – one innocent wrong word on my part and he'd be in my knickers like a ferret down a rabbit hole!"

Vaughan proffered a boyish snicker, both at the metaphor and to think that he might have one up on the randy bus driver.

"I suppose I should take that as a compliment," he thanked her. Then his countenance darkened and his gaze drifted to a distant place.

"It's not the only shock I've had this week," he admitted. "I found out that once upon a time Mom gave birth to another son who she's never told me about. Then, to compound the shock, Mom told me she's not my mother after all; but that my Auntie Angie – who I am staying with – is actually my *real* mother."

"Gosh! No wonder you looked like the bottom had dropped out of your world when I opened the door to you just now."

"Come here," she then leaned over and threw her arms around him, having observed how he was on the verge of tears.

She swept her hair out of her face and nestled his head against her own. Rocking him gently in her enveloping arms, it permitted him to release all the emotion he'd been bottling up inside.

"Go ahead, it's okay to cry," she spoke softly. "And contrary to the old saying, real men *do* cry. They cry because they care. And caring is another wonderful quality that I can detect every time I look into those eyes of yours," she lifted him away, compelling him to make eye contact with her grey-blue ones. Then, to further cement her act of solidarity, she sat up in her chair again to address him in earnest.

"I know how you must be feeling, Vaughan. You see, my dad left my mom for another woman when I was seven. I look back now and can still remember the hurt I felt; and how I also took what he did personally – as if maybe I'd done something wrong. What made it worse was that, after he left, my mom started behaving like she was less than a woman unless she had some other bloke on her arm – sometimes a different bloke at the end of the week to the one she had on her arm at the start.

"It left me wrestling with all manner of insecurities of my own. Then, when I was a twelve, these things popped out of my chest," she glanced down at her bosom with that familiar weary sigh. "Suddenly, boys at school were taking an interest in me. One or two of them even offered me their dinner money if I'd get them out for them to ogle at – and a bit more money still if I'd let them touch them and hold them.

"To my shame, when no one was about I took them up on their offers. Inevitably though, some of them couldn't resist bragging. And so word got round – ''Ere lads, Tina'll get her tits out for you if you stump up fifty pence!' After that, the girls in class started shunning me and calling me a prostitute," she looked away from him, appalled. "But it was never about the money. Maybe after the way my father had rejected me, and my mother's attention was always elsewhere, it felt empowering to know that somebody valued me for something – even if it was only because of these two ridiculous lumps of flesh!"

Vaughan frowned in righteous indignation on her behalf – as well as feeling profound guilt that so much of his own interest in this affable, if emotionally-scarred young lady had also been predicated upon those colossal 'lumps of flesh'. Suddenly, he regretted that self-pitying 'interested-in-you-for-something' remark he'd made.

"One of Mom's boyfriend noticed them too because he made a point of being nice to me," she continued with dark foreboding. "I guess I was flattered by his attention. After being cold-shouldered by my schoolmates, he became one of the few friends I had. Perhaps being an older man, I just trusted him more. Or maybe I'd come to look upon him as the father-figure I no longer had. He used to compliment me and tell me how pretty I was – just like my real dad once did. He helped me with my homework. He bought me an expensive present for my fifteenth birthday. And he would patiently listen to all my silly ramblings about why David Cassidy was so much better than Donny Osmond."

"And both were better than the Bay City Rollers!" Vaughan attempted levity. However, Tina wasn't laughing.

"Then, one day, he also asked me if I'd take them out; to let him see them… and touch them…" he watched her face crumple remorsefully. "One thing led to another… and we ended up in bed together. I guess you could say he raped me," she sobbed.

"So now I really did feel dirty – the class 'prozzie' brimming with even more self-loathing – again as if what he'd done was my fault; that I'd led him on and encouraged him to behave like that towards me. I never told anyone at the time – and certainly not Mom, who thought the sun shone out of this guy's arse. Uh!" she sneered and dabbed her tears, "At least until he became the latest in a long line of ex-boyfriends whose arm she'd once clung to!

"You're the first person I have ever spoken about this to, Vaughan," her sad, wandering eyes finally met his own.

He felt compelled to return the gesture of solidarity, brushing her hair from her face to dab at those tears with the handkerchief he'd retrieved from his pocket. Tina took it from him and blubbed apologetically, commending his thoughtfulness.

"For a long time afterwards, far from getting my tits out for the boys, I tried to hide them. At college I'd flatten them inside these big, thick jumpers I'd taken to wearing – ashamed of them. But then one day a little voice inside said: why should I be ashamed? After all, God made me this way. It's not my fault if men can't deal with that; nor if they're so superficial that they're uninterested in the real Tina Brown to whom they belong.

"Neither was I going to sleep around and so conform to their stereotype of how girls with big boobs behaved – like Mom was doing. In fact, I'm convinced that was the reason why Paul – my sailor boyfriend from Birmingham – left me: because I refused to just whip my knickers off and be a convenient lay whenever he was home on leave. Sadly, my best friend proved a more reliable lay – and now she's got Paul's kid to prove it!

"On the contrary, I'm determined that the love I have to give will be kept for someone who will treat me with respect; for the right man at the right time – and for the right reasons."

It was a laudable goal; one Vaughan had set himself too. However (as he had intimated to Aimee on the bus that day), he feared his reluctance to 'play the field' or 'put it about' with girls had made him something of a laughing stock amongst his more dissolute workmates. More grievously – and having assumed that a born-again Christian girl would be impressed by such chivalry – it hurt to reflect that Aimee too considered him a wimp when it came to sex. And that, perversely (or so he feared), this might be why she'd rejected him in favour of that lecherous hotel manager (who, Shelby had confided to him, was forever drooling over her best friend). This was the real reason why he'd been tempted to vandalise the car of his supposed 'half-brother'!

He so wanted to unburden all these things to Tina and to seek her counsel about how he might put them right. However, he fumbled for the right words – as he often did at moments like these. Instead, observing how recounting the trauma of her rape ordeal had enervated her, he cast aside his own preoccupations and sought instead to put the smile back on her face.

"*I* appreciate the real Tina," he assured her emphatically, taking hold of her hand. "You've been a good friend to me. You taught me how to dance. You never poke fun at me because I'm shy with girls. You listen to all my problems. And you've never made me feel like some sort of pervert whenever you've caught me admiring your enormous…!"

Suddenly, he too glanced away, ashamed that he'd actually admitted to such a thing. However, he needn't have worried. She kept hold of his hand, fondling the back of it with her thumb.

"I'll take that as a compliment too then," her eyes glowed. "Besides, it's what you men do, isn't it – most of you without even realising you're doing it. So please don't go beating yourself up about it – especially you being a Christian and all that," she added – perhaps a telling acknowledgement of the fount of his otherwise gallant and thoughtful disposition.

"No, Vaughan, you're a gentleman: someone who knows how to conduct himself in the presence of a lady – even if that sometimes comes across as shyness or reticence. For that, you will always have my profound gratitude – which, I suppose, is just as well really," she then sat back and joked, "because if you were hoping I'd get them out and show you then you can form an orderly queue behind Colin and the other blokes down the depot – who'll also be waiting around a long time, I promise you!"

He shared the amusement, realising as he did that they had just engaged in some pretty eye-popping conversation. And yet there was a grace and sincerity about Tina that left him strangely warmed and edified by her candid confession. Furthermore, her wise words about the healing of emotional pain being the outcome of rediscovering self-respect (rather than appeasing the false gods of sexual promiscuity – however tempting) compelled him to pray that he might yet understand what pain and inner turmoil Aimee might be going through. Perhaps this was what had caused her behave the way she had – towards him and towards that snake of a hotel manager.

They talked some more before dusk gave way to a darkness moderated by the benign glow of a half-moon. Vaughan eventually glanced at his watch and realised that his mother – both the real and the acting one – must by now be fretting that he'd hurled himself off Culver Cliff!

"It's been wonderful to talk to you. Thank you for being... so understanding," he fumbled for words again as she walked him towards the front door.

"Thank you for being so understanding too," she insisted, rubbing his forearm in a final gesture of solidarity. "And remember: your life is far from over just because you've found out that – like mine – *your* family are human beings too."

However, from the glint in each other's eyes the evening was not quite over yet. Neither of them was sure whose lips pursed first; but before they knew it those lips were touching. She placed her dainty hands upon his shoulders and they drew closer, Vaughan's hands curling around the small of her back while a more prolonged kiss blossomed. He was tempted to permit those hands to explore and maybe close their spans around those objects he'd spent the holiday fantasising about. Her breasts certainly felt ample and inviting when pressed against him, her nipples firm and aroused. He suspected she would not be averse to him toying with them in ways that might further arouse her. However, reluctantly she eased herself from his embrace until only a pair of regretful eyes remained trained upon each other.

"Vaughan, you're a great guy. And I would be really flattered to think you fancied me," she sighed. "But I suspect I'm not the girl you really want... am I."

Without saying a word those eyes directed away in anguish told her what she sought to know.

"Not to worry," she pined, loosing him and opening the front door. "You'll always be my friend – you know that. I hope I'll always be yours too. But I guess the honour of being your true love belongs to Aimee – even if she doesn't yet realise it. So go out there, Vaughan... and find her. Maybe tell her one final time how you feel about her. If she has any brains about her then she'll recognise that, in you, she has found the most wonderful man any woman could ever want."

He was visibly humbled. She'd certainly given him a reputation to uphold! But as he reached over to offer her a more beseeming goodnight peck on the cheek, he knew she was right: Aimee-Marie Eichelberger remained his first love. Even though time was fast running out before the summer would draw to a close and they would both go their separate ways, he had to make one more attempt at winning her heart (though, as yet, he hadn't a clue how he might even begin such a herculean task).

"But Vaughan…" she called after him as she finally motioned to close the door. He turned. "If she still says 'no'… then you know where you can find me."

22

Saturday, August 21st 1976

Every time John Lawton took to the air he experienced an adrenalin rush like no other. Not even bedding a beautiful woman could better the sheer exhilaration of hurtling down the runway at the controls of a plane.

Alas, the Beechcraft Bonanza F33A that was climbing over Whitecliff Bay was not one of those supersonic Lightning fighter jets that he'd dreamed of piloting during his schooldays. However, having a few years back acquired his pilot's licence, this modest light aircraft had enabled him to at last indulge his childhood passion for flying.

Today's flight from Bembridge Aerodrome was a very special one. For beside him at the controls was none other than one General Charles F. Eichelberger USAF (ret). Levelling off at five thousand feet, Lawton banked to port and steered a west-north-westerly course that brought them parallel with Bracklesham Bay on the Sussex coast. Ascent completed, the General glanced across at him through his mirror sunshades and nodded, well impressed with the sure touch with which his British host and devotee handled the plane.

On such bright, cloudless day it was possible to see for miles. Ahead of them was Southampton Water – and the eponymous port city, famous for being one of the few places on Earth to benefit from double tides. Below them, V-shaped wakes marked the progress of ferries back and forth across the shimmering waters of Spithead that separated island from mainland. The Ryde-Southsea hovercraft was meanwhile skimming across those waters at speed. Off to starboard lay the great naval citadel of Portsmouth, where they could make out the grey shapes of Her Majesty's warships moored at their berths.

"Look," Lawton cried above the drone of the plane's engine, pointing down to one of those warships that was making haste through the Harbour entrance. "That's *HMS Sheffield* – one of our new Type 42 destroyers, armed with Sea Dart surface-to-air missiles. That's the second time in as many weeks that she's put to sea. Her captain's probably anxious to shake down his crew,"

"Best not get too close then," Eichelberger quipped. "One of those SAMs would make short shrift of both of us – especially in the hands of a novice crew too jittery to distinguish between the radar plot of a light plane and that of their target drone!"

As they passed over it, Lawton observed how the General continued to study the warship, perhaps making out those bright red missiles in their launcher abaft the vessel's for'ard gun. He tried to imagine what terror must have assailed his son during those final few minutes of his life upon realising that a similar missile that had locked onto his B52 bomber was defying every counter-measure that had been executed to shake it off.

"You know, on a day like today flying is rather a joyride," he began to approach the subject crablike. "Once upon a time it must have been so different for you: death or capture hanging over you every time you took off for hostile skies. I can't tell you how much I admire you... and guys like you."

"John, at times it was sheer hell wondering whether one of those Nazi cannon rounds had your name written all over it. Few men can face that day after day and not be changed forever by the experience. It's why Eisenhower was right when he said there's no greater pacifist than the ordinary serving officer."

"Quite. I hope my account of the war you Mustang pilots fought did justice to your courage and tenacity."

"John, your book was one of the most stirring accounts I've ever read. You have a real talent for bringing the story of aerial combat to life. It's why it's been a privilege to have helped you with your new book. It's just a shame you never approached me earlier – to help you with the first one. That said, it's seems you did a pretty swell job without me!"

For John Lawton, second only to the buzz of flying was that of receiving the approbation of his hero. It made him aware of how immensely privileged he was. The good looks he'd been born with (and from whom, on his mother's side, he now knew he had inherited); the recipient of an expensive private education, as well as the social capital that had accrued from being the adopted son of a decorated air marshal; and a fortune pocketed from five years of trading in the City, and which had enabled him to 'retire' at the height of the commodity price boom to indulge his love of aviation. Yet still self-doubt lingered – not least on account of not knowing who his real father was. It was a missing piece of the jigsaw of his eventful life that his mother had been unable to assist him with. The name 'Paul' (and that he had been a Cockney soldier) were the only clues she'd been able to offer regarding who this elusive character might be.

Overflying the squadrons of white-sailed yachts racing off Cowes, he set a south-westerly course down The Solent towards The Needles. Meanwhile, drifting columns of smoke to starboard indicated the smouldering remains of fires that had recently raged through the New Forest on account of the exceptional dry weather. Indeed, it was only from this altitude that one could truly appreciate just how brown and parched Southern England had become after months without significant rainfall.

"Talking of the weather, when I was over here all it seemed to do was rain. That first summer of '44 was especially unsettled. Bad weather nearly scuppered the D-Day landings. Then for several weeks during the winter of '45 our planes had to be dug out of deep snow ahead of missions."

"I'm sure when the weather does finally break we'll end up with a year's worth of rainfall in just a few torrential downpours. This is England, after all!" Lawton smirked from behind his own mirror sunglasses.

Eichelberger acknowledged the aside. The firm, if intriguingly symbiotic bond that had been established between the retired American general and the awestruck British historian certainly looked set to provide more valuable insights for the latter's new book – *'The Boeing B52 Stratofortress And The Air War Over Indochina'*. As with their previous correspondence, Lawton found himself once more probing Charles Eichelberger for his reflections – which (apropos that symbiosis) the General was eager to recount. Indeed, it seemed that doing so had provided some kind of welcome personal catharsis for him.

Crucially, his appointment as commander of the US Seventh Air Force in April 1972 had come at a point when things were coming to a head in Vietnam. The United States was finally winding down its involvement in this controversial war when, on Good Friday a few days earlier, the North Vietnamese had launched a massive offensive throughout the South, testing President Nixon's resolve to defend America's ally in Saigon.

Throughout the war so far, the B52 – a strategic bomber designed to deliver nuclear retaliation to the Soviet Union – had been used tactically to provide close air support to US and South Vietnamese ground forces. Hence, one of the first orders Eichelberger had issued was for their crews to recommence flying tactical *'Arc Light'* mission intended to smash North Vietnamese troop concentrations in the South.

"Dick Nixon was livid with air force commanders in Vietnam. He charged that they'd been insufficiently aggressive or imaginative in their prosecution of the war so far. He despatched me there with express orders to change all that," he now intimated to his host. "On my watch we flew six thousand sorties alone between April and June. In particular, I was determined to employ the B52s' massive firepower to repel the invasion."

"Of course, An Loc was your real test. If the enemy captured this strategic town then Saigon lay open before him," the Englishman reminded him, showing off his erudition.

"That's right. Realising the North Vietnamese intended to throw everything they had at this battle, I ordered every B52 in South-East Asia to go after their massing tanks and infantry. We established numbered 'strike boxes' covering the town – each measuring one kilometre by three. With my aircraft guided onto these boxes by ground-based radar, over one two-day period we managed to send in an *'Arc Light'* mission every hour for thirty hours solid, deploying one hundred-and-seventy B52s in rapid succession. We were obliterating entire enemy regiments in the process. By mid-June – chastened by the losses we'd inflicted upon him – he called it a day. An Loc was saved – and with it Saigon too. But it was damn close-run thing – as your Duke of Wellington might have said."

"Nixon also ordered you to send them in to bomb Hanoi and Haiphong – which was risky. The Russians had equipped the North Vietnamese with their latest sophisticated anti-aircraft defences. And your B52s were rather large targets!"

"We knew we would take losses. Of course, we could have gone in with smaller, faster jets – as I cautioned the President at the time. However, Nixon wanted to go for broke. And *'Linebacker II'* did just that, catching Hanoi totally off balance. We hit them so hard that by the end of the mission they'd run out of SAM missiles. With my B52s roaming their airspace at will, we'd left them with no alternative but to sue for peace."

"Which I guess must make it all the more galling that the campaign turned out to be such a pyrrhic victory. Moreover, one that had meanwhile cost the life of your son," Lawton decided the time had come to grasp the nettle, as it were.

Glancing across at him, those mirror sunshades left him unsure how mention of this most personal aspect of the war that Charles Eichelberger had waged had been received.

An answer of sorts came when he heard the General expel a deep breath down the plane's intercom and sigh "It grieves me to say it, John, but you're right. While we'd been pounding the enemy from the skies, public support for the war back home had finally evaporated. Nixon knew this. And so too did the North Vietnamese. Henceforth, with a peace agreement signed and the last of our troops headed home, all the enemy had to do was bide his time until first Watergate, and then a hostile Congress slashing military aid to Saigon removed the last obstacles to his ambitions. When his next big offensive opened in December 1974 the absence of US air support – in particular, the threat of those B52 strikes – emboldened Hanoi to press on to final victory. By then, we'd washed our hands of South Vietnam and abandoned its people to their fate. It was a shameful end to a struggle that had cost so many lives – yes, including that of my own son."

Upon that harrowing admission the confabulation ceased. Instead, the brooding general gazed down at The Needles as his host executed a sharp bank to port so that the tall cliffs of Tennyson Down could also be viewed (from which these impressive chalk stacks had once broken away). Lawton could only pray he hadn't tweaked a raw nerve and thereby brought to an abrupt end the fulsome collaboration he so desperately sought. Therefore, once he had over-flown Freshwater Bay to set a course along the wild, sparsely-populated southern coastline of the island, the historian had a sudden brainwave. Nudging his taciturn passenger, he suggested he should take the controls from him.

"No kidding?" Eichelberger seemed startled at first.

"Be my guest. I can think of no safer pair of hands to be in than those of one of the world's greatest living aviators!" Lawton commended him sportively.

Eichelberger grasped the joystick and felt the plane responding to his control. All at once his despondency vanished. It was someone else's turn to experience a rush of adrenalin.

To be sure, John Lawton could be too ingratiating for his own good at times. The object of his awe was prepared to put this down to traditional English politeness; as well as his tendency to betray a certain insecurity about his considerable achievements to that same English propensity for understatement. However, none of this lessened the General's admiration for this man who had lavished such hospitality upon his wife and himself; a man who (it appeared) had doted on and looked after his daughter too during the time she'd been working at his hotel – as would a supportive older brother.

The trauma of losing Lawrence – a young man who'd been set for a glittering air force career *après le père* – had indeed been a terrible blow. Meanwhile, rebuilding his tenuous relationship with Aimee was proving a fraught undertaking which (he suspected) she inwardly resented. However, in this affable, aviation-loving son of a famous British air marshal it was almost as if Charles Eichelberger had stumbled upon the perfect repository for his frustrated paternal yearnings. Though he could never replace the son he had lost, one could almost say that, in John Lawton, he had found the second son he'd never had.

* * * * *

Its approach could be discerned by the gathering drone of its engine. All eyes strained to pick out the small plane in the empty afternoon sky. Then it appeared, emerging around the headland to race past at low altitude. As the three women jumped to their feet and waved, so the pilot at the controls waved back.

"Hey, that's my dad!" Aimee leapt up and down, excitedly pointing out the Bonanza waggling its wings in salute before it made off into the distance, the drone fading Doppler-like to permit tranquillity to return.

"Yes, John said he might take him on a spin around the island. I'm afraid he does so love showing off his latest plaything," Veronica Lawton cussed as she returned from the kitchen with some refreshments.

The bikini-clad Aimee returned to the sun lounger she'd been relaxing on. Next to her a similarly-clad Shelby was also once again supine – just the merest dash of sun lotion enough to equip her to top up her enviable tan. Meanwhile, on the opposite side of the wrought ornamental table from them (and upon which she had placed the tray of drinks), Veronica sat down on an easy chair next to Natalie – whose brimmed straw hat and long, patterned summer dress belied a skin type that (like her daughter's) took rather less kindly to being toasted by the intense August sun.

"I'm really sorry you girls can't dive in and cool off," Veronica called over, plopping her own stylish sun hat back over her dark brown locks. "But only in Britain can a swimming pool be declared out of bounds just when one needs it most! Unfortunately though, these are desperate times. Of course, it'll be such a chore to have to trot up the hill to fetch water from one of those abominable standpipes. I'm afraid John will simply have to roll up his sleeves and wander up with some buckets."

Aimee inwardly seethed. Though it tickled Natalie, Veronica's snooty aside was indicative of the woman's patronising disdain towards a man who – for all his quirks – the American history student had come to feel a strange and symbiotic bond.

"Yeah, you Brits have sure got it bad. So much for me telling Aimee to pack all those raincoats!" her mother observed, taking a moment to gaze about at the bistred lawn and withered hedges, and repenting of at least one stern admonition she'd drummed into her daughter upon her departure for England.

Meanwhile, Aimee reached over to the table and took a sip of the vodka and tonic that Veronica had furtively mixed for her, contemplating a further stern admonition she'd spent the intervening year conveniently ignoring.

It had been Veronica's idea that, while Charles and her husband were indulging their shared passion for winged flight, Natalie and the girls join her at the Edwardian property they had bought and renovated in the pretty little village of Bonchurch, near Ventnor. With its spacious lounge, lavishly-equipped kitchen, four tastefully-furnished en-suite bedrooms, pine-clad summer house, and sea-facing terrace with commanding views of the English Channel, it was the perfect place to withdraw from the travails of running a busy hotel. It boasted a swimming pool too – even if it had been drained and covered over on account of the worsening water shortage. However, it had not gone unnoticed by Aimee that her boss was apologising so profusely for them being unable to use it. In fact, it represented a startling sea change when contrasted with her previous grudging attitude to her two employees using the pool at the hotel.

"Say, isn't that that ship we saw the other day in Portsmouth. The one Vaughan pointed out us," Shelby meanwhile sat up and cupped a hand to her eyes. "*HMS Sheffield*, wasn't it?"

"From here one sees all sorts of ships passing. I often find John studying them through his binoculars. You see, he's into ships, planes – anything to do with war. Sadly though, he's not into things to do with the day-to-day running of a hotel. Those things he leaves to me!" his wife huffed, sipping from her Chardonnay.

Also not unnoticed, her remark reminded Aimee that Veronica Lawton would normally have been hard at work this afternoon overseeing the weekly influx of new guests. However, something had transpired over the last week or so that had caused the demeanour of this invariably sour-faced woman to lighten and so pull out all the stops to make the two room maids welcome in her home. This uncharacteristic complaisance made a refreshing change to the haughty scowl with which she usually entreated them. Aimee, for one, was of a mind that there must be an ulterior motive behind the transformation.

"Say, it really is a swell place you got here," cooed Natalie, leaning back in her chair and admiring the views.

"I like to think so," Veronica replied with a hint of self-satisfaction. "John would have you believe it's his money that has made all this possible. And yes, I suppose he did put up the capital to purchase and restore both this house and the hotel. But neither investment would have amounted to much without the hard work that *I've* put into managing them," she crowed.

"See what I mean, girls. Knuckle down and study and then one day you too can own real estate like this. Why, I keep telling Aimee to quit chasing boys and concentrate on graduating instead. Every night I pray to the Good Lord that my daughter might actually listen to me!" Natalie rolled her eyes and whisked a hand in faux despair.

Unseen, Aimee also rolled her eyes behind her bulbous sunshades, otherwise pretending not to have heard. She recalled a sermon her grandfather had once preached around Christ's admonition that 'a man's life consisteth not in the abundance of the things which he possesseth'. That said, marrying a man who could afford to buy a hotel, a mansion and a private plane – and still have money in the bank – had its attractions.

"Oh, I don't know. There's nothing wrong with having a little fun every now and again. You agree, girls...?" Veronica looked to the two youngsters for affirmation. "I said, you agree?"

"Oh... I'm sorry, Mrs Lawton?" Shelby hastily swivelled to acknowledge her boss – otherwise still strangely fascinated by that warship making haste to round St Catherine's Point.

"I said there's nothing wrong with having a little fun."

"Sure. Me and Aimee have had lots of fun together while we've been on the island. We've been dancing; and to some swell parties too. But trust me, Mrs Eichelberger, it's all been good, clean fun. 'What would Jesus do?', and all that. I've been looking after your daughter real good while we've been in England."

While Shelby lacked the heart to admit that, of late, her best friend had ceased being amenable to being 'looked after', Aimee was thankful that her breezy assurance seemed to assuage the perpetual fussing of her God-fearing mother about her moral welfare. Meanwhile, a sly, cognisant grin flitted across Veronica's bronzed and comely face – again unseen.

While it had been good to catch up with her folks again, these last few days had witnessed Aimee back on her best behaviour. Furthermore, her father seemed most eager that she recount what she'd been up to since they'd last met – of which she had offered him a sanitized version (as befitted her conviction that 'what Mom and Dad don't know won't hurt them!'). However, to her surprise, she had found her father commending the opportunity for independence and self-discovery that her year abroad had afforded her. She couldn't make up her mind whether this sudden professed interest was just another pitch to try and make up for all those years when – apropos being an 'afterthought' – it had been her brother's endeavours (and no doubt his similarly sanitized exploits) that had interested her father more.

"Yes, this really is a beautiful house," Natalie commended their host. Then she glanced across at her and noted that "All it needs to complete the homely atmosphere is the sound of children's laughter. I listen to your gentle voice and sense the Lord telling me you'd make a really excellent mother?"

Aimee rolled her eyes again, both at her mother's crass remark and that the Lord's estimation of this frequently gruff and impatient chatelaine (or at least her mother's interpretation of it!) was so wide of the mark.

In fact, she'd heard enough. While Veronica was graciously explaining that – regardless of John's enthusiasm – she still had so many things she wanted to do before she could contemplate putting things on hold for something as inconvenient as a baby, Aimee rose to her feet, tied her rayon sarong around her hips, and lifted her sunshades onto her head.

"Could I use your bathroom, Mrs Lawton," she requested.

"Of course," her host stared up and beamed obligingly. "Up the stairs; final door at the end of the corridor."

"Thank you."

Yes, Aimee pondered as she stepped over the threshold into the welcome shade of the house: that woman was definitely up to something. Otherwise, wearily plodding up the stairs, she recalled how – contrary to Shelby's resumé of their hectic social life –

these last few days she'd been too fatigued to care about dancing or partying. More tellingly, once she'd located the bathroom and bolted the door behind her she sank to her knees over the pan and wretched. Lifting herself to her feet, she then dabbed her lips with a tissue and fretted over her reflection in the mirror. When allied to the period she'd missed, it was another worrying sign that her body might be trying to tell her something.

Exiting the bathroom, she came over queasy again, halting to steady herself against the wall. As she did so, she availed herself of the moment to nudge open a door on the landing that was ajar. Peering inside, it turned out to be the opulent master bedroom. She lingered to admire the décor, the furnishings, and the painting above the bed by David Hockney.

Yet what struck her was the complete absence of 'ships, planes or anything to do with war' – either here or (upon reflection) elsewhere around the house. This place was most definitely the wife's domain, the husband's less aesthetic collectibles having been banished to his office at the hotel. Still, at least she'd permitted him a pair of binoculars with which to play look-out!

Stepping inside, she took the liberty of seating herself upon the sumptuous king-sized bed, where she imagined those little Lawtons that her mother had alluded to would be made – if only, that is, their prospective mother would suffer to open her legs wide enough and often enough for her husband to perform his role in their procreation. Once again, Aimee found her burning resentment towards Veronica Lawton matched by sympathy towards her longsuffering husband. She brushed her fingers along the soft sheets, wondering what this poor man had done to end up locked in a loveless marriage to such a fastidious harridan!

"*'Someone's been sleeping in my bed and she's still there!'*" there suddenly chortled a voice from behind her.

She turned with a start and a sharp intake of breath to behold the object of her contempt standing in the doorway, spying her.

"I'm sorry, Mrs Lawton," Aimee leapt to her feet. "I didn't mean to pry. I was just admiring how nicely you've…"

Veronica had fire in her eyes redolent of a woman gleeful at having caught the flirty room maid *in flagrante* snooping around her private quarters.

"*'Goldilocks and the Three Bears'*," her eyes locked onto Aimee as she paced forward and pondered aloud that "Surely American children are taught this tale by their parents too."

Her riddling put her employee on the spot. "Er, yes... W-w-we do. I m-m-mean, we are," Aimee stuttered.

"But then neither a bear nor a suspicious wife will take kindly to discovering that a young girl with fair hair has been sleeping in her bed – behind her back; and with her husband in it!"

"I'm sorry, Mrs Lawton. But I'm not sure I follow what you mean," the American protested.

"Come on, Aimee. You've been to Oxford University – so I know you're not stupid. I've noticed the way you and my husband are always looking at each other in that certain way."

Then she stepped forward to finger the string of Aimee's bikini top in a move that was at once menacing and (as that finger brushed slowly and purposefully against the underside of her pert little breast) electrifyingly sexual.

"I've noticed too that you clearly enjoy having *these* things on display whenever he's around. So I can understand why John might be tempted to get to know them – and their owner – a little better," she offered her a back-handed compliment.

Thereupon, Veronica inserted the tips of those fingers into the bikini top to unveil the supple orb and marvel at it. It seemed her husband wasn't the only Lawton who, all this time, had been tempted to get to know them – and their owner – a little better!

Electing to lift her gaze, she re-engaged eye contact with the dumbstruck student, who juggled a lump in her throat as she stared into her boss's dark, appetitive eyes. Aimee felt a thumb gently roam back and forth over the proud nipple. Rooted to the spot, she winced and drew breath again when Veronica grasped the teat between her thumb and forefingers and squeezed it hard.

"I think there m-m-must be some m-m-misunderstanding, Mrs Lawton. There is nothing going on between J-J-John and me. I promise."

"Of course not... If you say so," she feigned to believe her. Grinning warily, Veronica then released her pinch – though for several long, tense seconds she continued to stare out her terrified visitor.

"You see, John is a very fickle man. So, my dear, whether there is or there isn't anything 'going on', please don't flatter yourself that these things will always keep you in his thoughts," she insisted, roughly inserting the boob back into the bikini top and withdrawing the hand. "Therefore, it's as well you heed your mother's advice and concentrate on graduating... And not keep floozying yourself in front of my husband. Agreed?"

Aimee so wanted to protest this outrageous imputation. However, recognising that discretion was the better party of valour (and by now completely cowed by this adroit and intimidating woman), she nodded stiffly.

"Good. I'm glad we understand each other."

This time feigning sisterly solicitude, Veronica then looped an arm around Aimee and led her back out onto the landing, closing the bedroom door behind her.

"Of course, *were* you to find yourself getting intimate with John he'd probably flatter you with some bullshit about sex with you being so much better than it is with his 'frigid' wife. Alas though, were he not so wrapped up in his obsession with aeroplanes he would realise that his 'frigid' wife has been rather hotter when it comes to arranging our financial affairs. And in such a way that were he to fly off in that plane of his – with some fancy young bimbo by his side – then he wouldn't get very far. After all, there has to have been some advantage to me from his attention always being elsewhere!"

Then, in a demonstration of why Aimee had been wise to choose discretion, she had a final observation to make as they descended the stairs to join the other women on the sun terrace.

"Your parents are very religious, aren't they, Aimee. The kind of upright churchgoers who might not be well pleased were your mother to sense the Lord – or maybe even me – whispering in ear that the 'fun' their daughter has been having in my hotel has been anything but 'good' or 'clean'."

23

Sunday, August 22nd 1976

"Take a seat. Drink?"

"I won't say no."

"If I've got it, you can have it," John Lawton chortled, opening wide his drinks cabinet and pointing proudly to the assortment of bottles and decanters on display. "Was that a scotch on the rocks I noticed you imbibing at Aimee's party the other evening? If so, I have scotch; and there's ice in the fridge," he announced, holding up the requisite bottle.

Charles Eichelberger appeared to agonise for a moment.

"Why not," he yielded.

However, instead of taking a seat as offered he chose instead to roam the office, hands clasped behind his back, studying the many paintings and photographs mounted upon the walls. In common with every visitor who the hotelier privileged with an invitation into this inner sanctum, eventually he alighted upon that huge portrait of an austere-looking figure with a clipped moustache, who stared back at him. From the pressed grey-blue uniform and the array of braid and medals on his chest he spotted straight away that it was a senior Royal Air Force officer.

"Your old man?" he turned to his host.

"Air Marshal Sir Hugh Lawton KBE VC," Lawton beamed proudly, sidling up to the General to hand him the glass he had poured before returning to mix something for himself.

"Yeah. Name rings a bell. I guess it's always possible we've met. When I was at Ramstein with 17 EAF I got to work closely with you Brits on NATO liaison."

"Then it's a small world!" Lawton noted, repeating an expression he'd found himself using a lot lately.

Raising a toast to their enduring friendship, he mused that it was indeed intriguing to think that these two veteran aviators might have worked together once upon a time. It was to share more of these sorts of fascinating vignettes that he had invited the General to his office for a nightcap

As was their custom, the Eichelbergers had attended church this morning – the little gospel hall in Shanklin that Aimee and Shelby also attended. After evening dinner, Aimee had then retired to her room, complaining of once again feeling nauseous. Shelby had later checked and found her friend fast asleep. Convincing her parents that their daughter must have spent too long in the sun yesterday, she volunteered to accompany Natalie to the hotel's cabaret show, where some crisp and clean-cut young pianist was entertaining the guests with a selection of Barry Manilow hits. It afforded Charles the excuse he needed to join Lawton for a more earnest late-night *tête-a-tête*.

"You know, John, when I was in England I used to drink this stuff a lot," he recalled, having finally sat down on the long leather sofa, where he held his glass up to stare at it warily.

"Understandable, I suppose – given the enormous stress you guys were working under," Lawton opined, joining him at the opposite end of the sofa.

"Nowadays I only do so on special occasions. Natalie doesn't like me drinking alcohol. Says it sets a bad example to our daughter. Not that Aimee any longer considers me a role model to emulate. Heaven knows what she must have gotten up to while she's been in England!" he shook his head and frowned.

"I couldn't possibly comment!" Lawton smirked.

Their light-hearted moment soon passed. In its place, Lawton took a swig from his own whisky-and-dry and donned a demeanour to match the occasion.

"You and Natalie profess quite a deep faith – if you don't mind me saying. In fact, didn't I read somewhere that you were training to be a minister when war broke out; and that nowadays you're an elder at your church back in Minnesota? And that your wife leads the ladies' prayer chapter there?"

"That's right. We both gave our lives to the Lord more years ago than we care to remember. Natalie's old man's a pastor. My parents too are very devout."

Lawton was touched – even as he confessed that "I'm afraid I'm a somewhat irresolute believer myself; the sort you only tend to find in church at christenings, weddings and funerals – or hatchings, matchings and despatchings, as the old saying goes."

The General murmured indulgently, listening with interest as his host went on to concede that "I suppose it must make me the kind of wayward soul who needs your wife's prayers rather a lot – a Prodigal Son who has 'wasted his substance with riotous living', as the Good Book puts it. In my case, I'm afraid, on fast cars, a private plane, and one or two regrettable romantic entanglements," he grinned cryptically. "But then they do say seducing women is rather like fox-hunting – insofar as the thrill of the chase usually outweighs anything one can conceivable do with the thing once one's caught it!"

Eichelberger stared him out for a moment – his host unsure whether his throw-away remark might have offended this godly man. Indeed, by rights Charles Eichelberger should have been horrified by such a cynical aside. He certainly wouldn't want a man trifling with his own daughter's affections in such a cavalier manner. However, before the General could raise his voice in rebuke, recollections of his own 'riotous living' suppressed it – as did recalling the 'foxes' he'd once 'chased'.

"We're all sinners, John – if that's what you're driving at. But the important lesson about the Prodigal Son was that he came to his senses; and sought forgiveness for his past mistakes. And when he did, the response of the Father was to fall upon him in compassion," the General observed, standing up for his faith while side-stepping his own guilt. For, far from sermonising, there was a look of penitent sorrow in Charles Eichelberger's tight brown eyes that belied an awareness that one or two 'regrettable romantic entanglements' of his own might yet be about to catch up with him.

"Maybe. But then I can't imagine an All-American hero like you has done anything that might conceivably be in need of forgiveness," Lawton expressed amusement (as well as attempting to side-step this uncomfortable talk about religion).

"I might be an 'All-American hero' to some people," the General replied. "However, there are probably others out there for whom I am a far from heroic figure."

"You mean because of Cambodia?" Lawton presumed – wrongly as it happened. However, at least the presumption afforded his guest a while longer to summon up the courage to maybe broach a more personal matter that had lately been troubling him. Therefore – religion suitably side-stepped – he was instead willing to offer his thoughts about his latter-day involvement in this small, benighted country.

"Right from the start Congress was adamant it would not grant the White House *carte blanche* in Cambodia as it had in Vietnam. The President was therefore left scratching about for a response to the North Vietnamese using the country as a base for their operations in the South; and to the mounting threat to Phnom Penh from its own communist insurgency. Forbidden to use US ground troops, the only option Nixon had left was to employ air power to blunt the threat from both. For example, in '72-'73 our bombing sorties were almost certainly what prevented Khmer Rouge guerrillas from overrunning the country."

"They were deeply controversial operations though," Lawton reminded him, settling into this new dialogue. "The bombing probably resulted in the deaths of thousands of innocent Cambodians. One of your own analysts even went public and admitted that it was virtually impossible to configure a B52 'strike box' that didn't involve the risk of hitting a settlement."

"We tried hard to minimise casualties. All B52 strikes were preceded by LORAN-equipped F4 reconnaissance aircraft, enabling us to plot the precise location of enemy units. My staff turned down many requests from the Cambodian government for strikes precisely because of the risk of incurring civilian casualties. But damn it, John! I couldn't vouch for the precise location of every single Cambodian civilian at any given moment of the day or night."

"And then came the catastrophe at Neak Luong," Lawton pressed him. "In August 1973 a lone B52 dropped its entire payload of bombs on a town along the banks of the Mekong River. Hundreds of civilians were killed – ironically many of them refugees fleeing from your bombing campaign."

"There was a mix-up involving the homing beacons that led to the pilot misjudging his position relative to the target. It shouldn't have happened; but it was human error – pure and simple."

"I accept that. Yet surely it must trouble you that in some quarters Nixon and Kissinger are regarded as war criminals because of what they ordered in Cambodia – and that fingers are being pointed at you too as the military commander who oversaw those *'Freedom Deal'* missions."

Eichelberger sat up and propped his elbows upon knees that he had spread apart.

"My conscience is clean," he then proceeded to lecture his understudy with his empty glass. "And besides: is what I ordered in Cambodia any more a 'war crime' than what your own air force did over Germany?" the increasingly prickly General snapped, angrily pointing the glass at the portrait of Lawton's father. "Neak Luong was an accident, John; Hamburg, Dresden and Berlin were not."

Shocked by the outburst his interrogation had unleashed, Lawton desisted. A lacuna thus descended upon the two men that enabled each to pause and reflect. Eventually, it was the General who elected to break the silence.

"I'm sorry," he huffed, contrite for his loss of self-control. "It's just that when you're the guy in charge those are the kind of dilemmas you have to wrestle with every single day. War is cruel, John – let's not pretend otherwise. Neither is it ever black-or-white. But what was the alternative?" he stared at him indignantly and then into his empty glass, as if to observe a dreg that was left. "If even half the reports about its new communist government are true, then by our abdication we have surrendered six million Cambodians to the tender mercies of a regime that is plumbing new depths of barbarism; one that is engaged in the systematic genocide of its own people. It's the leadership of the Khmer Rouge who are the real war criminals, John – not me!"

"Another one?" an emollient Lawton hinted at the glass still in his hand. The General stared into it again.

"Sure," he handed it back to him and watched while his host wandered over to the drinks cabinet and returned with it refilled. Then he ventured upon the real reason why he felt his heroic 'All-

American' image had been irrevocably tarnished by the dilemmas he had once had to wrestle with.

"You know, to be frank, I'd don't give a damn what all those cosseted college professors and posturing Congressmen think about me. Nor the *'Washington Post'*! But it does grieve me that maybe my own daughter is appalled by the things I had to do. And that maybe she despises me because of it."

"Surely not," Lawton attempted to console him. "You're her father. She has certainly never given me any reason to believe she 'despises' you. So maybe if she seemed wilful at times, then it was just Aimee dealing with the normal issues that all young people go through – the daughters of four-star generals included."

Eichelberger huffed as if unconvinced, but grateful anyway for his host's kind words. He recalled his own wild youth and how he too had pushed against the boundaries of decorous behaviour that his strict and devout parents had drilled into him. And – like he suspected Aimee had been doing – that once packed off to England (and thereby liberated from their oversight) he too had 'wasted his substance with riotous living'. Studying his anxious features, Lawton picked up on this gnawing guilt that there might once have been a time when this man had been far from a glowing role model for his headstrong daughter.

"For what it's worth, I rebelled at university too," the hotelier confided, hoping to leaven the General's despondency. "More so when I discovered that I was not going to be accepted for pilot training in the RAF. That was all I'd lived for as a teenager – to fly, and to make my father proud by following in his footsteps. I guess being rejected served to further fuel my resentment at having found out that I was an unwanted child."

"'Unwanted'?" Eichelberger suddenly puzzled. "But you told me your parents both loved you."

"That's right. They did. But when I turned eighteen I made the shocking discovery that Sir Hugh and his wife were not my real parents after all; but that I had been adopted by them when I was two years-old. Apparently, I was the illegitimate outcome of some wartime fling. My real mother had surrendered me to an orphanage in order to escape the shame of what she had done."

"Really?"

"Yes. All I knew was that her name was Nora and that I'd been born in Suffolk. But then – by a series of amazing coincidences – the other day I finally got to meet her for the first time in over thirty years. I can't begin to describe to you how that moment felt. It was as if I had stumbled upon a precious piece of the jigsaw of my jumbled life that would enable me to at last make sense of who I am."

For one brief moment that Lawton – lost in reflection of his own – never noticed, an almost visible shudder coursed through Charles Eichelberger. He stared at his host and listened with mounting disbelief to his candid lament.

"Alas, as far as the final missing piece is concerned, the entry on my birth certificate says simply 'father unknown'. My mother has told me very little about him – only that he was soldier billeted at the coastal defences that had been constructed nearby. However, I suspect she's keeping his real identity from me even now – such is the shame she still feels after all these years. But then I imagine it must match the shame she still feels for abandoning me at birth, knowing that one day I would discover that I had been the unintended result of her hasty affair."

The General's taut face had turned white as a sheet.

"Listen, John," he felt compelled to point out. "You don't have to feel that way. Whatever happened back then was just one of those unfortunate things that go on all the time during war. People sometimes come together in desperate circumstances. Sometimes they part that way too. I'm sure somewhere out there is a man who still feels bad about fathering you and then abandoning your mother. But were he to be sitting in this room now, seeing all the amazing things you've achieved – your fortune, your hotel, your writing career – I know he would be mighty proud of you. Heck, if you were a son of mine I'd be mighty proud of you too."

Lawton cracked a smile. Compliment though it was, lately a conflict had been brewing within the wealthy womaniser between the carnal and calculating side of his nature and the nobler, if more vulnerable side – the outcome of what he now knew about who he was. He looked away, the latter nature bidding a rare tear trickle from his eye. As he angrily dabbed at it, the General reached over and alighted a paternal hand upon his shoulder, pressing it with manly assurance – the kind of act he'd undertaken many times when seeking to steel up the men he had once commanded to face hardships and dangers.

"I'm sorry," Lawton apologised, downing the contents of his glass. Meanwhile, his eyes sought to ape the resolve those brave pilots must have shown upon understanding how they too enjoyed the confidence of this most esteemed leader of men.

Eichelberger withdrew his hand. Then he downed some more scotch in order to firm up his own faltering resolve.

"And this Nora woman – who you say is your mother – she's here? On the island? Right now?"

"That's right," Lawton nodded his head at how preposterous such a coincidence must seem. "She's holidaying here with her sister, who's a nightclub singer. In fact, her sister is that Angie Ashby who you've probably seen advertised around the hotel."

By now the wistful historian could discern that his guest was uncomfortable about something. In fact, he was squirming.

"You know Angie, don't you," he ventured, recalling that wartime photograph he'd come across of the two of them enjoying a moment of Christmas revelry in 1944.

The moment of truth was upon him. Like Jacob's sons in the Book of Genesis upon discovering that the brother they'd bundled into a pit and left for dead was actually alive and offering them alms, so the past had finally caught up with the horrified and guilt-stricken Charles Eichelberger. He swallowed hard and looked his host in the eye.

"Yeah," he shrugged awkwardly, "Sure I know Angie. You might as well know that I dated her while I was in England. In fact… we were engaged to be married," the story dribbled out. "But, well… sometimes relationships forged in the haste of war don't always seem so clever with the more leisurely reflection afforded by peace."

Lawton was astounded. It really was a small world. To think, he would never have met his mother had her sister's glamorous good looks not caught his roving eye. And he would never have met her sister's one-time fiancé – a man she had up until now only alluded to – had he not needed to fill in the gaps of the research project that had been obsessing him. Therefore, astounded by this happenstance, he had a further coincidence he wished to toss into this extraordinary mix.

"Then it might tickle you to know that your daughter dated Nora's younger son, Vaughan – that bus conductor chap she might have told you about. If something had come of it that would certainly have been a turn up for the books: your daughter and my half-brother standing at the altar; with my aunt – your ex-fiancée – watching you give her away!"

It had taken over thirty years, but at last the cock was crowing for the terrible thing that Charles Eichelberger had done that night on the dunes. The grievous sin that he had left unspoken and unresolved for so long was finally catching up with him – as was the remarkable *dramatis personae* of his life who were now gathered together on this small island for what was turning out to be a long, hot and exceedingly revelatory summer.

24

Tuesday, August 24th 1976

PRESS STATEMENT

The Prime Minister has today announced that he has asked Mr Dennis Howell, Minister of State at the Department of the Environment, to co-ordinate all matters connected with the supply of water during the period of drought and the measures being taken to deal with it. Mr Howell, who was present at the meeting of ministers held at 10 Downing Street today to consider the situation, will begin work immediately.

Individual ministers remain responsible for their particular functions and Mr Howell will continue to work within the Department of the Environment.

10 Downing Street,
London, SW1

24 August 1976

Note to editors: Mr Howell's press conference will be held at 3.00pm today.

* * * * *

"Good evening, both. Lovely to see you down here nice and early to reserve the best seats in the house."

"Thank you, John. We really enjoyed last night's show. You've booked some amazing acts," the husband commended the hotel manager who was looming over their table.

"Well, we've an even better show for you tonight. And may I say how absolutely radiant Mrs Williams looks. There must be hearts breaking all over Shanklin tonight!" Lawton smirked, complimenting the blushing wife for the way her bobbed hair danced upon sun-bronzed shoulders left exposed by the expensive evening gown that was hanging off them.

"Now I trust you and Mr Williams have been sharing baths to save water," the smooth-talking hotelier teased as he leaned in to address her directly. "And in no more than five inches of the stuff, mind – just like our new Minister for Drought told us to do at his press conference this afternoon.

"And I don't know what you're all laughing at," he then turned to playfully berate guests on neighbouring tables who had overheard. "I'm going to be coming round each of your rooms tomorrow to personally place a brick inside the toilet cisterns – something else Mr Howell has asked me to do. And if I catch any of you not joining in the show tonight I shall be inserting *two* bricks inside yours!"

There was hearty laughter. Indeed, it was a toss-up whether John Lawton's true calling in life was to chronicle the exploits of great aviators; or to be a one-man welcoming committee for his exclusive hotel. He slipped into either mode with a natural flair.

Tonight the latter gift was very much on show. However, touring the room to make small talk, or to chivvy his guests with his witty asides, he eventually alighted upon one table where the gracious welcome was genuinely heartfelt.

"General Eichelberger, sir," he offered his outstretched hand to his hero, wishing it was permissible to salute him instead.

"John," the stocky commander stood to his feet, gripping and shaking it.

"The beautiful Mrs Eichelberger," Lawton then progressed around the table, tenderly lifting Natalie's dainty paw and placing the gentlest of kisses upon the back of it.

"Thank you, John. You are so kind," she gazed up at him through fluttering eyelashes.

"The stunning Aimee – to whom it is plain the mother has bequeathed her incredible good looks," Lawton moved to greet her, taking her hand and kissing it too, as well as savouring the sight of the maiden from Minnesota blushing at the compliment.

"And Shelby."

"Mr Lawton, sir," Shelby insisted on addressing him formally, her tiny hand grudgingly accepting his own.

The pint-sized lass from Jasper County was shrewd enough to discern the artful thought processes going on inside her boss's head whenever he was in the company of her taller room mate. For his part, Lawton was shrewd enough to discern that 'Little Miss Perfect' had long since gained the measure of him. He returned in kind the bristling smile she offered him.

"Isn't he such a nice man: a true English gentleman – and he has made us so welcome here," Natalie gushed. "Veronica is so blessed to be married to such a wonderful guy. And you girls should be grateful too: to have worked for him. See, Charles," she then turned to her husband, "didn't I tell you the Good Lord would look after Aimee while she was in England."

"I still think he's a creep," Shelby muttered under her breath once Lawton had moved safely out of earshot.

Watching while this 'wonderful man' lavished his glib charm upon another duo of attractive young ladies (who were sat at their table looking out of place amidst the sea of couples and families), someone of her sexual probity could recall the Shakespeare she'd read at college and muse that – vain, boastful and lecherous – truly John Lawton was Falstaff minus the girth!

Something else Shelby had picked up on was that she and Natalie were the only ones around the table who seemed to be looking forward to tonight's show. Aimee was still under the weather (literally maybe; but Shelby sensed something else was burdening her normally vivacious best friend). Meanwhile, her father was comporting himself as if a whole squadron of Focke-Wulf 190s was about to pounce upon his Mustang from out of the clouds. When he wasn't giving the impression of being impatient to be somewhere else, he was easily startled by passing waitresses or late-arriving couples enquiring after untaken seats. Something was clearly burdening Charles Eichelberger too.

"Look, if you ladies don't mind, I think I'll retire early," he eventually piped up, motioning to stand up.

"No you will not, Charles!" Natalie thundered, hauling him back into his seat. "Sunday evening you disappeared and left me here on my own. Now stay and watch the show – especially now

John has taken the trouble of getting us a table on the front row. Besides, everyone here's been talking about tonight's act."

Realising there was going to be no escape, Charles grudgingly settled back down and – upon his wife's insistence – signalled the waitress to fetch another round of drinks. He pondered whether to further risk Natalie's displeasure and order himself a neat scotch while he was at it!

Once that traditional British hotel fixture – the nightly game of bingo – had been wrapped up, the compère strode onto the stage to introduce the magician booked as the warm-up act. Once he, in turn, had sawn his pretty assistant in half and pulled a white rabbit from out of his hat, the compère returned to this time introduce the star turn with his usual panoply of superlatives. Suddenly, the stage lights were bathing the whole room in dramatic hues of swirling colour. Suddenly, *she* was there!

It was the first time in over thirty-one years that Charles Eichelberger had set eyes upon this Englishwomen who he'd once impulsively proposed marriage to, and who now advanced onto the stage to launch into a sultry swing rendition of Cole Porter's seasonally appropriate *'Too Darn Hot'*. Like the rest of her audience, Natalie and Shelby were rendered spellbound by Angie's gripping performance.

Thereafter, she slowed the tempo to follow on with the evocative *'Night And Day'*. As she did so – and like an eerie reprise for a time in his life he hoped had been closed forever – it was almost as if she had purposed to assail her one-time fiancé with that very same melody she had performed upon a memorable night in the summer of 1944 when they had first set eyes on each other. He'd fallen head-over-heels in love with her there and then. So much so that – against his better judgement (and in careless disregard of the sweetheart he had left behind in Stearns County) – the young fighter ace had plucked up the courage after the show to ask if he might date her. To his surprise, she had agreed. It had been love at first sight on her part too. Thereafter, they had embarked upon nine months of unbridled passion – interrupted only by the exigencies of the war it had been conducted amidst.

Meanwhile, Aimee spotted her father palpitating with disbelief when Angie stepped down from the stage, placed a hand upon one of her shapely hips, and sauntered over to their table. Stooping, with the forefinger of other hand she then lifted his chin and drew almost nose-to-nose with him, staring into his skittish eyes so that she might address those lyrics to him personally...

> *"...Night and day, under the hide of me,*
> *There's oh, such a hungry yearnin' burnin' inside of me.*
> *And its torment won't be through,*
> *Till you let me spend my life makin' love to you,*
> *Day and night, night and day."*

For a moment as she too observed her husband's discomfort, Natalie Eichelberger wondered if there was something she ought to know. However, no sooner had her indulgent smile turned to a nascent scowl than Angie had stood erect again and was striding off to address another front row table. Eventually, she stepped back onto the stage and drew the number to a close to a round of ecstatic applause.

"See, I told y'all she was good," Shelby chortled innocently – the only one around the table who had failed to read anything untoward into what had just transpired. Otherwise, it had been a brush with remembrance that had clearly spooked Charles Eichelberger – as the vampish chanteuse had intended.

Mercifully, the more contemporary melodies that followed afforded Charles the opportunity to breath easy. However, while his wife appeared to have dismissed the incident as a piece of (admittedly risqué) stage theatrics, Aimee's eyes met her father's as if to demand an answer. However, she guessed she already had it: as she had suspected all along, Charles Eichelberger and Angie Ashby had once been lovers. She recalled that interview in which the latter had hinted that – even were 'a thousand chapters' to be devoted to it – her study of the fraternisation that had taken place between GIs and local girls in wartime Britain would never do justice to the 'heartache and misery' of 'love betrayed and promises unfulfilled'. Suddenly, that senior thesis Aimee had spent her year in England researching and writing up had become chillingly personal.

Angie's final number was a full-throttle rendition of Carole King's soulful *'(You Make Me Feel Like) A Natural Woman'*. It had the entire house on its feet in a standing ovation – including the Eichelberger party. As she exited the stage, she once more gave Charles 'the eye' – this time a defiant eye that spoke of a woman who had put her life back together again after an epic fall. Once more, it was a gesture that Aimee decoded, turning to her father to observe him offer Angie a mangled smile.

"MORE...! MORE...!" the cry meanwhile went up.

"Shelby's right, honey. She is good," he thought to cover his tracks by speaking into the ear of his wife above the din.

If, by that grudging approbation, Charles Eichelberger thought his purgatory was over, he was mistaken – for all that hollering and foot-stomping was not about to go unrewarded. Within the minute, Angie Ashby was back on stage, her figure-hugging sequin dress spangling beneath its powerful spotlights.

"Thank you... Thank you..." the teary starlet called out, bidding the audience to be still.

"I'd like to dedicate this final song to those of you husbands and wives who are lucky enough to still be as in love tonight as you were on the day you first met. So if that's you, why not take this opportunity to step onto the floor and celebrate that love."

With that, the guy on the sound desk unleashed the opening bars of *'Strangers In The Night'*, prompting Natalie to turn to the first and only love of her own life. She fired him an inviting stare that needed no accompanying words.

"Yay! Come on, Dad, you romantic old fool. Go take her by the hand!" his daughter cheered him on as he rose to his feet and gazed into his wife's eyes – for Aimee was desperate to banish the thought that someone other than her mother might once have been Charles Eichelberger's 'first and only love'.

Natalie unhesitatingly accepted her husband's outstretched hand and permitted him to lead her onto the dance floor. Watching them glide serenely in each other's arms, Aimee instead gave thanks that her parents' thirty long years of happy marriage had indeed been a blessing. She was minded to mention this epiphany to Shelby – only to discover that her best friend was about to be whisked onto the dance floor by a handsome young man who'd been eyeing her from a neighbouring table. Suddenly, Shelby and her new admirer too were now gazing into each other's eyes while slowly revolving in the other's arms – as if love might indeed be just 'a warm, inviting dance away'.

That cynical question that Aimee had once posed now returned to mock her: what is love? She thought back to that afternoon at Freshwater Bay and how she'd envied that girl aboard the yacht that had been riding at anchor. Thereupon, she grieved for the terrible mistake she realised she had made by similarly offering herself up to be a rich man's love interest.

Except where had 'love' figured in what had since transpired? Glancing about the room, she spotted that love interest busily 'exchanging glances' with some glamorous female guest he had sidled up to at the bar (and who it appeared had also found 'something' in his searching blue eyes that was 'so inviting'). Seething with hurt, she cursed how foolish she'd been to believe her smooth-talking boss would ever regard her as anything more than just another passing outlet for his habitual philandering.

For Angie, the lyrics to this song also had a hollow ring to them. Physically reminded that, for her, love 'at first sight' had patently not 'turned out right', she could only gaze on with bitter impotence while Charles Eichelberger and his wife gently swayed around the floor in each other's embrace. What's more, it was almost as if her one-time lover was now exacting his own revenge for her unsubtle act of spite by purposely avoiding eye contact with *her* while staring resolutely into Natalie's instead. Only professional self-control enabled Angie to dam the tears that were welling up behind her own anguished eyes as she drew this final song to a close and exited the stage for the last time.

* * * * *

The remainder of the evening was given over to the disco, which would continue until the midnight hour drew all entertainment at the Shanklin Heights Hotel to a close. Kicking off with Tina Charles' chirpy *'I Love To Love (But My Baby Just Loves To Dance)'*, younger (and young-at-heart) revellers were soon drifting onto the dance floor to strut their stuff. As they did,

Shelby's little legs started tapping beneath the table, impatient to be up and joining them.

"Come on, Aimee. Let's you and me show 'em how it's done – like we always do!" she chivvied her friend when the DJ dropped The Trammps' *'Hold Back The Night'* onto the turntable.

Aimee appeared less than animated by the request, but permitted her friend to drag her from her seat anyway.

"Come on, Mrs Eichelberger. You join us too," Shelby hollered after her mother for good measure.

With the three of them dancing, Charles Eichelberger decided the time was long overdue for grabbing a little fresh air. Aimee looked on from the dance floor as her father made for the exit, concerned for the fate of their purses that he'd carelessly left unattended. Mindful of this too, Natalie headed back to their table to catch her breath when the opening bars of Abba's brand new, up-tempo *'Dancing Queen'* single pounded out (and which tempted even more guests to excitedly crowd onto the floor). Aimee promptly traipsed after her mother, once again feeling the effects of the lethargy that had been afflicting her of late.

"Oh, come on, Aimee. This song is awesome!" a manifestly disappointed Shelby pleaded with her, to no avail.

However, the girl from Dixie wasn't dancing by herself for long. Her friend's departure was swiftly followed by the reappearance of that young man who she'd slow-danced with earlier on, and who was now endeavouring to impress her with some 'awesome' moves of his own.

"Phew! I need air," Aimee meanwhile called to her mother above the music, fanning her face with her hand.

"What is it with you guys? Why does everybody keep leaving me by myself?" Natalie threw her hands up in faux despair as she watched her daughter breeze past the table on her way out.

* * * * *

"Why?" she wanted to know.

Yet summoning up an answer to her simple question felt like the hardest thing Charles Eichelberger had ever been tasked to do – far harder than engaging in lethal combat over the skies of

Germany; far harder than supersonic dog-fighting over Korea; far harder indeed than controversially ordering death and destruction to rain down from the skies over Vietnam and Cambodia. There ensued a long, guilty silence before he finally shook his head and conceded defeat. He could give her no answer.

"Don't you think after all these years I deserve an explanation of why you just... walked away?" it frustrated Angie to have to verbalise how their passionate affair had abruptly ended.

Perhaps the busy ambience of the hotel's moonlit terrace – with other guests milling about around them – was not exactly conducive to this kind of intimate confrontation (less so when odd ones would spot and rush up to Angie to commend her on her performance). However, having spotted Charles there, deep in anguished reflection – and with only a few days to go before he and his wife jetted out of Britain (almost certainly for good) – she'd reasoned it was now or never. Thus, having changed out of her stage attire, she'd marched up to him and uttered that monosyllabic request. Gripping the rail of the balustrade, he stared out across the darkened bay and drew breath.

"It's not that I never loved you. For nine long months you were my every waking thought. Part of me never ceased loving you. It's just that... I had made a mistake. There was Natalie – back home. I'd promised her I would return for her. I couldn't just..."

"You made promises to me too. Or are promises made to girls on foreign shores somehow worth less than those made to American girls? Were we English girls just convenient playthings for you while war was on, to be tossed aside once you could return home to the lives and loves you had back in America?"

"No, it was never like that. Heck, what is love anyway! It's just some crazy feeling we all get," he turned and snapped. "Look, the truth is something happened – something that brought me to my senses; something that made me realise what a terrible mess I'd made – of my life; of your life; and of...."

He didn't get to complete the sentence that would have spelt out the awful truth. Instead, Angie pounced, unburdening herself of three decades of pent-up hurt.

"Oh, you made a mess of my life alright. And you excuse it by trying to tell me you wouldn't even recognise love if it smacked you in the mouth – which is what I feel like doing to you right now! For pity's sake, Charles, it took me years to get over you. The pain and grief I nursed I carried into my marriage to Frank. And now, as if all that were not punishment enough, your daughter has walked into my son's life and has forced me to watch while history repeats itself all over again!"

"*Your* son? I thought the boy was…"

"Yes, Vaughan is *my* son – not Nora's. The son I ended up giving away because of mental scars that *you* inflicted that never properly healed. It was Nora who raised him though. But then you've probably met Nora's *real* son: John Lawton – the guy whose hotel you're staying at. You see, he was the illegitimate outcome of a hasty wartime affair Nora once had. She says by some soldier she met. But I have my suspicions it was one of you lot from the base who put her up the duff."

"So John Lawton *is* Nora's son!" Charles gasped – his eyes suddenly gaping wide. Confirmation from a second source, as military parlance might have it.

"Yes," she repeated, too caught up in righteous indignation on her sister's behalf to notice how his countenance had changed. "But that's another story. Another tale of how the mess you Yanks left behind blighted the lives of me, of my sister, and of thousands of girls like us up and down the country."

Amidst the guests still coming and going on this balmy evening, neither Charles nor Angie had noticed that Aimee had spotted them both while out searching for a cooling breeze. Having concealed herself out of sight behind one of the decorative colonnades that lined the terrace, she'd been listening to every single word of their conversation. Tears were cascading down her face as the realisation sunk in that she was not the first Eichelberger to have found herself assailed by youthful lusts while far from home (and thereby from the moral constraints of her devout upbringing). Nor, alas, the first Eichelberger to contemplate the comeuppance that now awaited those who had meantime foolishly bade the Devil take tomorrow.

"Ah, there you are, young lady. I've been looking all over for you…" she suddenly turned to catch the inimitable rasp of her mother's accent above the hubbub of the other guests.

"Gee, you okay? Why are you crying?" her mother's voice then softened.

"It's nothing, Mom. I'm okay. Just a little tired, that's all," she snuffled, trying to summon up a smile.

"Maybe we both need our beds. That said, I think we oughta' leave Shelby down here. The kid's having the time of her life dancing with that young man she's just met."

Aimee smiled again at the irony of her friend having turned out to be the most vivacious party animal of the two of them.

"Say, where's your father?" Natalie also wanted to know, her anxious eyes roving the terrace. Then she spotted him strolling out onto the floodlit lawn in the company of some flaxen-haired broad. Onto the lawn the vexed wife strode also – her daughter hurrying after her and fearing the worst.

"Mom... Mom..."

"Say, if you don't mind me saying, lady... Oh, it's you!" Natalie's indignant rebuke was halted in its tracks when that mysterious broad turned to face her.

"Yes, it's me," Angie offered the hand of greeting, Natalie momentarily unsure what to do with it. "And you're Natalie, aren't you. I've so been looking forward to meeting you."

"Listen, lady, don't you think it's getting' kinda' late to be out here all alone with my husband," she continued, her eyes ablaze in the quest for answers. Banished now was any notion of not wanting to know what he might have gotten up to during those wartime years spent in England.

"Look, it's okay, Nat," the General chipped in. "You see Angie and I were... well..." he burbled, willing himself to alight upon a perfectly innocent explanation.

"What Charles is trying to say..." the impish singer interjected, staring up at him and deliberately leaving the sentence hanging in mid-air for a terrifying split second.

It was split second during which Charles Eichelberger knew his thirty years of happy marriage was, in all likelihood, over. Aimee too closed her eyes to await the sentence's completion – for surely this embittered woman would never have a better opportunity to deal a vengeful killer blow to her father for his part in her unhappiness.

Indeed, it was a split second too during which this seductive Englishwoman savoured the power that had finally been granted her to break this pathetic man – albeit she'd been kept waiting for this moment for over three decades. Maybe revenge really is a dish best served cold! And yet… And yet…

"What your husband is trying to say is that we once met when I was performing on stage at the camp where he was based," she recommenced. "He and some of his fellow airmen had come backstage at the close looking for autographs. We had a laugh and a joke – as you do. If I'm honest, I was rather taken with him. And I could see from the look in his eyes that he was taken with me too," she added, glancing up at the perspiring aviator (whose lips crumpled resignedly as if to concur – though mortified by the terrible truth he knew she was about to divulge). Meanwhile, Angie turned to address his wife directly.

"Eventually, he asked if he could take me out to dinner. And so we met up at this quiet little restaurant, where we got chatting about what we were hoping to do when war was over. We talked too about how it felt to be apart from those you love. That's when he explained to me that he was indeed in love – with a girl back in Minnesota who remained his every waking thought. So though he admired me, his deep Christian faith meant he could never betray her. He was grateful for my friendship though – for being someone he could talk to about how much he missed her. And grateful too, of course, for my understanding of his situation.

"Alas, the next thing I heard he'd returned to America," the maudlin lilt in her voice then lifted – Charles' incredulous heart lifting with relief too. "Then I read somewhere that he'd become one of its most decorated generals. Meanwhile, I pass my days here on the Isle of Wight entertaining love-struck holidaymakers. Still, it's been good to catch up with your husband after all these years. And it's heartening to know he made the right choice in the end. I can see you are both very happy together – and that you have raised a beautiful, talented daughter who will one day achieve great things and make you both very proud," she eyed Aimee up and down – who, like her father, had been teetering in fear of what this jilted ex-lover might confess to.

The relief was palpable, though Natalie seemed unsure whether to believe what she'd just been told. However, she looked up at the humility gushing from her husband's eyes and blinked with eyes of her own that now mellowed.

"Those war years were difficult for all of us. And if I'm honest too, there wasn't a day went by when I didn't fear waking up to find Charles had returned home with another girl on his arm – some English girl who was much prettier than me," she paid her one-time rival the subtlest of compliments.

"But I guess placing your trust in the Lord never goes unrewarded. I wish you well, Angie. You too are one mighty talented lady. If ever you get to sing on my side of the Pond, drop me a line. With a voice like that I reckon you could do a great line in hymns at our church."

The agnostic nightclub singer doffed to thank her, warmed with hindsight to know that her sister had been right about one thing: forgiveness really can be a strangely liberating emotion.

"Anyhow, like I said, it's getting late. Aimee has to be up for work tomorrow. Maybe we'll see you around again before we fly home," Natalie bade her goodnight.

Then she looped her arm into that of her broad-shouldered husband, who flashed his old flame an indebted half-smile of his own before turning to escort his wife back to their room.

It left Angie to train a searching eye upon the young woman towards whom she'd harboured such gathering suspicion, if not outright contempt, these last few weeks. Then, swallowing her prejudice, that eye softened to indicate that she had pardoned Aimee too.

The relieved student flashed a grateful half-smile of her own before turning to trail after her parents. Even if some dark and painful deeds from the past can never be entirely forgotten, they can surely be forgiven.

25

Wednesday, August 25th 1976

"Come in."

The voice behind the door was brusque – as Veronica Lawton's voice invariably was. Thus he found himself entering her office for a second time with a bulging folder under his arm, called upon again to unearth that vital piece of missing evidence upon which she could well and truly hang her husband out to dry. This time her hired sleuth was insufficiently poker-faced that she hadn't already deduced that within that bulging file was what she was looking for. He placed it down upon her desk and stepped back to await her reaction.

From the moment she opened it and began thumbing through the black-and-white photographs her face was contorting with both fascination and revulsion. No ambiguity in these images – they had captured coital passion alright.

"So who is she? And how did you...?" Veronica at last managed to haul her eyes away from this troubling treasure trove, bidding him draw up a chair.

"Her name is Sophie Wiseman. She's thirty-two years-old; the youngest daughter of a senior diplomat. She studied at Somerville College, Oxford, from where she graduated with an honours degree in PPE. Nowadays, she heads up her own fashion business. She's married to no less a personage than Sir Clive Wiseman, the Permanent Secretary for the Ministry of Defence – who is fifteen years her senior. She's his second wife. He has two grown-up sons from his first marriage. She has no children – as yet. However, she has ambitions to enter politics. It's even rumoured she's looking to stand for Parliament."

"Good grief!" Veronica swooned – both at her philandering other-half's colourful choice of *inamorata* and at having alighted upon an image of him being subjected to a particularly bizarre sexual practice. Did men and women really get up to such things, suggested the incredulous, petitioning stare of a woman who had only just come to terms with the missionary position?

Her sleuth paused to study it too. Thereupon, he shrugged as if to suggest that certain adventurous types obviously did.

"As to the means," he continued, "all it took was a small camera and a recording device. Wire both up to a motion sensor planted in her bedroom and, hey presto! So not only can you have these stills I've developed, but there's enough footage to create a motion picture show from it too."

"What? You mean you have moving images of their shenanigans?" she retorted, twisting yet another photograph this way and that in order to work out exactly what this 'adventurous' woman was doing to her husband.

"Absolutely. You can have it in standard sixteen-millimetre film; or in super eight-millimetre, if you prefer. I can even copy it onto that new Betamax video format if you like," he replied, twisting the photograph around the right way for his client.

Whereupon a wicked smirk on her part alerted him to the realisation that footage of this particular sex game would come in very handy indeed for some vengeful scheme or other that he imagined Veronica Lawton might yet be hatching.

"But how did you manage to sneak the camera inside this woman's bedroom?" she marvelled.

"One thing about this heat-wave we've been having lately is that people will insist on leaving their windows open when they're out – as I noticed Mrs Wiseman had been doing at her *pied-à-terre* in Bayswater. It's where your husband has been dallying with her. I noticed too that the apartment next door to hers is for sale. So I rang the estate agent and asked for a viewing. While he was showing me around I managed to take an imprint of the key to it and get a copy cut. All I needed to do then was come back later, let myself in, clamber around the balcony, and climb in through the open window of Mrs Wiseman's flat. Having set the device up, I returned a few days later, climbed in again, and retrieved it."

"Goodness! You are resourceful," she commented, glancing up from perusing the photographs in the file.

"Yes, a bit like something out of that American private detective series on TV; the one starring James Garner – what's it called: *'The Rockford Files'*...? *'This is Jim Rockford',*" he then squeezed his nose to impersonate the answer machine message that famously opened each episode. "*'At the tone, leave your name and a message and I'll get back to you'.*"

Veronica broke from perusing to offer him a cutting stare. Mindful that this joyless woman had no time for humour, he donned an earnest face and qualified his explanation.

"The Wisemans' marital home in Surrey is nowadays guarded like Fort Knox. Understandable, I suppose, what with the IRA going round assassinating top people – like our ambassador to Ireland, who they blew up in Dublin last month. After all, Sir Clive is one of the country's top civil servants, holding one of its most sensitive posts. So it's fortunate your husband wasn't meeting up with her there because I'd have never been able to plant the camera. Mind you, had he been foolhardy enough to have done so then he would've almost certainly have had MI5 on his case. They might even be on it now, for all we know. So if I was you, I'd keep an eye open for any dodgy-looking characters in dark glasses checking in to your hotel!"

He could see he was trying her patience. However, his rambling at least reminded Veronica of another matter for which she needed closure.

"Talking about Americans," she glared at him. "Have you unearthed anything more about that room maid of mine?"

He sat back, scrunched his mouth, and shook his head.

"Nothing. Zilch."

"And that Angie Ashby woman?"

"Same. No more car park liaisons since that day I caught them on Brading Down. That said, on two occasions since I've followed his car to the address in Sandown where she lives. On both occasions he's been greeted by another woman."

"That'll be Nora Lewis – his real mother. She's Angie Ashby's sister. You see, I've since found out that John was adopted – conceived out of wedlock. He was placed in an orphanage when he was born. Nora's been searching for him ever since."

"Really?"

"Yes. Believe it or not, Nora also happens to be the mother of the lad who's been going out with that American girl. We live in a very small world – as my husband is fond of saying."

"Clearly. But then I suppose it wouldn't have done for your husband to be knocking off his aunt, would it!" he sniggered, his face straightening again when he realised she didn't find that indelicate aside particularly amusing either.

"Anyway, at least I've finally nailed the woman who he *has* been carrying on with," he commended himself, folding his arms smugly.

Veronica hummed with relief – or with as much relief as a wife betrayed could be expected to show.

"Of course, I've had to stump up quite a bit of dosh to purchase all these state-of-the-art surveillance gadgets…"

"Just add it to your bill," she waved a hand insouciantly. Instead, she carried on perusing the file, insisting that "What you have handed me here is worth its weight in gold."

"It also means I've exonerated the two original suspects," he added. "Though I can see why they had you worried."

"I suppose," she sneered, "though I'm still not entirely convinced my husband hasn't been cavorting with at least one of them. Still, at least with your evidence in my possession John will think twice before divorcing me in preference for this Sophie woman – or any other woman, for that matter. All that remains is for me to think of a way I can break the bad news to him."

* * * * *

Thursday, August 26th 1976

"Why?" she wanted to know.

Aimee could give no answer why she'd turned her back on a decent boy whose intentions were honourable; no answer why she'd fallen instead for the charms of an older married man whose intentions clearly were not; And certainly no answer why she'd allowed herself to get into the predicament of possibly having this man's child growing inside her.

Shelby's mien of horror eventually softened into one of Christian charity as she leant upon her mop and put a further question to her tearful best friend.

"And why didn't you tell me all this before?"

Aimee dabbed a knuckle to her cheeks to wipe away those tears. Mindful of their shared faith, it was sufficient for Shelby to know that the cock had crowed – so to speak. What's more, she was nursing guilt of her own that she hadn't acted on her nagging suspicions and confronted Aimee sooner. Resting the mop in its bucket she sat down beside her fellow room maid on a half-made bed and looped an arm across her shoulder.

"I knew you would be angry with me," Aimee snuffled, permitting Shelby to haul her in close and be hugged.

"You bet I'm angry with you," she admitted, though with an indulgent voice that assured her that "You're still my best friend though. And I still care about you. So right now I'm desperately trying to think how I can help you. Does *he* know?"

Aimee shook her head.

"Not that it would make much difference. I think I can guess what he'd tell you to do," Shelby hissed.

"And what about his wife? Does she know you two have been carrying on behind her back?"

Aimee shrugged despondently.

"I don't know. But she must have her suspicions. The other day she threatened to tell my parents if she ever found out that we were."

"Yeah, well. Just a few more days and we'll be outta' here. Then hopefully she need never know," Shelby pointed out, still glancing around the room while metaphorically scratching her head in the quest for a practical solution to her friend's lamentable predicament.

"Look," she then hastily suggested, "you'll just have tell your folks you met some guy on a night-out and that one thing led to another. But you know next to nothing about your baby's father so there's no point in anyone going looking for him. It's sordid, I know. But hey, these things happen – even to Christian girls!"

Even to Christian girls! The very words jolted Aimee into remembering why Veronica Lawton's threat carried such potency.

She buried her head into Shelby's shoulder in despair and released a torrent of repentant tears.

"When Mom finds out I'm pregnant she'll be mad as hell and will never speak to me again. Neither will Dad. And then I'll be left to bring up a child all on my own – a child who'll never know its real father. Oh, Shell," she wept, "I'm so scared."

Shelby hugged her again, shedding a tear of her own and sensing there was going to be no happy outcome to this sorry saga. However, one thing was for sure: sooner or later Aimee would indeed have to tell her parents.

* * * * *

"Be off with yer', yer' young hooligans!"

The indignant old lady tore out of her front door as fast as her spindly little legs would carry her to turn off the tap and preserve her street's precious liquid treasure. The standpipe silenced, the three young lads fled who'd been soaking each other by pressing thumbs over its spout – though not before offering the woman all manner of rude gestures.

"Bleedin' kids nowadays. I'll be glad when they're back at school!" she squawked after them before turning to Vaughan as he was cycling past. "…And I'll be glad when this bleedin' drought's over too," she hectored him breathlessly.

The summer heat and the lack of rain had long ceased being a talking point and now constituted a civil emergency. Vaughan had heard on the news that hundreds of million of pounds worth of crops had been ruined by the unyielding heat-wave, while industry was facing the prospect of working three-day weeks in order to preserve water. And in one of the more fanciful developments so far, it was rumoured that the new Minister for Drought was consulting meteorologists about the practicalities of ordering the RAF to artificially seed clouds in the hope of coaxing desperately-needed rain.

Detouring before clocking on at the bus depot, Vaughan propped his bike up outside the entrance to the Shanklin Heights Hotel and was about to wander inside. Then he stopped, returned to the bike, and took a moment to chain it up properly. Bleedin' kids around here!

This was now his third unannounced visit. However, this morning Vaughan had resolved there would be no skulking about. As such, he marched straight up to the reception desk. Neither did he falter when he caught sight of Veronica Lawton craning over that pretty redhead who was manning it, running through some paperwork she'd presumably deposited for her attention. He had resolved too that he was no longer going to be cowed by this woman.

"Can I help you, sir?" the young receptionist broke to glance up and offer him her best customer service smile.

Veronica too looked up and spotted the busman's uniform "Oh, it's you... Vaughan," she noted, her tone strangely lacking its customary abruptness. What's more, she was even smiling! And she was addressing him by his name too!

"Yes, it's me. I would like to see Miss Aimee-Marie Eichelberger if I may," he swallowed hard and insisted.

"I see." Veronica was taken aback, deigning to ponder his request. Then she glanced down at her receptionist.

"I'll take care this, Vicky," she assured the girl, whose deferential upward gaze suggested she was as daunted by her strident manager as the rest of the workforce in this place.

Veronica then strode around the desk and, to Vaughan's surprise, hooked an arm into one of his in order to usher him across the lobby.

"Listen, I know all about you," she halted him once out of earshot, turning him about to face her.

"Know?" he puzzled, astonished that again there was that unexpected clemency in her clipped, velvety voice.

"About John... and your mother. It must have been a terrible shock for you – to find out you have a half-brother she's never told you about. It would appear too that this makes me your half sister-in-law. Therefore, perhaps it's time we got to know each other better. So allow me to make a start by introducing myself. I'm Veronica," she offered him her dainty, feminine paw.

It was an unexpected expression of upper-class matiness that left Vaughan lost for words. Perhaps this woman was not the out-

and-out virago that Aimee had led him to believe. He stared down at one of his own sweaty palms before thrusting it into hers.

Touched by his jejune clumsiness, she smiled indulgently. "Now, you say you want to see that young lady friend of yours," she reminded him.

"Er… Yes. I want to give her this," he showed her a letter he now pulled from his trouser pocket. "However, if she's busy then maybe you can pass it to her for me."

"No, that's okay. I'm sure you would prefer to hand it to her in person. Take a seat in my office and I'll go find her."

So it was that a bewildered Vaughan Lewis found himself in the office of *'Veronica Lawton – Manageress'*, perched upon her expensive leather swivel chair, while the woman in question (who he'd previously dwelt in fear of) disappeared to run an errand on his behalf. This unrelenting heat really had induced madness in people. Meanwhile, the door ajar, Vicky on the reception desk peered inside and fluttered him an inquisitive Irish smile.

* * * * *

"Aimee! You're required down to my office. Now!" the two room maids were alarmed to find the door to the suite they were preparing burst open and Veronica Lawton standing in the portal, glaring at the one of them.

Aimee looked to Shelby before nervously glancing at her boss.

"This instant, girl. If you don't mind," she repeated, hinting at the open door behind her.

Aimee laid aside the vacuum cleaner she'd been about to wield and made her way out onto the corridor – past her boss, who glanced her up and down (Aimee's reddened eyes suggesting that her troublesome employee might have been crying).

"You, meanwhile, can carry on as you were," she then offered Shelby a slick grin.

And with that Veronica closed the door behind her, leaving the anxious Southerner alone to ponder whether the fate her best friend feared was about to break upon her head. She glanced up to Heaven and offered up another silent prayer.

* * * * *

"One Aimee-Marie Eichelberger – as requested," Veronica Lawton announced, having led the palpitating room maid down the stairs and into Vaughan's waiting presence.

"Vaughan! What are you doing here?" Aimee expressed surprise.

"And what was all that about?" she couldn't resist commenting once her boss had pulled the door to, leaving the two youngsters alone together. Tentatively, she sat herself down across the desk from her erstwhile boyfriend – upon the chair the curiously obliging manageress had pulled up for her.

"Search me. I swear she must be schizophrenic or something. One minute she's bollocking me; next minute she's nice as pie."

"Same here. Though I have to say it's usually a sign she's up to something," Aimee cautioned with the benefit of experience.

"Anyway, it's good to see you again," she summoned up a nervous smile, reaching across the desk to squeeze his hand.

"You too," he flashed his soft brown eyes. "But what I really came here for is to give you this."

He drew up the envelope he'd been clutching in his hand and held it out for her to take.

"What is it?"

"It's an invitation – for you and Shelby. To Mom's fiftieth birthday party," he mumbled. "Its just a little get together we're having at the flat on Sunday afternoon. That's if you're both free, of course. She'll understand if you have other things planned – what with your parents still being over here,"

Aimee was touched, gently tearing the envelope open and perusing the handwritten note inside – a note penned in a woman's elegant handwriting.

"Oh, Vaughan. This is so very kind of her. But we couldn't possibly accept. We don't even know the lady," she pleaded, a coded excuse for felling guilty that she'd purposely not invited Vaughan to her own birthday celebration the other day.

"No problem. I asked her and she said yes," he confessed cheekily. "But then I know she wants to meet you and Shelby before you fly home. She's truly grateful that you two have helped make this summer such a memorable one for me."

Aimee winced. "I'm only sorry that *I* may not always have made it memorable for the right reasons," she pleaded again.

He gazed into those big remorseful eyes of hers and shrugged magnanimously.

"That's okay. At least you were honest with me. I'm just sorry if I freaked you out by coming on all serious. It's just that I'm not terribly very clued up about the ways of women," he lowered that gaze, embarrassed to be making such an admission.

"Maybe that's makes two of us – in my case about the ways of men," she shrugged too, Vaughan oblivious to the shocking discovery that tempered her own shameful admission.

"Still, we had some good times together. It's a shame that this time next week we'll be thousands of miles apart. Then all this – the island; the sunny weather; you and me – will all be just a memory. I hope they will be happy memories."

"At least you have made it memorable for the *right* reasons," she assured him through doleful, alluding eyes.

"You okay?" Vaughan picked up on the subdued edge to her reassurance, gentlemanly concern compelling him to ask.

"Yeah, I guess," she sighed unconvincingly. "It's just that maybe this holiday will turn out to be kinda' memorable for other reasons too: for uncomfortable things that I've had to find out about myself; that I'm not the wonderful perfect human being maybe you imagined I was. Neither is my family perfect too. Boy, do we Eichelbergers have some mighty impressive skeletons in our cupboard – as you Brits might say!"

"My family too," Vaughan wanted to explain – but reasoning that doing so would take up far too much of her time when he was already keeping her from her work. "Maybe we can meet up one final time before you leave: to tell each other all about it."

"Sure. That would be good."

"You see, despite the fact that our backgrounds are so very different, I get this funny feeling that your family and mine have more in common than we could ever have imagined."

"Yeah. Me too," she chuckled knowingly.

"Anyway, I best be getting back to work. Shelby will be wondering what's happened to me," Aimee suggested, rising from her chair and urging him towards the door.

Once out into the lobby, there they spotted Veronica Lawton over by the reception desk, where she was once more talking Vicky through all that paperwork that needed sorting.

Vaughan followed the trajectory of Aimee's eyes and glanced over just in time for Veronica to fire the two of them that peculiar, doting smile.

"So will I see you and Shelby on Sunday?" he turned to beg Aimee in closing.

"Sure," she nodded. "We'll be there."

As she leant forward to offer him a tender hug she glanced over his shoulder to observe her boss's doting smile morph into one of cunning. The woman was definitely up to something.

26

Friday, August 27th 1976

The Bank Holiday weekend had finally arrived. Surely the unprecedented spell of sweltering weather must break soon. After all, didn't it always rain in Britain on bank holidays! What's more, most people had now had enough of it. The crowds at Lords had even cheered the heavens when a cloud had briefly passed and light rain stopped play for the grand total of fifteen minutes before the blue skies returned again.

It was just such an endless clear blue sky that greeted Nora Lewis as she made her way out onto the steps of the verandah, where Chico's tall cage was parked in its usual spot overlooking the street. There another passing family had halted to converse with its feathered occupant. Thankfully, Chico was entertaining the two children with a selection of the less saucy phrases he'd picked up, as well as whistling *'Rule Britannia'* and *'La Marseillaise'* for their delight and amusement.

"Nice arse!" he squawked at Nora as she made her way down the steps, prompting the little boy and girl to huddle together impishly and snigger.

Meanwhile, Betty had spotted the onlookers gathered around the cage and was hurrying across the road bearing two shopping bags brimming with groceries,

"Oh, Nora. I do hope Chico hasn't been saying naughty words to people again."

"I'm afraid so, Betty. That said, it's been a long time since the male of any species has complimented my bottom!"

"I hate to disappoint you, my dear, but Chico thinks most of the ladies in Sandown have nice bottoms," Betty chortled in her dulcet tones. "Mind you, you do look smart in that pretty summer dress. You wouldn't be off to meet up with a young man, would you?" she proffered a mischievous grin.

"Unfortunately not, Betty," Nora chuckled. "More like an expedition to pick up an outfit to wear on Sunday."

"Oh, of course. It's your party."

"That's right. You will pop in, won't you," Nora pleaded. "You've been such a good friend to my sister. And any friend of Angie's will always be a friend of mine!"

"Thank you. Of course I will."

"As for my outfit, I did see a little peach number in the boutique on the High Street, but I'm undecided. Therefore, I thought I'd take myself off to see what I can find in Ryde."

"Well, good luck to you, my dear. Walking around shops in this heat is murder," she puffed, her shoulders limp from lugging those heavy bags. "I swear I haven't experienced weather like this since I was a midwife in Rhodesia, where I worked at a little clinic for African mothers and their babies. They were such happy days! I loved my job and I loved the people. However, since I retired four years ago all this fighting has started. And now I can't bear to watch how it's tearing the country apart."

Much as she enjoyed listening to Betty recount tales from her years in Africa, time was pressing if Nora intended to have a good tramp around the shops. Therefore, she politely disengaged from the conversation. Crossing the road, she made a point of turning to offer her a parting wave. As she did, she spotted Angie peering from behind the curtain of her bedroom. She offered her a parting wave too, her sister smiling wanly in return as she watched Nora round the corner into the High Street.

* * * * *

Mercifully, she didn't have long to wait in the sun before a Number 16 bus arrived. Hopping aboard, she settled into a seat upstairs. It would have been preferable had her sister been accompanying her to proffer a womanly opinion about whether that comely behind Chico assured her she possessed would look okay in a shorter dress. However, Angie had wanted to practice her repertoire for tonight's cabaret appearance. Nora knew she often availed herself of the solitude of the flat while Frank was at work to rehearse numbers – notwithstanding that, first Vaughan's presence, and now her own, had lately robbed her sister of this valuable time alone.

No sooner had the bus pulled away than a pretty conductress with long, flowing hair trotted up the stairs and made her way along the saloon to where she was sitting. Nora held out some change, watching while the pleasant young lass twiddled with the dials on her ticket machine. As she spun the handle and tore the ticket, she glanced at Nora and their eyes met... and lingered.

"Do I know you?" the girl quizzed aloud.

"No, probably not," Nora grinned. "But I think I know you. Are you Tina, by any chance?"

"Yeah. I am," her gorgeous grey-blue eyes glowed with amazement. "How d'you know that then?"

"My son works on the buses – Vaughan. He's a conductor at Shanklin depot."

"Oh, yeah. I know Vaughan. He's a smashing guy. We've had such a great laugh together this summer. So you're his... his mom then," she hesitated.

From her wary stare, Nora sensed the girl might just be in on the terrible family secret. After all, Vaughan had oft times spoken about how this 'Tina' was one of his closest friends at the depot.

"Yes, I'm his mom," she played along, simpering politely.

"Well, it's great to meet you," Tina acknowledged. "I can see now why he's such a handsome chap. The good looks obviously run in the family."

Even as she said it, Tina knew it was not the most tactful thing to say to this woman who (she now knew) was not Vaughan's biological 'mom'. Nora offered her a magnanimous smile, Tina veiling her embarrassment by pleading the need to collect some more fares. She then retreated downstairs.

The awkward encounter reminded Nora again of what a mess both she and Angie had made of their lives: the younger sibling who had given away her child because it had been born out of wedlock; and the older sibling who had given away hers while in a state of mental meltdown. Following the revelation about his true parentage, things were still raw between Vaughan and his adoptive mother. She knew that, however much she protested her love for him, inwardly he resented her. And he most certainly resented John, unable to even articulate his name in her presence. She wondered whether he would ever be ready for her to break to him the third and final instalment in the story of just how tangled had been the lives and love of the Ashby sisters. *'If we confess our sins, He is faithful and just to forgive us our sins, and to cleanse us from all unrighteousness,'* she recalled a scripture that had been chiselled into her heart. To that end, she prayed once more that her Saviour would expedite the right moment for her to unburden herself of this last remaining secret.

The bus had not reached Brading when it pulled up at a stop with steam pouring from beneath the bonnet. Glancing out of the window, Nora spotted Tina hop off the platform to converse with driver. Sure enough, the regrettable news she had relayed downstairs she now climbed the stairs and proceeded to announce to the passengers on the upper saloon too.

"Sorry, folks. I'm afraid it's conked out. But if you'd care to make your way downstairs there will be another bus along in about fifteen minutes."

"Fifteen minutes!" an irate youth choked, gazing at the bulbous diver's watch hanging from his wrist. "I'm supposed to be meeting my girlfriend at three o'clock. Now I'm gonna' be late and she'll think I don't care about her and dump me instead."

"Don't sweat, darlin'," Tina placated him in her chirpy southern ling as he traipsed down the stairs after her, "a goodlooking bloke like you – she'll wait!"

Nora too glanced at her own watch as she stepped down onto the pavement. "Fifteen minutes, you say?"

"Yeah, should be," Tina repeated.

Such a sweet and bubbly young lady, Nora pondered as she joined the other passengers who had congregated to wait in the shade of a big old tree. She certainly sounded much more down-to-earth than this American girl her son was still besotted with – and whom he had pleaded she invite to her party. Not that Nora needed too much persuasion. Curiosity alone had been enough for her to agree to Vaughan's request, which would enable her to finally meet the daughter of the famous Charles Eichelberger.

"Bloody old bone-shaker. They should buy themselves some decent buses!" the kid who was on-a-promise had meanwhile lit a cigarette and was chuntering between puffs.

Nora glanced at her watch again, fanning herself with her free hand. Betty was right: she was no longer sure she had the stamina for traipsing in and out of shops in this heat. Besides, the peach outfit was very nice and the price tag was within what she could afford. She would have liked to have chatted some more with Tina though – eager to understand why Vaughan hadn't hit it off with her (Brighton was certainly a more promising option for a long distance romance for a boy from Dudley than was St Cloud, Minnesota!). However, the bonny conductress had nestled her ample bosom on the mouth of the open bonnet and was busy nattering to her driver, who was peering inside to second guess why his bus had overheated. Instead, Nora now spotted another bus approaching in the opposite direction.

"It's been nice meeting you, Tina," she bade her,

"Yeah, you too, Mrs Lewis. You take care," Tina looked up and called back, watching while Nora stepped up to the kerb, looked left and right, and hurried across the road.

* * * * *

Having arrived back in Sandown much earlier than planned, Nora treated herself to a stroll along the Esplanade – that trendy little peach dress now wrapped in a paper bag that was proudly swinging from her fingers. There she located a spot on a bench from which she could observe the seaside crowds enjoying this final glorious weekend of the summer. She'd overheard someone on the bus say the forecasters were predicting rain before the bank holiday was through.

Watching the children playing on the beach reminded her of the times when Vaughan too had played on those fabulous golden sands as a child. By then the cracks in his parents' tenuous marriage were already beginning to show. It would not be long before he would find himself, to all intents and purpose, without a father; and Nora without a man in her life. Six long years after her separation from Jim, she was still without a man in her life.

Like little girls down the ages, when she'd been a child, growing up in a sleepy Suffolk town, Nora too had dreamed of one day marrying a dashing prince who would sweep her off her feet and usher her to some magical fairy-tale castle, there to live happily ever after. Alas, like so many girls who had come of age during those turbulent wartime years, the Elysium had proved as elusive as the dashing prince. Only through her faith had she come close to finding fulfilment in this life.

No sooner had the couple sat next to her vacated their places on the bench than a tall, rugged man sporting tennis shorts and a white Levi's T-shirt spotted it and enquired if it was free. Nora awoke from her daydream and gestured accordingly.

It was one of those spine-tingling moments when two strangers of the opposite sex suddenly find themselves in close proximity to each other. Nora sensed him glancing her up and down in curiosity. Therefore when, from out of the corner of her eye, she spotted him turn away again to also observe those holidaymakers at play on the beach, she elected to throw a quick sideways glance of her own to study him in more detail.

She guessed he was late-twenties – though the trimmed bandito moustache made him appear older (if, paradoxically, more alluring). He had rich brown eyes that roamed the horizon; and dark, wavy, shoulder-length hair – like the moustache, all the fashion for men nowadays. With his not excessive body hair on his arms and legs, all told he was quite a dish. However, she made the fatal mistake of lingering to study him just a moment too long. He had spotted her interest! Embarrassed, her eyes darted dead ahead, unconvincingly studying the horizon too.

"Lovely day again," he lifted his purview skywards before making eye contact with her anxious returning gaze.

"It is," she hummed coyly, looking away again.

"They say it's not going to last though."

"No, so I hear."

"Just as well really. Sometimes you can have too much of a good thing. If you know what I mean."

"I suppose," she concurred, coaxed to offer him a smile.

There then followed a lull in the conversation during which they both pretended to spy out a posse of excited prepubescent youngsters emerging dripping wet from the surf.

"Your children down there?" he enquired.

Aside from the absurdity of why she would be sitting up here if her children were playing down there, the remark was sufficiently fanciful to elicit another coy smile.

"My son is thirty years-old," she replied, as if daunted by the fact that she herself was just two days short of her half-century.

"Oh, I see... It's just that... if you don't mind me saying, you don't look old enough to..."

She was flattered. As he clearly intended she should be. Meanwhile, he offered her the smile that a man does when he wants a woman to know he finds her attractive.

"Ah, there you are, darling," some woman barged into their bashful love-in, thrusting an ice cream cone into the hand of her startled husband, while curling a slobbering tongue around her own. Meanwhile, peering from behind each of her broad hips, a small boy and his even smaller sister trained their beady eyes upon Nora as they bit chunks out of their *'Funny Feet'* ice lollies.

"I didn't have enough change, so I had to borrow fifty pence out of Jemima's pocket money. Of course, it would be nice if *you* paid for the ice creams for once," their mother lamented. "After all, you are their father!"

And with that rebuke, this stranger whom Nora Lewis had shocked herself by flirting with offered her a wistful parting smile before being hauled off in the direction of the amusement arcade on the pier (where she presumed he would be shamed into making amends for his omission).

Ah well, what could have been, she pondered wistfully too.

* * * * *

"Hi, Frank. How's business?" Nora popped her head inside Tring's Toys on her way back from the seafront, the bell above the door duly alerting its pudgy proprietor to the surprise visitor.

Busy shuffling stock on the shelves behind the counter, Frank Tring was attired in his faithful bog-house brown cow gown, a line-up of chewed pencils poking from its breast pocket like the pipes on a church organ. Meanwhile, a biro perched behind one ear was jutting half-skywards like a wonky TV aerial. This he now removed to jot down the figures he'd been tallying on the notepad he kept on the counter.

"Brisk. Second time this month I've sold out of inflatable rubber dinghies... Wholesaler's out of them too... This warm weather's been a boon for sales," he replied laconically.

While Nora was glancing about, she spotted that huge model plane that Vaughan had made, and which now had pride of place suspended by wires in the shop window display.

"Yes, superb piece of craftsmanship. You must be so proud of the lad, Nora. Angie and I are certainly grateful for the way you've cared for him and brought him up. He's turned out to be a fine young man. How can we ever repay you!" he simpered.

Coming from a man of Frank's frequent aloofness, such sincerity was all the more clawing. Nora recalled the story of Ruth in the Bible, and how the unmerited love and favour of a generous, adoptive kinsman had enabled a downtrodden nobody to realise her destiny as a woman of God (and which, she knew, mirrored the unmerited love and favour of her Lord and Saviour towards His 'adopted' children – herself included). She prayed that her youngest son – nay, the adopted son of two people she loved – might one day also become a man who God would use.

"You look like you've been shopping," Frank meanwhile noticed the bag in her hand, subtly steering the conversation back to a subject less likely to induce a watering of the eyes. Mindful of how this buttoned-up character was loathed to show emotion in public, she was happy to oblige.

"Yes. Just a little outfit for Sunday. I'm going to show it off to Angie when I get back. I hope she'll like it. I'm afraid it's all I can afford. Unfortunately, money's been tight of late, what with all this inflation going on. And we hairdressers don't belong to a powerful trades union capable of winning big pay rises."

"Neither do we struggling shopkeepers!" Frank huffed in sympathy. "Anyway, I'm sure you'll look splendid. You always do. In fact, you and Angie would look classy dressed in potato sacks," he offered her a bumbling compliment – for which she blushed. "I've been so lucky to be married to such a beautiful woman. And to have such a beautiful sister-in-law too."

"And my sister is so lucky to have had a husband who stuck by her when the chips were down" Nora insisted gratefully.

"I know there were times when I could have treated her better…" Frank struggled with tearfulness that was plainly just a whimper away. "I'm sorry too that our little hiccup helped destroy your marriage to Jim. But then I hope one day the Good Lord will find you another man. A better one maybe."

"Yes, one day," she tried not to build her hopes up.

The dingling of the bell and the entry into the shop of a young girl and her mother brought their awkward reminiscence to an abrupt halt. The youngster then made an animated bee-line for a boxed-up Pippa doll that she spotted on display.

"Can I, mummy? Can I?" she squealed with delight, lifting the box and claiming it as her own.

"You better ask Daddy, my dear," her mother insisted as her husband too wandered into the shop, having tarried outside to admire with boy-like awe that giant jet bomber that was suspended in the window from wires.

"But then you know what Daddy's like. One look from you and you can get whatever you want out of him," her mother looked up and rolled her eyes at Frank and Nora.

Nora winked at Frank knowingly as she motioned to leave. That's dads for you, her eyes reaffirmed.

* * * * *

"Cor! Sex!" Chico greeted Nora as she remounted the steps to the verandah upon her return.

There was a warning in the bird's remark that became apparent the instant she strolled up to the front door of the flat and motioned to open it. Staying her hand, she overheard a sound unlike any of the sassy ballads she'd previously caught Angie rehearsing. Not so much Tina Turner belting out *'River Deep, Mountain High'* as Donna Summer moaning her way through *'Love To Love You, Baby'* – the raunchy hit that had earlier in the year been banned from *'Top Of The Pops'* on account of its orgasmic overtones. Nora pressed her ear to the door again and was convinced that was exactly what she could hear.

She glanced at her watch and panicked. Vaughan must have come home from work early. And brought Aimee back to the flat with him! And now here they were… in his aunt's bedroom! Gripped by a moral reflex to storm inside and berate such unbecoming behaviour, her hand was stayed upon recalling a similar first frenzied teenage encounter of her own.

As she paused to listen further, the realisation dawned that the sporadic coital utterances she was furtively overhearing were not the outworking of two young people fumbling their way to conjugation. That wasn't Vaughan's voice doing the grunting; and neither was the more fricative female voice Aimee's. Then, all of a sudden, the grunting and the panting reached its climactic crescendo. The inside of the flat fell deathly quiet.

Seething with indignation, Nora's hand folded around the door handle and twisted it. However, no sooner had she marched over the threshold than she was confronted with the spectacle of her sister tumbling from the bedroom in a state of total undress. Angie hurriedly launched her arms around the most unseemly aspects of her nakedness the instant she spotted the horror and incomprehension blazing from those eyes now trained upon her.

"Nora, what are you doing…?"

"I was about to ask you the same question," she glared angrily.

A further suspicion was confirmed when Nora pushed past her sister to peer inside the bedroom. There, upon a corner of a marital bed that had been literally and metaphorically trashed, was perched an equally shame-faced John Lawton hurrying into his underpants. Turning to offer his mother his hirsute back, he then struggled into the rest of his garments before pushing past her to make haste through the front door, stopping neither to make eye contact with her, nor offer an explanation.

"Nora, I can explain…" Angie implored instead, having meanwhile grabbed a dressing gown with which to cover up.

"What's to explain?" Nora seethed with tears in her eyes. "My own sister – making out with *my* son – *her* nephew – in the bed she shares with *her* husband!"

"It was not like that when we started out. Neither of us had any idea that we were… that…"

"That you were blood relatives!" she screeched, spelling it out. "Well, you know now, don't you! There's a word they use to describe the relationship you two have been having!"

It was a terrifying word that must surely have entered Angie's consciousness at some point over the last few weeks; when what had started out as an illicit affair between a virile young man and an emotionally-starved older woman became instead an incestuous relationship between two people who had discovered, to their horror, that they were aunt and nephew. That terrifying word now made Angie shudder with remorse. If ever there was a nadir to the drawn-out saga of the Ashby sisters and their abject love lives then this was surely it. Nora was so appalled that she found herself unable to face her sister, preferring to divert into the sitting room and slump into the sofa, there to press her hand to her mouth, close her eyes, and shake her head in disbelief.

"I'm sorry, Nora. We had no idea at first. It just felt so good, and so right. To be in his arms made me feel alive again – and for the first time since my relationship with Charles," Angie pleaded, resting an arm against the door lintel at the entrance to the room and pressing her forehead against it.

"Have you any idea how difficult it is to then forsake that kind of love and passion once it's been tasted?" she wept, lifting her head away and gazing about in despair. "Have you any idea what manner of punishment it is to find out that the bit of joy in your life that you have been waiting for all these years turns out to be something that is forbidden? We tried, Nora! For God's sake, we tried…! Uh!" she then cussed. "Talking of which, that God you worship must have one hell of a cruel sense of humour!"

"But it was *always* 'forbidden', wasn't it. Or have you forgotten about Frank?" Nora countered, reminding her.

"Uh!" Angie huffed again, this time making no attempt to suppress her bitterness. "Thirty years I've been locked in marriage to that man – someone who spent one half of it being serially unfaithful to me; and the other half mostly ignoring me."

"'Locked'?" Nora spat back at her in contempt. "You could have walked out at any time. Perhaps it might have spared us all heartache and misery if you had. But I guess the regular income he brought home had its uses – especially once the performing work had dried up!

"Besides," she then continued to Angie's mounting dismay, "what makes you so confident you're such a delight to live with? How do you think Frank must have felt to see you wallowing in self-pity over some bloke who dumped you years ago? How do you think he must have felt watching you go merrily off your rocker because you failed to get over it and move on? How do you think it feels for him now, watching you doll yourself up to amuse boozed-up holidaymakers while trying to kid yourself it's 1944 all over again? And how do you think he would feel if he knew you'd been screwing his nephew – *my son* – because that too makes you feel less like the pathetic, embittered old tart you really are? The real miracle is that Frank has put up with you for so long. If he didn't have his shop and his television, I swear he too would have gone off his rocker by now!"

It was a catty, wounding diatribe that Nora regretted as soon as she had spewed it out – notwithstanding that her sister couldn't counter the essence of truth it bore. It induced Angie to shove herself away from the lintel and slump into her husband's favourite armchair, there to launch herself into a fit of tearfulness made all the more harrowing by her sibling's determined refusal to acknowledge her contrition. Instead, Nora stood up and wandered across to the open window, where the first stirring of a cool, refreshing breeze was in the air.

"Uh!" Angie thereupon huffed once more, eschewing the seeking of forgiveness and responding in kind. "But then you're no saint either – are you, Nora. The woman who thinks rattling a tambourine in church every Sunday gives her the right to judge others – conveniently overlooking the circumstances in which that 'son' I have been 'screwing' came into this world in the first place. The woman who allowed herself to be used as a rubbing post by the soldiers of the Sizewell battery; the woman who stole *my* son as a replacement for the one she gave away; the woman whose own loveless marriage was in trouble long before she stumbled upon the convenient excuse of blaming the poor kid for driving a wedge between her and her husband.

"So carry on revelling in your abstinence and your 'born again' religiosity. But you know it's just a way of making yourself feel better because you have *never* been loved by a man in your entire life – I mean really loved. At least I know what real love feels like. I *know* Charles Eichelberger loved me!"

There ensued a hanging silence while Angie looked up through mascara-streaked eyes to see if her return salvo of catty, wounding observations had hit home. Instead, Nora maintained her back to her sister, continuing to stare through a net curtain that was rippling in the gathering breeze.

"You're wrong, Angie" she eventually insisted in a voice that was curiously devoid of anger or indignation. Absent too was any indication about which bit of her sister's own diatribe was 'wrong'. However, when, after another pregnant pause, clarification came it contained a new and devastating charge.

"You see, there never was a soldier called Paul; but there was an American airman called Charles. And while this 'Charles' might have loved you – once – it was *me* he loved in the end."

Angie's eyes suddenly opened wide. She listened with mounting disbelief – and in appalled silence – as Nora finally stumbled upon the right moment to calmly and purposefully unburden herself of that third and final family secret she'd kept to herself for over thirty long years.

"It all began in the Christmas of 1944 – that night we gathered to celebrate in Woodbridge. It was the first time Charles and I had the opportunity to chat together. Before the night was over though, we each knew enough about the other to understand that some kind of chemistry existed between us.

"To start with, maybe we were both too scared to acknowledge it – terrified of what an awful thing we would open up if we did. However, it was while you were away singing during that winter that our affair began in earnest. At first, it didn't amount to much. He would sometimes walk me home, holding hands when no one was looking. Maybe the odd snatched kiss here and there. Then finally the moment arrived when we both knew we wanted more. It was VE Day – May 8th 1945. Everybody was getting drunk and singing their hearts out at the street party. Maybe we got a little merry too. But then all of a sudden we were looking into each other's eyes and just knew the time was right.

" And so he walked me down to the beach; and… well, I'm sure you don't need me to explain how these things happen. How 'it felt so good, and so right'; or how 'to be in his arms made me feel alive'; or 'how difficult it is to forsake that kind of love and passion once it's been tasted'," she quoted her sister's excuses back at her.

"And you have kept this from me all this time?" Angie was mortified, symbolically emphasising each word in the sentence – though with a similar strange absence of venom or indignation.

Instead, bizarrely, there suddenly dwelt within Angela Tring a closet admiration for the chutzpah of her little sister, who had subtly turned the tables so that neither of them could any longer claim the moral high ground. Perhaps Nora's God was not so cruel after all. In fact, His sense of humour was rather apt.

At last, Nora turned about in the window bay to address Angie and to put this belated revelation into some kind of context.

"I guess we will never know why Charles Eichelberger left England in a hurry – and without telling either of us. Did he really love you, but was too ashamed to tell his fiancée that he'd gotten her little sister pregnant? Did he love me, but was too appalled to tell his fiancée that to her face? Or all along was he still in love with Natalie, and now needed to wipe the slate clean of the mistakes he'd made while overseas – proposing marriage to you while seeing me behind your back?

"Of course, it's always possible he never actually loved any of us. Instead, he married Natalie in order to lend convenient respectability to the real love of his life: his promising career with the United States Air Force. Men do that sometimes: they choose their mates primarily as an adornment with which to further cement their social and career advantage."

It was a fascinating thought, Angie grinned wryly. Charles Eichelberger would indeed have had his work cut out explaining to his devout parents (and maybe to his air force superiors) why he'd jilted his All-American sweetheart in preference for some brassy English nightclub singer.

"But then I suppose there is only one person who can answer that question. However, I suspect that, for the sake of the illusions we each cherish – you, me, his wife; and, yes, his daughter too – none of us really wants to hear the truth tumble from his lips.

"So now you and I are quits. Neither of us has covered ourselves in glory, have we. Both of us have been guilty of allowing our desire for a bit of sensual excitement in our boring lives to override our loyalty to – and our love for – each other as sisters," Nora noted poignantly, staring her out.

"So I guess we can either spend what time is left to us on this Earth despising the other and plotting how we can exact some kind of revenge upon her. Or we can resolve right now to forgive, to forget, and to instead cleave to the one thing that hopefully still unites us: our desire to continue offering Vaughan all the love and support I fear he will need to get over these terrible truths we have had to tell him. Which is it to be, Angie?"

27

Saturday, August 28th 1976

"A penny for your thoughts."

Aimee looked up from her daydream to observe that her father had wandered out onto the balcony to join her, admiring the unrivalled views of Sandown Bay to be had from her parents' exclusive rooftop hotel suite. She said nothing. It prompted Charles Eichelberger to wonder whether he might need to up the price if he wanted to get inside his daughter's head, the better to understand the melancholy had come over her of late.

Already her mother had made several attempts to encourage her daughter to confide in her, only to be fobbed off with excuses as varied as 'worn out by all this heat', 'anxious about my final year at college' and 'feeling sad to be finally leaving England'. Though Natalie had prayed with her (as she often had at key moments in Aimee's life), and though Aimee herself had gone through the motions of praying too, her father knew something more profound had come over his daughter, of which the Good Lord was party to but they were not.

"It was very kind of Veronica to let you off work today," he launched the first probing sortie to find out – even as he realised that, for a variety of reasons that he'd come to regret, his chances of penetrating the hostile air space that was his daughter's reticence were equally remote.

"Yeah, I guess," was all she would say.

"She told me you'd been throwing up," he followed on.

"Yeah. It must have been something I'd eaten. I'm just sorry I had to leave Shelby to carry on without me – and on the hotel's busiest day of the week too."

"Veronica was very understanding. She said she'd find another member of the house-keeping team to help out. Besides, Shelby's a hard worker. She'll be just fine."

"Yeah. She is."

Taking advantage of another pause while her father pondered something to say, Aimee was once more fretting that Veronica Lawton had smelt a rat. Sooner or later the truth was bound to tumble out. So contrary to the hastily-agreed plan Shelby had concocted that she should blame her predicament on some one-night stand, Aimee would tell her parents the awful truth about how she had come to be with child – and who the father was! Maybe the respect in which he held John Lawton would cause her father to somehow view what had happening less disapprovingly. A forlorn hope, she conceded.

All she could do was pray that the Lord would find a way for her to break the news to them – because determining the ends and willing the means were two different things. Therefore, when her father drew up a chair and sat down beside her what he had to say felt like her prayer was about to be answered.

"You know, I guess you and I are long overdue for a good talk," he opened, resting a reassuring paternal hand upon her shoulder, Aimee encouraged by the fond smile he offered her. "Not least, because there are a whole load of things I guess I need to tell you too," it pained him to add.

Then, looking up at the sky – and at the first flocculent clouds they'd seen in many days – he noted that "They say the weather's gonna' break soon. We best make the most of it. Fancy a walk?"

She reflected for a few moments before staring up at to him and nodding. She rose and joined him in re-entering the room.

"You guys going somewhere?" Natalie cried above the roar of the hair-dryer she was wielding at the dresser, observing their reflections pass by in the mirror.

"For a stroll," her husband called over.

"Can I come? I've almost finished here."

"No," was his emphatic reply.

And with that they were out the door.

Whatever dejection Natalie might have felt at being summarily left behind was tempered by the tentative gladdening of her heart that Charles and Aimee might be about to undergo some kind of long overdue reconciliation after the years they'd spent seeming to talk past each other. She glanced up to Heaven, trusting that at least one longstanding prayer of faith for her daughter might be about to be answered.

* * * * *

"Penny for your thoughts."

John Lawton had stumbled upon Aimee perched pensively upon one of those expansive leather sofas that were dotted about the hotel lobby. She was attired in her uniform – that short black skirt that always turned him on, along with the matching blouse – but with neither mop, bucket or any other cleaning utensil in her hands. Having been waiting for her father to return from a visit to the washroom, she looked up to observe looming over her the last person she wanted to talk to right then.

"Trust me: you wouldn't want to know," she replied, testily firing him a sullen glare as he attempted to offer her that ingratiating smirk she had so come to despise.

"Well, whatever it is it's clearly keeping you from your work," the jovial charmer switched to terse employer mode, removing the hands he had slunk in the pockets of his beige, bell-bottomed trousers and propping them indignantly on his hips.

However, she'd witnessed too much of the mercenary side of this man's nature to either respect him or be intimidated by him. Therefore, she rose from the sofa and snubbed him by feigning to studying the adjacent entertainment board that was propped on its easel outside the restaurant.

"Well, does Veronica know that you're slacking on the job?" he played on what he thought might be a more effective means of whipping this insolent young thing back into line.

"Yes. Although again, trust me: you wouldn't want her to know the reason why I'm 'slacking' either," she snapped back.

John Lawton wasn't normally a man to take no for an answer from a woman. However, he was alarmed by the allusion he thought she'd let slip. Therefore, both his tone and his blue eyes softened and he abandoned his brief and unimpressive attempt to browbeat this recalcitrant employee.

"Look, I'm not an ogre," he was at pains to emphasise. "If you have a problem you need to deal with, then maybe I can be of assistance. You see, I know people… people who help girls like you. And I have money to help you to…"

"To do what, John?" she fumed, turning about and cutting him off mid-sentence. "To help me kill my baby? Or should that be *our* baby?"

"Keep your voice down," he hushed her through ventriloquist's lips, glancing about to see who might perchance be within earshot. "Look, if you're half as smart as your expensive education suggests, then you will indeed get rid of that bothersome bundle of cells – sharpish! For both our sakes."

It was not so much the advice that shook Aimee to the core as the callousness with which it was offered. Whatever affinity she had once felt towards this odious man had now completely evaporated. The scales had finally tumbled from the pretty little eyes of Aimee-Marie Eichelberger.

Meanwhile, Lawton's own eyes were still scanning the lobby on tenterhooks. Maddeningly, it was invariably his wife who was hovering about whenever he and this attractive American room maid bumped into each other. However, today those flitting eyes alighted upon someone else up at the top of the list of individuals he did not want to be overhearing this exchange.

"Ah, Charles," he greeted the reappearance in the lobby of Aimee's tall, stocky father, offering him his hand, as well as that look that told the General he was about to be deluged in Lawton's usual gushing flattery.

"John," Eichelberger acknowledged him, though pointedly ignoring his outstretched hand. Instead, he slapped one of his own down upon Lawton's shoulder in the manner he might once have done to a subordinate to whom he was looking to break bad news. Further ambiguity was added to this encounter when the General drew breath and looked him in the eye paternally.

"You know, John, we really ought to have another little chat before I fly back – just you and me. You see, a little matter has come to light that I really think you and I need to talk about."

Had Aimee already told her father, Lawton's anxious eyes swivelled back and forth between them? However, without elaborating further, the General removed the chunky hand to alight it protectively upon his daughter's shoulder instead.

Thereupon, he employed it to lead her out into the morning sunshine. It left the womanising hotelier more fearful than ever that, of all the many extracurricular balls he had – so to speak – been trying to juggle, potentially the most troublesome one of them all had just slipped his grasp.

* * * * *

"You know, John's a great guy," Charles confided as he emerged with his daughter from the public lift that transported guests from the cliff top hotels down onto Shanklin Esplanade. "But, I don't know. I'm beginning to sense there might be another side to him. And that this 'other side' is a dark place indeed."

Where to start! Aimee frowned, but otherwise said nothing. Instead, joining her father on a leisurely stroll along the seafront, both of them would stare across at the bay from time to time as they made exploratory small talk – each angling for a way to unburden themselves to the other.

"I know you must think I'm an old square sometimes; someone who doesn't understand what it's like to be a young person caught up in these so-called 'liberated' times we're living in. But my generation knew what the temptation of the flesh was too. And if I'm honest, then I'm not without sin myself when it comes to... well, you know. And, I suspect, neither are you," he probed, as if expecting an affirmative response.

If ever there was an invitation for Aimee to unburden herself, this was it. However, though she shrugged her shoulders and pursed her lips, before she could even string together a form of words by which she might break her terrible news to her father he had commenced the baring of his own soul. Yet instead of serving up reheated morsels of his conversation the other evening with Angie Ashby (as she was expecting), he digressed.

"I guess I owe you an apology."

"You do?" she played along.

"Yeah. For my head kinda' being somewhere else these last few years. I'm guessing it's why you and I haven't always seen eye-to-eye. I'm guessing too it's because you maybe resent that for so long it might have seemed like I only had time for your brother. And that this might have led you to think I didn't care about you; that you were perhaps… an afterthought."

His innocent use of a word she'd frequently employed herself was eerie. However, it prompted her to generously observe that "I get why you were proud of Ike – especially when he followed you into the air force. And why, when you lost him, it shook you the way it did."

"But none of this ever meant I didn't love *you*. It's just that…"

She watched while he struggled to recount how he'd first learned the terrible news that both son and the promising air force career he'd been pursuing had been prematurely snuffed out. Then – to her amazement – he also laid bare a terrible secret about her older brother that until now he had kept to himself.

"Aimee, Ike was no stranger to temptation either. I've never told either you or your mom about it; but there was this girl he met when his wing was based at Andersen during the fall of '72."

"Girl?" Aimee puzzled. "What girl? He'd announced his engagement to Mary-Ann a few weeks earlier. They'd been going steady since he'd graduated from the Air Force Academy."

"Yeah, exactly. Except like the young butthead he was, he'd not been only two-timing Mary-Ann, but had gone and got this other girl pregnant too."

"Pregnant?" she gasped.

"That's right. The last conversation I had with him he was begging me to do what I could to help him with the predicament he'd gotten into; to pull strings maybe. He was in a real panic that being court-martialled would jeopardise his career."

"Court martial? Career? Why? Who was this girl?" the questions kept coming.

"Alas, not some two-bit dame on a foreign shore who he could just wash his hands of and return to the States. Heck, this woman was a clerk on the base. And if word of their affair slipped out then the son-of-a-gun was going to wind up on a charge of fraternising with enlisted personnel."

A 'two-bit dame on a foreign shore'! Recalling the testimonies she'd transcribed for her senior thesis, there was an uncomfortable cynicism about her father's throwaway remark that sat ill with what she now knew about how he'd treated Angie. Surely he hadn't meant it to come out that way.

"In the end though, your brother never had to face a court martial. And I never had to pull any strings. Though I'd been agonising about whether to intervene and have Ike posted back to Barksdale – away from this girl – the following day the President ordered me to effect *'Operation Linebacker II'*. You know, when my staff drew up the order of battle I had this terrible feeling that my boy was not gonna' make it. His squadron would be hitting Hanoi – facing everything the enemy could throw at them. But what could I do now? I couldn't be seen to be posting my own son away from combat while ordering others to face it."

"Dad, what happened was not your fault," she pleaded, dismayed he was still taking her brother's loss so personally. "You were following orders – as any commander is under oath to do. And besides, Ike would not have wanted you to have had him scrubbed from those missions. He loved his job. He loved the air force. He accepted the risks he would be running."

"Maybe. But you know what really tore me up about your brother's little escapade? A terrible awareness that history was repeating itself. You see," he halted her to look her in the eye, "when I was his age – in England – I too got a girl... pregnant."

It was a revelation that should have shocked his daughter; except that – thanks to that overheard conversation the other evening – she already had her suspicions.

"Really?" she feigned surprise. "Angie Ashby?" she surmised, returning his troubled stare.

He looked away for a moment, vaguely amused by her presumption. Then guilty eyes returned to lock onto hers again.

"No. It was her sister," he blurted out the awful truth.

"What? You mean Nora? Vaughan's mom? The mother of the boy I dated?"

"Yes. Look, I'm sorry. I know it must be such a shock to you. In fact, I can't tell you how much I've beaten myself up ever since over what I did; over how shamefully I behaved; how I betrayed first your mother… and then Angie."

"And Mom doesn't know about this either?"

He shook his head in shame. Otherwise, he was as freaked as she was that she'd found herself inadvertently dating the son and nephew of two people who had once been so intimately connected with her father. It almost had the feel of divine judgement about it. However, what Charles Eichelberger could not perceive was the far more portentous alarm bell that was suddenly ringing inside his daughter's head – peeling a warning that she now began to verbalise.

"But isn't Nora also the mother of... John Lawton?" she gasped, spilling out something else she'd overheard the other evening on the terrace.

"That's right," he affirmed, though intrigued at how well briefed his daughter was about the hotel manager's true parentage. "I never realised it when I first started corresponding with him; nor when I arrived on the island. However, I now know that John Lawton is indeed *my* son – the child I sired by Nora while I was in England. The child I abandoned, along with his mother – to say nothing of the woman I'd rashly pledged myself to marry: Angie Ashby – Nora's sister."

Aimee was dumbstruck. She had been disabused of the assumption that her father's 'first and only love' was her mother, as well as (until his untimely death) that her brother had similarly been faithful to his beloved sweetheart. Furthermore, she now understood why John was forever waxing lyrical about her country – even to the point of intimating to her that he wished he'd been born an American. It was because – whether or not he was aware of it – he *was* half-American! By *her* father!

Unpalatable as she found this deluge of revelations, she found herself being assailed by a more urgent one: namely, that the child she had growing in her womb was the result not just of a similarly stupid and illicit affair; but of a sexual relationship that she had engaged in – however unknowingly – with a man who was her *half-brother*! Yet, bizarrely, at this moment when her world was suddenly caving in around her, she found herself troubled too by a further crazy, abstract thought.

"What happened to the girl?"

"I'm sorry?" her father woke from his guilty introspection.

"The girl. On Guam. The mother of Ike's child."

Her question flummoxed him. He shrugged his shoulders. He didn't know. She wondered if her father even cared. He had lost his son and had yet to come to terms with his hand in it. Consequently, he seemed unconcerned that out there somewhere was a young woman whose air force career had ended in disgrace, as well as maybe a three year-old grandchild who he had never seen and, unnervingly, seemed to possess no pressing desire to seek out. For the first time, she understood how expediency – as well as a base instinct for self-preservation – might have compelled Charles Eichelberger to turn his back upon both Angie and her younger sibling.

Meanwhile, it was the turn of his daughter to descend into guilty introspection. The knowledge of both her father's (as well as her brother's) misdemeanours had completely up-ended her own crablike attempt to break news of her unwanted pregnancy to him – never mind to her mother! How could she possibly do it now? And, more pertinently, how could she reveal *who* the father of her baby was? Suddenly, she wondered whether she would have to fall back on Shelby's wheeze about being seduced by some guy she'd met in a bar. But what if the child was afflicted by those genetic abnormalities she'd read somewhere often attended incestuous conceptions?

For the first time, she too suddenly contemplated an expedient and self-serving solution of her own: she would indeed have to abort her child – even though doing so would fly in the face of her Christian faith; the faith that had been rendered so tattered and threadbare by her wilful disobedience to God (wilful disobedience that seemed to run in the family!). Perhaps she might be in need of both John Lawton's friends and his money after all.

* * * * *

"So you didn't find out what's wrong with her?"

Charles shook his head regretfully.

"I was this close," he replied in frustration, gesticulating like so with a raised thumb and forefinger.

Sat alongside her on the opulent king-sized bed of their luxury hotel suite, he draped an arm around Natalie's shoulders and gently drew her in close.

"Well, something's clearly bugging her," she rested her head upon his broad chest and sighed. "The poor kid's been on edge ever since that afternoon at Veronica's place. Something is going on and I'm not sure I like it. I can see it's got you on edge too."

Indeed, if Aimee was having great difficulty verbalising to her mother what was on her mind, then so too was her father. Now that he had shared with his daughter both Ike's dark secret and his own then it was only right that he finally let his wife in on those secrets too. But how to confess to Natalie that not only had he (unbeknown to her) proposed marriage to another woman, but he had then seduced that woman's sister and sired a secret love child by her. And, by some extraordinary twist of fate (or divine judgement), that secret love child just happened to be the man whose hotel they were staying in!

More troubling still, Charles Eichelberger couldn't get out of his head the thought that, somehow or other, this secret son of his was the cause of Aimee's unsettled behaviour. He'd noticed how John Lawton had a soft spot for his daughter. Up until a few days ago the feeling had evidently been mutual. And, thinking back, what was all that shouting and bawling about that he'd caught wind off in the hotel lobby earlier on? Had they perchance been having some kind of lover's tiff? Indeed, were they conducting some kind of affair behind his back? It was a prospect that really didn't bear thinking about. *Id quod circumiret, circumveniat* – 'what goes around comes around'. Suddenly, the true cost of that reckless night of passion with Nora Ashby – and the disturbing manner in which it kept on echoing down the years – had truly come back to torment him.

"Charles, I guess there's only one thing we can do in these circumstances," Natalie sat up and suggested. Observing the striated brow of a man lost in thought (and maybe assailed by unspoken torment), she nudged her husband.

"I said there's only one thing we can do in these circumstances," she repeated.

To look into her expectant eyes was to know what that 'one thing' was. Instinctively he bowed his head in prayer, permitting Natalie to place her hand upon his and petition the Almighty.

"Lord, whatever's on Aimee's mind, I pray You will continue to honour the word You gave us when she left for England: that You will guide and protect her, and be the Rock that she turns to should she ever find herself in trouble.

"I also pray for my husband, Lord: that, whatever may be troubling him, You will guide and protect him too. Your Word tells us that *'if we say that we have no sin, we deceive ourselves, and the truth is not in us'*. But it also tells us that *'if we confess our sins, He is faithful and just to forgive us our sins, and to cleanse us from all unrighteousness'*. I pray that Charles will know Your forgiveness – right now. May he also be reminded that I love him and always will; and that, Lord, you will help me to forgive him – no matter what he feels he may be in need of forgiveness for. Amen"

"Amen," he concurred.

Lifting his head and brushing aside a tear, he hugged his wife and kissed her forehead. It was always so moving to hear Natalie pray and quote Scripture. So many times he'd felt himself unworthy of such a devout and spiritual woman. He knew the time had indeed now arrived to tell her everything – and to seek her forgiveness for the terrible things he had done.

* * * * *

"So you didn't actually tell your father?"

Aimee shook her head regretfully.

"I was this close," she replied in frustration, gesticulating like so with a raised thumb and forefinger.

Sat alongside her on her single bed in their small, yet functional living quarters, Shelby draped an arm upon her friend's shoulders and gently drew her in close.

"But you were right about John. He said he knew people who could 'help me'. He even offered me money too."

"Sounds like he makes a habit of getting his female workers in this situation," Shelby scowled, aware of rumours that had done the rounds amongst the hotel staff. "Ironic really, for a man who talks so much about wanting to be a father!"

"Yeah, and someone who was himself an 'unwanted' child!" Aimee sniffed, reflecting upon how cynically her boss had exploited the awe in which she had once beheld him. What price now the forbidden thrill he had personified when she'd first permitted him to flatter and seduce her?

Shelby was minded to say 'I told you so'. Instead, she rested her head against her friend's to assure her of her continuing friendship and support.

"Well, if nothing else at least he knows what he's done. It won't hurt that despicable sleazeball if you leave him to sweat a while longer," she replied indignantly.

"However, that's not all, Shell. Dad opened his heart to me big time this morning. He told me he too got a girl pregnant when he was in England."

"Angie?" Shelby made an educated guess based on what Aimee had told her of the story so far.

"Uh-uh," she lifted herself from her friend's embrace to shake her head. "It was actually her sister – Vaughan's mother."

Shelby's eyes popped.

"Wow! That's scary," her voice trembled, staggered by what an epic tale their working holiday was turning out to be. Then the penny dropped.

"But you told me John is *her* son too. So that means that... Oh, my goodness!" her heart correspondingly thumped.

"Exactly! Look, maybe John's right," her friend pleaded, "I will have to consider an abortion. Oh, Shell. I am so sorry for everything I've done. I've betrayed my parents; I've betrayed your friendship; and I've let myself down. But most of all, I have grieved the Lord."

Shelby too had strong views about the sanctity of unborn life. However, observing her friend once more descend into tears of pitiful self-reproach – and having been touched by her penitent confession – she recognised that now was neither the time nor the place to pass judgement. Right now what Aimee needed was to know the loving and forgiving embrace of the Heavenly Father she was seeking anew. The Georgian reached over to her bedside table and picked up the bible that had been her other companion during her time in England. Flicking its well-thumbed pages to the Fifty-first Psalm, she read the passage aloud...

> *"Have mercy upon me, O God, according to Thy loving kindness: according unto the multitude of Thy tender mercies blot out my transgressions. Wash me thoroughly from mine iniquity, and cleanse me from my sin. For I acknowledge my transgressions, and my sin is ever before me. Against Thee, Thee only, have I sinned, and done this evil in Thy sight: that Thou mightest be justified when Thou speakest, and be clear when Thou judgest..."*

Aimee's heart began to lift as those timeless words sank in – the repentant confession of King David of old once he too had been brought face to face with how great was his sin in taking another man's wife; and then compounding his offence by conspiring in the death of her husband. Like Aimee – and like her father and her brother before her – his sin had also resulted in an innocent child being conceived.

> *"...Hide Thy face from my sins, and blot out all mine iniquities. Create in me a clean heart, O God; and renew a right spirit within me. Cast me not away from Thy presence; and take not Thy Holy Spirit from me. Restore unto me the joy of Thy salvation; and uphold me with Thy free spirit."*

Shelby laid the bible aside and lifted her gaze to Heaven. Closing her eyes, Aimee did likewise.

"Lord, we know You are gracious and You are merciful. Be with Aimee during this difficult time. Whatever Your plans are for her and for the tiny life she is carrying inside her, I pray You will restore to her 'the joy of Your salvation', because 'a broken and a contrite heart, O God, You will not despise'. Amen."

"Amen," Aimee snuffled, opening her eyes to receive another hug from Shelby.

All of a sudden – and for the first time this summer – it felt like these two inseparable friends really were back on the same wavelength, as it were. To be sure, they were no nearer to alighting upon a practical solution to the problem Aimee was confronting – including the awkward matter of how to break the news to her parents. However, they drew comfort from knowing that this pressing problem had now been offered up into the hands of the One who had its solution already worked out.

28

Sunday, August 29th 1976

The heavens had darkened and the rain was sheeting down when the blue Austin Princess rental car drew up in Victoria Road at four o'clock on the dot. There, waiting inside the verandah to greet its occupants, were Angie, Nora and Vaughan – with Chico, as ever, looking on from his tall cage.

First out of the car, emerging from its wide rear seat and running up the steps, were Aimee and Shelby, huddling beneath raincoats that had made their first appearance of the summer. Dashing inside and shaking off the precipitation, each one planted a kiss on Vaughan's cheek before moving along the line to plant a kiss on Angie's cheek too.

"Hello, Mrs Lewis," Aimee nervously drew up to his mother and offered her outstretched hand.

"Hello, Aimee. I've been looking forward to meeting you," she smiled disarmingly as she accepted it. "But let's dispense with the formality, shall we. Please call me Nora."

Upon which, she stepped forward to plant a kiss upon Aimee's smooth cheek before flinging her arms open wide and embracing her. Likewise Shelby when she too presented herself.

While these pleasantries were being exchanged, there stepped from the car its front seat occupants. Charles Eichelberger hauled himself out of the driving seat, hastily opened an umbrella, and wandered around the car to shield his wife from the downpour. Together they mounted those same verandah steps.

Natalie was greeted first, accepting a kiss on the cheek from Angie before offering her cheek to Nora's disarming kiss too. Her husband likewise greeted Angie. Then, for the first time in three decades, he too moved along the line and accepted a kiss of salutation from someone who had been an impressionable, lovestruck eighteen year-old on the last occasion he'd been physically this close to her.

"Hello, Charles. It's been a long while," she smiled graciously. "But it's so wonderful to see you again."

Charles offered her the kind of mangled smile that spoke of awkwardness pickled with embarrassment and remorse – one he had become accustomed to summoning up these last two weeks when confronted with so many powerful reminders of the past. And above all things, to have felt Nora's soft hand and tender lips alighting again upon his rugged cheeks was to be reminded that the past had never really gone away.

Meanwhile, looking on, Angie couldn't help but be touched by the powerful symbolism of Nora's kiss. It was a most potent act of forgiveness and magnanimity on the part of her sister – as had been her own kiss. Maybe someone up above had indeed brought them together at this time and in this place for this reason: to find closure at last for the regrettable mistakes that these three imperfect, yet chastened individuals had once made.

"It's turning out to be quite a storm," Angie glanced up at the rain hammering on the roof of the verandah.

"Yeah, looks like you Brits have finally got your rain at last," Charles did likewise. "Why, we even spotted some folks dancing in the streets back there – celebrating it. Can you believe that?"

"Just as well I brought Chico inside," said Vaughan.

With perfect timing, the bird whistled the opening bars of *'The Star-Spangled Banner'*. It prompted amusement on the part of the Americans present – including Aimee's parents, who bade their farewells and motioned to hurry back down the steps to their car.

"You can stay if you wish," Nora insisted, grabbing Charles' arm, though addressing his wife also. "Forgive me. When I sent Vaughan round with the invitation I should have made clear to him that it was to be extended to you and Natalie as well."

The Eichelbergers hovered in the doorway. It was a most generous offer from a charming lady. Natalie glanced up at her husband and seemed open to accepting it. Charles too pondered the invitation. Sure, they could skip church. However, gazing at the beautiful hairdresser – whose good looks had stood the test of time far better than his – he was reminded why he had once fallen for her so completely. As he did, he wrestled with how he could possibly endure being in the same room as Nora while all the time having to train his eyes anywhere but upon that manifest beauty, lest she (and maybe Angie and Natalie too) spot his discomfort.

"Er, no – if that's okay. It's very kind of you, but, well... right now Natalie and I have a few things we need to talk over," he offered Nora that mangled smile again.

"We do?" his wife expressed surprise.

"Well, if you're sure," Nora was disappointed, but understood. Upon which, she offered them a parting smile.

Standing at the edge of the verandah she watched him usher a bemused Natalie back down the steps to the car, brolly in hand and opening the door for her like the gentleman he always was. Then he wandered around to the driver's side. However, before stepping inside he had one more thing he wanted to say to her on this, probably the one and only occasion they would meet again during the remainder of their time on this Earth.

"By the way, Nora," he called up to her from beneath the umbrella, offering her his most sincere deportment, "I wondered if you would be so kind as to say thank you to Vaughan for me – for looking after Aimee. My daughter is very precious to me."

"Thank you. He'll appreciate your kind words," she beamed.

"And I guess you might as well know that my gratitude extends to you personally for bringing the boy up so well. You know, there are a lot of dubious characters out there who would only too readily take advantage of a girl as hopelessly wide-eyed as my daughter. It's kinda' been a big answer to prayer to know she's been safe in the company of a true gentleman like your son – someone who knows how to respect a woman. You will never know what that means to me."

Nora sensed his heartfelt compliment was also a coded and belated apology to her for things that had happened a long, long time ago. She smiled again – this time through welling tears of magnanimity and prayerful goodwill that rendered that smile as mangled as his.

"So long, Nora," it only remained for him to bid her.

"So long, Charles," she replied, her gorgeous sable hair glistening from the damp air.

And with that, she watched the car pull away, splashing through puddles as it drew up to the junction with the High Street – at which point it turned off in the direction of Ryde.

"Hey, where are we going?" Natalie protested, recognising that this was not the way to church. "And how come you didn't want to stick around for the lady's party?"

"Like I said, Nat, there are some things I have waited an awful long time to tell you."

"Am I going to like what you're gonna' to tell me?" she riposted, only vaguely in jest.

"Well," he glanced across at her, "you did tell the Lord yesterday that you will always love me; and you asked Him to help you forgive me, no matter what I may be in need of forgiveness for. So right now I'm taking you some place quiet to see if He intends to answer that prayer."

* * * * *

"Ah, the beautiful Aimee... and Shelby," John Lawton glanced up and heralded the entrance into the room of the two American students, his effusive greeting grudgingly returned.

Neither girl knew for certain whether the smirking hotelier and his wife would be present at Nora's party (though, aware of John's newly-discovered relationship to their host, it could not be discounted). However, with her long overdue period having thankfully put in an appearance this morning, at least some of the resentment Aimee felt towards him had dissipated – to be replaced instead another, familiar sort of resentment: namely, that Charles Eichelberger's secret 'other son' miraculously walking into her father's life might yet result in her being consigned to second place in his affections once more – the 'afterthought'!

Neither was Vaughan impressed by Lawton's attempt to butter up the girl whose heart he'd still not entirely given up hope of winning. Neither (as was to be expected) was Veronica, who was seated demurely on the sofa.

To be sure, Lawton's presence seemed to provoke unease all round. Angie was putting on an unconvincing show of pretending to treat the wealthy hotelier as just another member of her extended family. Maternal indulgence and a seemingly bottomless reservoir of Christian forbearance helped Nora laugh off her son's demonstrative urge to organise everything and everybody (though even she appeared dismayed at times by his pooterish bombast). Meanwhile, Veronica would discreetly roll her eyes as if to question whether her husband could really the offspring of this gracious, mild-mannered 'birthday girl'?

Only Frank (with his perpetual inability to think beyond the day's television viewing) seemed relaxed in his company. Lawton himself was kneeling on the floor, showing off some clunky great machine he'd rigged up to his television set. The curious toy shop proprietor was clearly impressed by his demonstration of what this amazing device could do.

"Yes, what is that thing you've brought with you?" Angie enquired, watching Lawton rewind coverage of the cricket and hoping he hadn't given her couch-potato-of-a-husband ideas.

"This, Auntie Angie, is a Betamax video cassette recorder," he proudly announced, not noticing Vaughan cringe at his appropriation of that familial term (Angie too seemed wearied by its constant use). "Simply route your TV aerial through it and then you can use this built-in timer here to set the machine to record the programmes you want to watch. No more having to miss *'Crossroads'* because you're off out to a singing engagement. Instead, you can record the episodes and watch them at your leisure. What's more, you can fast-forward the playback... like so," he demonstrated, pressing another clunky switch so that the white-clad batsmen were racing back and forth to the crease at sixteen-times normal speed. "That way you can skip all those annoying adverts."

"Fascinating," warbled Betty. "So how much did this 'video' thingy set you back?"

"Seven hundred pounds."

"Seven hundred pounds!" Frank spluttered. "Out of our price range. I'm afraid watching *'Crossroads'* at your leisure will have to wait, love," he broke the disappointing news to his wife.

Angie grinned ironically. It was disappointment she guessed she could live with if it prevented Frank from disturbing her favourite soap opera by playing back all the daytime sports coverage he'd missed while attending to the shop.

"Trust me, Uncle Frank, the price will soon tumble. And mark my words, Auntie Angie, in ten years time every household – including yours – will have one of these things," Lawton counselled with boastful prescience.

'Uncle Frank' this! 'Auntie Angie' that! Vaughan could feel steam metaphorically escaping from his ears. These terms of endearment had once been exclusively his, but now grated every time his so-called 'half-brother' parroted them.

Talking of parrots, he decided he needed some space with which to come to terms with the outworking of this unwanted new domestic arrangement. While the other guests chatted or helped themselves to the spread Angie and Nora had prepared, he grabbed himself a sausage roll or two and slipped out of the room to join Chico amongst the triffids in the verandah.

* * * * *

By now, the skies overhead were positively evil. Black clouds had massed and, in the distance, the first peals of thunder were making their presence known.

"Chi-co!" the bird sang, clambering around his cage in agitation. However, the slither of sausage roll that Vaughan offered through the bars soon tempted him to halt on his perch.

"Looks like the summer's drawing to a close in style," he commenced a maudlin monologue with the animal. "By this time next week it will be a memory – like my extraordinary island adventure. I'll be preparing to start my first term at polytechnic. Mom," he mused (having determined to address Nora the way he always had), "she'll be shampooing hair at the salon in Gornal. Uncle Frank and Auntie Angie will have their flat all to themselves again. And I dare say the kids who pass by in the street will be teaching you yet more naughty words. And Aimee…?" he sighed.

"Back in the United States, missing a very good friend," he turned to behold the said Miss Eichelberger simper alongside him, joining in staring up at the rain pounding on the roof.

"Oh... Hi. I didn't hear you creep up," he twittered, self-conscious that he had been caught pouring out his heart to his feathered friend.

"Sorry if I startled you. But I guess, like you, I have a low tolerance threshold for smarm and hypocrisy."

Vaughan emitted a wry grin, aware of who she was referring to. Meanwhile, they both spotted a flash of lightning touch earth somewhere out in Sandown Bay. The thunderclap that followed startled Chico and halted his chobbling on the sausage roll.

"It's alright for you and Shelby. You only work for him. I'm related to him!" he grunted.

"Well, that makes two of us," said Aimee, easing herself into one of the wicker chairs. Once seated, she winced and began rubbing the small of her back.

"You okay?" said Vaughan, sitting himself down opposite and momentarily not registering what she'd just said.

"Yeah. I'm just a bit achy, that's all. I guess this is what comes from making beds all summer long," she replied. Then another flash of lightning illuminated her leaning forward to drape her arms across her knees and stare at the floor despondently.

"You spoke truer than you knew when you said our families have more in common than we could ever have imagined. I've since found out that John Lawton is *my* half-brother too," she looked him in the eye before glancing away in shame. "The son of an illicit relationship *my* father had with *your* mother in 1945."

Vaughan ought to have been shocked. However, nothing about this bizarre holiday surprised him any more. Besides, he was no longer so naive that he hadn't rumbled his mother's evasions about this soldier called 'Paul'. Like Aimee, he too had witnessed the tense and hesitant manner in which *his* mother and *her* father had interacted in the verandah just now.

"So was that why you pushed me away?" he needed to know. "If it was, then I understand. In fact, it was Auntie Angie who pointed out to me that, by spurning me, you might even have done me a favour – for which I will one day thank you. Well, I guess now is the opportunity for me to thank you – even though I can't pretend I don't wish things hadn't turned out differently."

On that they could agree – even as it seemed convenient to have him believe she'd shunned him on account of being aware of this fateful coincidence of birth. However, with no blood link between them, surely there was no moral or legal barrier to them restarting their romantic relationship. What's more, the pregnancy she'd feared had revealed itself to be a false alarm – albeit an immensely sobering one. How she wished it were possible to turn back the clock to a warm Saturday in June when a working-class boy from the Midlands and a vivacious exchange student from the United States had first arrived on the Isle of Wight.

"I love you, Aimee," she heard those words tumble again from this young man's lips.

"I love you too, Vaughan," she replied, still staring at the floor. Maybe she'd simply misheard him. After all, why would he want her back after the shameful way she'd treated him.

Either way, she'd finally said it: what she realised she should have felt towards him all along. Moreover, she wished she could tell him that this was never about him, or his supposed omissions; but about her and her crazy, mixed-up emotions – and (though she couldn't bring herself to further hurt him by confessing to it) about her fateful decision to become a rich man's love interest, which she now bitterly regretted.

She lifted her gaze to observe the look of (not unpleasant) surprise upon Vaughan's face. That look of surprise then slipped into one of mild amusement.

"I love you, Aimee," the disembodied voice repeated.

"Oh – my – God!" she gasped. "You said that without even moving your lips!"

There could only be one culprit! She fired an accusing stare over his shoulder at Chico, who was busy breaking open a monkey nut he was clutching in his claw. There was a mischievous glint in the beady black eye he'd trained upon her.

"Show us yer' tits!" he dropped the nut and squawked.

"You taught him to say that?" Aimee gasped a second time, training a beady and incredulous eye of her own upon Vaughan.

"No. Like I said, it's the school children who've taught him all these rude words."

"No, I mean you taught him to say 'I love you, Aimee'?" she clarified the charge.

It was Vaughan's turn to momentarily drop his gaze to the floor – guilty as charged, yet wickedly unashamed.

"My aunt was right when she warned me Chico copies everything he hears," he looked up at her half-apologetically. "I must have said those words a lot on lonely evenings when I was sat in this chair feeling sorry for myself."

Suddenly, her heart had been cracked open as deftly as one of those monkey nuts, her beautiful eyes moistening as she watched Vaughan rise from the chair and close the gap between them. He took hold of her delicate feminine hands and motioned for her to rise also. This she did, entranced again by those doleful eyes that spoke of a boy wanting nothing more than to be able to hold in his embrace again this girl he had never ceased to adore.

"I love you, Aimee," she this time witnessed those words tumble from his own lips – lips that now formed to fashion the kiss by which they sought to make up for wasted time.

Shelby had meanwhile drifted out onto the verandah, curious to know where her friend might have gotten to. When she spotted the two of them there, locked in a loving kiss (and thereby oblivious to her presence), she couldn't disguise that frisson of jealousy she'd oft times had to suppress. However, such is the cross to be borne by those who are destined to love 'pure and chaste from afar'. She offered up a grateful prayer and rejoiced that at least one legacy of her best friend's eventful working holiday was coming right for her.

As she turned to tiptoe back inside, her pocket-sized frame suddenly collided into the tall, solid physique of John Lawton – the contempt in his eyes causing her to draw breath as she looked up into them.

"Ah, how pleasing to witness my half-brother find true love," he side-stepped her and strode out onto the verandah to observe the two youngsters break apart upon spying his presence, "... And with my best-looking employee too! I'm so envious of him. Why, had I been ten years younger I might have been tempted to seek out her affections for myself," he then smirked.

Vaughan longed to say something, but didn't. Aimee longed to say something, but couldn't. Instead, their Adam's apples both bobbed self-consciously when the grinning hotelier reminded Vaughan that "If you're not too busy canoodling, your mother requests your presence for the audio-visual highlight of the afternoon. If you'll kindly follow after me all will be revealed."

* * * * *

With all the guests parked on chairs in Frank and Angie's sitting room – Aimee next to Shelby, and Vaughan over by the dining table (where he could work out his frustration by pigging on the fairy cakes) – Lawton commenced his eagerly-awaited *pièce de résistance*. As he stood ready to address them, a flash of lightning flittingly illuminated his impressive stature – as well as his gaily-coloured cravat and snakeskin shoes. Thunder too crashed loudly to add dramatic effect.

"Ladies and gentleman, this summer will be remembered for many reasons – not least an incredible run of hot, sunny weather which it appears has now come to an end," he observed, the relentless pitter-patter of rain upon the sill of the open window further heightening the sense of expectation.

"But what you may or may not be aware of is that, for me, this summer has been memorable for a more personal reason. Once upon a time there was a happy little boy growing up in a warm, loving family. However, one day that little boy – by now an assertive teenager – discovered that these wonderful people were not his real family after all. Rather he had been adopted by them when he was a baby. Alas, it transpired, his real mother had been put in the predicament of having to give him up at birth."

Nora visibly winced, sensing a dozen or more eyes glancing her way. Therefore, Angie – who was sat next to her on the sofa – discreetly placed a sisterly hand upon her arm. Veronica too offered her new mother-in-law an empathetic smile.

"Of course, I know now that my real mother never stopped loving me, or thinking about me," he cast a forgiving eye upon her, "nor praying that we would one day be reunited again," he added, conceding that some heartfelt longings are so preposterous that they can only ever be assuaged by miraculous intervention.

"And so it was that, as a result of a seemingly chance conversation with the good lady who has very kindly thrown her home open to us this afternoon," he announced, offering Angie a more sinuous smile, "my mother and I were put in touch with each other for the first time since I'd been born."

The genteel Betty led the soft chorus of touching sighs that coursed around the room. Even the undemonstrative Frank couldn't resist dabbing the non-tear that he imagined might have escaped from a flickering eye. Vaughan too felt compelled to divert his attention away from the last tempting chocolate éclair and warm to the hotelier's emotive tale.

"Mom," Lawton now turned to address Nora, who stared up at him, also on the cusp of sobbing. "All those years you must have wondered what had happened to me: where I was; what I looked like; how I was growing up. Yet all these things remained a mystery to you. How you must have yearned to be present at all the most memorable moments during my childhood – treasured landmarks on my journey in life that you sadly missed.

"Well now, I'm pleased to announce that – thanks to the wonders of modern technology – you are going to be able to do just that. So, Mom, please accept from me a very special gift on this, your fiftieth birthday."

And with that, the guests gazed on in heartfelt awe as Veronica trawled from her bag a small, rectangular, gift-wrapped package that she now placed in Nora's hands.

"What is it?" she twittered, looking up at her son.

"There's only one way to find out," he urged.

Upon which, she gingerly pawed at the wrapping, removing it until all that remained in her hand was a strange black plastic object. This she now permitted Lawton to take from her. Then he knelt down, pressed open the lid of the VCR machine, and slotted it in. The device swallowed the object with a hefty clunk. Pressing the 'play' button he then drew back to slide onto the sofa alongside her as all eyes were drawn to the TV in the corner..

Suddenly, to Nora's amazement, there was her long-lost 'little boy' on the screen of Frank's television set. Riding around on a tricycle, he was determined to show his adoptive (and camera-wielding) father that he could master riding it all the way from the officers' quarters to guardhouse. Once there, the cute, blonde-mopped toddler began steering it in circles around the bemused corporal on duty. Aimee emitted a grudging smile, for such seeming ephemera reminded her of her own military childhood – remarkable similarities in their life stories that had first drawn her to this complex and troubled man.

Then the edited footage switched to a childhood birthday party, with lots of jelly and ice cream and jolly party games. Attired in short-trousers, John Lawton was excitedly opening his presents before the air marshal's all-seeing lens – so all-seeing that, by twiddling with the focus, it had caught his adopted son stealing a crafty kiss from one of the better-looking little girls who'd been invited.

"Ah, RAF Benson – 1954... And that's Melody Fraser – the daughter of the station CO. I remember her well. She was a stunning young lady – even at eight years-old!" he recalled, turning to his real mother, who smiled back indulgently at the full-grown man. In contrast, Veronica's face remained stubbornly inscrutable: some of her husband's foibles hadn't changed with the passage of time!

And so the footage he'd painstakingly stitched together from the air marshal's old cine-films progressed to a family holiday in some exotic place. After panning around to set the scene of powdery white sand, swaying palm trees and a turquoise sea, that searching lens alighted upon the growing youngster, legs spread apart at the waters edge, enjoying the sensation of the frothing, milk-white surf breaking upon them.

"That was Singapore in 1959. My father was based at RAF Sembawang. I used to visit my adoptive parents there during the school holidays."

Once more, Aimee was visibly moved upon by these frames he'd spliced together for his mother's delectation. She recalled an idyllic beach that she had similarly frolicked upon during a fondly remembered vacation with her parents in the Philippines in 1968, when her father had been stationed at Clark Air Base.

"Of course, I haven't given up hope of one day being able to show off all this footage to my real father too – wherever in this big, wide world he may be. One day I will find him. I know I will," Lawton promised the assembled guests.

At that moment there were several different pairs of eyes in the room darting back and forth at each other knowingly. Indeed, it was almost as if only John Lawton himself was unaware of just how close he had come to completing that search. Was it really asking too much to believe that he was as much victim as perpetrator of the tragic catalogue of events that had kept him in the dark these last few days? Aimee was tempted to speak up and put him right. Nora too pondered whether she owed her family and friends this final momentous confession.

Instead, she squeezed her son's hand guiltily when the footage progressed to his anxious first day at Eton, as well as his graduation ceremony from Cambridge University (where he had bagged a first class honours degree). Touching or ironic (depending on how well acquainted those present were with the couple), the footage concluded with John and Veronica exchanging vows on their wedding day – 'forsaking all others', the groom had promised his stunning bride; 'with my body I thee worship', she had promised him in return.

Thereupon, the object of his mother's indulgence bounced up from the sofa and begged to be excused.

"Ladies and gentlemen, give me just a moment while I announce another little surprise for my beloved mother," he explained, ejecting the video cassette and handing it back to her. Then, taking another one that Veronica passed to him, he slotted it into the machine and again pressed 'play'.

"Just keep watching. In my absence I'm sure Veronica will talk you through this one. It contains footage of some of the things I've been up to since we got married," he said, grabbing his jacket and disappearing out of the flat, car keys in his hand.

Watch was precisely what the guests continued to do. However, Lawton's parting admonition did prompt more curious souls to train their eyes upon his wife, who had suddenly come over all self-conscious now that her husband had landed her with the invidious task of narrating the footage.

Alas, she promptly clammed up. For it had certainly captured what he'd 'been up to' alright, opening as it did with the lascivious hotelier – in his capacity as a local business worthy – on the judging panel of this summer's Miss Shanklin beauty pageant. Whoever had wielded this particular roving photographic lens had taken a series of still shots capturing Lawton's incorrigible eye for such things similarly roving up and down the bikini-clad contestants' 'particulars'. After the contest, it had even zoomed in to capture him furtively chatting up the owner of an especially head-turning pair of 'particulars'.

It prompted a laddish ripple of hilarity on the part of Frank and Vaughan. Let no one say this wealthy playboy wasn't able to laugh at himself and his predilections. Neither Aimee nor Shelby shared the amusement however. Neither did Angie or Nora. And neither too did Veronica, having suddenly realised what had happened. For a moment her every instinct was to jump up and hit the 'stop' button. But then something gripped her that rendered her a passive spectator in this unfolding happenstance. Indeed, commentary was superfluous – for by now there was palpably darker edge to the playback.

To be precise, there was more stills footage – this time of Lawton's Jaguar (with its distinctive number plate) drawing up alongside some pretty girl, who was attired in hot pants and a plunging vest top. Furthermore, it was possible to discern the enticing contents of that top when the camera zoomed in to capture her leaning forward to converse with the driver before hopping inside his motor.

Aimee was mortified. All of a sudden those darting eyes were trained upon her. Neither was there hilarity on the part of any of the assembled guests when that journey concluded with more snapshots of that same sexy student storming out of the car to angrily offer her chauffeur 'the finger'.

Vaughan closed his eyes and prayed there was an innocent explanation. Aimee broke to fire Veronica Lawton an accusing glare before the anger was wiped from her face by the grimace induced by a sudden cramping pain in her belly.

For better of worse, no one noticed – for the tape was still rolling and all eyes were glued to the collage of shots of someone else receiving the *'Candid Camera'* treatment. At first it wasn't possible to make out who the woman was that Lawton was this time conversing with in his car. However, when she was captured stepping out of that car to face the photographer's lens – unawares, and with smouldering eyes and shark-like grin – no one in the room was left in any doubt that Angela Tring had been caught *in flagrante* engaging in something decidedly chancy. It was the turn of this second secret assignee to wish the floor would open up and swallow her.

Some of the guests were beginning to wonder if Lawton was aware of the explosive content of the tape that he'd carelessly left running. Had he made a cock-up when editing it? And why was his wife still sitting there stone-faced on the sofa, making no effort to halt it?

Meanwhile, the montage progressed to the footloose hotelier parking up in some upmarket mews. The Routemaster buses, clear skies and skimpy fashions suggested it had been taken in London at some point during this remarkable summer. The object of this surveillance was captured in the act of bidding some scantily-clad beauty step out of the passenger side of his car, thereafter to usher him inside her apartment. Then suddenly there was moving footage too! What's more, it had captured these two individuals hurriedly undressing each other!

Jaws dropped. What on Earth was this woman about to do to him? No, surely not! Nora drew her hand to her mouth in horror. Betty was aghast. Frank was gobsmacked. Shelby closed her eyes and prayed. Vaughan – at first tickled by *schadenfreude* – was soon dumbstruck too, having been taught nothing about such things in sex education classes at school! Meanwhile, neither Aimee nor Angie could bear to watch.

Only Veronica Lawton seemed unfazed. Buddha-like, her eyes were shut tight and her lips were pressed together – as if she had transcendentally removed herself from the proceedings. This was not how she had planned to use that surveillance footage. But then maybe fate, or the Good Lord above, had forced her hand – and in a most spectacular fashion.

"Turn it off, Frank! For goodness sake, turn it off!" Angie raged, leaping from her seat and shoving him aside to bodge this button and that in an attempt to halt the playback.

"Happy Birthday to you, Happy Birthday to you, Happy Birthday, dear Mother..." sang one of the participants in these unspeakable acts when – dripping wet from the rain – he re-entered the room bearing in his hands a beautifully-decorated cake that he had removed from its box.

A powerful flash of lightning lit up a face transfixed in horror the instant he realised what everyone was staring at. No sooner had footage of his adulterous conjugation with Sophie reached its climactic consummation than an almighty clap of thunder shook the room like a herald of divine wrath. In that instant too, Angie jabbed a button that finally froze the screen. Thus did the moment that this long-lost son collapsed in a sweaty heap upon his lover's naked torso become the abiding image for those present (and who were now recovering their composures sufficient to be able to reflect upon what they had just seen).

"Mom!" said Lawton, who hurriedly laid the cake aside on the table, stooping down to console Nora. However, she pushed him aside, leapt tearfully from her seat, and fled the room.

Veronica too followed after her, snatching her raincoat and her husband's car keys to brush past him with not a flicker of emotion in her eyes. It was certainly going to be a birthday to remember.

"If you don't mind, Angie, I think I need your bathroom," Aimee was meanwhile gasping, rising from her seat to stagger disconcertingly towards the door, clutching at her stomach.

"I think I better go with her," said Shelby, seizing her by the arm to steady her. It was the turn of the diminutive Georgian to fire Lawton a look of blazing contempt as she too brushed past.

Meanwhile, Vaughan glanced over at the chair Aimee had vacated and noticed a large vermilion stain where she'd been sat.

* * * * *

The minute Aimee closed the door behind her and sat down she was suddenly confronted by more blood than she'd ever seen. Then a terrifying cramp tore through her stomach.

"You okay in there?" Shelby called out, hearing the squeal.

"Is she alright?" Vaughan popped his head into the hallway and called out, aware she almost certainly wasn't.

Shelby offered him an expression that gainsaid any reassuring words she might have been tempted to offer. Meanwhile, John Lawton hurriedly pushed past Vaughan on his way out of the flat, that clunky VCR machine tucked under his arm. Other guests too had concluded that the party was, to all intents and purposes, at an end. Another flash of lightning lit up the hallway as they too began making their excuses and leaving.

* * * * *

"You okay, Aimee?" Shelby called out again, having overheard further muffled squeals.

"Look, girl, I'm coming in!" she finally tired of waiting, grasping the handle and stealing herself inside.

"Oh, my goodness! What's happening to you?" she cried upon discovering her friend doubled up on the toilet pan. Everywhere around it was dappled crimson.

"I guess I was wrong about being pregnant," she panted, clutching her stomach. "It looks like Aunt Flo has returned with a vengeance!"

No sooner had she completed her hopeful sentence than a further violent cramp caused her to claw at her abdomen.

"This sure doesn't look like a period to me," Shelby insisted. "I think you need to get to a hospital. Now!"

* * * * *

"Can I use your phone?" Shelby sidled up to Angie in the kitchen and begged. With their guests having abandoned them, she and Nora were making themselves busy tidying up, too shell-shocked to articulate what they had just witnessed.

"Is Aimee okay?" was her instinctive response, vaguely aware that something was awry down the other end of the hallway.

"I'm not sure. She says she's menstruating badly; but I think it's much worse than that. I think she might be having some kind of... miscarriage," Shelby explained in anxious tones.

"Miscarriage?" Nora exclaimed. Her angry gaze immediately alighted upon Vaughan – who she turned to observe pacing about the sitting room, pretending to listen to Frank lecturing him about the pitfalls of dallying with 'those sorts of women'

Angie stared accusingly too, dismayed that all her admonitions about being 'prepared' and taking 'precautions' had gone unheeded. Suddenly history really was repeating itself!

Vaughan perchance looked up to spot their eyes burning holes in him. He wondered what he might have done to warrant their censure. Hence he broke to head into the kitchen and find out.

As he approached, Shelby felt compelled to insist that "It's not Vaughan's child, Mrs Lewis. Honest, it's not!"

"What's not my...?" he wondered aloud. Then, realising what he was being fingered for, his eyes opened wide in dismay.

"What? Aimee? Are you saying she's...? NO!" he exhaled forcefully, raising his hands in protest.

"If it's not Vaughan's, then whose is it?" Angie proffered the logical response.

Just then, they heard the unmistakable roar of John Lawton's XJS being revved up outside. Everyone craned to the kitchen window to observe it crunch and splash its way across the gravel car park at the rear of the block. Veronica was slumped in the passenger seat, arms folded sullenly. They turned to glare at Shelby. Once again, her cherubic face couldn't tell a lie.

While that shocking realisation was sinking in – and Vaughan understood at last why Aimee had pushed him away – they were jolted by a fiendish howl emanating from down the hallway.

* * * * *

Fortunately, less smitten with playing 'who-done-it' and instead drawing upon her experience as a midwife in Bulawayo, Betty had heard Aimee's cries and had taken it upon herself to offer her services. The other women burst into the bathroom to observe her reassuring arm cast around the girl's shoulder.

"I'll call that ambulance," said Angie, appalled by the blood splattered everywhere.

"I'll get some towels," Nora added, barging past her and flinging open the cupboards.

Vaughan wanted to enter and console her too.

"Uh-uh!" he found his way barred by Shelby. "No place for a man. You go pray and leave the icky bits to us," she ordered.

Reluctantly, he rejoined Frank in the sitting room. While the women dealt with the crisis that had suddenly befallen the house, Vaughan did indeed pray... as well as chew his fingernails and feign to watch *'Jim'll Fix It'* (Frank having switched the TV on in the vain hope of taking the lad's mind off all this kerfuffle).

* * * * *

By the time the ambulance drew up in Victoria Road the skies were in uproar. Amidst flashes of lightning, loudly-clapping thunder, and hammering rain, Vaughan could only look on impotently as Aimee was stretchered down the steps towards it. Shielded from the downpour by Betty holding aloft a brolly, she glanced back to observe him standing there in the verandah. She could only offer him her most sorrowful and apologetic smile.

"Only one relative in the back with the patient please," the ambulance man insisted as he secured her to the litter.

"Relative?" Angie's eyes flashed from beneath the hood of her coat. She turned to her sister. "Look, we really ought to get in touch with her parents," she fretted.

"I guess they'll be at church right now," Shelby piped up, studying her rain-splattered watch.

"I'll get the car out. Where about is this church?"

"I can't recall what the street's called. However, I can direct you there," Shelby offered, anxiously glancing inside the back of the ambulance at her best friend still doubling up in pain.

"In which case, *I'll* go with Aimee," Nora insisted, glancing inside too before turning to Shelby and suggesting "You go with Angie and fetch them. Then join us as fast as you can."

And with that, Vaughan watched from the verandah as his mother stepped into the back of the ambulance and the doors were closed behind her. Off it sped through rain-filled puddles, its flashing blue lights bathing the surrounding buildings in yet another hue of colour to add to those fashioned by the dramatic Wagnerian storm still streaking across the heavens.

29

Sunday, August 29th 1976

"You have humiliated me in front of my relatives. And in front of my mother too, for pity's sake!" he yelled at her without irony, having simmered with rage during the half-hour journey back to their Bonchurch mansion.

However, if Veronica Lawton felt guilty for subjecting innocent bystanders, as it were, to at least some of the stark reality of what her philandering husband had been up to then she didn't let it show. Instead, having poured herself a glass of wine, she kicked off her shoes and sat down in her favourite armchair, strains of Chicago's *'If You Leave Me Now'* drifting lazily from the hi-fi she had meanwhile switched on. The lyrics grating, her furious spouse promptly strode across to switch it off again.

"Why did you have to do that to me? All these years I've been searching for my real mother. And now – because of you – it looks like she's never going to want to speak to me again."

"Then you underestimate a mother's love, darling – even towards a worm like you!" she eventually deigned to address him. Placing the glass back on the table, she then shuffled about on her bottom in order to tuck her legs beneath it.

"Anyway, I've already told you: it was not my intention to tell her what you've been up to. How was I to know you'd pick up the wrong video tape and then broadcast it to your family!"

She could see he didn't believe her. However, her lame excuse – plus her refusal to be fazed by the vile temper he was in – only enraged him even more. His anger was deepening to the point where he really did wish this joyless woman dead.

By virtue of the humiliation he'd piled upon her, Veronica was nursing enough of a grievance towards her husband to feel the same way – for she suspected that during their four years of marriage he'd probably been in and out of more beds than the gardener's spade! Even now she was not convinced there hadn't been another during the time he'd been seeing the Permanent Secretary's wife. Rising from her chair and wandering over to the mantelpiece, she thought she'd have a final stab at seeing if truth and contrition would ever tumble from her husband's lips.

"Anyway – and talking of mothers – that American girl hasn't been feeling very well of late. In fact, I let her take Friday morning off because she was sick. She didn't look too good at the party either. Perhaps it's time I had a little chat with *her* mother; and maybe with her father too," she mused wickedly. "After all, my hotel can't afford to keep having its prettiest domestic staff going down with this strange 'morning sickness'."

Lawton pretended not to twig the pun – or be perturbed by the subtle blackmail it implied. However, the culpable look in his eyes was sufficient answer for his wife. He had indeed been carrying on with 'that American girl' – just as she had suspected. Otherwise, he was in no mood for either her crass humour or her odious mind games. He squared up to her at the fireplace. Outside, the electrical storm that was still periodically illuminating the evening skies lit up the room again.

"*Your* hotel? *Your* hotel? Good grief, woman, I swear the *'Manageress'* plaque on the door of that office has gone to your head. Just remember: you would be nothing without me – just another air-headed, aristocratic totty in need of a rich husband to keep her in the means to which she's become accustomed. Uh! Perhaps it's true what they say about women like you. You really do chase after men for one reason and one reason alone: to acquire and retain social and economic advantage," he stared down at her with misogynistic contempt.

"So whose money do you think has lavished all this upon you?" he fumed, the sweep of his hand drawing her affronted gaze to the luxurious furnishings all around. "And how do you repay me? By denying me your body and then humiliating me in front of my family. Why, you ungrateful bitch! It's high time I sent you packing and instead found someone who's capable of demonstrating at least a flicker of gratitude for my generosity. A woman who knows how to properly attend to a man's needs. They do exist, you know."

"I'm sure they do, darling: giggling little tramps who'll happily attend to those 'needs' in return for a ride in your car and a flight in your aeroplane," she snarled, countering his barb while remembering her game plan. "However, think again. While you might treat these bits of skirt as trifles to be discarded at will, when the trifle in question is your wife, your business manager and your accountant then such cynicism will cost you dear."

"What are you suggesting?" he eyed her up warily.

"Merely that *your* hotel is also *my* hotel now. Have you forgotten the agreement we drew up to transfer half of the assets and investments into my name?"

"But that was just a convenient piece of paper we signed to reduce our tax liability," he scoffed.

"To you it might be. But in the eyes of the law your signature on that paper means that half of the hotel is now mine," she reaffirmed, adding for good measure that "Of course, if you're foolish enough to force me to play dirty, then I would imagine Her Majesty's Inland Revenue will take a dim view of the way you've been siphoning the profits from *your* hotel into all those offshore bank accounts; and falsifying the hotel's accounts to cover your tracks. After all, darling, your paw prints are all over that paper trail too."

His eyes darkened at the threat. "But you assured me what we were doing was all legal and above board."

Smirking at his naivety, Veronica wandered back to the bottle on the table beside her chair and topped up her glass. She sipped from it as she sensed her husband glowering behind her back. Eventually, she turned about to stare him out.

"Being a full-blooded Alpha Male has its drawbacks. While your risk-taking personality makes you an unrivalled player when the game is exhilarating and the stakes are high – like gambling with other people's money on the commodity markets, or secretly screwing a senior civil servant's wife – it means you're too easily bored by the minutiae of actually managing a business. Did you really think that I was content to play dutiful little book-keeper while you were hobnobbing with that American general – and screwing his daughter too?

"So I'd forget about running away with this Sophie woman, darling – or indeed, any other woman, for that matter. You've been lucky so far: only 'Mommy' and her friends have had the dubious privilege of witnessing the means by which you derive sexual pleasure."

Her scathing stare left him visibly smarting. 'Attending to a man's needs' indeed! However, she then calmly, but firmly placed his deviancy in a more deadly context.

"When I first saw what was on that video I was sickened enough to want to plunge a knife into you there and then. But then I thought again. If instead I was to post that film to the Sunday newspapers then maybe destroying your reputation – as well as that of the kinky parliamentary hopeful you've been seeing behind my back – would be the next best thing."

"You bitch!" he seethed.

"Alas, darling, I wish you well with your latest book. I think you'll find you'll need every penny of the royalties from it should you ever be so stupid to think you can walk away from our marriage unscathed," she taunted him.

Meanwhile, a lightning flash illuminated the wide, self-satisfied grin of a cheated wife who – while she hadn't planned for the day to turn out this way – had even so pulled off the perfect act of blackmail and revenge.

* * * * *

"Why are they keeping me here?" she winced, her body still racked by sporadic pain.

"The doctors need to know that everything inside you has passed. Once they're sure of that, they will let you go home."

"Does that mean I've lost my baby?"

Nora nodded regretfully. Aimee glanced away, her face contorting as she fought back her tears.

"Maybe it was for the best then," she grimaced, trying to be brave and philosophical – even though she knew she was failing miserably.

"Yes, maybe," Nora leant across and squeezed her hand as it rested on the hospital bed.

"More to the point, why are you here?" Aimee wanted to know. "You ought to hate me with every bone in your body because of the way I've treated Vaughan," she insisted before glancing away again – this time in shame.

"Perhaps I should. But I don't. But then maybe you should hate me too – because of the way John has behaved towards you," Nora replied.

Aimee's gaze returned to spend a moment studying the sorrow that belied Nora's own vicarious shame.

"I try to ask myself would he have behaved that way had I been a proper mother to him," her comforter agonised. "Instead – and against my every instinct – I gave him away at birth, thereby denying him my love during those crucial early years of his life; maybe commencing the process by which he would one day be filled with all manner of insecurity and resentment."

"But it wasn't your fault that attitudes to unmarried mothers were so unforgiving back then," Aimee pointed out. "Neither did you deserve to have my father abandon you: nor to betray your sister the way he did. So I ask again: why do you and your family not hate me and mine for everything we have done to you?"

She watched while Nora pondered the question again.

"Angie did indeed spend many years hating your father. All it achieved though was to almost rob her of her marriage, her child – and her sanity. Thankfully, she's realised her mistake and forgiven your father at last. Indeed – remarkable as it seems – I believe the reason you and Vaughan were destined to spend this summer together was so that both our families might yet find release from the prison that has been our terrible mistakes."

For the first time since she'd arrived at the hospital, Aimee managed a touching smile. Nora responded in kind. Then, once again dispensing with formality that seemed so inappropriate, she drew up to this tangible reminder of the man who'd once wronged her and trailed her fingers through Aimee's dishevelled locks.

"Aimee, you and I have both been shown grace and mercy that we didn't deserve. After all, didn't I too betray my sister by stealing her man? Yet when we truly realise just how much God loves us and has forgiven us, then loving and forgiving others becomes a whole lot easier."

* * * * *

How easy it had been to seize her by the throat in a fit of rage. As John Lawton sat on the living room floor tearfully cradling his wife's body and lovingly running his hands through her silky chestnut mane, the magnitude of the terrible thing he'd just done finally sank in. At first in denial, he reluctantly accepted that life had departed her limp frame, never to return – and irrespective of the tender words he was still whispering in her ear.

And yet, laughably, it was at this very moment of finality that he realised how much he still loved Veronica. Had he really been so deluded to believe those other women he'd chased could ever supplant her? After all, what had sex with those diverse others been – except the outworking of a contemptible base urge that he had despised himself for no sooner he'd surrendered to it? Furthermore, he now despised those women for tempting him to indulge those urges in the first place.

Above all, he cursed the God who had frustrated his desire to channel those urges into the pure and constructive outlet of a fulfilling marriage. Veronica had been his wife, his soul mate, his trusted business partner. And yet this cruel God had caused her to be repelled by his advances, thereby denying him the right to be a loving father to children of his own. This God had also latterly planted in her heart the wicked legerdemain that had defrauded him of the hotel into which he had sunk his fortune.

However, all that was by-the-by. He had to work out a plan for the here-and-now. Casting sentimentality aside, he lowered her body to the floor and drifted over to the drinks cabinet to mix a whisky-and-dry. Briskly downing it for courage, glass still in hand he wandered over to the French window to pass a moment contemplating the rumbling storm and the driving rain.

* * * * *

Drenched from the short walk from the car park to the main entrance, it was after ten o'clock by the time Charles and Natalie Eichelberger stormed into the hospital and raced up to the reception desk, Angie and Shelby in tow. Startled, the woman behind the counter looked up from her paperwork.

"I believe you've admitted an Aimee-Marie Eichelberger," her breathless father demanded, raindrops dripping from his angular nose and jaw.

The receptionist consulted her notes before pointing the anxious party in the direction of the ward where his daughter had been deposited. Off the party raced, bursting like a tornado through the each of the hefty fire doors en route.

It had taken Angie and Shelby some time to round up Aimee's parents. No one at the church or back at the hotel knew of their whereabouts. Then, just when this two-woman search party had been on the verge of rejoining Nora without them, the couple had wandered into the hotel lobby. Apparently (or so Charles had explained) they had passed this stormy evening partaking of a *tête-a-tête* on some lonely car park overlooking the bay. From Natalie's stern silence on the half-hour journey here, Angie could guess the subject matter. Indeed, only patent anxiety about her daughter had kept the lid on the things she guessed Natalie might want to confront her about. However, neither the time nor the circumstance lent themselves to recriminations. Meanwhile, even the rigidly honest Shelby had not been able to admit the real reason why her friend had wound up in hospital. Instead, she'd dissembled about Aimee being taken ill with some sort of 'feminine' malady.

Finally, the troop wound up at the ward in question, barging inside and past the nurse station. However, the duty sister in charge promptly swooped out her hands to bar their way.

"I'm sorry, visiting time was six till eight," she scolded them.

"Look, I'm Charles Eichelberger, and this is my wife, Natalie. I believe you have our daughter on your ward – Aimee. She was rushed here this evening," he panted.

"Yes, she is here. She's poorly, but she's stable. I'm afraid she's lost a lot of blood, but hopefully there will be no lasting complications. So she should be able to conceive again."

"Conceive! Complications! Blood! What on Earth has happened to my girl?" Natalie beseeched her, drawing her hands to her trembling lips.

"Mrs Eichelberger, I'm afraid your daughter has had a miscarriage," the sister broke the news.

"Miscarriage! You mean she was pregnant?" was the horrified response.

Charles put aside his own incredulity in readiness to catch a wife he feared was on the verge of fainting. Surely the poor woman had been dealt enough shocks already tonight. Meanwhile, Natalie stared in turn at Shelby and then at Angie.

"Would one of you ladies kindly like to tell me exactly what my daughter has been up to these last few weeks!" she demanded.

From the way Angie was being stared out, Shelby feared that Vaughan's name was about to become mud for a second time. As such – and aware that she could stall them no longer – she gulped and blurted out the truth.

"Mrs Eichelberger, I'm afraid Aimee got herself involved in some kind of affair."

"Affair?" Natalie gasped. Her accusing eyes alighted upon her husband, who raised his hands and shook his head.

"Honest, Nat," he burbled, "I know nothing about this either!"

"So who is this man she's been having this 'affair' with?" she demanded. "And who is presumably the father of..."

"John, Mrs Eichelberger. John Lawton was the father of Aimee's baby," Shelby finally spat it out, as daunted to be using the past tense as to be uttering the name of the cad himself.

"What! John? You mean that nice man... the hotel manager?"

Though for Angie this appalling news was now several hours old, hearing it again didn't lessen the humiliation of knowing she'd been double-crossed by a lover for the second time in her life. She blanched and looked away in a manner that Charles noticed but couldn't hope to comprehend. Truly revelations had broken like thunderbolts on this tumultuous night when there had been plenty of both.

"But earlier you told me that John was *your* son," Natalie arraigned her husband again. "If that's so, then that makes Aimee's baby... OH – MY – GOD!" she exclaimed, snatching at her head of permed auburn hair. It was the only time he'd ever heard his wife come close to taking the Lord's name in vain.

"Mrs Eichelberger, Aimee didn't know. None of us did," Shelby leapt gallantly to her friend's defence.

"Look, I have no idea what you people have been smoking," the ward sister shook her head and interjected, "but kindly save these arguments for elsewhere. However – sir, madam – if you would like me to escort you to your daughter's bedside then do try to keep the noise down. The rest of you, wait here."

And with that, Aimee's parents trailed after her, leaving Angie and Shelby to grab a stack-up chair each and stake out a vacant spot on the corridor where they might sit down.

"Boy, this has sure turned out to be one crazy summer," Shelby puffed, slumping in the seat and staring demonstratively at the ceiling.

"You can certainly say that again!" Angie concurred, sinking her tired face into her hands and wondering what else the Bank Holiday that had marked its end had yet to launch at them from out of the blue.

* * * * *

"Petty Officer Crosby, present yourself to the First Officer at the double. Left-right-left-right-left-right...! Atten-tion! Off cap!"

Having been wheeled in front of the Number One by the master-at-arms, the nervous NCO drew up to him, saluting stiffly and removing his cap with equal rigidity.

"Petty Officer Crosby," the officer sighed impatiently, "this is now the second time you've had cause to come before me for slacking on the job."

"Yes, sir. I'm sorry, sir," Crosby acknowledged, gazing dead ahead. A lump was bobbing discernibly in his throat.

"Or should I say it seems your mind appears to be somewhere else *other* than on the job. Your weapons officer has brought to my attention the little matter of your failure to execute in timely manner an instruction that, had we been under an actual attack by enemy aircraft, could have placed your ship and its crew in serious jeopardy. I will not tolerate such a situation happening again. Do I make myself clear?"

"Aye, sir," he barked a second time.

"Crosby, you are privileged to serve aboard the Royal Navy's newest destroyer – twenty-three million pounds worth of state-of-the-art kit. Neither Captain Drake nor the British taxpayer would have been impressed if your daydreaming had resulted in an accidental misfire of the ship's principal weapon system.

"No, sir."

"Of course, what makes these omissions more inexplicable is that up until now you've proved an exceptionally capable warfare specialist, with an exemplary service record. Presumably that's why you were promoted to petty officer rank at such a relatively young age," the First Officer noted, eyeing him up and down.

"Aye, sir. Thank you, sir."

"So, tell me: what's gotten into you, Crosby?"

There was a pause while the lump in his throat bobbed again.

"My girlfriend, sir. She's expecting our first child. I'm just a bit concerned, like. We're planning to get married soon, sir," the anxious NCO explained in his broad Brummie accent.

"Well, unfortunately these things happen, Crosby – although I must say it makes more sense to marry the girl first and *then* put the bun in the oven," the First Officer huffed sarcastically. For a split second even the unyielding master-at-arms looked as if he might be tempted to smirk.

Warfare Specialist Petty Officer Paul Crosby had neither the heart nor the courage to tell the Number One that his life was in turmoil. Having ditched the bubbly and buxom student from Brighton who he'd been going steady with, he'd then latched onto her best friend – only to find a few months into the relationship that she was carrying his child! However, with a promising career in the Royal Navy still beckoning, he wasn't sure he was ready to be a father. And although he was 'doing the right thing' in standing by her, still he was assailed by doubts. Ominously, the most nagging doubt was that he now realised he'd chosen the wrong girl. Come back Tina Brown, all is forgiven! Except he doubted she would ever forgive him for his betrayal. To make matters worse, it now looked like that promising career was on the verge of going as belly-up as his complicated love life. What price now permitting this caring girl to believe she had been just 'a convenient lay' while he was ashore on leave?

"Meanwhile, I'm sure I don't need to tell you that Captain Drake does not tolerate fools – and neither do I, for that matter. He is determined that *HMS Sheffield* will be the finest ship in the Royal Navy. That's why he's been working us all so hard."

"Aye, sir."

"We will be docking at Portsmouth the day after tomorrow. Crosby, I want you to use you time ashore to put your domestic situation in order. It's just unfortunate that the teething problems we've suffered on this voyage so far mean you'll have to make it snappy," he regretted, alluding to the catalogue of issues that had led to this sophisticated new ship breaking down at sea.

This embarrassing incident had rendered their notorious martinet of a captain even more determined to whip its two-hundred-and-fifty-man crew into shape ready for when it set sail again to practice live missile firing on the ranges off Scotland.

"Captain Drake intends to use our remaining time at sea to practice further air attack drills," the Number One informed him. "Petty Officer Crosby, you will perform your part in those drills to the expected standard. If you do not, then when you step ashore on Tuesday you will find that you will have completed your last posting at sea – and possibly in the Royal Navy itself. Do you understand what I am saying?"

"Aye, sir."

"Dismissed."

"Petty Officer Crosby, atten-tion! On cap! About turn... Left-right-left-right-left-right...!"

* * * * *

The pain having receded, Aimee was asleep when her father first entered the room to observe her lying there. However, the very next thing he spotted was the woman who was by his daughter's side – and who was tenderly clutching Aimee's hand. Her head was bowed and her lips spoke in whispers. Nora Lewis was praying. Suddenly those revolutionary words that Jesus had once taught his followers flooded into his head...

"Love your enemies, bless them that curse you, do good to them that hate you, and pray for them which despitefully use you."

However, he had only the most fleeting moment during which to ponder both the words and this woman he had once 'despitefully used' – and who was interceding with the Almighty on behalf of his child. Soon enough his wife's tearful clucking broke the spell, awoke his daughter, and caused Nora to look up and spy their presence looming over her.

"Mom! Dad!" Aimee grimaced, battling sudden discomfort to lever herself up in the bed.

"Oh, honey! We've been out of our minds with worry about you," Natalie raced in to steady her and then to clutch her.

Her vigil complete, Nora rose quietly from her chair and lifted her raincoat from its back. Without fuss, she then side-stepped around the bed and made for the door. Before she could reach it however, Charles Eichelberger had seized her arm and halted her.

"Nora. Once again, thank you," was all he needed to say, though his eyes glistened with unspoken emotion.

She smiled and acknowledged him. Once his grip was released she then continued on her way, silently slipping through the slither of door she opened and quietly closing it behind her.

"I'm so sorry for the trouble I've caused," Aimee was meanwhile wittering repentantly.

"Shhh! You're safe now – and that's all that matters," her mother consoled her.

Aimee glanced away and stared up at her father. The sorrow in his eyes spoke of an elementary spiritual truth: that trouble had befallen her because, at a point during her impetuous youth, she – like her father and brother before her – had strayed from the path of simple trust in, and obedience to, the Author and Perfector of her faith. However, the smile that then dawned reminded her of another elementary spiritual truth, the essence of which had been conveyed in those awesome words of the one-hundred-and-third Psalm with which Nora had been comforting her…

"The LORD is merciful and gracious,

Slow to anger, and plenteous in mercy.
He will not always chide;
Neither will He keep his anger for ever.
He hath not dealt with us after our sins;
Nor rewarded us according to our iniquities.
For as the heaven is high above the earth,
So great is His mercy toward them that fear Him.
As far as the east is from the west,
So far hath He removed our transgressions from us.
Like as a father pitieth his children,
So the LORD pitieth them that fear him.

Charles Eichelberger reached over, planted a tender paternal kiss upon his daughter moist brow, and quietly gave thanks for her safekeeping. He had forgiven her. He hoped she had forgiven him too.

30

Monday, August 30th 1976

"Morning, Mr Lawton," Vicky looked up and greeted him.

He fired the receptionist a gawky smile in what passed for his less-than-usually jovial and effusive salutation. Hurrying past the cleaner buffing the marble floor that his heels were clicking upon, she received a similar terse acknowledgement.

While Veronica Lawton was a notorious early bird, rare it was for her husband to turn up at his hotel this early in the day. And on a bank holiday too! Vicky watched him halt outside his wife's office, delve into his jacket pocket, and fumble with the key before hurrying inside. He was plainly a man with something on his mind.

* * * * *

The low pressure front that had swept north from the Bay of Biscay had predictably brought foul weather it, having dispersed the area of benign high pressure that had been squatting over the United Kingdom for most of the summer.

Somewhere at sea in the English Channel, the symbolism was not lost on the crew of *HMS Sheffield* – for it had turned Captain Martin Drake's countenance foul as well. The forty-five year-old commander was certainly in no mood for any further balls-ups aboard his new command lest it become a laughing stock – both in navy circles and (he feared) in the press. As he stood on the bridge surveying the convulsing grey seas through the patch of glass that the wipers kept clear of spray, he was determined his ship would perform like a well-oiled machine.

"Bring her midships," he ordered.

"Aye, aye, sir... Midships... Maintain twenty knots."

"Midships. Twenty knots," the cry went out.

"Rudder midships," it was repeated from the conn.

"Maintaining twenty knots," likewise from the engine room.

"Commence hostile aircraft attack drill, Number One."

"Aye, aye, sir."

As the instruction was relayed, sirens brought her crew to readiness. Hands raced to action stations, while in the ship's operations room Petty Officer Paul Crosby and his section hurriedly hauled on their flash gear. Soon all that was visible of their faces were anxious eyes waiting for information about the potential target the vessel's Type 965 radar was tracking. Meanwhile, out on deck, the turret of the ship's single Mark VIII gun was trained off the starboard bow. Abaft of it, a pair of Sea Dart missiles emerged from the magazine to swiftly lock into their launcher. This too was then trained off the starboard beam.

* * * * *

It had taken him an hour or two, but by rifling through every drawer in her filing cabinets John Lawton had pieced together a pretty comprehensive picture what his wife had been up to. Wading through the reams of correspondence in the files he had strewn across her desk the names of several companies kept cropping up; companies he'd only vaguely heard of that had supposedly undertaken work at the hotel – work that seemed grossly overpriced. For example, over the years one of these companies had invoiced the Shanklin Heights for 'consultancy' work running to hundreds of thousands of pounds.

What consultancy work? To the best of his knowledge he'd never approved the hiring of any 'consultants'. Furthermore, he strongly suspected these were fake companies that his wife had set up and of which she was the sole director. In other words, she had been skimming off the profits from his hotel by overpaying these 'contractors' and then funnelling the proceeds into offshore bank accounts that she probably controlled. What's more, he realised he'd been an unwitting player in these shenanigans, his frequent flights to Jersey thereby helping to launder this money. Meanwhile, falsified accounts had indeed been submitted to disguise what she'd been doing.

How could he have been so stupid to have taken his eye off the ball in this way! And to have thereby rendered himself an accessory to her despicable scams! For the first time he began to appreciate the true cost of those consuming obsessions of writing war stories and bedding beautiful women.

Just then there was a knock on the door. Startled, he looked up.

"Come in," he thought he'd better acknowledge whoever it was, hurriedly scooping up the papers he'd spread out and bundling the files back inside the cabinets.

"Sorry to disturb you, Mr Lawton," Vicky poked her head around the door. "It's just that a policeman was here this morning," she entered and informed him matter-of-factly.

"Police?" his ears pricked up. He swallowed hard and turned around to hear her out.

"Yes. Apparently, two dangerous convicts escaped from Parkhurst prison last night and are on the run somewhere on the island. The officer called by asking that local hotels keep an eye open for them," she explained, waving in her hand a 'wanted' poster of the two lags that the police were circulating.

"Er... well..." Lawton mumbled, Vicky surprised to observe that he was not at all his usual suave and unflustered self, "In which case, just... pin that flyer up somewhere."

"Oh... Er, yes... Of course, Mr Lawton."

The tell-tale arching of the teenager's eyebrows indicated that she was as baffled by this nebulous instruction as he was embarrassed to have spluttered it. Perhaps in need of a more resolute response, she asked whether his wife might perchance be popping by this morning.

"Er, Veronica... Well, no. You see, Vicky, she's had to return to the mainland... at somewhat short notice, I'm afraid. What's more, she may be away for some time. You see, she's had to stay with an elderly aunt who's very poorly at the moment."

"Oh, I am sorry to hear that, Mr Lawton."

"Yes, unfortunately it looks like the old girl might be losing her marbles. It's all been very distressing for my wife."

Even as he bumbled his way through this cock-and-bull story, Lawton knew it sounded far-fetched. As if an incorrigible workaholic like Veronica would ever summarily abandon the hotel in such a manner. However, the saving grace was that the eighteen year-old receptionist was sufficiently besotted with her debonair boss that she might just be swallowing his tale. Yes, Vicky was such a naïve and impressionable young lady. Perhaps it was why Lawton had had his eye on her of late. Of course, it helped that the bonny Galway lass possessed a nice slim figure, flame red hair, fawning pond green eyes, and cute little dimples that put in an appearance whenever she smiled at him. As she was doing now, convincing the dissembling hotelier that she could so easily have been his next conquest.

"Well, please convey to her my best wishes," those eyes meanwhile dipped tactfully. "In the meantime, if you need me to help you with anything in her absence, please don't hesitate to ask," she forced a warm smile, those girlish dimples beguiling him once more as she watched him guiltily nudge shut the half-open drawer of a filing cabinet.

"Thank you, Vicky. That's very kind," he replied, heartened by her ever-obliging good nature. "However, things are a bit up-in-the-air at the moment. That's why I'm sorry if my head appears to be elsewhere."

That was understandable. Therefore, she shrugged awkwardly and backed herself towards the door, Lawton breathing a sigh of relief when it closed behind her.

"Oh, by the way," she immediately popped her head around it again, startling him a second time. "About that kind offer you made the other day: you know, to take me up in your private plane sometime. Well, I've been thinking and… I would very much like that. In your wife's absence, perhaps I can accompany you on one of your flights to the Channel Islands – if that's okay, Mr Lawton…. well, John. You did say I could call you John, did you not," she blushed, barely concealing her excitement at being on first name terms with such a dashing, handsome and successful man (someone who was certainly a much more engaging character than his haughty and demanding wife. Janey Mac, how in Heaven's name did he put up with her!).

Notwithstanding the trepidation bearing down upon him at that moment, the randy old charmer couldn't help but raise a smile.

"Yes, of course," he nodded, observing those eyes sparkle with delight as she quietly slipped out of the office a second time.

Now there was a metaphorical open door if ever there was! Alas, it was an open door the threshold of which fate had decreed he was not going to be granted the opportunity of crossing.

* * * * *

It was gone ten o'clock by the time he'd finished loading up the car with the things he reckoned he'd need – passport, money from the safe, and paperwork to enable him to access his own offshore bank accounts. Thereupon he glanced up from his labours to spot Charles Eichelberger gazing at him through the window of the dining room. Rising from the table, the General abandoned his wife to her breakfast and made haste to intercept him.

Ordinarily this most valued guest would have been treated to one of those effusive 'good-mornings' for which the hotelier was renowned. However, today – and with similar haste – Lawton slammed the boot shut and hopped inside the Jaguar, slotting the key in the ignition and firing up its powerful V12 engine. Reversing out of his marked parking bay, he never spotted the General come dashing up to the car and then having to leap out of the way of it. The burly American stumbled to his feet and raced back in to seize the driver's door handle.

"John…! John…!" he yelled, tugging at it and banging his fist on the window "Wait! There's something I gotta' tell ya'… John… John…! *I'm* your real father!"

However, the central locking had been activated and Pussycat's *'Mississippi'* was blaring from the stereo to drown out his cries. Unwilling to face him, Lawton rammed the car into 'drive' and hit the accelerator, compelling the General to let go of the handle as it spun off the car park. He glanced back at a breathless Charles Eichelberger diminishing in the reflection of his rear view mirror.

* * * * *

The weather might have improved. However, Captain Drake's countenance had not. The officers on the bridge could see from the way he stared ominously out to sea that he was not a happy bunny, annoyed that his crews were still not taking evasive action swiftly enough to assure the ship would survive an air attack sweeping in beneath her radar. What's more, earlier trials of the Sea Dart missile that was his ship's principal defence against such an attack had demonstrated the worrying inability of the weapon system to engage such low-flying targets.

"Stand down the crew, Number One," Drake broke his gaze to order his second-in-command. "In due course we will commence another drill. And this time they *will* get it right."

"Aye, aye, sir," the First Officer replied, wondering whether to tactfully remind the captain that the men under his command had been worked hard enough already. Surely, even he could understand that it would take longer than a week at sea for his new crew to gel as a team.

However, he kept his counsel. Like everyone else aboard who had been cowed by their unrelenting skipper, he pinned his hope on the fact that the window of opportunity for safely practising such high speed manoeuvres was closing now that *HMS Sheffield* was approaching the busier cross-Channel shipping lanes on her return to Portsmouth.

Down in the operations room, Petty Officer Paul Crosby tugged off his perspiration-drenched flash mask and mopped his brow. How he wished the ship would just make haste back to 'Pompey'. He'd barely been able to sleep worrying about how things were going to play out with his girlfriend now that her pregnancy was into its final trimester. And all he would get with her would be three days shore leave! What's more, he knew she wasn't happy about the prospect of him departing for further weeks at sea when *Sheffield* sailed again on Friday.

Crosby desperately wanted to do right by his kid. Having been raised by a single mother himself, he knew the heartbreak of growing up without ever knowing one's father – and of facing playground taunts for being 'a bastard'. Therefore, he'd resolved not take the easy option of just abandoning his offspring – like his own father had done – no matter the cost; and no matter that he wasn't really in love with the child's mother. Indeed, in his heart, he was still pining for Tina.

* * * * *

So why had the General been so desperate to halt him? Lawton agonised as he headed north on the main road.

The most likely explanation, he feared, was that Aimee (or more probably that toadying little companion of hers) had blabbed to the Eichelbergers that their daughter was pregnant with *his* child. No wonder her father was on the warpath! Compounding their anger, he didn't doubt that the prissy Shelby had also told them about the discomfiting acts she'd witnessed that Veronica had hired someone to record. No doubt his accursed wife had added such snooping to the list of overpriced 'consultancy' work for which the hotel had been billed!

Right now though, all that was academic. Today – and for a while to come, he knew – he would have to operate in survival mode. As such, that would entail abandoning his cliff-top hotel (along with his paying guests and – it pained him – the loyal staff who'd worked for him) and abandoning the island he'd come to love; indeed, abandoning the United Kingdom altogether.

He had a plan – of sorts. He reckoned he'd have about a week before someone at the hotel would be sufficiently concerned to contact the police and advise them that, to all intents and purposes, John and Veronica Lawton had disappeared off the face of the Earth. In that time, he would endeavour to withdraw what money he could from his accounts in Jersey and then make his way overland through France to Spain. *Floreat Etona*: once there he intended to contact an old friend from his schooldays and his time in the City who could lend him a bolthole to hide out in. With a fake passport and an altered identity, he could then slip out the country to begin a new life in Australia or South America.

Would it work? He could only hope so. With charges of tax evasion and murder hanging over him, he no longer had a choice! Besides, Lord Lucan had got away with it. After famously murdering his wife's nanny in 1974, the wealthy aristocrat had also disappeared off the face of the Earth – and had not been seen since. The Labour minister John Stonehouse had almost gotten away with it too – until he'd been spotted in Australia and extradited back to Britain to stand trial.

No, South America it would have to be then. Maybe the long, hot summer had been a worthwhile preparation for spending the rest of his days chatting up sun-bronzed beauties on the Copacabana, he smirked in anticipation.

* * * * *

Police! They appeared to be everywhere – presumably on the hunt for those escaped prisoners. As they wandered down the queue of cars they had halted on the approach to Sandown, Lawton hurriedly summoned up the composure to greet them.

"Morning, officer," he smiled politely.

"Morning, sir. Your car?"

"Yes, it is."

"In which case, can I see your driving licence?"

Lawton fumbled in his jacket pocket and hauled out his wallet, taking the said documentation and presenting it for the officer's perusal. It was a long, agonising moment during which the hotelier fought to maintain his repose – mindful of what he was carrying around in the boot! With one car having meanwhile been ordered aside to be searched, his hastily-cobbled-together plan looked set to stumble at the first hurdle.

"Thank you, sir," the officer handed him back his licence before waving him through.

Lawton let out one almighty sigh of relief. Like those elusive convicts, he had to get off the island – and get off it fast.

* * * * *

Turning up a quiet side street not far from the railway station, Lawton parked up and stepped out of the car to slip his coat on. As he did, he took a moment to admire its classic lines. He marvelled too that the bank holiday downpours had given the XJS its first wash in weeks – even if the end result had been to replace a coating of dust on the bonnet and roof with splashes of mud up the sides! It was still a superlative driving machine though – yet one more thing that he would sadly have to abandon.

Before saying goodbye to it though, he sat back inside and ran his hands across the leather trim of its passenger seat, recalling as he did the succession of beautiful women whose posteriors had once graced it: Sophie; Angie; Aimee; Vicky; and Veronica, of course. He recalled too the one and only time that his mother had ridden in the car – the Jaguar symbolic in her eyes of how her son had made good his life, despite her tearful regret that she'd caused it to open so inauspiciously. And now tears began to well in Lawton's wistful eyes too. For that brief journey could almost be an allegory for how lamentable it was that – after thirty years of searching for each other – their similarly fleeting time together had to come to such an abrupt and shameful end.

No less lamentable was that the manner of its ending would mean the search for his father was something else he would now be compelled to abandon. He would never know of whose seed he had been fashioned; and what part it had played in making him the man he was. He stared at his reflection in the rear view mirror and posed an ironic question: what if his father had once upon a time booked in as a guest at the Shanklin Heights Hotel – and been subjected to Lawton's customary gushing welcome – and yet both father and son had remained blissfully unaware of who the other really was?

He dabbed an angry tear. It was the sort of mean trick some cruel deity would no doubt have taken exceeding pleasure in playing upon him; the same cruel deity that, all his life, had found ways of reminding this flawed and embittered man of his shortcomings: *"...that Thou mightest be justified when Thou speakest, and be clear when Thou judgest"* he seemed to recall reading in the Bible somewhere. Maybe those flaws had rendered him unworthy of his real father. In that sense, he sighed, maybe it was a trick that he had deserved to have had played upon him.

Snapping out of such self-pity, he stepped out of the car, opened the boot, and removed a suitcase, as well as a travel bag containing documents and personal effects. Then he stared with maudlin regret at the remaining item in the boot that would not be coming with him – a sturdy canvas sheet that had been left lying about by the builders Veronica had commissioned to work on their Bonchurch mansion (something else he would now be compelled to abandon). It was a sheet into which he had bundled the mortal remains of his deceased wife.

"Goodbye, darling," he bade her without rancour. "We made a good team. We achieved so much together. You know I'll miss you. But for now – sleep tight."

And with that he closed the boot, locked the car up, and made off down the street with his suitcase in his hand and his bag over his shoulder – to all the world just one more holidaymaker saying a final sad farewell to an island upon which he had passed an unforgettable summer.

* * * * *

"So I tell you, he just drove off – without saying a word. He knew I was there. But he just ignored me. It was most strange."

"Not strange at all, if you ask me," Natalie Eichelberger begged to differ. "He must know you're mad as hell over all that business with Aimee. Or at least you should be," she chided her husband, concerned that righteous indignation appeared to have rather too hastily given way to paternal forbearing.

"And you've no idea where he was heading?" Aimee ventured to ask, glancing nervously at her father and then at her mother – unsure whether they were still 'mad as hell' with *her*, despite having come close to losing their daughter the previous evening.

Otherwise, her father elected not to respond to his daughter's anxious question. Instead, he looked up from loading the trunk of the rental car with the last of their baggage, cupping his hand to his eyes to spy a small plane droning in the broken blue sky overhead. Could it be, she witnessed those eyes imploring, certain her father recognised its type and markings.

Alas though, there was no time left to say the things that had been left unsaid; no time for John to express remorse or to seek the forgiveness of his real father for the wrong he had done; no time for her father to express his own remorse for abandoning his love child all those years ago. The brief return visit Charles Eichelberger had made to England was drawing to a close. Before the day was over he and Natalie would have checked-in at Heathrow Airport and boarded the long overnight flight back to Minneapolis-St Paul – back to the good life they had made for themselves since those fateful wartime years spent apart.

Aimee would be making that return journey too in a few days time – the first time she would be back in the United States in a while. So much had changed while she'd been away. Once she had brimmed with resentment towards her father, believing that he somehow valued her less than her older brother. Hence, like the parable of the Prodigal Son, her year spent in England had been as much an act of rebellion against her father as a milestone on the road to graduating. And now, like that Prodigal Son, she too had finally come to her senses and returned to the succour of her father's love and compassion.

Just then, as father and daughter watched the plane disappear over the headland, Vicky the receptionist came scurrying out of the lobby, racing over to them bearing a large box file that she now held up in front of the departing guest.

"I'm so glad I caught you, Mr Eichelberger, sir," she panted. "I almost forgot: Mr Lawton left this behind the desk, he did. He told me to hand it to you when you checked out."

Charles took the file from her and unclipped the catch that had fastened it closed. Peering inside, in gathering disbelief he thumbed through the typed-up reams of paper the file contained, as well as the maps, photographs and illustrations therein.

"What is it?" Natalie was anxious to know, craning in to sneak a glance. Then she watched her husband stare up at that now empty sky as if to try and make sense of why these documents had been gifted to his care.

"It's the manuscript for his new book," he replied.

"But why?" Aimee, like her father, was at a loss to explain.

"Maybe one day he'll tell me. In his own good time," he said, clipping the file shut and setting it down lovingly inside the trunk.

Charles turned and accepted the hug his daughter drew forward to both offer him and then her mother. Then, as he opened the door of the car to permit his wife to step inside, Aimee witnessed him once more prayerfully search that empty sky. It brought to her recollection the words with which the father of the Prodigal Son had justified his own extraordinary compassion…

> *"Thy brother was dead, and is come to life again;*
> *he was lost, and is found."*

Unlike Lawrence – the son he'd lost over Vietnam (and whose fate he might never know for certain) – Charles Eichelberger was quietly rejoicing that this other secret son 'was dead and is come to life again', 'was lost and is now found'. Likewise – and for all that he had behaved like a scoundrel – some still small voice inside implored Aimee not surrender to the temptation to hate or despise her half-brother.

Above all, she gave thanks that her father was at peace with himself, having lain to rest these ghosts from his past. As such, there was hope at last that – with the page turned and the chapter finally closed – in Christ who was their hope 'all things' might indeed 'become new'.

* * * * *

"Action Stations, Actions Stations! Air attack red! Air attack red!" the stark warning blared through the ship's tannoy.

Once again the sirens screamed and throughout the length of the ship its narrow gangways were alive to the scramble of ratings hurrying to their stations. It might only be (yet another) drill. However, by now the crew of *HMS Sheffield* had been so psyched up by the pressure they were under to 'get it right' that it might just as well be the real thing. Meanwhile, the gathering roar of the turbines hinted that the ship was once again accelerating to its maximum thirty knots top speed. Here we go again.

Down in the ship's cramped operations room the tension was further ramped up by the presence in their midst of Captain Drake himself, his eagle eye panning around to observe the bank of glowing screens and consoles that illuminated it.

"Hostile contact bearing green forty!" they meanwhile heard the radar plotter holler.

"All engines full ahead... Steer seventy degrees starboard rudder," the instructions from the bridge kept coming.

"All engines ahead."

"Steering starboard seventy."

"Contact twelve miles out and closing," the radar plotter updated them, his eyes fixed upon the blip he was tracking.

"Bring main weapon to bear," they heard the ship's anti-air warfare officer order.

"Main weapon arming!" Petty Officer Crosby cried back, flicking the appropriate switches on the console beside him.

Thereafter, in Crosby's head, the vague whirring of Sea Dart missiles being propelled from the magazine to the elevators (and thence upwards into their launcher) merged like background noise with the stream of announcements from the bridge and the animated responses of his fellow crewmen. Though he was desperately trying to concentrate on the job he had to do, memories of Tina (and of the happy times they'd spent together) continued to flit in and out of his thoughts. Then, lips trembling behind the veil of his flash mask, he looked up to observe Captain Drake staring straight at him.

Crosby swallowed hard. For the sake of his unborn child and of its anxious mother – both of whom were depending upon his love and support – he would get the drill right. He gazed down at the missile trigger he was gripping in his sweaty, tremulous palm before closing his eyes in silent prayer.

"Contact closing... Range seven thousand yards..."

No, this time there must be no mistakes.

* * * * *

"Good evening. Here is the news... More than a hundred police officers have been taken to hospital following clashes at this year's Notting Hill Carnival in west London. Around sixty carnival-goers are also reported to have needed hospital treatment.

"The trouble started after police attempted to arrest a pickpocket near Portobello Road. Several black youths went to the pickpocket's aid and within

minutes police found themselves under attack, defending themselves against stones and other missiles with dustbin lids and milk crates. Over sixty people are reported to have been arrested..."

With Frank cussing at the television set, Angie looked up from her novel to observe her sister quietly place down her knitting, rise from her seat, and head into the hall – as she had done several times already on this tense bank holiday afternoon.

"...Meanwhile, in other news, the Conservative Party has announced the selection of its candidate to fight the forthcoming Birmingham Lea Hall by-election. Sophie Wiseman is a married thirty-two year-old fashion entrepreneur from Surrey. With Mr Callaghan's government still trailing in opinion polls, Mrs Wiseman said she is confident that her party can win this normally-safe Labour seat..."

As on those occasions, Nora first dialled his Bonchurch mansion – only to hear the phone ring out with no response. Then she dialled the Shanklin Heights Hotel – only for the girl on the reception desk to again inform her that her son had not been seen since he'd left there in a hurry this morning. Neither had anybody been able to contact Veronica.

Politely, she thanked the girl, placing the receiver down. Though it was hardly conclusive enough to justify her fears, Nora Lewis sensed in her heart that – after all the years of searching – something terrible had happened to her son. Therefore, this time, instead of returning to the living room, she drifted into her bedroom. There she lifted from the dressing table a framed photograph that John had presented to her in the brief time they'd been reunited. She stared at the image of this most dashing and handsome man posing proudly beside his private plane.

Then, placing it back on the dresser, she sat down on the bed, closed her eyes, and began to weep.

31

Saturday, September 4th 1976

"Thank you, Auntie Angie – for a wonderful summer. It's certainly been one I will never forget."

His aunt picked up on the unintended pun in her nephew's heartfelt words and shot him a wry smile.

"Thank you, Vaughan. It's been a pleasure to have you stay with us. You know you will always be welcome here," she insisted as she drew him tight into her embrace. "And, what's more, now you know *why* you will always be welcome."

It was Vaughan's turn to twig a pun. He tightened that embrace for a further few precious seconds.

"Will you keep Mum posted if you hear anything?"

As they drew apart, Angie dutifully nodded while trying to mask her own concern.

To be sure, Nora had departed the island herself on Tuesday, still desperately worried about what might have become of John. Then later that morning it was confirmed that her son's plane had taken off from Bembridge Aerodrome the previous day, but had failed to arrive at its destination. A major search operation had been mounted to scour the English Channel in the vicinity of the flight plan that had been filed. It had even been assisted by *HMS Sheffield* – the Royal Navy's new Type 42 destroyer – which had been exercising in the area. However, to date that search had drawn a blank. His plane was missing; and Lawton with it.

That said, there remained a whiff of foul play about the sudden disappearance of John and Veronica Lawton. Rumours suggested the couple might have been fleeing because the Inland Revenue were about to catch up with them over some sort of tax swindle they'd been party to. Either way, their unexplained departure had left the hotel in such turmoil that Aimee and Shelby had yesterday departed for the United States minus a week's pay!

"Chi-co!" someone meanwhile interjected as if to bid his own farewell to Vaughan.

There was time for a quick stroke of the bird's head before Vaughan made his way down those familiar verandah steps, lugging his suitcase down with him.

"Who's you friend?" Angie enquired, folding her arms and resting them upon the balustrade. There she gazed down at the prepubescent nipper who was waiting rather presumptuously alongside an old pram that he'd converted into a luggage trolley. It was the sort of contraption upon which she'd often seen youngsters hauling holidaymakers' belongings.

"This is Tom, Auntie. He's my personal taxi service," Vaughan chirruped, heaving the bulky case onto it.

"Tom? Hang about," Angie straightened herself up and stared down at the lad accusingly. "You're Helena Mills' son, aren't you – from up the road? Weren't you one of those lads I overheard teaching Chico rude words the other day?"

"Wot? Me, missus?" the youngster stared back with a cocky self-assurance that spoke of butter not melting in his mouth. "Nah, you must be mistaken."

She seemed unconvinced. Hurriedly, Tom turned about and made off after his customer. Angie lingered to watch the convoy round the corner out of sight, offering Vaughan a parting wave when he glanced over his shoulder at her one final time.

"Nice arse!" Chico meanwhile complimented the way Angie's posterior padded out that short skirt she was wearing.

* * * * *

"'Ere, 'ow come you wanna' go this way then?" Tom piped up, his pram squeaking incessantly as he steered it in and out of shoppers milling about on the High Street.

"Slight detour. It'll only be brief. And don't worry – you'll get paid extra," Vaughan assured him.

Tom was instructed to halt outside the familiar frontage of Tring's Toys. While Vaughan disappeared inside, the youngster pressed his face to the window to study the fabulous model of a huge American jet bomber that was hanging there.

"So this is it. You're leaving us," Uncle Frank simpered, placing his hands firmly upon Vaughan's shoulders.

"Yes, for now, Uncle. Maybe I'll visit at Christmas. Or perhaps I can stay again next summer," he wondered aloud.

Frank's clipped moustache twitched its fond consent. Then, eschewing his usual aloofness, he drew the lad forward in an emotional embrace. As a father would a long-lost son.

* * * * *

"So whatcha' been up to this summer then?" Tom interrogated his client once they had recommenced their journey to the railway station. "It's certainly been a scorcher, in' it."

"Oh, the usual things: a bit of sightseeing; plenty of swimming in the sea; been to a few parties here and there – that kind of thing," Vaughan replied, glancing down at him matter-of-factly.

Then, with a mischievous glint in his eye, he confided that "While I've been on the island I've also found out that the aunt I've been staying with – the woman you just met – is really my mother; and that my mother is actually my aunt. And that my uncle – the man who owns that toy shop – is my real father.

"Then I further discovered that I have a half-brother I never knew about, to whom my mum gave birth many years earlier – but who is not really my half-brother because his mother is my aunt, who I *thought* was my mum. Oh, and now this 'half-brother' – who is not my half-brother – has disappeared with his wife, and no one knows where they've gone."

Tom looked up at Vaughan mystified, having lost the plot after the bit about his aunt being his mom. Either way, it all sounded rather far-fetched. Vaughan must be pulling his leg. After all, this was the bloke who'd tried to kid him he'd been offered – and turned down – the chance to play the next James Bond!

"So how did yer' enjoy working on the buses then?" the youngster probed, wondering what other flannel he might offer.

"Uh! You were right about the school kids, Tom!" he shook his head, firing the lad a weary frown. "But never mind. It's been useful experience. And I've made lots of friends too. Perhaps I'll come back and work on the buses again one day."

As he spoke those words, his mind drifted back to endless sunny days spent riding the platforms of big green Lodekkas. He recalled those pearls of wisdom about girls, music and life in general that Colin Garrett had inveigled him with. He recalled Tina Brown too, and her wise counsel about love and relationships; about the importance of maintaining one's self-respect, and of refusing to tolerate dishonourable behaviour in others in order to gain – and retain – their affection.

"And did yer' get to see any nice tits while you were 'ere?"

Vaughan offered Tom that same glare of faux disapproval that he had the first time this precocious youngster had broached the subject. He paused before answering, pondering the question.

"Well, yes… actually… Now you mention it, there was one rather nice pair I got to see…"

Tom was all ears. However, from the distant expression that had suddenly come over his companion, he could see that he was going to keep that particular flannel to himself.

In the pause in the conversation Vaughan's thoughts did indeed return to a warm July evening when he'd suddenly been confronted with Aimee's proud, pink nipples. He recalled who it was who had squawked the crude, chauvinist remark that had occasioned their exposure. Chico had certainly proved the most adept matchmaker a boy could ever wish for!

With Vaughan still lost in misty-eyed contemplation, it was just as well Tom was keeping an eye open for cars when they arrived at the zebra crossing on the main road. There a battered blue Austin 1100 with a mountain of luggage strapped to its roof rack drew up at the head of the traffic. When they stepped off the pavement, its driver suddenly let out a loud and tuneful blast on its air horns, startling both boy and daydreaming teenager.

It was Phil and Dave from the depot – and on the seat behind them staring between their heads was Sally – all waving to him. What's more, the rear passenger door suddenly opened and out leapt Tina. Launching her arms around Vaughan, she seized this unexpected opportunity to bid him a final excited farewell.

"You take care of yourself, darlin'," she insisted, releasing her grip to permit her hands to rest upon his hips.

Meanwhile, Tom's disbelieving eyes had popped out of his head upon beholding that heaving bosom being crushed flat in the encounter before perking up again beneath her top.

"Yeah, you too," Vaughan bade her, savouring her radiant smile. Then that bosom was crushed flat again when he threw his arms around her for a final embrace of his own.

"You've got my address?"

"Yes. I promise I'll write to you when I get back," he nodded.

"Good. Maybe we can visit each other one weekend."

However, with drivers in the cars behind reaching for their own less tuneful horns there was no time to indulge in further demonstrative valedictions. Tina hurriedly dived back into the car, waving to him as Dave crunched it into gear and Vaughan's ex-depot colleagues headed off for their appointment with the car ferry at Fishbourne.

"Wow! You mean you got to see that enormous pair?" Tom's jaw dropped open.

"I might have," Vaughan teased as they continued their journey to the station, Tom tugging at his squeaking trolley to keep up.

"You jammy bleeder! So what are they like then? And did you get to touch 'em... and squeeze 'em?"

"You're far too young to know about such things," he rebuked the lad playfully. "Besides, Tina's not that kind of girl."

Though Tom was peeved at being denied any salacious details, Vaughan was content for him to assume it was the busty beauty from Brighton that he'd been ruminating upon. Instead, he resumed daydreaming about Aimee, appreciating only too readily that seeing her again would present a more daunting challenge. Though they too had promised to write to each other, and maybe to phone, with her year at Oxford complete Aimee had no reason to return to England. And now that bus conducting would be giving way to a cash-strapped regime of study at polytechnic Vaughan would struggle to raise the funds needed to visit her in the United States. Perhaps, like other heady holiday romances – and, indeed, like that fabulous summer during which they'd been passed – those precious weeks that Vaughan Lewis and Aimee-

Marie Eichelberger had spent in each other's company were only ever destined to be a season in the sun.

* * * * *

Having paid Tom handsomely for his services ("Forty pence," the youngster had cheekily insisted, "It's inflation, don't you know!") Vaughan continued to ponder these things on the short journey aboard the electric train to Ryde Pier Head.

Once aboard the Sealink ferry he further mused how pathos invariably accompanies a holiday that has finally come to an end – more so when that eventful holiday had lasted an incredible eleven weeks *and* coincided with the longest period of glorious sunshine this normally rain-sodden little country had ever experienced. Today – as if to emphasise the return to normal weather (as well as to the reality of a tired, 1970s Britain still buffeted by the same old political and economic woes) – the sky was sufficiently damp and overcast to deter all but the hardiest of passengers from remaining on deck.

One passenger alone with his thoughts who did brave the inclement weather could be found lingering on the stern of the vessel, employing hands he had sunk in the pockets of his black leather jacket to draw it tight around him. Staring out at the island retreating from his gaze, he recalled other such instances during his childhood when he had found himself similarly staring back at this vista – sad to be going home and wishing instead that he could somehow turn the ferry about.

It was not that Vaughan would never see the Isle of Wight again: this beloved holiday playground would still be there when Frank and Angie again invited him to stay. It was just that now, as then – and in some small, yet poignant way – another milestone on the journey that was his life was also retreating from view.

In due course, the ferry drew alongside Portsmouth Harbour railway station, where it tied up. Suitcase in hand, a passenger alone with his thoughts then shuffled his way along the docking ramp to locate and board his waiting train.

However, before he did he moved out of file of the other queuing passengers to lean upon the guide rail and snatch one final glimpse of a 'blue remembered hill' that was still just visible across the grey, choppy expanse of Spithead. Though the memories would last a lifetime, with a heavy heart he accepted that the summer of '76 was – in the words of the poet – 'a happy highway' upon which he had once been privileged to travel, but could never come again.

* * * * *

Wednesday, September 8th 1976

The white Jaguar the police had been looking for had finally been tracked down to a side street near Sandown railway station.

Thus it was that on this cold wet morning a young copper was instructed to unlock the car using the spare keys that the local constabulary had in its possession following a search of the Lawton's Bonchurch residence.

As the boot lid sprung open the detectives gathered around were greeted by the unmistakable odour of a decomposing body. As one of them carefully lifted aside the canvas sheet in which it had been bundled it became apparent they had established the whereabouts of at least one half of the wealthy couple whose faces were suddenly all over the newspapers.

POSTSCRIPT

Arlington National Cemetery, Virginia, USA,
Tuesday, September 2nd 2008

The flags were already at half-mast as the solemn procession made its way through this verdant and most hallowed ground – the final resting place of some four hundred thousand of America's fallen, from battles spanning the Civil War to the ongoing conflicts in Iraq and Afghanistan.

To strains of a military band playing *'America The Beautiful'* the honour guard of United States Air Force personnel bore the last mortal remains of one of its fallen into the chapel, the coffin they attended draped in the stark red-white-and-blue of his country's flag. For this day – almost thirty-six years after being reported 'missing in action' – Captain Lawrence 'Ike' Eichelberger USAF had finally come home.

Many mourners had gathered to hear the chaplain eulogise a life offered up in sacrifice for his fellow Americans – as Christ had offered up His own life to atone for the sins of mankind. Leading them was the tall, stooping figure of his father, the comforting arm of the eighty-eight year-old retired general cast upon the shoulder of his tearful wife. Alongside them – also ashen-faced and sorrowful – stood their daughter, Senator Aimee-Marie Forrester, the fifty-three year-old Minnesotan Democrat also placing a hand of comfort upon her mother's arm.

For so many years her parents had carried the torment of not knowing for certain what had become of their son when *Turquoise 2* had been blasted from the sky over Vietnam. Briefly during the 1980s hopes had been raised that there were indeed US service personnel who were still being held in the country. However, gradually those hopes had faded as supposed sightings of Caucasian males dwelling in lonely jungles outposts invariably turned out to be hoaxes.

Then, earlier this year, while dredging an irrigation canal on the outskirts of Hanoi, construction workers had come across human remains encased in a flight suit that had lain undisturbed in the mud. DNA testing subsequently confirmed they belonged to the missing B52 radar navigator, who had sadly activated his downward-firing ejector seat too late for his parachute to open. The grim discovery had permitted a grieving father to be reunited at last with his beloved son.

Amidst her own mournful reflections, Aimee pondered that the same could not be said for Charles Eichelberger's other son, whose whereabouts similarly remained a mystery – ever since that fateful day in August 1976 when he had murdered his wife and disappeared without trace.

Several different theories had grown up around John Lawton's fate. The generally-accepted version was that, having attempted to flee to Jersey (where it was suspected he had deposited significant sums of money), his private plane had been lost over the English Channel – possibly due to a navigational error on the part of its pilot. Neither could it be discounted that the wealthy hotelier – perhaps remorseful at having killed his wife in an impulsive crime of passion – had deliberately crashed his plane into the sea in a spectacular suicide bid. Either way, no wreckage from his Beechcraft Bonanza was ever found. It too had disappeared without trace.

However – as often happens with bizarre, unexplained events – it would not take long for conspiracy theories to abound. It was said that Lawton's plane had been accidentally shot down by the inexperienced crew of a new Royal Navy destroyer that had been exercising in the area at the time. It was indeed chilling to surmise that the life of Charles Eichelberger's other son might also have been snuffed out by an encounter with a surface-to-air missile! What's more, Britain's tight-lipped defence establishment had form for covering up such embarrassing mishaps. For example, when investigating this very possibility many years later, Aimee had unearthed that in October 1969 a Sea Slug missile misfired from the destroyer *HMS Glamorgan* had almost destroyed a farmhouse ashore!

Further embellishment suggested that maybe Lawton's disappearance had been no accident – and that his plane had been shot down on orders from the top because one of his affairs risked causing embarrassment in British defence and intelligence circles. It was even suggested that he'd been spying for the Russians under the guise of being a military historian, and that MI5 might have silenced him by less spectacular means. The story was given legs when it came to light that the private investigator Veronica Lawton had hired to expose her husband's philandering was shortly afterwards found dead in suspicious circumstances, his office ransacked. Certainly no trace was ever found of that compromising photographic and video footage either. Meanwhile, the woman who'd also been compromised by it went on to become a Conservative MP and a British government minister.

No less intriguing for his former employee and *amoureuse* was the possibility that her half-brother had actually fled and resettled abroad under a new identity. After all, his car had been found abandoned several miles from Bembridge Aerodrome (from where his plane had taken off on that fateful morning) – and yet a mere stone's throw from a railway station! It was known too that John Lawton had friends in France and Spain who could have afforded him succour and assistance. Finally, those two prisoners who had absconded from jail on the Isle of Wight that weekend were never found either – fuelling speculation *they* might have stolen Lawton's plane and been attempting to pilot it when it crashed into the sea.

Though it spooked Aimee to think that somewhere in the world a wizened and well-spoken Englishman might be passing his exile flattering and charming gullible young women, in a small, yet touching way John Edward Lawton indeed lived on.

You see, her father never did run for the White House in 1980 (although, as a respected military strategist, he would later advise President Bush during the Gulf War, and President Clinton during the air wars over Bosnia and Kosovo). However, what Charles Eichelberger did do that year was to publish a book: *'The Boeing B52 Stratofortress And The Air War Over Indochina'*.

Much lauded in aviation circles, it has endured as a masterful study of the role this mighty warplane played in what – to this day – remains the most controversial and divisive war the United States has fought on a foreign shore. As well as the glowing tributes it paid to the aircrews that flew in them – men he had once commanded in battle – when thumbing through this important reference work the reader will come across this simple anonymous dedication...

'To John – who I will always look upon as my son'.

With prayers spoken and the benediction given, it was time for the honour guard to reform and bear the coffin to a horse-drawn caisson for its final committal. Family, friends and ageing comrades from Lawrence's old squadron – including the rear gunner of *Turquoise 2* (its sole surviving crewman) – followed in its train as the band struck up *'Shenandoah'*. Eventually, instruments stilled, the only sounds to disturb the procession as it completed its journey to the freshly-dug grave was the rhythmic clopping of horses' hoofs and the clattering of their bridles.

As with her full-blood brother, likewise the many supposed sightings of her half-brother also proved to be hoaxes. Yet whatever his fate that day, Aimee had long since put the more regrettable events of that remarkable summer behind her. Graduating with honours from Wellesley College, she would subsequently pursue a successful career in journalism (aided by the publication of her senior thesis, which proved to be a groundbreaking study of the social aspects of the US military presence in Britain during World War Two – as recounted by the young British women who'd experienced it first-hand). Subsequently entering politics, in 2006 she won the election to represent her home state in the United States Senate – Minnesota's first-ever female senator. And although her father never quite reconciled himself to her politics, the father-daughter bond that had been re-established during their time together on the Isle of Wight was such that it would never again be broken.

It was during such moments of quiet reflection that Aimee was given to recalling happier memories of that long, hot summer she had spent on the island – and of wondering what had become of the other two people who had made it so memorable.

For instance, what had become of Shelby – the friend who had been so close back then that they could almost have been sisters? Though they had gone their separate ways upon graduation, the two girls had made a vow to meet up at least once a year to reaffirm that friendship. However, as so often happens – despite the promises and the best intentions – their correspondence and their get-togethers had dwindled and they'd eventually lost touch. The last Aimee heard her friend had landed a top PR job and had moved overseas. *'Shelby is a good Christian girl who loves the Lord. You'll never find a better friend'*, her mother had once averred. She resolved anew that she would seek out that friend again – if only to remind her that she never had.

And what had become of Vaughan? Again, in their letters thereafter they'd talked about finding the means to visit each other. However, in the end nothing had come of it – as she guessed it wouldn't. Eventually, they too had lost touch. That was not to say she didn't still think about him from time to time – idle moments spent wondering where he was and what he might be doing; and whether her prayer that he would one day find the true love he deserved had been answered. Perhaps he'd dated and eventually married that bonny conductress who Aimee had been introduced to that day on the Number 12 bus.

To be sure, in 1980 Aimee had herself married an ambitious young congressman, though twelve years later they would divorce. Though there had been relationships with men since, she had never remarried. Perhaps Senator Aimee-Marie Forrester was still asking herself the question: what is love?

Perhaps too she had found an answer of sorts. For amongst the eight pall bearers conveying the coffin from the caisson to the graveside, a mother's eye proudly alighted upon one Captain Rhona Natalie Forrester USAF. Bearing herself with precision and dignity – despite her proximity to all that remained of an uncle she never knew – the sight of this twenty-four year-old F16 fighter pilot attired in uniform was more than enough to swell with pride both her mother and her beloved grandparents.

Finally, the time had come for the chaplain to commit Captain Lawrence Eichelberger into the arms of God's mercy – arms that, in truth, had never deserted him. The rifle company cracked off a saluting volley of shots and all heads bowed while a lone bugler sounded *'Taps'* – the haunting lament that had been played at American military funerals since 1862. Finally, the flag was lifted from the coffin and carefully and respectfully folded before being presented to his father.

However, with impeccable timing, the United States Air Force had one last salute to offer its fallen hero. Above them, the mourners could make out a loud, gathering roar. Suddenly, a lone B52 Stratofortress bomber drew all eyes skywards to behold it thundering low overhead. Charles Eichelberger cupped his hands to his eyes too, the huge plane a reminder that his son had – in the words of the air force poet – *'slipped the surly bonds of Earth and danced the skies on laughter-silvered wings'*, whereupon at last he had *'touched the face of God'*.

* * * * *

Dudley, West Midlands, England, Monday, August 29th 2016

The rain had stopped and the sun was shining – something of a rarity in England these last few weeks. Taking advantage of this break in the weather, today's gathering of Nora Lewis's friends and family had decamped to the garden of the sheltered housing complex where she was nowadays living out her twilight years. Everyone present was eager to wish this frail, white-haired, yet still discernibly beautiful lady many happy returns on this, her ninetieth birthday – including her adopted son, Vaughan.

Though in his element organising proceeding, while the big surprise was about to be sprung he took a moment to give thanks for God's goodness in his life. *'One day you will make a superb husband. And a great dad, I'm sure'*, Tina Brown had once confidently assured him. Gazing around to behold his handsome son and beautiful daughter – as well as to spot his bossy little grand-daughter playing hide-and-seek with his two mischievous grandsons – Vaughan Lewis was finally tempted to concede she'd been right!

Recalling Tina's words and feeling the warmth of that sun once more upon his arms and face, it seemed apt to cast his mind back forty years to a very different summer when they had first met. And while Denis Howell's much-mocked appointment as

'Minister for Drought' had indeed expedited the arrival of the rain that had brought it to an abrupt end (torrents of the stuff – throughout one of the wettest autumns on record), many of the measures to combat that drought would remain in place for months afterwards as the nation's reservoirs took time to refill. However, for Vaughan, for Tina, and for so many men and women who had come of age during that era, the long, hot summer of 1976 would remain the benchmark against which all subsequent British summers would be judged.

With hindsight, in many ways that summer had been a watershed too. Trite glam rock bands were still parading about in platform boots and glitter suits when 1976 had opened. Likewise, over-earnest prog-rockers were still serving up their grandiose 'concept' albums and lavish, theatrical stage shows. By year's end however, all that would be eclipsed by the raucous iconoclasm of punk rock – famously dubbed a greater threat to the nation's way of life than Soviet communism following a seminal incident in December when band members of the infamous Sex Pistols had effed-and-blinded their way through a primetime television interview. Yet despite inducing a moral panic at the time, Britain would survive its fleeting punk explosion. As would prog-rock: three of the best-selling albums of the closing years of the 1970s would include compilations by Yes, ELO and Pink Floyd.

Meanwhile – and despite the music press similarly loathing it – disco music too would vastly outsell punk. Transcending barriers of race, class, gender, and even generation, it would complete its conquest of the dance floors of both Britain and the United States (a triumph immortalised in the movie *'Saturday Night Fever'*, which would be released the following year). It was an ascendancy it would retain for the remainder of the decade.

1976 also proved a watershed year on the political stage too. Britain's 'Butskellite' commitment to 'full employment' and an expanding welfare state – which had guided governments of both main parties since 1945 – was already proving unsustainable in an era of raging 'stagflation'. The value of the pound would continue to plummet during that torrid summer, prompting Prime Minister Jim Callaghan to warn starkly at September's Labour Party

Conference in Blackpool that "For too long we have postponed facing up to fundamental changes in our economy. We've been living on borrowed time. The cosy world we were told would go on for ever – where full employment could be guaranteed by a stroke of the chancellor's pen – that cosy world is gone."

To hammer home that message, two days later Chancellor-of-the-Exchequer Denis Healey broke from crisis talks at the Treasury to head up to Blackpool himself. Confronting those MPs and delegates who were accusing the leadership of 'betraying socialism', in a florid fighting political speech he braved fierce heckling to urge his party accept the harsh monetarist medicine the country was being asked to swallow. Even so, before 1976 was out Healey would be compelled to go 'cap in hand' to the International Monetary Fund and negotiate a huge loan to stave off national bankruptcy – the terms of which would include further savage cuts to public expenditure. It was a symbolic moment of humiliation for a country that a mere generation before had boasted an empire that spanned the globe.

Meanwhile, that stifling summer would have a hand in magnifying that other great running sore of 1970s Britain – the power and status of its trades unions. On August 20th workers at the Grunwick film processing plant in London had walked out, complaining about having to work long hours in hot, oppressive conditions, and demanding the right to join a union. To the Left this was an example of an exploitative employer in need of reining in. To the Right however, the often violent mass picketing of the plant during the two-year long dispute – as well as the boycotting of Grunwick's mail by post office unions – was a textbook example of why it was the trades unions themselves that urgently needed to be reined in.

All this time, Margaret Thatcher had been honing her message of trades union reform, lower taxes, and curtailing subsidies to loss-making state industries. The Conservative Party she led was winning by-election after by-election at the expense of a tired Labour government that would lose its parliamentary majority the following year. To be sure, Jim Callaghan's administration would soldier on until May 1979. Thereafter, it was the Lady and *her* legacy that would temper political discourse for the remainder of the twentieth century.

In the United States too, the election of Jimmy Carter to the presidency in November would prove little more than a passing post-Watergate backlash. Four years later, the hapless Carter would be trounced by a resurgent Republican Party led by Ronald Reagan, whose own brand of strong defence and free market capitalism would finally rally America to shake off it post-Vietnam crisis of confidence.

The long, hot summer of 1976 would also prove to be the swansong of the traditional British holiday – of which the Isle of Wight had always been a magnet. As Colin Garrett had correctly foreseen that scorching afternoon in the restroom of Ryde Bus Station, the indifferent summer weather of subsequent years, as well as the advent of cheap air fares (Freddie Laker would launch his 'no frills' Skytrain in 1977), would fuel a boom in foreign holidays that accelerated the decline of many once-proud British seaside resorts. In 1971 the British had taken four million holidays abroad; ten years later that figure had surged to more than thirteen million – most of the growth accounted for by ordinary families becoming ever more adventurous. And while the island ambience has spared Ryde, Sandown, Shanklin and Ventnor from the worst of this decline, they are quieter places today than when Colin and Vaughan had once plied between them aboard packed summer buses.

"Come on, Dad, how much longer is Mom going to keep us waiting?" his son hollered, expressing the bemused impatience of them all that it was taking so long for his mother to put the finishing touches to Nanny Lewis's 'surprise'.

"It's coming, it's coming," Vaughan insisted, attempting to quell a nascent family mutiny. "In fact... here it comes now!"

On cue, his daughter reached her hands around Nanny Lewis's face to veil her eyes as the door from the kitchen opened at last. She then released them so those eyes could behold this token of the enduring respect and affection in which she was held.

"Happy Birthday to you, Happy Birthday to you..." everyone launched themselves into the refrain, *"Happy Birthday, dear Nora... Happy Birthday to you."*

"Happy Birthday, Mom," Vaughan raced in to alight a kiss upon one of Nora's wizened cheeks.

"There ya' go, you guys. Didn't I say y'all would be impressed by this," his diminutive wife cooed proudly.

Upon the table in front of her mother-in-law Shelby now placed the huge, sculpted cake she had carried out, and which was spangled with ninety – yes, ninety – glowing candles. These Nora was encouraged to extinguish (though aided by the eager, inflated lungs of her great grandchildren rallying around!).

"Thank you, Shell. You've done my mother proud," Vaughan cast his arm around her shoulder, pulling his wife in tight so that he might further express his gratitude with a loving kiss placed upon her forehead. "But then you Yanks never do anything in half-measures, do you," he jested.

"Yanks?" she looked up at him and scowled – for all that she had made England her home, playfully reminding her husband of which side of the Mason-Dixon Line she hailed!

After his whirlwind romance with Aimee during that now distant summer, Vaughan's love life would return to the doldrums. Alas, cheap transatlantic air fares had failed to rescue their long distance relationship. Gradually, their letters to each other had become fewer and far between. Soon they would lose touch altogether. And even though his correspondence with Tina had been interspersed with a weekend visit, their friendship too would fail to blossom into romance. They too would eventually lose contact.

Since then though – and thanks to the wonders of social media – he'd managed to reconnect with both of them. He follows with interest Aimee's career as a respected US senator and one of the Democratic Party's 'rising stars' (a future president even). Meanwhile, Tina regularly uploads photographs of herself with the man she would eventually marry (as well as with the three stunning daughters – and six gorgeous grandchildren – they have been blessed with).

What's more, it was through Facebook that Vaughan would eventually catch up with Colin again. With the retiring of its elderly Lodekkas, the ruttish bus driver had left the employ of Southern Vectis in 1980. Thereafter, he'd drifted in and out of a succession of both jobs and relationships before eventually meeting and marrying the buxom blonde lass with whom Vaughan had spotted him sharing his 'profile' photo. Thirty years of wedded ups-and-downs later and today the couple can be found pulling pints in their popular 'English' pub in Torremolinos – just as his old friend had promised one day he would.

Like Vaughan, Shelby Carmichael had also looked set to be unsuccessful in love. Romantic interludes had come and gone without progressing to the peel of wedding bells. However, disappointment had failed to quench her determination to trust that God would one day fulfil her own yearning to be a wife and a mother.

In 1986 she would return to England – this time working as a senior consultant for a leading public relations agency. As if by chance ('as if' because, to a believer, nothing in this world ever happens 'by chance'), it was in this capacity that she would attend a business reception in London two years later where she would bump into an old friend; an old friend who just happened to be a marketing executive for the newly-privatised Southern Vectis bus company – one Vaughan Francis Lewis!

Mrs Shelby Lewis (they had married in 1988) would therefore return to the Isle of Wight, accompanying her husband as his career progressed with the same company he'd once worked for as a lowly bus conductor. Soon after, they returned to the mainland – he to become a senior manager at one of Britain's largest bus companies; and she to become a full-time mom.

It had been a brief sojourn tinged with mixed emotions, for so much on the island had changed. Though the Shanklin Heights Hotel (where she'd once made beds and mopped bathrooms) still dominated the cliffs overlooking Sandown Bay, it had long since been renamed by new owners anxious to erase the memory of its darkest chapter. Meanwhile, Shanklin bus depot (where her husband's interest in public transport had first been kindled) had been demolished and redeveloped as a supermarket.

Still there had been that fondly remembered apartment block in Sandown, though its deteriorating façade and increasingly transient compliment of tenants lent it a marked air of *gloire perdu*. Betty had passed away and Chico was longer there on the verandah steps to keep watch over Victoria Road, as well as to entertain passing holidaymakers with his saucy quips.

Sadly, neither had the silky, sensual voice of Vaughan's beloved Auntie Angie – his real mother – been there to greet them on those steps. She had passed away too in 1979 after a courageous battle with cancer. She was just fifty-seven.

His uncle Frank had sold up Tring's Toys not long after his wife's untimely death. Symbolic of the change in the nation's eating and shopping habits, the High Street premises it had once occupied had re-opened as an oriental takeaway (in 1976 the number of Chinese takeaways in Britain would officially exceed the number of fish-and-chip shops for the first time). Thereafter, he would pass his days frequenting dwindling reunions of his old naval comrades. Vaughan and Shelby had made a point of visiting him as often as they could, and were present at his bedside when he too passed away in a care home in 1999.

Thankfully, at least one of Vaughan's real parents had lived long enough to witness their son find happiness with a beautiful girl who – apropos Frank's words that day on the pier – possessed noble qualities that hadn't been immediately obvious when Vaughan had instead raced after her leggy companion in a crowded disco. Meanwhile, had she lived to witness this day, Angie too would have been heartened to know that, in the end, her son would find himself a mate who has treasured *his* heart every bit as much as he has treasured hers.

Recalling his aunt's pearl of wisdom goaded Vaughan to hug Shelby possessively while everyone was helping themselves to a slice of the cake their daughter was busy dividing up.

"How could I have ever been so blind?" he turned to his wife, shaking his head in chastened reflection.

"So blind about what?" she looked up at him, eager to know.

"I mean, how could I have not seen that it was *you* I should have been chasing all along – back then… during that summer?"

"There's none so blind as he who will not see," she prodded him flippantly before crowing "Me? I knew you were something special the day I first set eyes on you."

"So why didn't you tell me? Or muscle in when Aimee was having second thoughts?"

She shrugged as if the answer was self-evident.

"Back then you were besotted with her. And she was my best friend. I guessed there was little point in making a big show of *my* feelings towards you until such time as you two had worked whatever you felt for each other from out of your systems."

It prompted Vaughan to recall something his mother had once counselled: *'Lay it before the Lord and let Him lead you to who He wants you to be with – and in His own good time'*. He glanced at Nora – forty years on once again basking in the adulation of her family – before turning to stare into Shelby's lush brown eyes. In their glow he marvelled at just how completely that prayer had been answered – once he had eventually learned to 'lay it before the Lord' and trust.

"The end of a matter is better than its beginning, and patience is better than pride," a wise man in the Old Testament had once mused. While everyone's attention remained fixed upon the 'birthday girl', it seemed an opportune moment to steal from Shelby a kiss – which he now lovingly planted upon her soft, receptive lips. As he did, and his arms closed more fully around her, he gave thanks that meeting this wonderful woman – as well as the shining example of patience and faith she had been to him then and since – was the most apposite reason why, as long as he lived, Vaughan Lewis would never forget the summer of '76.

Though the wider events mentioned in this novel took place, I confess I have taken two big liberties with historical accuracy.

* * * * *

The first concerns the Type 42 destroyer HMS Sheffield.

Commissioned in 1975, the ship's first few years at sea would indeed be dogged by 'teething problems' – as was to be expected of the lead ship of a new class of destroyer armed with a sophisticated new weapon system. However, her August 1976 deployment – as recounted in this novel – is my own invention.

Like Captain Martin Drake, her actual commanding officer at this time – Captain John 'Sandy' Woodward – had a reputation for being abrasive and of not tolerating fools. Promoted to the rank of rear admiral, in 1982 Woodward would head up the British naval task force despatched to retake the Falkland Islands following their occupation by Argentina. Addressing the men under his command on the eve of battle, he was typically blunt: "You've taken the Queen's shilling. Now you're going to have to bloody well earn it. And your best way of getting back alive is to do your absolute utmost. So go do it."

It was during this campaign that the deficiencies of his former ship would be cruelly exposed. On the morning of Tuesday May 4th 1982 a low-flying Argentine Navy Super Etendard attack aircraft fired two French-built Exocet anti-ship missiles at HMS Sheffield, *one of which struck her amidships.*

So taken by surprise were her crew that there had been no time to execute defensive counter-measures. The resulting fire eventually engulfed the ship, occasioning the loss of twenty of her crew, as well as her abandonment. While awaiting rescue, one of Sheffield's *officers famously rallied her surviving crew members by leading them in the singing of the sardonic ditty* 'Always Look On The Bright Side Of Life'*!*

Noting the inability of the Sheffield's *Type 965 radar system to engage low-flying targets at close quarters, the Court of Inquiry into her loss also concluded that her crew had been inadequately trained in simulated realistic low-level target acquisition. Neither did the ship possess any electronic jamming equipment that could have foiled the missile's homing radar.*

During the conflict, seven Argentine warplanes would be lost to Sea Dart missiles – ironically two of them low-flying jets shot down by HMS Exeter *– a Type 42 destroyer that was fitted with the newer and more advanced Type 1022 radar system.*

Admiral 'Sandy' Woodward was knighted for his part in the successful retaking of the Falklands Islands. He retired from the Royal Navy in 1989, and passed away in 2013.

The burnt-out hulk of HMS Sheffield *was eventually scuttled at sea and is today a war grave.*

* * * * *

The second liberty I have taken is that the man who actually commanded US air power in South-East Asia during 1972-73 was General John W Vogt Jr USAF.

Like Charles Eichelberger, General Vogt was born in 1920. Like Charles Eichelberger, during 1944-45 he too served in England as a distinguished fighter ace with the US Eighth Army Air Force. In 1969 he also joined the Joint Chiefs of Staff, becoming its director the following year.

On April 7th 1972 President Nixon appointed General Vogt commander of the US Seventh Air Force and deputy commander of US Military Assistance Command Vietnam, with a remit to shake up air operations in response to the communists' Spring Offensive. "The bastards have never been bombed like they're gonna' be bombed this time," those soon-to-be-infamous White House tapes had revealed Nixon confiding to an aide.

General Vogt did not disappoint the President. During the nine months that followed he successfully deployed American air assets – including its B52 bombers – to 'bomb the bastards' so relentlessly that on January 27th 1973 Hanoi agreed the ceasefire that enabled US forces to finally withdraw from South Vietnam.

Following the signing of the Paris Peace Accord he redeployed US air power to arrest the advance of communist forces in neighbouring Cambodia – controversial bombing missions that were halted by Congress on August 15th 1973.

General Vogt retired from the United States Air Force in 1975 and passed away in 2010. He is the only officer ever to have commanded both the US Pacific and European Air Forces.

To the best of my knowledge, General Vogt's private and family lives bore absolutely no resemblance to the colourful ones experienced by Charles Eichelberger in this novel!

I do hope you have enjoyed reading *'The Summer Of '76'*. If so, then can I beg one final indulgence: that you very kindly leave a review of this book on the Amazon site you purchased it from....

United Kingdom/Ireland – amazon.co.uk
United States – amazon.com
Canada – amazon.ca
Australia/New Zealand – amazon.com.au
India – amazon.in

Reviews greatly assist authors to promote their books as widely as possible. A review needn't be a long essay. Even a simple 'I enjoyed this book' will suffice.

Thank you, and God bless.

Ray Burston

If you have enjoyed reading this, why not stir your heart with another tale of love and tragedy involving a young English girl and a handsome American airman…

During the darkest days of the Second World War, Eileen Kimberley – a pretty teenage girl from the backstreets of Birmingham – makes her bid to escape a claustrophobic home life by enlisting in Britain's Women's Auxiliary Air Force.

What follows proves to be not just the adventure of a lifetime, playing her part in her country's desperate war in the skies over Germany; but also a painful voyage of self-discovery in which a tragic past impels this gifted young woman to seek out that special someone with whom she can share her crazy dreams.

Printed in Great Britain
by Amazon